CW00486705

The Devil's Crossing

HANA COLE

CONTENTS

Part One – The Age of the Father

Prologue

Chartres, 1201

Gui did not mean to look up. The previous day he had transcribed the interrogations without laying eyes on the souls condemned to burn. Far better the dull scratch of his nib on the parchment than an indelible portrait of the damned. But at that moment, a beam of early morning sunlight danced over his desk. He raised his head.

A girl stood in the flood of light from the open door. She was wearing a yellow dress, embroidered with flourishes at the hem, and Gui could see the outline of her body beneath the gown. Eyes the pale blue of winter light, she surveyed the room earnestly, as though despite her fear, she expected to find reason among the venerable. Gui's heart hammered as Inquisitor Bernard de Nogent asked her name. His whole body burned but he could not look away.

'Sir, I am Agnes. Daughter of Estève Le Coudray, the salt merchant.'

'Cleric!' The inquisitor's voice was sharp. Gui's attention flew from the girl to the scroll before him. He scratched at the parchment although he had forgotten to ink the nib of his quill.

De Nogent continued, 'The same Estève Le Coudray condemned here as a recalcitrant heretic.'

'Sir, please. He is no heretic.'

'You question the authority of this investigation?' The black, avian eyes blinked.

Agnes clapped her hand over her mouth. Stammering an apology she searched the faces of the court for clemency. Before Gui could avert his gaze, she found him. Sweat pricked his lip. He dropped his head - the power to help her was not his. Reaching forward, he re-arranged the flayed skin on the table before him.

Master Bernard began. 'Tell us, Mademoiselle Agnes, is God in all things?'

Gui held his breath. *God is in no evil thing.*

'Only in good things, sir.'

'Only in good things? You have been taught this?' A pause, then the inquisitor said, 'Good. This is good. There are some people who believe that God is in all things. Have you heard this?'

Her eyes widened. 'I do not believe that, sir.'

'That is not what I asked.'

'No, sir. I cannot think I have heard anyone speak such a thing...Not in those words. Sir.'

'Not in those words.' The inquisitor tapped sharply on the desk, summoning Gui's attention. 'The deposition.' He thrust forward an impatient hand. Face puckered, he opened the scroll.

'Omnia Deus sunt et omnia unum.' Another pause; a test of her nerves.

1

The courtroom filled with the pressure of silence.

Agnes Le Coudray hesitated. Inwardly Gui urged her to keep her counsel - to debate with the inquisitor was as good as signing your own death warrant.

'God is in everything,' she muttered eventually.

'God is all and thus all things are one.' Master Bernard's words boomed around the vaulted room. 'So you have heard those words.'

Agnes shook her head vigorously. 'That's not what I meant. I mean I have heard something of that sort. But I don't remember where.'

De Nogent raised an imperious brow. 'You don't remember where.'

'Tis a commonly known phrase, sir.'

With a controlled, heavy sigh, the inquisitor dipped his eyes to the parchment. '"That's what I heard Le Coudray say. God is in everything, even the Devil. I swear it by the Virgin, God bless, he said them very words",' de Nogent read, the testimony sounding absurd in his scholarly Parisian.

'No, sir, it's a lie! My father never said such a thing,' cried Agnes. 'Who are these witnesses, my lord?'

He slammed the document down. 'You may not question the proceedings of this court!' The a surge of violence in de Nogent's voice made Agnes flinch.

Shame crawled in Gui's belly. The witnesses claimed to have been Le Coudray's housemaids. 'Pay them for their courage and service', de Nogent had instructed him. From the sly smiles and quick fingers that pocketed his coin, Gui knew they were lying.

'Please sir, with your permission. May I ask a question?' Agnes asked.

A spiteful grin played on the inquisitor's lips. 'It would seem the grounds are greater for me to ask further questions of you.'

The girl's face crumpled. Now she understands, thought Gui. Closing his eyes he reached for his inkwell, and prayed the interrogation would be counted in hours not days. With careful method, the inquisitor lead Agnes into confusion, contradiction and inevitably, falsehood. Grim-faced de Nogent pronounced his verdict, offering her the chance to avoid the fire if only she would repent.

A furrow dented her brow. 'How can I repent of something that I do not believe?'

The inquisitor, sitting on the corner of Gui's desk, pressed the tips of his fingers together.

'I am no heretic, sir. Tell me, please, what must I say?'

Gui's chest was drum-tight with the effort of his silence. Only a truly repentant soul could be forgiven, and only the inquisitor could judge the truly repentant. Bernard de Nogent nodded to the guards.

'Please. What must I say?' She drew back as the guards approached, cradling her arms across her body. 'For the love of God.'

Two guards strong-armed her to the door. Twisting under their grip she craned over her shoulder, casting around until her eyes fell on Gui. She did not look away until the guards had dragged her out of sight. And neither did he.

That evening, drawn by the noise from the streets below, Gui laid aside his manuscript and peered over the balcony. Three men shuffled in irons behind a plough horse. The prisoners had been sentenced to suffer for their own good. The purifying flame would cleanse their souls, and bestow a last chance of salvation before the fires of Hell. Although he had been clerk to the inquisitor for weeks now, this was the first time that he had witnessed a blood punishment and seen the faces of the convicts; faces just like any other. Among them, he knew, was Estève Le Coudray. A salt merchant from the Languedoc with a kind face and a hearty laugh who had been condemned by a testimony the Inquisition had paid for.

As the procession drew level with the balcony, someone in the crowd threw a chunk of masonry. It struck Le Coudray with such force that Gui heard the man's jaw crack. Large crimson gobs spilled from his mouth. Gui felt his legs yield beneath him. A fist squeezed inside his stomach, releasing a wave of nausea - I did this. Staggering backwards onto his bench, he sat, heart racing, as the jeers of the crowd built to a crescendo. Any moment now he would smell the smoke.

Transcription scattered at his feet, Gui ran his fingers through his hair, trying to chase out the images from the morning's trial. But all he could think of was the girl as they took her away, eyes locked onto his as though there were no other living soul in the world. He jumped up and closed the shutter. The noise of the crowd dulled. Gui paced the cell. The day after next, Agnes Le Coudray would be in shackles, stumbling along the cobbles below to her final agony. *So whoever knows the right thing to do and fails to do it, for him it is sin.* The words of St James had his heart pumping hard against his better judgement.

The wooden shutters muffled the din, but they did not impede the vapours of oak moss, garlanded by spectators to veil the stench of burning flesh. It was the same perfume that his mother used on her deathbed to disguise her decay. Gui felt his gorge rise. He reached for the rosary attached to his belt. It was his mother's gift to him just months before he entered the Cathedral. On his twelfth birthday he had sat at her bedside, her icy hand in his, as death made its mask of her face.

'Deliver the weak and needy from the hands of the wicked.' She pressed the rosary into his palm. 'For the love of God, may you never falter in your devotion to His mercy.'

Her last words told him of her pride at his calling. He wondered now, as he recalled that beautiful girl blinking back her tears, if his mother would still be proud.

3

Outside the crowd exalted. Plumes of smoke curled over the rooftops. Blood thrummed urgently in his ears. He pressed his palms together and drew a deep breath. *Deliver the weak and needy.* Fist clenched tight over the coral beads, he fled the room before the screams began. Sandals slapping on the stone, he hurried to the chapel and he prayed. First, for those poor souls who burned for denying Rome, then, head lifted to the Heavens, he remembered his mother.

Gui crossed the courtyard hooded in the cloak of a cathedral canon. He knew the corridors well enough to walk them blind. Palms slick with sweat, he stole into the scriptorium, a jumble of standing desks, loose parchments, and ribbon-bound ledgers. He tugged at a locked drawer of the Abbot's desk until it yielded, rummaging through the seals and scrolls to find the key to the Cathedral's prison. Then, fingers moving light, he thumbed through his documents until he found the pages he had transcribed from Agnes Le Coudray's interrogation. The urgency of his endeavour pressed the air from his chest. Still, he paused to tear them up before stuffing them into his cloak. He peered out into the empty hallway. Quickening his pace, he glided over the cold quarry tiles to the courtroom, and the cell that lay below.

There was an hour to go before the Canons roused for Lauds - the noose of time was tightening around his neck. In a matter of hours her bones would be ash. He tasted bile at the thought. Before him, narrow steps spiralled down to blackness. Rust from the stolen key scratched at his damp palm. Barely breathing, he placed one foot on the stone, as though he were testing its solidity. Then he squeezed his eyes shut in prayer to a merciful God, and, heart in free fall, stepped down into the abyss.

Gui squinted through the door's grille. Agnes was hugged into the corner of the cell, a shadowy outline in the near dark. She started at his presence, inching back further against the wall, as though there were succour to be found against the wet stone. A word of reassurance pressed at the base of his throat, but it would not come. Not in this place, with the Devil at his back.

One hand steadying the other, Gui weaved the crudely-cut key into the keyhole and hunted for the lock. Voices from outside echoed above. A moment of panic: if I fail we will both die here. It summoned brute force and, clunk, the door yielded. Agnes inched forward until she was close enough for him to hear her breath. In a moment that seemed to stall the world, he felt her searching his intention. Then, bobbing her head, she pushed at the door. He reached for her hand.

'Quick,' he managed. 'Come with me.'

Chapter One

Montoire-sur-le-Loir, 10 years later.

Gui rode through the village before sunrise. Most of the houses on the square were stone, set around a fountain with his church in the far corner, its pink façade still grey at this pale hour. None of the shutters on the square were open, but Gui knew that when they were, there would be tattle on the tongues of those who poked out their heads to shake their coverlets at the new day. And they would be right.

Priest of their modest parish for ten years this spring, he did not delude himself that no one speculated on his circumstances. He had been exiled to this backwater under suspicion of freeing a heretic. With the trouble he had made for himself he was lucky to get that. His only regret was that it was not his burden alone to wonder if the day would come when idle chatter would harness malicious intent. Then the sacrament he administered would be worthless, and everything would fall. His stomach shrank at the thought. Even from behind closed doors he felt as though eyes were upon his every step. Just one careless regard or fond smile was all it would take. The very comfort her presence kindled could betray him in a way he knew his words never would.

He followed the bank of the river Loir out of the village for a mile or so before crossing. The morning mist dissolved under the mantle of dawn light, and he stopped his mule on the bridge to look across the plain, savouring this rare moment of solitude. For the next few hours he was free from his duties as intercessor between the living and the dead, negotiator between man and the angels. On this road he was just a man, with all his flaws, grateful for the few breaths granted him where he might dare to imagine a life free of the obligation to hide his love.

There were early bluebells on the floor of the copse. He dismounted and walked through the trees, the bracken and leaves of forest floor a welcome change from the muddy road. Although she usually arrived before he did, today Agnes was not there. Gui took a seat on a fallen branch while his mule drank from the stream and cast around for a distraction. Soon enough he was fingering his rosary, mind lurching from anticipation to concern and finally irritation. He was at the mercy of some force of the heart beyond his control.

The same force that had turned the key to her cell so many years ago and kept that autumn night as vivid as ever it had been - the smell of burned char cloth and dampened hearths, their breath hot and fast on the air as they fled through the city streets to the sanctuary of her godmother's house. He could still recall the heat of his body at the sight of her standing

5

by the water wheel of the little dyer's cottage. How long it had taken him to separate desire from shame. Seasons passed, realisation dawned; he hadn't freed her because he could not stand to see her burn, he had freed her because she was meant to be his. And so it was.

Where was she? Gui rubbed his face vigorously and exhaled. The long, familiar sigh that he knew as companion to affairs of the heart. From the day he left for Montoire and realised he could leave every thing else behind except her, to the day she stood before him, eyes brimming with hope and fear, trying to find the right words. He had known straight away that she was with child. That he was soon to learn the true meaning of the word responsibility. *Obligare,* to bind. Also *religare.* Religion.

Gui kept his family under his own roof by the well-worn feint of many a parish priest, with Agnes playing the role of housekeeper. Still, for all the weight in his heart caused by the deception, Gui knew their son had to remain ignorant of his father's true identity, and of his parents' intimacy. To spare him the shame of illegitimacy, yes, but also to seal the truth from those villagers who, necks craning, tried to bring their woes across the threshold of Gui's home. Was it their desire to claim familiarity with God's representative, or the human bent for power over another that drew them in, seeking a confidence from his hearth? He did not know and he would not risk finding out. Thus it was that he and Agnes made love in fern-concealed copses, upon the moss and grasses of the forest floor - the thickets of woodland groves their covenant, a certainty they would never be discovered.

When the foliage crunched behind him, he swung round. Agnes gave a yelp of surprise. Arms folded in front of him, Gui was laughing. 'Were you trying to creep up on me?'

'Don't,' said Agnes, the light of self-mockery dancing in her eyes.

Gui drew her into his body. She rested her head against his chest.

'What is it?'

'That Claire was by the washing brook again. She had no laundry with her, so I stopped now and then in case she was following me.'

'The furrier's wife?' Gui snorted as though someone were asking him if he knew the Lord' prayer. The haughty wife of an artisan, Claire was one of the habitual gossips who congregated on the square after mass, chin jutting back and forth as she exchanged tattle.

'Agnes, a woman like that would never venture beyond the boundary of the village unaccompanied, let alone hazard the forest.'

For a moment they stood in silence. Gui closed his eyes and lowered his lips to the crown of her head. They inhaled as one, the shrill of the spring birds, the twitch of a rabbit in the undergrowth, and the deep, low breath of the forest around them. Thumb and forefinger under her chin, he gently raised her head. Her eyes did not quite fix onto his. She was still listening. He stroked his thumbs along the plaits that ran from her temples, holding the loose hair from her face. She shook her head. There was no one there. Face hardening in defiance, she dismissed the air with the back of her hand. Her eyes were a deeper water now, flint-edged. 'You're right. She would never dare.'

'There are few who have your courage.'

Gui took the weight of her hair in his hand. He pressed his mouth onto hers, and felt her body exhale beneath his touch. It had been four weeks since their last union. Without breaking their embrace, they sat on a tree stump, hands searching each other's clothing for access to the warm skin beneath. Gui brought Agnes down to kneel on the cushion of moss beneath and gathered up the skirts of her dress. She placed her hand over his and drew it up to the flesh of her buttocks. Guiding him down to the ground, she sat astride him.

'I've missed your touch,' he said.

Her hips rocked against his as above their heads, wisps of cloud raced by on the morning breeze and the sun flickered through the canopy of leaves.

'And I yours,' she replied.
*

Inside the vestry lanterns smoked and guttered in the draught. Gui pitched forward onto the edge of his writing bench and flipped the letter over, examining it. The seal was a simple lamb of God, the address written by a novice scribe, suspiciously anonymous. He felt uneasy, as though someone were standing behind him. Under the protest of Reason, he looked over his shoulder. A shadow moved across the apse; the branches of the apple sapling in the churchyard. He refused to allow himself to go over and check if that was all.

He filleted a letter opener under the hard, cherry wax and the parchment fell open. It was like seeing a ghost. The hand he knew by heart. Shakier than once it had been but unmistakeable nonetheless; a tight, rounded cursive learned in the Paris schools fifty years before and long since fallen out of fashion.

His eyes fell down the page, soaking up the content. A hollow sensation seared his chest. It felt as though someone had scooped out his heart. He stared up at the wall before him. High above the doorway, a wooden angel offered up a chalice. The wisdom of the covenant - an unbreakable bond. He scanned the letter once more. The words swirled around inside his head, making his ears ring. He was dimly aware that he should be feeling something else, sorrow, pain, maybe even fear. But all he felt was confusion.

Hidden under his maniple and a hundred other scrolls, there was a locked chest. He swiped the clutter off the top and heaved it opened. Inside were scores of letters in that same hand. He pulled one from the bottom. It dated back to his arrival in Montoire.

Dear Gui, I am so very glad that you are settled and have remembered that those most in need of succour may not be those who appear so…

In the familiar, paternal tone was the casual generosity of a great teacher. An understanding he had found nowhere else. He picked up another letter, and another. Before long, he was thrown back to those dark days when he had been thrashing about in the sea of doubt, the weight of his own judgment pushing him further under with every passing day. A decade gone and he could still relive it, palms slick, shoulders drawn up high against some invisible assailant. His childhood barely over, Gui had stumbled into an abyss beyond the threshold of everything life had taught him to expect. Without this man's compassion and insight, he knew he might never have found his way out. The memory brought the realisation he was in shock. My heart is breaking, he thought, I just can't feel it yet.

That evening Gui made his way home, his shadow wandering out before him under the lantern light. His cottage lay on the outskirts of the village, and a handful of day labourers were bivouacked under the oaks that lined the road, heating whatever roots they had found for their pot. Reaching for his pouch to give them alms, he found he still had his fingers curled around the letter. For a moment he was drawn by the urge to pull it out, as though there might be some chance he had misread it before. That he wouldn't have to find the words to tell Agnes.

He arrived home to find her hovering at the threshold of the cottage, skimming a broom back and forth across the same spot. She snapped up her head as soon as he closed the gate, lips pressed together.

'That was a long day,' he said and tried for a smile.

'The coughing sickness?'

Gui nodded. 'Four burials this afternoon. It's cold tonight, let's go in.'

Agnes gestured inside with a formality intended to check him.

'I thought you weren't going to hear Vespers tonight,' she said.

'I wasn't. I got held up with some paperwork, then the sacristan arrived and we haven't held it since Wednesday, so…'

'You thought you'd hold Vespers for the empty pews.'

'Agnes, please.'

Her eyelashes flickered downwards. 'I was worried, that's all. You said you'd be back before dark.'

'I know. I'm sorry…It's just,' Gui pulled his hands down his face.

'What? What is it?'

There was an urgency to her voice that made his stomach lurch. His hand fell to his cloak. 'Abbot Roger has written to me.'

Agnes cocked her head. 'Roger of Chartres?'

Gui inhaled. 'He is dying.'

She drew breath as if to speak, but instead enveloped him with the warmth of her body. He buried his head into her hair and inhaled the soft, woody smell of cedar that she burned to keep the air clean.

'Oh Gui, I am so very sorry.'

Gui rubbed at his collarbone and smiled, grateful that she did not need him to speak. Once tutor to the royal court, and of the noblest lineage himself, Abbot Roger was Gui's mentor and confessor. The only living soul who knew the truth of it all, of his childhood, of Agnes, and of their boy. Although nothing but suspicion had ever been found against him, it was at Roger's venerable intervention that Gui had been granted his parish along with the benefit of the doubt, rather than expulsion from the Church and the penalty of losing his livelihood.

Agnes drew back, studying his face. In the lantern light he could see his own pupils reflected in her eyes, solemn and black.

'Gui, let there be no doubt. You must go to him.'

'It would take me two weeks, maybe more if I can't get loan of a good horse. I will not leave you for that long.'

'You think I cannot defend myself against those jealous old harridans?' She gave the wry smile of the battle hardened.

'I don't doubt it,'Gui laughed. 'It is not you, Agnes. It's something I cannot place. Something is happening. The language in these new proclamations from Rome unnerves me...'

'You say that every time the diocese sends you another sermon against heretics.'

He took her hand. 'I know. And every time they get more...' He wanted to say violent, but the word caught in his throat.

In the diffuse glow of the flame, Agnes regarded him fiercely.

'You cannot let Roger pass away without paying our respects. They would have hunted me down like a dog if he hadn't told the Inquisition I was drowned. It is on his account that we have this life at all.'

And your life is the most precious thing I will ever have, he thought. Her face softened, sensing his heart, 'I know the love you have for him, Gui. Go. I know you must want to.'

'I would be at his deathbed before my own father's.'

At once, from the hedgerow beyond, came the crunch of stones on the track. Instantly they dropped each other hands. Agnes's eyes roved in the direction of the sound.

'Etienne?' Gui said.

'He's not back.'

Gui shrugged. Still as statues, they listened. Nothing more.

'Just an animal,' he said. Agnes raised her brow – how foolish we are. Moments later a fox screamed and they both laughed with relief.

Reaching the door, Gui hesitated, wanting to express his gratitude, but the unspoken warmth between them served better than any words he might find. He brought her hand to his lips.

'Very well,' he relented. Opening the door for her, he glanced into the

9

darkness, a final sweep before he shut out the world for the night.

Inside the blast from the fire was a welcome contrast to the damp evening. The smell of Agnes' pine oil mingled with the lingering aroma of the soup pot. An earthen floor, swept speckless, was covered with two braided rugs. To one side, a writing bench brimmed with parchments. Half concealed by an alcove, it led to Gui's room, the corner of his pallet just visible through the door. On the other side of a wide, brick hearth, was the oak trestle he had hewn himself, terracotta bowls set in place upon it.

'Where is Etienne?' he asked.

'Lambing.'

'Of course.' Gui staged an earnest smile but it felt starched and formal. 'He has already spent two evenings at the lambing pens this week. I thought they took it in turns.'

Agnes shrugged and started fussing in the kitchen, fetching bread, wiping off the spoons. It was not a conversation either of them wanted to have again. Gui padded around the living area, seeking a comfortable silence, and found himself prodding aimlessly at the fire. Lost in the hypnosis of the flame, he didn't hear her approach and his shoulders tensed as she rubbed them.

'I'm sorry,' he said. He took the letter out from his cloak, and laid it down on the stool by the fire.

'I know,' she said softly. 'I know the others make him do their share of the hard work, and I know it's not fair. But it's not your fault either.'

Gui gave a stiff nod.

'Telling him the truth won't make a difference,' she said.

'You can't know that.' Gui's voice pitched. 'He'll know.' He tapped his hand to his chest. 'In here.'

'How do you know what he'd do if he found out we have kept the truth from him all these years? All we would be doing is burdening him with our lie.' Agnes looked down. 'And we both know how difficult a lie it is to keep.' Then, her eyes lifted, blazing into his soul, and he knew they were asking him what would become of their son if a slip of the lie sent them both to the pyre.

Gui's eyelids flickered as guilt sank, leaden, in his belly. He was bursting with protestations and counter-arguments, but despite the pull on his heart, he knew that to tell Etienne would be to wilfully betray his promise to Agnes, to unloose her worst fears and watch those beautiful, limpid eyes crack and overflow. Worse of all, he was afraid she might be right.

She pressed her hand onto his chest. 'You are a good man, Gui of Courville,' she said and rising to her tiptoes, kissed him softly on the cheek.

Chapter Two

The wind is battering the barn like a giant shaking a child's toy. On his hands and knees, Etienne sniffs at the floor of the lambing pen. It needs more lime. He shovels another layer down, then jabs at the brazier with his spade to kindle it against the spring gale that pokes its fingers through the gaps and weaves its chill through the beams.

From his round the previous evening he reckons on about four or five dropping today. It's hard to tell for sure though. Sheep are tricky, especially the saggy older ones. Outside the other boys roam around the pastures, heads lowered into their cloaks, looking for any stragglers, the ones who like to hide themselves away in the farthest corners as their time comes on. He is glad to be inside for now.

Above the racket of the wind, the bleating draws closer. There is something so desolate about it, such a sad little cry. It reminds him of being alone. He braces himself against the weather and opens the barn door. It hasn't started to rain but the air feels damp. Four sheep trot in under Marc's crook, steam rising from their coats. Etienne takes a flick to his backside as he turns round. Sometimes, when he is fast enough, he is able to grab the crook off Marc and smack him back, but the day started early and he isn't in the mood, so he throws a resigned glower. Marc pats him on the shoulder and says he'll be back shortly.

The sheep are bunched over in the far corner of the barn. Now it is a waiting game. He is supposed to have another shepherd with him for lambing but he has done it so many times now and he knows Marc won't be back until noon. Etienne puts a pan of water on to heat and sinks down into the sheep's bedding, listening to the gale, wondering if there are secret messages hidden in those moans and screeches. When sheep bleat, or birds shrill, most often they are sending messages to each other, warning each other of dangers. Priests say the weather is one of the ways God sends messages to man and he wonders if that is always so, or if bad weather can happen by itself for no reason.

From the corner of the barn, one of the ewes lets out a cry as her labour begins. He kneels down beside to check all is well, then, whispering a reassurance to her, withdraws back to the fire. Usually they are better off if you just leave them to get on with it. In a few hours, there will be a lamb and god willing it won't take any pulling on his part.

Marc returns after the first lamb is on its feet. He slumps down by the brazier, cursing the weather with such vigour that it half makes Etienne feel it is his fault.

'Where have you been?' Etienne asks.

Marc ignores the question, and starts gnawing at a hunk of bread. Etienne opens his mouth but thinks better of it. One of the sharpest shepherd boys, Marc's ravenous eyes are always darting around, hunting. Etienne has often thought that Marc would get on better if he didn't have to act angry all the time.

One of the sheep starts stamping and bleating. Marc's head swivels over to the pen. 'It's stuck,' he says. 'Must have its legs twisted about.'

Etienne rolls up the sleeves of his tunic while Marc stokes at the fire for want of something else to do. The first time Etienne birthed a stuck lamb it was strangled inside the mother and he pulled out the tiny body, slimy and cold. The ewe licked and licked at the stringy carcass and he hadn't had the heart to take it away for burning, so he had stayed there with it, helpless witness to her distress, desperate for one of the shepherds to get back and take it away for him. But no one came. In the end the ewe sat down with the lamb's body nestled into her, trying to warm it up.

The ewe is bleating piteously. Etienne sighs. He has heard the cry often enough, the cry that says her baby is dying. 'Please not another one,' Etienne whispers as he roots around inside the mother, feeling for her baby's legs.

'One of the legs is back,' he yells at Marc, pulling his shirt off. Marc tosses him a lambing rope with a shrug.

He manages to loop both legs, pushing back the lamb's head. The ewe's cries pierce through him as he gropes frantically, trying to pull the legs forward. Several minutes of tugging and the lamb slithers free. Its mother's head slumps to the ground. She is slick with sweat, exhausted. Etienne can hardly bear to look. He lowers his ear to the little body. It is still warm.

'Please God.' He holds his breath.

A few moments later the bundle stirs and he hears the weak little cry that tells him his prayer is answered. Still kneeling, he collapses forward and lays his head between his arms.

On the way home they come across Marc's older cousin huddled with a couple of others in the village square. It's nearly dusk now and there is a tear of ochre bleeding into the purple sky. Etienne knows his mother will be ready to serve up dinner but he wants to linger a while. In the winter, when the night comes early and leaves late, there is nothing much to do but sit indoors by the fire and listen to his mother complain the way that women do, about the mud, the cold, or other women. By the time that Lent comes around he is tired of early nights and waiting for time to pass, so he joins the group.

'Guess what we've got!'

Marc has snatched a small square parcel from his cousin and is waving it around. Etienne looks at Marc enquiringly, not wanting to put his hand out only for Marc to snatch the mysterious package away.

'Swear not to tell anyone?' Marc beckons Etienne closer. His cousin and the others are whispering and Etienne feels the quiet little voice in his gut tell him they are about to play a trick on him. But curiosity defeats the voice and he leans in. 'I swear.'

Marc prizes open the box. Inside there is a scroll of parchment. He picks it up between his thumb and index finger and shakes it gently, relishing the suspense. Etienne peers at the parchment. On it a woman lays prostrate with her breasts exposed whilst a man penetrates her with a long-handled device.

'Antoine found some books at the lord of Magny's manor when they were working up there. There were other books on the tortures of St Agatha and Catherine. The Fall, too, with demons fucking. Loads of other stuff,' Marc brags to the open-mouthed Etienne.

'Do you think people really do that?' Etienne asks.

Marc nods sagely. 'They do it in Paris. My oldest brother went once. He's going to take me next time.'

'No he's not, you liar,' someone chimes in, but Etienne can't tell who as everyone has their heads turned towards a shrill voice coming from the other side of the square.

'Here.' Something is thrust into Etienne's hand. The boys leap to distance themselves from him as the voice approaches. He looks down to see he has the parchment in his hand, and by the time he realises what is about to happen it is too late.

'What's all this?' yells Marc's mother. 'Give me that.' She grabs the end of the scroll. Etienne hesitates, tussles for a moment, then against his better judgement, he unclamps his fingers. Behind his mother's back, Marc is shaking his head and mouthing something that Etienne can't understand. Marc's mother readies herself for a tirade as she unrolls the parchment, but its contents stop the words from coming, and she stands there, mouth wide open, 'I..well…I…' The noises coming from her throat make it sounds like she is drowning. Her eyes are on stalks, her jowls wobbling like an old running-hound and Etienne has to cough to suppress his laughter.

Antoine glowers at Marc from his great height and Marc starts blabbing. 'It was Etienne, mother. He made us look at them, mother. I tried to tell him it was wrong. I did, mother. I did.'

Etienne stares helplessly at Marc. He wants to protest his innocence but he knows it won't make any difference, so he stays silent.

'You filthy little bastard.' Marc's mother grabs Etienne by the ear. 'I'd beat you myself if I didn't know that you'd be crying for that priest to come scuttling out and save you.'

The others are looking at the ground now. Etienne wants to throw the old bag's hand off him and run.

'I'm not a bastard,' he mumbles. 'My father died fighting bandits.' To his horror he feels tears beginning to sting the back of his throat. He pulls away from the woman's grip.

'Not even your mother tells that lie,' she spits. 'Fighting bandits! Did you hear that, boys?' Marc and his brother laugh along sheepishly. Etienne sets his jaw and glares furiously ahead, hoping that his eyes aren't glistening noticeably.

As cross as he is with Marc, he is even angrier with himself. For giving up the stupid scroll in the first place, for taking the blame again, and for letting Marc's nasty old sow of a mother talk about his family like that. He knows that Marc will justify his betrayal to everyone later by saying it was better that Etienne take the blame. Agnes wouldn't even raise her hand to a dog, let alone to her own son. Even worse, Etienne knows that he will end up saying it's alright, because Marc's father is a violent drunkard who would thrash him black and blue. But also because that's just what you have to do to keep friends when you are an outsider who came to the village without a father.

Chapter Three

The abbey sat at the bottom of the hill, towering stone that dwarfed all the other buildings around. The buttresses reached out like arms, drawing in all that might chance to pass under it. Above them, the ancient bell tower stood watch, armoured in masonry against the hammer and blade of bygone invaders. The abbey had been built hundreds of years before Gui's birth for the glory of St Peter and he wondered how many more hundreds it would stand. Perhaps thousands. A silent witness that would endure when no one would be alive to know of Bishop Reginald, of Abbot Roger, or of him.

Now, nearly two decades on, and every step along those cobbled streets had already been made by a thousand former versions of himself. Gui paused under the cool, thick arches of the abbey's gate, felt his lungs expand and release, clearing the dust and fetid humours of the road. No matter the events that had occurred afterwards, there was still a strange comfort to the place. Here his twelve-year old self had found refuge from his father's unpredictable violence, and his mother's sad hopelessness that turned to sickness and finally to death. He had never quite been able to shake the notion that she had chosen death over spending another day under the fists of that man.

Glancing the limestone blocks, Gui fingered the memories, recalled the purpose with which he had stepped through the gates for the first time. Finally certain that God was on his side, he had vowed to work every day to make sure he served the meek, just as Christ instructed. It had been his deliverance and, also the place where he had first met Abbot Roger. The man whom he had wished a thousand times was his real father.

The old man was seated in the window alcove. There had been a time when Gui would have found him in meditation, but now he was dozing gently in the sunlight, the leaded window shadowed upon his face. Abbot Roger started at the knock on the door, face broadening as he recognised his former pupil.

'Gui. Please.' He beckoned Gui to sit with arthritic fingers. He had been old as long as Gui had known him, ancient even, but he had a frailty to him now that spoke of the end, his bones visible under the dry, papery skin.

'Tell me how long has it been?' The old scholar's rheumy eyes searched for the memory.

'Several years, master. Too many, I know.'

'No, no. Since we baptised your son.'

'Etienne?' Stalled by the ease with which his old mentor could still read his heart, Etienne's name caught raw in Gui's throat. 'Ten years

15

gone.'

'Ah yes. Of course. He must be big now.' Roger laughed like a child who had got away with a biscuit from the cooling racks.

'He is.'

'Tell me how he fares.'

The confessor reclined against the back of his chair, body sagging contently as he listened to his student's tales. Gui entertained him with his news, local gossip, then fell back on the past, the preferred resting place of the time-weary mind. The confessor rallied and he talked of how it had been when he was a novice. When a different king had ruled France, long before Jerusalem had been lost to the Saracen and the great lords had grown fat and complacent. And he had believed that Bernard of Clairvaux would lead them all to a better world.

'But man is not made for a better world. He is made for this one. The world has chosen a dangerous path.' He sighed and lapsed into silence. Gui could feel time passing - in the echo of footsteps along a distant corridor, the chirp of a bird outside, the breath of the old man as he tired.

'I should leave you to your contemplation, Master.'

The old monk smiled and gave the arm of the chair a resigned pat.

'I do not think that you will see me again, Gui.'

Gui made to protest but Roger halted him with a tremulous hand.

'I used to believe that the life of those born to pray need only be passed in prayer. But prayer is not enough to keep evil at bay.'

'Master, you have done more than pray. Much more.'

'I have risked very little. What of the rising tide of intolerance that I should have done more to dam?' Regret moulded the scholar's face. 'But this body has no more to give.' His lips parted with a sigh.

'Where you are going you will have no need of it.' The corners of Gui's mouth turned up just barely, as though they were unable to support the weight in his eyes.

Abbot Roger's brow rose fleetingly. 'You think that you would have served the world better by living an ascetic life as I have?

Gui edged forward in his seat, readying his objection, but Roger continued, 'And what of those priests who served the early church before marriage was prohibited, do you find them corrupted? They believed all love is of the Lord and is the Lord.'

'If I have lived my life true to love then why do I still find myself living in fear for the lives of those I cherish?'

'The bars of your prison are fashioned with guilt. As long as you try to silence the truth in your heart, another absolution from me gains you nothing.'

'Master, I came only to see you, not to trouble you with confession.' Gui shifted in his seat.

'Look at me, Gui.' Roger draped his hand over his chest. 'This casing

16

of flesh fails us all and Death is a quick-fingered accountant. Don't wait until you feel his approach before you balance the weight in your heart.'

Gui took in the old man with a steady gaze. It was hard to look him directly in the eye and not see the end. But as much as he wanted to break the exchange, he found he could not. Abbot Roger nodded, encouraging Gui to pursue this strange exercise. Slowly, his beloved tutor's face began to change, fading into shadow, until it disappeared, and in its place he saw his own. Startled, Gui blinked, and the confrontation with his own visage vanished.

His confessor spoke. 'It is not the Lord's forgiveness that you require, is it?'

Gui dragged his hand across his jaw. It felt as though his insides might spill out if he tried to speak. Eyes shining kindly, the monk opened his palms - an invitation to Truth. A tidal wave of silence compressed Gui's lungs. He could feel his hands trembling.

'I have to tell Etienne I am his father.' The words tumbled out with an urgency that left him feeling naked. Gui smiled shakily. 'My son is nearing manhood.' His breath scorched as though he had been running. 'I'm afraid it will be too late.'

'Too late for what?'

'It is easier to win the forgiveness of a boy than undo resentment grown in a man.'

'So why do you hesitate?'

'Agnes thinks he is too young. That the truth is more burden than liberation. All it would take if one careless slip of the tongue and...' He shrugged off the familiar pinch that crept into his shoulders, ashamed to reveal how tight was the grip of this demon. 'Rome kindles hatred with every new directive. How can I defend us...' He stalled as he realised what he was about to say.

The old man smiled indulgently. 'You mean once I am gone?'

Abbot Roger gestured towards the bookcase, warped with the weight of the tomes, and with time.

'What does Augustine say about the lion of truth?'

Gui's eyes fell on the illuminated spine that rested on top of the vertically stacked books.

'Let it loose; it will defend itself.'

'Then really, what is there to fear?'

Roger pushed down hard on the window seat to stand on uncertain legs. Gui jumped up and took his tutor's arm. He was shocked by how light it felt, how insubstantial the flesh. His mentor was little more than a frame.

'It is not much at the end, is it?'

Gui found he could only shake his head in reply.

'Promise me, Gui. Promise me you will do it. God will protect his own. Have the conviction of your faith. There is no greater reward than Truth on earth. Or in Heaven.'

Gui squeezed the old man's hand and placed a kiss on his forehead.

'You have done more than any man could ask to protect me, and my family. For that I am forever in your debt. Thank you.'

'And I thank you for showing patience to an old man.'

Gui blinked back the emotion. 'Bless you, master.'

'God bless you, child. We are all poor sinners.'

Gui weaved his way back through the corridors and staircases of the abbey, but only when he was clear of the building did he allow himself to sit in the refuse by the roadside to mourn the old man, the wise compassion and faultless reasoning of which he would soon be bereft. And, more uncomfortably, to consider a world in which the tales and grievances that found their way back from Montoire to the bishop's office would no longer be brushed aside out of respect for the venerable scholar. The fork in the road was clear: compromise or truth. Gui raised his eyes to the heavens.

A passing cart flung a spatter of mud at him from the gutter. A man and a young boy were heaving the wooden frame along the pock-marked road, their gait sagging from a long day's work.

'Watch the wheels!' The man flicked a casual hand across the top of the boy's head.

'Sorry, father,' the boy replied.

The man raised his brow, poked his cap up out of his eyes and raised half a smile. 'It's been a long day.'

A long day. An honest day.

'Set it loose,' Gui whispered to the memory of his mentor. 'And come what may.'

Chapter Four

Etienne steps outside. The roar coming from the village sounds like a torrent of water. It takes him a few moments to adjust to the world; the shock of the rain on his skin, the biting wind, the half-light of dawn. He closes his eyes. The sound isn't water. It is voices. Lots of voices, and drums. Scuttling up the branches of a tree he scouts the horizon – flags are piked aloft, flashes of red and gold against the dull sky. He eyes the track that leads to the grazing pastures. If the others have heard the commotion, they will have gone to investigate for sure. And he isn't going to get stuck alone with the sheep for another day. No chance.

The road to the village is jammed with people; street vendors trudging with their wares, messenger boys on errands, women carrying bundles of laundry, kindling and who knows what else women carry. But there are other folk too, finer-dressed ladies, faces shielded from the weather under hooded capes, craftsmen, apprentices, and boys like him who should be somewhere else. Etienne weaves through the crowd, searching for a familiar face. When he reaches the square he sees banners marked with the cross, women praying, men rattling makeshift weapons. In their midst a group plays the pipe and tabor like they do to bring in May.

'What is this?' He tugs the sleeve of a shepherd boy called Jean from the next village.

'There is a holy preacher here. They say he has been to the Holy Land to see the suffering. They are marching all over the Chartraine against the infidel.'

Jean is nearly a head shorter than Etienne, a thin-boned boy who walks with a limp, but there is something hypnotic about him. His eyes are pale grey, almost translucent, and when he looks at you it is hard to look away.

'They say there is a shepherd boy called Stephen travelling with him, performing miracles for the love of Christ.'

'Let's go and see,' Etienne says, and they squeeze their way through the crowd. Marc and a few others are in the thick of it, jumping up and down for a better view. Etienne has never seen a collection of such afflicted people in the same place. Some are leaning on others for support or even being carried, others are bent over walking sticks, limbs wrapped in bandages.

The preacher is standing on a wooden crate, dwarfed by a chestnut tree behind him. He looks almost too old to be alive. Ragged and filthy too. A large crowd has circled round him.

'A piece of cloth from his robes can cure any disease,' Jean whispers, and for a minute Etienne feels the world around him grow perfectly still.

They wriggle further into the crowd, inching their way to the front

19

where people cry out for the preacher's attention. Penned inside the throng, Etienne can feel the expectation rising up like vapour as they huddle together. The preacher begins with a quotation from the gospels and then falls silent, searching them with his pinprick eyes.

'The way is clear. The humility that asks us to walk the treacherous path to the heavenly Jerusalem.'

People turn their heads, scanning the horizon as if it is possible to glimpse the holy city from where they stand.

'But we will not be received into paradise as long as Jerusalem, the earthly castle of the Lord, lies under the shame of infidel occupation. His sacrifice for us forgotten by the rich and powerful sons of France. Sorry are they when they pass on to face Judgement! Repent and take up the cross for Christ the Son!'

For a fleeting breath the preacher's eyes lock onto Etienne. He feels the hairs on his arms rise. The preacher moves forward to give a blessing. The crowd surges, and Etienne is lifted off his feet. Head tilted upward, he sups in some air as he is buffeted back and forth. When he regains his footing, in place of the preacher there stands a boy, not much older that he is, carrying a shepherd's crook in one hand and a sheet of parchment in the other. He thrusts a parchment skywards.

'It's him!' a voice calls out.

'Stephen, the miracle shepherd boy!' yells another.

'Rise up for the Holy Mother!' Stephen cries and the crowd goes beserk. All around people are throwing themselves to the ground, women wail, hysterical. The mass constricts, and with what feels like a blow from a pole, Etienne finds himself tossed down into the mud. Trampled by the weight of bodies that are squeezing the breath from his lungs, he thrashes out, desperately trying to win himself enough room to come to his knees.

Suddenly, everyone calms. A space before him clears. Etienne cranes his head up. The old preacher is there before them, arms aloft as though he is bathing in the rain. He passes his hand gently over the shepherd boys and as he rises, Etienne can feel heat radiating from the preacher's body, intense as the flame of a torch.

'Take heed of the holy one!' shouts Stephen.

From beneath his cloak, the preacher draws out a handful of small felt crosses. Jean inclines his knee and holds out his hands. His pale eyes are wide open. Tears stream down his face. The preacher places a cross into Jean's palm. The boy brings the preacher's white papery hands to his lips. The old man turns to Etienne and places his hand on top of his head. Etienne's mouth feels dry. He swallows.

'Peace be with you,' the preacher says.

'And also with you,' Etienne hears himself reply.

The old man puts his fingers to Etienne's face. They feel icy cold as they stumble across his features.

'The preacher has angelic powers.' Jean says as the holy man moves on. 'He must have seen something in you.'

'You took the cross.' Etienne surveys Jean, incredulous. 'You have to pay money if you take it and then don't go overseas you know.'

'Pay a conversion? Never. I am going.' Jean fingers the felt cross. 'I heard a voice. Not my voice. Not like when you talk to yourself. A voice from outside.'

Etienne isn't sure how to reply so he shakes his head in wonder. Jean's eyes are so transparent, so earnest, it is impossible to think he is lying.

'It was a low voice. Not frightening. Just deep and clear.'

'What did it say?' Etienne asks.

'It said, "kneel". As Jean speaks Etienne hears a strange ringing in his ear. He poggles it with his finger but the noise persists.

'I think you understand,' says Jean.

'Let's get out of here before we catch something,' Marc says, throwing a nod towards a group of supplicants, their wounds covered in rags. 'My skin is starting to itch.'

'I suppose,' says Etienne, but he doesn't want to leave. He is transfixed by the preacher as he walks among the suffering, calmly laying his hands upon them. He is so old, Etienne wonders how it is possible that he has never succumbed to leprosy or coughing sickness.

'His faith protects him.' Jean reads Etienne's mind.

'Witchcraft more like.' Marc tugs at the gawping Etienne. 'Come on, we can't leave my idiot brother up in the fields by himself all morning.'

Reluctantly Etienne turns to Jean. 'See you soon.'

'You will.' Jean's eyes shine like glass. They seem to have their own internal source of light, and although he looks right at Etienne, his attention seems far away.

The others have already set off up the hill, so Etienne trudges behind, casting the odd look back to the square to see if Jean is still there, but all he can see is the crowd, stuck to the preacher like iron filings on a smithy's floor.

'Hurry up!' Marc yodels.

'I'm coming,' Etienne yells, but he does not quicken his step. He feels as though he is labouring under a yoke, inexplicably short of breath. The rain has eased to a trickle. He stops to inhale the freshly-washed earth. The others have disappeared over the brow of the hill now. In his solitude Etienne feels calm, relieved.

Around him the treble of the birds seems very loud. He feels dizzy, as though he can sense the heavens spinning above him. He sits down among the long grasses, still wet from the deluge. Instantly sodden, his trousers cling to his thighs and buttocks but he doesn't care and his indifference makes him laugh aloud.

On the other side of the village, he can see his cottage. He can't go home because his mother will be there, fussing about the place, trying not to worry about Father Gui. He knows she loves him. It's obvious from the way her face looks when she is thinking about him. Etienne doesn't blame her. For all the problems it causes him, he suddenly feels very sad for her. He doesn't help his mother as much as he should, and his heart sinks as he recalls all that she does for him.

She is stuck. Her husband is dead and her family are poor and far away. She can't get married again. Etienne knows that unmarried women aren't really worth that much. Worst of all, his mother knows it too. He glances down at the departing crowds and considers those who took the cross. It's different for boys, he muses. One day soon he will be a man, and he will find a way not to spend his days stooped to the earth picking out weeds or milking sheep, always the butt of someone else's joke.

On the eastern-most horizon, storm clouds are eating up a strip of pale blue sky and he wonders what the people over there are doing – womenfolk bringing their laundry in, merchants on the road to Champagne taking cover with their fine silks and rare spices. Now that's a good life, he thinks, going to those far off places and seeing strange sights that he can't even imagine. The future is some far-distant land and he is not sure by what means he will travel there, but if he closes his eyes, he can see himself standing at a market stall in Chartres or maybe even Paris, picking out silks, watching the trader measure it out yard upon yard. His mother's face when a mysterious package arrives. He won't sign it. She will just know it is from him.

Etienne picks at a honeyed frond of cow parsley then tosses it down the hill. The square is nearly empty and the crowd is trooping away in a long chain, placards aloft, like ants carrying off breadcrumbs. He is troubled by the preacher's sermon in ways that he can't fully make sense of. Mostly because he felt a real, physical sensation that he had never felt before, and it told him Jean was right. Miracles happened all the time for sure, but not to someone like him. He shuts his eyes tight and asks God for a sign, just so he can be certain that the preacher's message was for him too.

There is something scratchy inside his sleeve. Etienne worms his finger in and picks it out, to find himself looking at a small felt cross, exactly like the one the preacher gave to Jean. He can't for a king's ransom say how it got there. Maybe Jean put it there? No, he watched the preacher give him only one. Etienne's chest feels too tight for his breath. He is sure he didn't receive one at the sermon.

He hears the rustle of grass and someone panting before he sees a figure scrambling up the bank towards him.

'Etienne! Etienne!' A cap of white blond hair appears over the brow of the hill.

'Jean!' Etienne slides down the wet grass on his rump.

'What is it?'

22

Jean gives him a triumphal smile. 'Come quickly,' he says as he starts back down, tugging Etienne's hand. 'It's the miracle shepherd boy. It's Stephen. People are saying he is gathering pilgrims for crusade now. You have to come.'

All his life Etienne has had to work that bit harder to win respect from other boys, always waiting for the trick that doesn't get played on anyone else. That's what it's like when you are different. Usually it is just a bit of fun for the others, like a test he has to take again and again to earn his place in the game. But he can tell from the bright, open smile of friendship, that with Jean it will be different.

Chapter Five

Gui's childhood friend, Philippe de Champol, lived half way up the cathedral hill. The three-storied merchant's house was a cross-hatching of timber frames, its top floors bowing out over the walls below. The windows were garlanded with pots of herbs upon which his wife lavished great affection in the absence of land. Philippe hailed from a cadet branch of a noble line, and as third son, free from the obligations of a family estate, he had started a trade in textiles.

His family owned a vineyard near to the Courville manor and the boys all had played together through the dry, bleached grasses of the dying summer when Philippe's father came to oversee the grape harvest. Although the four years that separated them no longer made a distinction, Gui had once been a nine-year old, looking up to the thirteen-year old friend who always intervened to save him from the mean tricks and accidental fists of the older boys.

Philippe opened the door himself, dressed in embroidered cloak of mustard-yellow wool trimmed with fox. He squinted at Gui, feigning not to recognise him, then ushered him across the threshold with a battery of jovial back slaps.

The more successful he became, it seemed to Gui, the more he delighted in embellishing his personality, so as not to disappear under the great waves of bright fabric that surrounded him.

Gui took a deep, velvet-cushioned seat by the fire. He had never desired the trappings of wealth that his own family might once have offered him, but sitting next to Philippe made him feel uncomfortable in his skin nonetheless. Though he could barely admit it to himself, the awkward itch came not from his coarse tunic but from the embarrassment that his old friend considered his asceticism childish. The wine Philippe served to revive his guest was full-bodied and aromatic. It tasted of some long forgotten pleasure and Gui fought the desire to drain the whole cup.

'The wine in that shit hole swamp is really so bad you rode a week to get here, huh?'

Gui gave a laugh that sounded a little too hearty.

'The old man?'

Gui nodded. Philippe swirled the wine round in his glass, nodding gravely. 'We must all meet our end I suppose.'

Gui flicked his hand in what was supposed to be a casual acceptance of the inevitable but Philippe knew him better than that.

'You know you are welcome in my house at any time. Come and visit me in Tours. It's closer to you than Chartres and besides I am there more often these days.'

'Thank you, my friend. You know I would visit you more often if my circumstances permitted.'

'I know, you have other…responsibilities.' For a moment a wry grin crossed the merchant's face, but today was not the day to goad a wounded friend.

Philippe ordered a plate of pig's trotters and more wine. It was Gui's first meal of the day and the second carafe of wine made him feel drunk. Nostalgia took an easy finger hold amidst the hazy warmth of rich hospitality, and they wound their way through the secret tree houses and ruined battlements of their youth until they arrived back at present circumstance.

'So, what goes on in that village of yours?' Philippe asked.

Gui shot him a look of exasperation. 'The same. Petty landowners pen their complaints against me to the bishop. Directives. Charters. Squabbles.'

Philippe shrugged. 'They say the bishop acquired a real taste for heretic flesh on that crusade down south. They are shaking the tree here for them. All sorts of diverting new creeds.'

'They send me the sermons I am supposed to use for the fight.'

'I just notice a tide is turning my friend. I am hearing things I don't like. The king's beloved tutor is an unassailable ally, but when the old man goes, there will be no one here to speak on your account with the powers that be,' he said. Then, seeing his friend was snatching sips from a now empty cup, Philippe reached forward and laid a steady hand on Gui's forearm. 'But I think you know that don't you?'

Gui flicked a nod of acknowledgement. In his mind's eye ashes were falling like snow onto grease-smeared cobbles – the remnants of a human being devoured by the pyre. Philippe was still sitting with his bulk craned forward expectantly. There were not many moments like this that came in life – when a friend stood on the other bank of a chasm that had defeated you a thousand times, hand in extension.

Pitching forward, Gui placed his palms together as though in prayer and said, 'Roger has been my only ally in that nest of vipers. Even my own father wouldn't suffer to hear my name.' He wasn't asking for a response and Philippe stayed silent. 'I have hardly acquired more friends since then.'

'There are friends to be had at the bishop's palace? I didn't know.'

He drew a smile from Gui. 'Then maybe it's time.'

'Time for what?'

Gui took a breath as though readying to plunge his head underwater. 'It's my responsibility to make sure my family is safe, Philippe. Mine.' He rubbed furiously at his collar. 'I promised the old man I would tell Etienne the truth.'

Philippe threw his hands apart – what's the problem? 'He's old enough.'

The pressure of what he had to say next forced Gui to his feet, and he began to pace the room. 'How can I tell the truth to my son and then ask him to tell the same lie? How do you teach a man to lead if not by example?' Holding up his girdle, knotted with the vows of obedience, poverty, and of chastity, he said, 'What if I can't live with this anymore.'

Philippe drew back his head, suddenly the stern older brother. 'Don't be so ridiculous. Why would you give up a good job? Not everyone's idea of fun, I admit, but you are housed, clothed, a small stipend. Every second priest has a family. Christ and his saints, Gui, you know that.'

'You said it yourself. With the old man gone I have no advocate left in the Church.'

'I meant only that you should take greater care now, not abandon your station to a life of hand-to-mouth scribe work writing out wills until your eyes fail.' Philippe pressed at the air with his palms as though cautioning a small child from running too fast. 'You are upset about Roger. It's natural, he was as a father to you. Give yourself time.'

'Time?' Gui batted away the counsel. Philippe was on his feet by now, gesticulating as though he was seeking to halt a moving wagon. Gui ignored him. 'You think the boy who thwarted the bishop's inquisitors and got a parish for his sins has more time?'

Heart pacing as rapidly as his mind, the conversation with Abbot Roger turned over and over. *Set it loose it will defend itself.* The rising moon was tracking across the window. Gui glanced out. The streets were dead, like the set of a play. Beads of sweat breaking on his brow, he closed his eyes. In the blackness he saw the night his son came into the world. Agnes, weeping for joy and exhaustion, he, staring at the bundle of swaddling in her arms, flooded with relief and sweating terror at the enormity of it. That night he had sworn he would be the best father he could, that he would do anything in his power to protect them both and that they would know only his love.

'I can't explain it Philippe, but I know in here.' Gui placed his palm on his chest and said softly, 'If I don't act now, everything falls.'

The merchant's arms flopped to his sides in defeat. 'Then may God protect you.'

*

Agnes sat up and rubbed off the fog of sleep. The dull glow of an overcast sky seeped through the shutters. It was long past dawn. The air felt warm on her skin – heat from the hearth next door. She threw off the bedclothes and raced to the living room. The floor was swept, the fire had a good flame, a large pan of water set to warm over it. She felt her face broaden with relief. *Gui is back.* Even though he had only been gone a week, Etienne was too obstinate to have undertaken so girlish a task as housework.

The joy fizzing in her veins ebbed as she surveyed the room more closely. The clutter of family life had been prodded onto shelves and patted into piles – Gui's parchments, her drying racks spilling with herbs, church candles stacked into a precarious pyramid with a carelessness that would only seem orderly in the eyes of a child. Etienne must have crept about like a mouse not to wake her before he left for the fields. The unexpected help should have been a comfort, but instead she found menace in the ordered stillness, and the foreboding of a mother's instinct; all was not its proper place.

Opening the shutters a jar she peeked out, hoping against reason to see the man she knew should still be in Chartres. There was no one. Not even beyond the hedgerows that separated their cottage from the washing brook, where faces often popped up, hawk-eyed, hunting for some little treasure of malice to report about the unwed woman left unsupervised. She craned to see the angle of the sun but it was obscured by cloud. Perhaps it was not yet mid morning when the women usually began to drift down, baskets of laundry on their hips and children criss-crossing their paths.

A week was the longest amount of time she had been without Gui since he had first appeared at the prison door with his wild, black curls and earnest walnut eyes, and she had mistaken him for the angel Gabriel. Fighting the creeping unease, she ran her palm over the smooth, oak table, remembering the dirty shell the house had been when first she arrived, a suggestion of pregnancy hidden under her housekeeper's apron and a sad tale of a husband suddenly lost. Gui had even held a funeral for him. She pressed her lips shut, sealing in her laughter at the memory, and crossed herself in reverence to her poor fairy tale man. How grateful she had been to see the spartan rooms, the cobwebbed corners, the damp larder. The two rooms they had cleaned and mended and made their home, the bed on which she had birthed her baby.

She poked at the loose bundle of threads that Etienne had stuffed haphazardly back into her darning box. It was the one possession Gui had managed to salvage from the lot sequestered by the Bishop of Chartres's bailiffs after her father's execution. Estève had been a broad–shouldered, squat man, with an honest charm and a keen nose that had taken him from a paludier on the blood-red salt flats of the Camargue to a merchant whose wealth exceeded many of the noblemen he supplied. Her mother, Céline, was noble born, ostracised by her family for defying them in a love marriage to a merchant - and one from the Langue d'Oc to boot. Not even the crystalline riches of the salt trade had been enough to undo the stigma of this swarthy foreigner, or the disgrace of such a wilful daughter. By the time Estève's fortune had grown enticing enough for those pinch-faced aristocrats it was too late. Céline had been taken birthing her second baby.

Agnes had only the vaguest impressions of her, she couldn't even call them memories; the scent of rosewater and lavender, a full skirt of green silk stretching up and up, a tear drop pearl that chinked on a silver bracelet. Rather, it was her father's expression as he reminisced that made the portrait Agnes had of her mother. His adoration declared in the shrug of Mediterranean indifference he gave to her dowry of familial fury, the riot of irreverence in his eyes capturing as no memory could the spirit of this woman.

Her father declared he would never re-marry, and Agnes found herself elevated to the status of a son. Her childhood was spent accompanying him up and down the salt routes, her world the blush-pink rocks of far-off mines, the grey, sandy crystals of Biscay, tiny particles that always seemed to be caught under her nails, and large, inviting chunks that looked like candied apricots. Salt, her father taught her, was the nourisher of blood, preserver of life.

By the time she was twelve she could read and write both French and Latin. Estève handed her his account ledgers, heavy as bricks. Creamy leaves of parchment tied in leather binders, embossed with his logo - a Roman coin laid over an 'S' shape. For, as he often told her, the Roman army had marched for its *Salarium Argentum*, its salt money. One day you will have a household of your own, he said. I will find you a husband worthy of sharing this with you once I am resolved into the earth. As she grew towards womanhood, the great guessing game began: who will he be, this worthy man? Will he be from Marseille, a merchant like her father? An Italian perhaps, the floppy-haired son of a banking family? Or a tall, fair Dutch Guildsman, like the ones who came to the Fairs to sell their wool and linen?

But no, papà, you brought me none of those, she thought, sweeping the breadcrumbs left from Etienne's breakfast into the fire. You brought me none of those power-hungry Italians, or petty French noblemen looking for a stipend to buy a larger army. The task of finding a suitor worthy of his daughter was interrupted just before her fifteenth birthday as they returned to Chartres, a mule- train of merchandise turned to gold. That's alchemy, he told her. But all the gold in the world could not have saved them. She knew that now. If only she had known it then. The key had been in her hands.

Voices carried on the air, waking her from the past. The ululating tones of women pierced with the shrieks of young children. Agnes looked outside for heads bobbing up and down behind the hedge line as they washed their garments; a blonde bun neatly pinned under a cloth bonnet, or a tangle of auburn, loose whorls twisting like Medusa. But there were only the branches of a sapling bending in the breeze, their shadows dancing back and forth across her face. The women must be making their way down from the village square, she told herself. Or else it is another one of those marches for the Holy Land, organised by charlatans to drum a pity penny for their own purses. They wouldn't have lingered so long if Gui had been here, that was for sure.

Shrinking away from the window, her gaze fell on Gui's disarray of parchments. She pictured him sitting at the desk in his long, black robe, lean, muscular hands turning the pages of the psalter as he taught Etienne to read. In a strange way, she thought, her father had kept his promise. He had brought her the worthiest of men. He's worth all the salt of the earth, father, she thought. He has taken more than a dowry of fury for me, he has taken the life-long menace of death.

For comfort, she bent to pick one up. And it was then that she saw it - the spider's leg scratches of a script she knew to be her son's. Her hand was already shaking as she let the sheet fall open. Suddenly, the voices from the village were deafeningly loud, the shrieks a clarion of comprehension. She brought both hands to her mouth and the note fluttered back down onto the pile.

Body shivering as though it were midwinter, she jumped up, mind racing ahead of her to the village square where those voices would become accusing screeches, fingers jabbing blame. She searched the room for an anchor. But he was not there. She felt as though she were being buried alive. Inhaling sharply, she caught the smell of his warm musk mixed with the frankincense that he used in the church. It was such a visceral assault on her senses, she crumpled down onto the writing bench. *Please God, no.*

'Where are you?' she whispered into the empty space. Louder now, insides crawling with desperation, '*Where are you?!*' Then, body thrown forward as though by a gale, she ran towards the fields, towards whatever the Devil had wrought.

Chapter Six

Water tumbled from the lip of the silver jug into the inquisitor's cup of wine. He watched as it mingled with the viscous, plum liquid, fighting the urge to touch the letter in his pouch. He knew Amaury, Lord of Maintenon, considered him a useful fool. France was riddled with nobility who used the clergy as a veneer of piety for their venal wants. It should have been a marriage of convenience between church and state, but the relationship between the two men had been unbalanced by the misfortune of happenstance. Finally, though, with this letter, Inquisitor de Nogent had acquired the power to make it a partnership of equals. He was going to savour playing this card as long as he could.

Slowly, he brought the vessel to his lips and allowed a few drops to roll over his tongue. From behind the brim of his cup, he could see his host massaging the knuckles of one hand with the spade-like palm of the other. They were hands that could snap a man's neck as though it were a guinea fowl. How long would he be able to draw out the other man's discomfort, he wondered? Not long, given the hot emotion he was about to kindle.

'And how goes the construction of your castle, if I may ask, my lord?' De Nogent began.

'If you may ask.' The big man rubbed the arm of the chair with a large, flat thumb. 'Awaiting the completion of my keep. Once unveiled, it will be the largest keep in France.'

Amaury of Maintenon was scion of a family who could trace back its line only two hundred years but, coffers full from booty won on the battlefield, he was determined to take his house from the backwaters of the Loire and into the royal court of France.

'And such an undertaking it is, my lord. What a testament that it is nearing completion in so few years.'

Maintenon folded his arms. A man satisfied with his efforts. 'Indeed. It is perfectly round, an entirely novel design. They tell me the king himself means to copy it.'

'I would not doubt it.'

Despite himself, de Nogent angled his head sycophantically, 'And the abbey..?'

Maintenon leaned the bulk of his torso forward. Tired of vying for the attention of the bishop against men of greater means, he had undertaken to build an abbey into which he could install his own man.

'Once the keep is finished, it will free up the necessary resources,' Maintenon said. 'As I am sure you have noticed, the foundations are set. It will be for the new abbot to oversee the rest. When I see fit to appointment him.'

The new abbot. The inquisitor gave a strained smile. 'There is more than one candidate?'

'For a seat of power outside the jurisdiction of the bishop, a direct line to the Holy See? There is always more than one candidate for the post of an abbot.'

De Nogent pressed his lips together until the thin line of flesh disappeared. After so many years of broken promises he had thought himself immune to such double dealing, but still he felt a stab of betrayal to hear it spoken aloud – and so brazenly to boot.

'One willing to wait ten years with nothing but a muddy field and a few lumps of sandstone to hope in?' De Nogent said tartly.

Maintenon's face soured.

Gazing carelessly into the contents of his cup the inquisitor continued, 'I remember well the nobleman who came to me denouncing a merchant and his daughter as heretics. Of course I agreed to investigate the case even before I learned the happy coincidence of their valuable estate.'

Maintenon's lip curled upward. 'Your piety has always been most commendable.'

'An abbacy hardly seems excessive recompense for the cause of righteousness.'

'The gift of the abbey is mine, but it is for Bishop Reginald to confirm the appointment of abbot.' Maintenon shrugged helplessly. 'All I can do is offer charity.'

'You know as well as I that the appointment by the bishop is a mere formality. The choice of abbot is a boon of the abbey's benefactor.'

The letter tucked inside his cloak was burning a hole in the inquisitor's chest. He smoothed his hand over it as though petting a cat. A scratch in his throat provoked a small, dry cough. Drawing himself up straight in his chair, he fought the urge to take a sip of wine. Enough of this insult.

'My lord Amaury, it pains me to have to remind you that you would not have acquired the means to fund such charity were it not for my assistance.'

Maintenon's nostrils flared. 'That was before the Le Coudray girl escaped,' he said. 'And you were dispatched elsewhere.'

De Nogent ignored the insult. 'An unfortunate mishap,' he retorted. 'If I remember the father's ashes gained near ten thousand acres of good soil and enough cash from the salt roads to field an army against a count.'

The inquisitor looked out the window, heart pattering in outrage. His eye caught the sharp veins of twisted lead and stone stumps of the abbey beyond - testament only to the greedy self-interest of a man whose insatiable appetites far outstripped his means. He cringed inwardly at the thought of how easily he had been duped. Had Maintenon ever meant forgo any of his income to build for the glory of God? Ignominy heating his blood, he narrowed his regard and said deliberately, 'Yet still you want more.'

'Warfare is an expensive business,' said Maintenon.

'As is purchasing the favour of those in the highest ranks of courtly circles.'

A vein in the nobleman's neck popped against taut muscle.

'Not as costly as purchasing the ear of the pope. I come from the ranks of those who fight, Inquisitor de Nogent. You think I can't tell ambition when I see it? Or do you think it reasonable to suppose I would put your ambition before my own?'

De Nogent could feel the other man's desire to do violence radiating towards him. Placing his cup down precisely on the table, the inquisitor brought the palms of his hands together. Ten years seemed as nothing. It was time to play his card.

'One of my informants intercepted this on the road from Vendôme.' De Nogent withdrew the letter from his cloak and perched keenly on his seat, ready to watch the Greek fire. 'It would seem, as I have long suspected, that Agnes Le Coudray is alive and well. And nearby.'

'What?' The Lord of Maintenon ground his teeth. 'That old fool at Chartres said she was drowned.'

'Abbot Roger?' De Nogent tutted. 'Trying to protect the de Courville boy no doubt.' He squeezed his fingernails into his palm as momentarily he re-lived the stinging humiliation. The utter shock that de Courville - a mere novice! - had freed a heretic, yet it was he who suffered the greater consequences of her escape. Chastened for his zealous approach, he had been sent to the southern lands, as lowly assistant to the inquisitors there. Six years it had taken him to make it back to the north, within striking distance of the Parisian courts. The rest of the time he had spent bartering with the man opposite him for his rightful due. Flexing his fingers he gave a dismissive shake of his head.

'And you did not know that at the time?' Maintenon studied him with a cold, predatory eye.

'Roger was the king's tutor. I was hardly in a position to interrogate him.'

'What has changed?'

'I'm glad you asked that,' de Nogent said with a sly smile. 'The old man will be dead within the month.' He placed the letter carefully on the table before Maintenon; the trump card of a winning hand.

A low growl bubbled in Maintenon's throat. 'Let me guess, Bishop Reginald of Chartres doesn't have you in mind to fill the vacancy?'

De Nogent's cheeks hollowed.

Maintenon snatched up the letter, shaking it out as though he were trying to hurl the words from the page. Shoulders hunched against the assault of his emotions, the grey eyes darkened to a storm. He placed the note back down on the table beside him, but the inquisitor saw how he struggled to withdraw his gaze, as though fearful it might make some move against him.

Bernard de Nogent gave a thin smile. He had been steeling himself for the explosive anger of the other man, but not this, not fear. *After all these years.*

'I have dispatched retainers to apprehend her and will depart immediately to verify. If it is indeed her, then I will bring her back to account for her heresy,' he said solemnly.

The nobleman's jaw muscles bulged beneath his beard. 'That is what you said last time.'

The prelate's eyelids fluttered at the affront. He reached deep for his composure. There were other cards yet to play. 'There were circumstances beyond my control. There is no need for my lordship to be concerned.'

Maintenon knuckles cracked as he rubbed his fists together. 'You dare to come talk to me of the abbey whilst all along the Le Coudray whore has been at large. She could have spread her lies to anyone with an ear to listen,' he spat.

'Lies?' De Nogent opened up an inquiring hand – what lies, indeed? 'Who would listen? She is a heretic.' He allowed the breath of a pause to whisper its doubt. 'Were she in the hands of another, well, after all these years, we might be concerned she could convince them of her innocence… And her title.' He let the last word echo into the high ceiling. 'But I can assure you my men have her under guard as we speak. And I shall be moved by no such clemency.'

'Are you threatening me?' Maintenon gripped the arms of the chair with both hands. De Nogent could feel the menace of the other's man's powerful frame barely restrained. Shrinking back in his chair, the prelate held out a defensive palm. 'Of course not, my lord.'

'Then see that you burn her.' Maintenon exhaled loudly, a bestial snort.

'The letter also talks of a boy.' The steel eyes spoke murder. 'An heir.'

De Nogent nodded gravely. 'I am making inquiries. It seems she may have sired a bastard.'

'Find him.' The big man shifted his bulk uncomfortably in his seat. 'Then perhaps we can consider the matter of the abbacy.'

'I understand.' The prelate placed his hand over his heart. 'But there is no need for concern. I doubt he even knows his grandfather had an income of the plumpest northern baron.' An apologetic bow. 'You are a busy man. A servant can see me out.'

Disappearing into the velvet comforts of his carriage, Bernard de Nogent packed away his smile and banged on the roof for his driver to depart. The meeting had been more instructive than he hoped. He knew Maintenon wanted the ghosts of the past consigned to their graves, but his reaction had been so visceral that de Nogent was sure he had stumbled upon something more – some other weakness ripe for exploitation.

Gazing out upon the embryonic columns of the abbey as he rode by, he could not help but see a future version of himself vigilantly surveying the grounds, the weight of an abbot's velvets on his shoulders, proud as any new parent. Unaccustomed as he was to dwelling on the sensations of his physical body, Bernard de Nogent felt his chest lift, and his spine straighten. Even seated in his carriage, he felt a head taller. Head of a monastic order fit for the new world of righteousness ushered in by His Eminence, Pope Innocent III. Then, wagon juddering over the deep, muddy ruts as the incipient building disappeared from view, he crossed himself for the sin of pride.

*

It was shortly before Compline and the royal purples of sunset had yielded to the cloak of night. The inquisitor had supped well; a Grave of small birds accompanied by thick, lightly-browned rounds of bread. Although his portion, naturally, had been no more than a few mouthfuls - a discipline to which he gladly submitted as befitted the austerity of his position.

Hands touching briefly in prayer, he stood and smoothed down his vestments in preparation for a final tour of the dungeons before turning in. Men less conscientious than he would doubtless have foregone this most difficult of tasks, but as hard as was the observance of human suffering, how great was the consolation of knowing the he was offering a gift to those souls. Each one, born in Christ, was receiving no less than a final opportunity to find their way back to salvation through His mercy.

The prison was silent but for his footsteps and the whine of his latest guest that put him in mind of a fox injured by a farmer's trap. It was the Devil's anguish at losing his grip, he reminded himself, and a sure sign that his ministrations were working.

'Mercy,' the woman raised her head, although she did not look him in the eye. Wrists bloodied and scabbed from the shackles that chained her, she wore only an under garment, torn from where his agents had inspected her for signs of the Devil. Jaw clenched against the stench of her soiled tunic, the inquisitor nodded in sympathy.

'Then you are ready, my child?'

'Please, my lord. No more.' The voice was barely audible. 'It was the Devil, like you said. He came to me.' She began to sob. 'He came to me and I did know it.'

A shudder of satisfaction rippled inside him. Bernard de Nogent extended a long, thin finger towards to bars of the cell.

'I know, my child. It is a terrible thing. But you will be at peace soon enough.'

Suddenly, as if powered by some unseen life force, the woman hoisted herself up on the bars. 'What of my daughter? Now will you tell me how she fares?'

The inquisitor drew his head back. 'Have no fear. All the innocents are taken into the bosom of the Church.'

The sunken eyes gripped onto De Nogent. 'Let me see her! Just for a moment. Please.'

De Nogent sighed as he turned away, shaking his head in sad contemplation of how vulnerable was the female sex to the temptations of the Dark One.

'My Lord,' the butler's voice rasped. 'Your guest has arrived.'

The man before him wore a blouson of blue and yellow silk, his beard waxed to a point at the chin. Christian he called himself, although de Nogent doubted it was his real name any more than it was his faith. He grimaced at such detestable vanity and the stink of the man's pomander. Initially receptacles for religious keepsakes, the latest fashion had them filled with perfumes, an innovation of which the inquisitor heartily disapproved.

The spy rubbed his hands lasciviously. 'An honour to receive another invitation so soon, your reverence.'

De Nogent rolled his eyes inwardly. For years his patience had been tried by the sloth of rag-tag informants - nothing but criminals whose good fortune had seen them cheat the gallows. But the Lord never failed to reward those whose work was just, and it had been this Christian who intercepted the letter sent by the Le Coudray whore. As much as he wished the Lord had chosen a less vulgar vehicle, the message was unmistakable. So much more than proof, it was a weapon. One that the Lord intended for him to strike not only at the black heart of heresy but also at the servants of Satan within the Church who suffered them to live.

Uninvited, an image of Gui de Courville assaulted his mind's eye. The scruffy curls and contrived air of distraction – mere childish dishevelment that Abbot Roger had mistaken for scholarship. Nothing but an upstart novice protected by a senile old man. How well that boy had played the wide-eyed innocent. How easily he beguiled others with false charm, whilst an authorised Church inquisitor who toiled tirelessly was left unrewarded. De Nogent ground his teeth at the memory.

'I need some more information,' he said to the spy. 'The letter you acquired mentioned a boy.'

Christian smiled broadly, revealing a full set of ivory teeth. Some price, thought de Nogent.

'I need to know his whereabouts.'

'Quite a task,' said Christian.

With a sideways glance, de Nogent followed as the spy's eyes wandered over the polished walnut table and the heavy, silk curtains that concealed the doorway into his main residence. Con men always have a nose for exactly what another man is prepared to give.

'Not a task beyond your…considerable ability, I trust?'

Christian brought his palms together in mock prayer. 'I pray you jest!'
'I never jest.'

The spy's hands sprang apart with a peel of laughter. 'Of course.'

'I require confirmation of the boy's parentage.' De Nogent's tongue hovered between his open teeth – what to tell this brigand without revealing the personal value of the information. An heir to the Le Coudray estate, whom, once cloistered inside a carefully selected monastery, would be an untouchable weapon with which to goad Maintenon. Equally as rewarding would be the satisfaction of having de Courville know that his spawn was in the hands of the Church.

'Le Coudray's, one assumes from the letter,' he continued, 'but assumption, Monsieur Christian, is the midwife of disaster.'

Christian chortled. 'How wise.' He rocked forward onto the balls of his feet. 'And compensation..?'

'The per diem will be as previously.'

Christian the spy ran his tongue over his lips, and gave a resigned twitch of his brow.

'Good.' De Nogent's gaze drifted to his aged butler as he dropped a coin into the spy's hand. Christian tipped his feathered hat and fell in behind the butler, sauntering down the hallway like a tourist at a Venetian palace.

De Nogent's eyes fluttered shut. Tomorrow he would go to Montoire sur Eure in person and interrogate Le Coudray. Maintenon was hiding something, he could feel it. And he was willing to wager that whore knew what it was. If he could prove the bastard was an heir to the estate then all the better. He would hold Maintenon to ransom, and burn both the parents.

Chapter Seven

Gui was two leagues from Montoire when a voice came skimming ghostly on the wind. At first he took it for boys labouring in the fields, but the cry did not abate and as it drew closer he was able to decipher it. Shrill and urgent, it filled his guts with frantic dread. *'Father Gui! Father Gui!'*

'I am Gui,' he cried out as he ran toward the small figure stumbling down the road.

'Father Gui, you must come quickly.' The boy panted out the words, legs buckling with exhaustion. Gui threw his arms forward to catch the messenger, his clothes instantly damp with sweat from the boy's body.

'You must come. They've taken Agnes.'

Blood thumped in Gui's ears. 'What do you mean? Who has taken her?'

'They came at dawn. The bishop's guard. They took the old farrier and his wife, a labourer and Agnes.'

Gui heard himself groan, a low, animal sigh. How could you have left her? *You fool.*

Wide-eyed with panic, the boy continued. 'They said they would do well to remember the fate of those fallen into falsehood. They said they would all burn the same.'

Gui turned his face away, heart pounding with a rage that no man of God should harbour.

'No-one will burn.' He put his hand on the boy's shoulder. 'Where are they held?'

'At the old monastery on the road to Tours.'

'What of Etienne?'

The boy looked agitated. 'He was not among them.'

Gui hoisted the child onto his mount and they set off, jolting along the ruts of the spring-drenched road. The uneasy instinct that he had convinced himself to lay aside scoured his gut. *How could you?*

The messenger boy's arms were a sweaty band around Gui's waist, and as they rattled down the pot-holed paths it put him in mind of Etienne as a small child - how hotly he clung to Agnes, even as he slept, hair pasted against his cherub face. Had those moments of grace really all been an illusion, his reassurance the necessary act of a desperate jongleur? Gui urged his old mount on, insides crawling with his worst imaginings.

*

The ragged silhouette of the monastery came into view from some distance across the plain. It had been abandoned centuries before as the ornamented Benedictine houses closed in the wake of reform. Weeds and brambles now chased their way around the carved stone capitals and through the vacant arches that had once housed windows and doors.

The façade partly blocked by a horse and wagon, Gui scraped past the protruding axles of the carriage. He threw his weight at the great doors, the screech of the bolt along the floor penetrating his skull as it swung open. He raced up to the crossing between the nave and the choir.

The villagers were knotted together on a bench. They seemed shrunken, like dolls slumped between the columns of the transept. Agnes was in the middle, sallow with exhaustion, her hair pulled loose from its pins. She cast her head down as his eyes met hers and suddenly the vaulted, echoing space felt vertiginous.

The two guards lounging in the choir jumped up.

'Who are you?' They approached Gui, hands hovering at their belts.

Gui shrugged off the challenge and dropped to a crouch before the prisoners. The story of their arraignment was clear from the dark shadows that circled their eyes. Gui took Agnes's hand and it turned it over to reveal red welts where her wrist was tied. Now he was closer, he could see the sleeve of her dress was torn. He looked up into her face but her gaze was distant. His hands shook as he worked his finger under the rope and, taking his fruit knife, severed the knot.

'What are you doing?' The guard gripped Gui's shoulder.

Gui uncoiled to face him, close enough to see the blood vessels fractured in the yellow film of the man's eyes.

'I am priest of this parish.' His tone was measured, but his eyes spoke differently. 'Why are these people bound?'

The guard lifted his chest. 'They are to be held for questioning on the bishop's orders.'

'The bishop's orders?' Gui let his voice rise. 'On what grounds?'

'Suspicion of heresy by public rumour.'

'Public rumour? Ridiculous. Release them.'

The guards exchanged sniggers. The squat one, hands wedged triumphantly on his hips, shook his head. 'An inquisitor is on the way.'

A knot of alarm tightened in Gui's gut. He pivoted back to the villagers. The farrier's wife wiped her cheek with a sleeve, pulling her husband's tethered arm up as she did so.

'Do they look like they might be able overpower you?' Gui made his way down the line, cutting them free from each other. Rubbing his wrists, the old farrier nodded in gratitude. His wife gave a sniffle as her husband put his arm around her and it rang in Gui's head, loud as any parish bell.

'Take courage. You will be released from this nonsense before the day is done.'

Gui spoke to Agnes's lowered head - the mat of pale golden yarn that she sometimes let him wash in the brook when it was warm enough. Pricks of perspiration lined his collar as his fingers lighted on her head.

'I will wait here with you.'

Agnes's head snapped up, features sharpening. He dropped to his knees, beaming at the recognition. But she was shaking her head. Lips moving, just barely, Gui could not make out the whisper, but he could sense she was asking him to look to their son.

At first Gui didn't recognise the brittle limbs and sunken face that stalked into the church, but then the man removed his hood and there was no mistaking him - Bernard de Nogent. The black hair was flecked with grey now, hairline receded to emphasise darting, vulturine eyes. Heart in his throat, Gui was on his feet. The last time he had seen de Nogent was at the Cathedral hearing when he was expelled to Montoire. The inquisitor's eyes, usually so impassive, had burned then in a covenant of revenge.

Bernard de Nogent pursed his thin, lined lips. 'Ah. The priest from Montoire,' he said. 'Aren't you going to ask me how I fare?'

'Well, it would seem from your robes.'

'It is easier to find decent cloth in the city.' The smile was triumphant. 'I would return to your parish for now if I were you, Father.'

The inquisitor walked away, fox-trimmed velvet swinging at his ankles. Gui felt his blood heat. How easy it would be to break it, he thought observing the fragile balance of de Nogent's head atop his skinny neck. He closed his eyes for a moment, swallowing down the rage. The old couple on the bench were staring at him, murmuring a prayer. Agnes's shoulders were hunched up high, her arms cradled across her chest. Gui lifted her face up in the cup of his hand. He brushed her cheek dry with his thumb.

'Please don't be afraid. Please trust in me.'

The thought that she might not made him nauseous.

De Nogent's breath was at his collar. 'Ah yes, could it be I recognise that lovely face?' A bony hand extended from the wide, black sleeve to caress the air before Agnes.

Gui pivoted, and met the inquisitor's eyes with murder. Bernard pinched his face, as though he were considering laughter. Gui's fingers gripped white around the inquisitor's cassock.

The inquisitor lent towards him and whispered, 'Return to your parish or you will be joining them on that bench.'

Gui staggered out into the setting sun. The sky above his head was a penumbra of birds roosting against the remains of the light. He felt as though he had been drained of blood. Resting on his palfrey's back, his head collapsed into his arms, the world reduced to the grate of his breath and the familiar smell of his animal's coarse hair. After a few moments the horse whinnied as though it meant to rally him from his paralysis.

He gave the old beast a pat on its haunches and mounted. Perhaps this was not punishment but deliverance - the liberating hand of God. There was no choice to it now, only necessity. One small transgression and he would return to wait for nightfall. The thought of Etienne at home alone tugged at his gut, but Gui knew it was too risky to return to his own church for this task. The neighbouring parish of Lavardin was closer than Montoire. Etienne must have heard the news by now. If he hadn't taken himself off to one of his hiding places, he would have sense enough to wait for Gui's return. In a matter of hours, God willing, they would all be together again.

Gui let himself into the church via the sacristy door. Although many prelates guarded their trinkets jealously, Father Michel of Lavardin was a jovial soul who cared more for a hearty meal and good company than candlesticks and silver plate. Gui easily located the parchment he needed among the other parish records. He traced over the words a few times with a clean nib to get a feel for the hand, then took a new sheet and began to write. Barely breathing, he took his knife and slowly teased the bishop's seal from the original document, attaching it to his forgery with a daub of candle wax.

A strip of coloured light flooded the nave from the stained glass panel behind the altar. It fell across Gui's shoulders as he knelt. On the central panel, the Supreme Commander wrestled with the Devil, foot upon his back. It took him back to Agnes, a prisoner on that bench. Determined not to waiver in the frailty of his mind, Gui pressed his hands together. Gathering his concentration, he set his gaze upon the raised hand of the Commander of Christ's Army, then closed his eyes.

'Lord save us, lest we perish.'

*

The walls of the crypt were green with slime. Much colder than the church above, the stink of mould choked the air. Agnes was curled up in a ball on the floor, her body trembling so violently she felt as though she were being shaken by some external force. She wanted to draw both her arms about her but one of her wrists was padlocked to a ventilation grille. There was no light in the sepulchral chamber. She craned for the sound of human voices, but all she could hear was the drip, drip of water as it slid down the walls.

She was hungry or at least she had been, but the pangs of her stomach now paled against other torments – the raw skin of her wrist, the cramping paralysis of the cold and worst of all, the voice in her head that needed to believe someone would come and tell her this was all a terrible mistake.

For the first few hours she had fought, contorting her body this way and that in the attempt to loosen the binds and find a position that offered her some relief. But they knew their job those guards. Strung tight enough to hurt, they had left some slack - the half inch of false hope they knew their captive must play with. As soon as she realised the game, she stopped and allowed her head to drop onto her arm, exhausted.

Closing her eyes, her body breathed a juddering sigh. There has been worse pain, she thought. It had started as a few spots of dark crimson when she was carrying her second child. At first she had thought nothing of it until her nausea stopped. The spots became a trickle, then a flood of cardinal red as the spasms began, far worse than anything she had experienced birthing Etienne. How she had fought to hold back the crashing waves she knew were expelling her unborn child. It had taken two days.

On the evening of the second day, she cried for God to take her along with the child back to the arms of her mother. Gui came into the bedroom. He wiped her brow and neck with a cool cloth, and placed a warm, firm hand on her belly. It felt like prayer, a commendation to the arms of the Father. She didn't need to see his face. Nestled in beside her, she could feel his body radiating sorrow. His grief a salve to her own pain, it gave her permission to let go of the baby that was not to be hers. When it was done, she knew she would never be able to carry another child again.

'Weep for me now', she whispered, and out of the blackness came the troubled eyes of his departing glance. I know you will come back for me if you can, my love. But do what you must. Make Etienne safe. The inside of her upper arm warmed with her breath and she realised she had spoken the words aloud. For a moment it lifted her heart. Even in the midst of this evil, a bond they could never tarnish. Then, torchlight flared in the stairwell and the fist of dread bunched in her gut.

The crack of footsteps echoed around the vault as the guard approached. Agnes blinked into the yellow flare. She could tell from the way the broad shoulders propelled his gait that there had been a change of guard. The man striding towards her was a trained soldier. Blood hot with alarm, she shook off the fog of reminiscence and braced her body.

Standing over her, the guard's face was a demon leer in the flame. He skimmed the mound in his trousers with a thick, calloused palm. Agnes felt the bile rise in the back of her throat. Laughing at the horror on her face, the guard stabbed the torch into a wall mount and unbuttoned his hose. Her skin felt like it was alive with parasites, muscles straining with the urge to wrench herself free. But this is what he wants, she thought. He wants to see your shame. Nausea swelled in her stomach as she realised the only thing she could do was deny him the pleasure of her struggle. She thought she would vomit if she opened her mouth, so instead she looked up at the guard, and from somewhere in the crucible of her imperative to survive, she forged a smile.

The guard moistened his lips. Agnes forced her eyes down to swollen flesh peeping from his hose. Dig deep, she told herself, now you must touch him. The guard gripped himself with one hand and unbuckled his sword with the other. Eyes roving over Agnes, he sent the metal clattering across the stone with his foot. Agnes's heart battered against her ribs. *You must.*

His eyes were on her bosom, where her mother's wedding ring rested.

'Nice piece.' He inserted the tip of his finger into the ring and pulled her towards him.

Breath raking her chest, she parted her lips to slacken her jaw. 'It will be easier if you untie me.' Her steadiness of voice surprised her. 'I can turn around then.'

The guard cackled. 'What did you just say you little whore? Want it do you?'

Grabbing the rough, hemp cloth, she drew his hose down to ankles.

'Yes.' The whisper scraped her throat. 'I want it.'

The guard lent forward. His breath stank of the beer and meat that lined his stomach. Agnes blinked away the tears as she felt the key pull in the padlock that bound her wrist. *You will never see my shame.* The pressure of the cuff released, and the lock fell open an inch from her fingertips.

'Up here.' She hauled herself onto a sarcophagus and raised her skirt.

The guard beamed. 'You dirty little bitch.'

She felt him grip her haunches. Then, blood pulsing acid in her veins, she turned and slammed the padlock into his groin. The guard paced backwards, bent double, and slipped. Arms windmilling the air, he grabbed for Agnes. A piece of her skirt glanced his fingertips but the mossy floor took his footing and he fell with a crack, his head against the tomb.

Beckoned by the half-light of freedom above, Agnes scrambled to the stairs, only to be halted by the realisation that there would be other guards at the top waiting for their friend. Waiting their turn. But she knew the panic that seized her could not afford the luxury of hesitation. *Please, hear my prayer.* Heart barely contained in her chest, she inched passed the stairwell door.

There was no-one in sight as she padded behind the great columns of the transept. When she reached the portal she saw a small rectangle of twilight against the dark wood of the huge vaulted frame – the entrance door was ajar. A shout echoed behind her, the scrape of movement. *Don't look back.* It felt as though she was falling through the air as she stumbled out in to the dusk, sobbing great, choking gulps of relief.

Agnes filled her lungs with the cool, fresh air. Salt stung her wrist as she wiped her face and ran, damp grass beneath her feet. Once she reached the cover of the tree line she dared to cast a glance over her shoulder. Two guards burst from the abbey's mouth, surveying the horse-shoe plain before them, then forked out towards the forest. Heart pattering, Agnes backed away, only to pivot into the restraint of a man's arms, her scream muffled by a strong hand. Blindly she thrashed to free herself from the brace, sinking her teeth into the black-sleeved forearm. The man spun her round to face his shining eyes.

'Gui!'

A moment of relief soaked through her body as he cradled her into his chest. Then, raising her head, she looked into the kind, brown eyes said, 'Run.'

Gui peered through the trees towards the abbey.

'Gui, we don't have time. They're right behind me.' She agitated at his arm, but his intention was settled on the guards' horses tethered at a water trough to the side of the building.

'They'll catch us if they are able to mount those horses. Mine is just beyond that thicket. Wait for me there.'

'*Gui!*' she hissed as he flew from the cover of the trees out onto the open grass.

He made twenty yards before the first guard saw him and, waving his mate on to Agnes's hiding place, he tacked to give chase. From the scrubland she watched Gui's robed silhouette streak across the indigo fields ahead of his pursuer. Throwing his cloak over the larger rouncey, he sent the other cantering into the woods.

'Come here you little bitch!' The other guard came wading through the brambles, hollering into the shadows of the forest.

Her skin shrank as she recognised the voice. *You dirty little bitch.* Grabbing the skirt of her dress she fled, ankles whipped by the branches and briars in her path, ankles scored by pine needles. She could hear her attacker thrashing his way through the scrub. Sweat stinging her eyes, she tumbled into the copse where Gui's palfrey was tethered.

'*Agnes!*'

Hooves thundered over the turf.

'*Gui! Over here.*'

Her attacker, encumbered by drink, could only swing his sword blindly as she threw herself up into the saddle and yarred the beast towards Gui. In echelon they zigzagged through the forest until they spilled from its dark arms onto an open road that shone before them, a brilliant white rivulet under the moon. The ghostly choreography of the trees behind them, they slowed and came together. Heads bowed over one another's shoulders, they caught their breath.

'Thank god you're safe.' Gui took her face in his hands.

'I thought I might never see you again,' she whispered.

'I would be dead before I would leave you to that demon.'

'I know.' She rubbed his hand. 'That is what I was afraid of.'

Gui peered into the gloaming. 'We should be gone from here,' he said. 'Let's head back to Montoire while the night is on our side.'

'Montoire?' The idea curdled her blood.

'Of course. I will go back for Etienne. You can wait outside the village.'

'Etienne?' Agnes's fingers tightened on Gui's cassock. 'Is he back?'

'Back?' Gui searched her face, confusion lining his brow.

Agnes felt her chest tighten. 'I thought you went back to Montoire, to look for Etienne.'

'Look for Etienne?' Gui eyes were wild now. 'I went to Lavardin to forge a release for you.'

'Oh Gui, I thought you knew.' Agnes pawed at his arm. 'Etienne has gone. He's gone, Gui.'

Her stomach shrank at the panic on Gui's face.

'Gone where?'

She opened her mouth but the pressure in her chest would not allow the words to come. She pushed her palm into her breastbone. 'He went with the other shepherd boys. He went on crusade.'

'Crusade?' Gui choked out the word as though it were a terrible affliction.

Around them the tendrils of the forest seemed to come alive, knotted fingers encroaching in the dark.

Agnes's hand ringed her neck. 'We should go to my godmother's cottage outside Chartres. You took me there when we first met.'

'I remember.'

'They won't find us there. Then we can look for Etienne from a place of safety.'

Gui leant into his pommel. 'Tell me what happened first.'

'I don't know. He only left a short note. After one of those holy processions. It said something about a vision of the Virgin. Someone had a vision and a group of shepherd boys were going on crusade. I don't know anything more. That's why I wrote to you to come.'

'You wrote to me?' Gui closed his eyes in terrible comprehension.

'At Chartres abbey. To call you home. I didn't know what else to do.' The cold stone of self-reproach sank in her heart. 'You didn't receive it.'

'It isn't your fault,' Gui said quickly. 'It's probably just a rumour. They'll get a few miles along St James's way and turn back. We'll find him, I promise.' His tone was keen, as though he were rallying his congregation to a paradise he couldn't quite believe in.

Agnes looked back down the luminous path that snaked into the trees. 'How?'

'We'll head for Tours.'

'Tours?'

'My old friend Philippe will be there by tomorrow. If anyone has heard of this crusade of children, it will be him.'

Chapter Eight

The birds wake Etienne at dawn. He rolls off his straw mat and stretches out the stiffness in his back. The air is already thick with the smoke from cooking pots. Yesterday's ash floats about like flakes of dead skin. He feels bereft, and for minute he can't remember why. Then the memory of disaster churns in his stomach. He tries to stifle it by turning his thoughts to the day ahead, but as he gets up to kindle the fire he sees the plains around and dismally he recalls.

The day before King Philippe had finally agreed to meet Stephen, the miracle shepherd boy. How his heart had soared to hear it. When he saw Jean, lolloping towards them with more news, his whole body felt weak with excitement. After all the weeks of waiting at the Fairs he was so tired of the stink of the camp and the hard, cracked fields where they made their beds, tired of surviving on the meagre charity of the pious or odd jobs traded for food, the promise of great adventures always just beyond their reach. This is it, he thought. But it wasn't. Instead, Jean, his face contorted with exertion, looked at them, shook his head, and said, 'The king has dismissed Stephen. There will be no crusade.'

Etienne sinks back down onto his heels, still dumbfounded. His mind feels like a spinning top without enough momentum, wobbling wildly as all his certainty drains away. He was so sure the king would say yes. He rubs furiously at his hairline. How could God abandon them?

He levers a poker into the heart of the fire and griddles it until the embers spark. Their little cooking pot lies upended next to him but there is nothing to put in it. He kicks it, just so he can watch it roll away. It would be more use as a helmet, he thinks. He remembers hearing stories of how ages ago, before the great lords of France had even claimed Jerusalem, thousands of peasants gathered together and journeyed off to the holy land armed with scythes, pitchforks, whatever protection they could find. They didn't turn back. They went all the way east before the great armies of the kings even left home.

He watches the departing boys gather up their belongings from their makeshift home. Packs on their shoulders, they traipse away through the fields. He digs his hand into his tunic and fingers his felt cross. To his relief, he stills gets the same tingling in his bones as before. A flutter of excitement stirs in his stomach, and it tells him that turning back is the wrong thing to do. Maybe there is a reason why the king sent Stephen away, he thinks. And maybe if I keep looking I'll find it.

Etienne picks his way through piles of rubbish and things abandoned. It stinks even more now that there aren't so many people and the distractions of their hubbub. Some of the things left behind seem good quality. A copper pot, a child's wooden toy and other such things you wouldn't really want to leave behind. He bends down and picks up the toy - a knight on a horse. The paint has chipped a bit and the knight has lost a hand but still, why would you leave behind such a reminder of home? Home. It is a few moments before he even realises that he is thinking about it, and by then it is too late to pretend otherwise.

Etienne sits down amid the refuse of their hopes. For the first time since he arrived at the camp he delves into the bottom of his pouch. He checks that no one is watching before he brings out the St Christopher pendant he stole from his mother. The saint carries a staff in one hand and a baby on his shoulder, crowned by a halo. She told him that her father gave it to her and it's pure gold. There's no way he wants anyone else to find out he has it. He cups it in his hand and plants a kiss on it.

A stab of guilt hollows his chest as he thinks of Agnes and how worried she will be. The note he left told her not to worry but he knows she will, and suddenly he finds himself swallowing hard, the sting of salt at the back of his throat. When he prays at night, he always remembers to ask God to make sure Father Gui is looking after her, and to make her happy so she doesn't miss him too much. It troubles Etienne that although he misses her too, it isn't enough to turn him around. Not even now, when everyone else wants to give up.

'I wish there was someway I could explain,' he says to the shiny disk in his hand. 'I know you won't understand yet. But you will.' He traces his fingers over the engraving and whispers into his cupped hands. 'You have travelled these roads, and so must I.'

By the time Etienne returns to his friends, over half of them have decided to turn back. It has been a great adventure but they are hungry and sore. They have had enough of loitering under a burning sun and wading around in so much filth. The shepherd boy was a fake. If not then the king would have seen it. Kings know that sort of thing.

'I heard Stephen is heading north. To Flanders,' says Jocelyn, one of Jean's friends. 'The Virgin appeared to him and told him to preach where the folk are more humble. He said the high born are not pleasing to God.'

'The only virgin that's appeared to him is in his dreams,' scoffs Marc.

'We are being tested,' Jean asserts. 'A fortune teller told me about this.'

'What? Crusade?'

Jean nods.

'Really? What did she say?'

'That one day I would be called by God. That I would go on a great adventure in His name.'

'Then what?'

Jean's brow knots. 'She said there would be much confusion. And to guard against deceit. And that I would teach the word of God in wild

46

places.'

Marc explodes with laughter. Jocelyn gives him a shove. Marc pushes him back as Marc's brother Piere ploughs in to help him, and soon there are four or five of them rolling around on the ground trading kicks and insults.

'That's enough!' Etienne wades in and pulls apart the warring boys. Marc gives him a feeble shove, then swipes the air and backs away as though he can't be bothered with it anymore. Silence descends like thick, low-lying cloud.

'I heard some older boys talking about going to Marseille. Going overseas,' says Etienne quietly.

'What?' blurts Jean.

'That sounds like a great idea,' Marc guffaws. 'With all the money and arms we have…'

'If you're not serious about going overseas then you don't have to come.'

'We would have better chance of success if we stick with Stephen. He can gather a new army of pilgrims,' reasons Jean.

'Maybe. But I don't want to go to Flanders. I want to go overseas.' Etienne's shoulders drop as he sheds the need to convince anyone else. 'What are we all here for if we aren't willing to take a chance? There are cities of French overseas, castles, knights. Maybe Stephen has been chosen by God to do this work and go with him if you want to. But there are still lots of boys here and maybe there is another way. If others are ready to find a ship, to stop all this talking and waiting, then I say we go and find them. And maybe God will help us then.'

The others stare at him. Even Marc is silent. Time feels like it is moving very slowly. Etienne doesn't know where those words came from, he can't even sure if he actually said them out loud. Jean squints at him from under the peak of his hand as though he is looking at the sun.

'You think I am mad?'

'No. I think you are right,' Jean replies. 'We followed this preacher boy because we thought he could lead us somewhere. But what if his purpose was just to bring us together?'

'If God wills it then there will be a way,' says Jocelyn. 'One of my mother's cousins, a saddler, moved to Acre and still lives there now.'

One by one the boys give the affirmation. 'God wills it.'

To Etienne's surprise, Marc's is among the voices.

Everyone agrees that approaching the older boys is a good idea, but no-one volunteers to go with Etienne, so he finds himself standing alone, fidgeting, as the older boys pack up their belongings. Even the youngest of them looks at least sixteen. Etienne knows he can't return to the others without at least trying to talk to them, but they seem so certain, polishing up their walking sticks, sharpening knives, forcing blankets and parcels of food into their packs.

Work has been easier for them to find. He has seen them skinning meat at the butchers' stalls, heaving consignments of timber, barrowing great containers of coins for money changers. Their confidence makes him shrink. What could his friends possibly have to offer? One of the boys looks over and instantly Etienne throws his glance away, prickles of discomfort at his collar. From the corner of his eye though, he can tell the boy is still looking at him. What's the worst that can happen, he asks himself? They will laugh at me. Come on, he scolds, how are you going to fight off the Saracen if you can't even approach a group of fellow pilgrims?

Fingers folded over the sleeves of his tunic, brow furrowed as though deep in thought, Etienne steps forward. At the very same moment, the boy who is looking at him comes over. Etienne guesses he is as old as eighteen. Not a boy at all. He has a thatch of black hair and a slightly paler beard that is patchy about his cheeks.

'You are watching us. Do you need something?'

Etienne feels his face flame. 'My friends are I were just wondering,' he says. 'We heard that you weren't following Stephen the shepherd boy anymore.'

He shakes his head. 'It was wrong to place our hope in the lords of France. We understand that now.'

'Cursed is the one who trusts in man,' adds another one of the others, joining them.

Etienne nods back with a keenness that makes him feels like a puppy waiting for a bone. 'And you are going to find your own way overseas?'

The dark-haired boy nods. 'Not just us. Come.'

The boy tells Etienne his name is Daniel and he is from Île de France. His eyes crinkle kindly as he talks, but there is something distant about them, or sad. Etienne can't quite place what it is but he feels as if he knows Daniel from somewhere.

'We are more than three score and we think there are many more groups of pilgrims like us.'

'Really?' Etienne beams. 'Some of my friends still want to follow Stephen. They say he will find a real crusader army further north.'

'Maybe he will but we do not think so,' one of Daniel's group chimes in. 'He was wrong to think the lords of France would rally.' The boy's face clouds.

'They are weak,' says another jabbing his finger furiously towards the distant pennants that stream over the royal tents. 'They have become corrupt. They wouldn't rally to the Virgin herself,'

'And the light shineth in darkness and the darkness comprehended it not,' says Daniel and his friends nod knowingly. Etienne feels as though they have knowledge of some great mystery that he too is supposed to know.

'Christendom is a sick man,' Daniel continues. 'If we show the Lord that we have not forsaken him then he will bless us with a new kingdom.'

'We were never meant to toil like slaves for the comfort of rich men,' another adds.

'I know,' Etienne says. 'Do you really think this crusade can change it all?'

'Of course,' the boys chorus, and Etienne can tell every single one of them means it. The air around them feels like it does just before a storm, all hot and sparky and full of untapped power. To be in the midst of such a swell makes his heart sing, and its song is vibrating through his whole body. This is not chance that brought me here, he thinks.

'God is giving us the opportunity to show that we can do better,' Daniel says as though reading his mind.

'There are great changes in the earth itself. The seasons are not what they were in the time of our grandfathers. The world grows cold. Rome would not have us hear it but we are coming into a new age,' adds Daniel's friend.

'Scholars in Paris are being burned for saying as much.'

Etienne swallows. 'Really?' He can hear a buzzing in his ears just like when he first met Jean. 'My friend Jean. He brought me here. He has to hear this.'

'Go and fetch him then,' says Daniel. 'Go and fetch all who you think have the heart to follow us.' He pushes his hair from his eyes with an impatient flick of his hand, and in that moment it comes to Etienne. Daniel reminds him of Father Gui. It isn't so much the dark, messy hair, but more the way that he looks at Etienne as though he is about to say something important. Now he has made the comparison, it is hard not to look at Daniel as though he knows him, even though he probably isn't like Father Gui at all. Still, there is reassurance in the fierce, dark eyes and the conviction of the older boy. This is it, he thinks as he races off to tell the others, this is why we came.

*

A few days later they leave the camp, their number the size of a small village. God must be able to see them, Etienne, thinks, covering the fields like they are part of the great Exodus. Others like them are bound to find the courage to join them. Then the heathen will see the error of their ways. God will see that the poor of France do not mean to stand by while rich Italian merchants take the spoils and leave the holy places to rot. There will be a boat at Marseille and there will be French landowners overseas ready to welcome them. The great lords have had their chance and they have spurned it. Now it is their turn, and he, Etienne, is going to put his fortune to good use when his time comes.

The sun is hot, the fields brittle as their column tramps through the long grasses, all but burned from the summer. Most of them have food for a few days - some hard bread, fruit. There will be ways, farmers in need of a day's labour, folk moved to charity for the pity of the Lord. One hand fingering the pouch with his mother's St Christopher pendant in it, Etienne swings his other arm over Jean's shoulder.

'Now we really are going to see those wild places,' he says.

Chapter Nine

The merchant was riffling through piles of fabric when his maid announced the visitors. He began an effusive greeting, but as they appeared in the doorway, pallid and dishevelled, the face of the jovial retailer fell away.

'Great heavens, Gui. Come in, come in.'

'Forgive me, my friend.' Gui patted the broad shoulders. The familiarity of his friend's bear-like embrace and his overpowering pomander felt like reassurance that not everything in his world had capsized.

Gui waited until the maid left the room and the heavy oak door had swung shut. 'We had to leave in some haste. It seems my fears were not without foundation.'

'That is most unhappy news.' Philippe tutted sadly, as though consoling a child who had lost a favourite toy. 'You know that friends are always welcome. More so if they are in need,' he said, extending his arm towards Agnes.

'At last. Madame.' One hand still clamped around Gui's arm, Philippe bowed as low as his belly permitted.

Agnes dug for the best smile she could. 'I have heard much of you, sir. And may I say that you do not disappoint in the flesh.'

'You mean I am fat!' Philippe guffawed. 'Oh what I would do for the honesty of an intelligent woman. I am rotten with envy.'

'You know that is not what I meant!'

'Ah! A real smile. See, a few moments in the company of Philippe and already your pallor lifts. Let me get you some refreshments.' Philippe gestured to a plush faldstool. 'I bought it from the Bishop of Aix.'

'Of course you did,' said Gui, deadpan.

Philippe summoned a carafe of wine and some Genovese panforte. Propping himself up on a daybed like some feasting Roman senator, Philippe's eyes followed the plate as the maid offered it to his guests. Taking a piece for himself, he licked the sugary spices from his fingers and said, 'Tell me.'

Gui rubbed his hands together, the quick, nervous gesture of a doctor considering an amputation. 'While I was in Chartres, Agnes was detained by the inquisition. Bernard de Nogent arrived to question her.'

The bushy eyebrows rose. 'Then that is a very unhappy co-incidence.'

'You understand.'

'I do.'

'By the grace of God we were able to flee. But we are hunted. I am truly sorry, Philippe. There is no one else whom I can trust. I am sure we were not followed.'

Philippe waved away Gui's fears with his thick palm. 'I don't care if the bishop sends a legion. You are safe here.' He poured a solemn draught from the carafe and inhaled from his goblet. 'I thought de Nogent had gone south to torture Cathars with impunity.'

'They said he came from the Île. I heard the University of Paris colluded in the latest burnings.'

'Then Rome's net widens.'

Outside a street vendor cried his wares. Philippe pulled at his beard.

'Do you know who informed him?'

'We don't.' The lie shifted Gui in his seat.

Agnes pitched forward, slipped a glance at Gui. 'It was my fault. Our son Etienne went missing while Gui was in Chartres. I sent him a note.'

'And it found its way to de Nogent,' said Philippe cracking another piece of panforte. 'Your son is still missing I take it.'

'It seems there was a shepherd boy preaching the cross in the Chartraine. He rallied a group of boys to crusade and we believe Etienne joined them.' Gui rubbed the back of his neck. The merchant's house gave onto a square and now the afternoon sun had made the roof line it was blazing in through the window, hot and oppressive at his collar. 'We haven't been able to find out anything more. Only rumours.'

'Such as?'

'They have been seen heading to the Fairs of Champagne, of Lendit, to the king, to the pope. They ascended into heaven.' Gui dragged his hands down his face. 'Can you keep Agnes safe here while I go to Paris?'

'Of course I can.' Philippe gave the same pout of reassurance he reserved for his customers fretful their fabrics would not arrive in time. 'But I can do better than that. I can keep you both safe here.'

'No, I cannot...'

Philippe raised his hand. 'The risk would not be worth the slim chance of reward for you to go alone. I have a much better chance of finding out where they are. 'I have contacts from Marseille to Flanders, my friend,' he said, articulating an arc with his hand. 'Your best chance is to wait here until I can find out more, or some of these children return home.' Philippe's face sagged solemnly. 'You have humiliated de Nogent for a second time, Gui. Don't go running after trouble. They'll kill you if they catch you.'

'I know,' said Gui. 'But Philippe, he is my son.'

'And he needs you alive.'

'I am so grateful, my friend, but I cannot have you risk yourself any further on our account. Agnes is a condemned heretic and I have sheltered her. I hardly need to tell you the consequences of helping us.'

Agnes took Gui gently by the arm. 'Philippe's right. He is in a far better position than we are to find out where Etienne might be.' She lifted her eyes to Philippe. 'If he can do so without personally putting himself in danger.'

'Of course, of course.' The merchant grabbed a fistful of his own flesh. 'Let me assure you Philippe de Champol does none of his own errands these days.'

A peal of relieved laughter filled the room.

'Good.' Philippe clapped his hands together. 'Then, let us attend to practical matters. You will both need a bilaud for the season, and a cloak for winter. Gui, we should fit you for a tunic and hose. We can't have you wandering around garbed in your employer's cloth.'

'I don't think I will be seeing this month's stipend.'

Philippe opened a chest, holding up different swathes of cloth as though it were a game of dressing up. He picked a dark green linen for Agnes, ushering her away to be measured up by his housekeeper. He was holding up a light, woollen cloak for Gui when his rangy, sullen assistant appeared, bringing with him a letter on a silver tray. Philippe's face darkened as he perused the seal.

'I recognise it but I can't place it,' said Gui.

'My cousin Amaury, you must remember?'

'Of course. The fox of Maintenon.' Gui wore his best smile. 'He sometimes played with us in the summer. I thought he had gone overseas?'

'To make his fortune on crusade? Ha! That is ten years gone, and the booty gone with it,' Philippe scoffed. 'The endless money pit that is fighting overseas has long since disabused him of trying it again.' He drew Gui closer to him by the elbow. 'For all the land he grabs locally, he rinses his estates twice as fast. I hear he's even stooped to money lenders at the Fairs.' Philippe waved his hand as though he were batting away a fly. 'He can vow to kill all the Saracens he likes, but the bishop won't lend him any more money that's for sure.'

'He has asked you?'

Philippe laughed a little too keenly. 'Half begging letter, half threat.'

Gui shook his head. 'He is really that hard up?'

'And now you insult me!'

For a junior son of a cadet family, Philippe had indeed advanced his name. Gui smirked. 'Jealousy is an ugly thing. It's a good job I am more handsome than you.'

'It's the priestly garb that really makes you irresistible I am sure.' Philippe slapped his thigh like a jester. 'Now. I shall send you to a discreet little tavern while I am away, just to be safe,' he said. 'I'll prepare you a note to take this to the innkeeper. Wait for me there. He and his wife will get you anything you need. At my pleasure, of course.'

The tavern was on an anonymous backstreet and the innkeeper's wife wore a cloth above her station that bore all the hallmarks of Philippe's generosity. Eyeing Gui and Agnes up and down with an arch brow, she flicked her head towards the stairs.

A neat little box tucked away at the end of the first floor landing, it was too warm for being above the kitchen but it felt safe. Gui took a jug of beer and sat down on a prickly mattress that sagged between three planks of wood. Agnes laid her head on his shoulder and they rested in silence, pinned by the weight of the past week and the passing luxury of safety. Her breath quickened, and Gui knew her thoughts had turned to Etienne.

'We will find him, my love.' He caressed her hair. Newly scented with cedar oil from Philippe, the smoky balsam took him home and he closed his eyes, immersed in the sound of birds, the rich, dark soil and the mossy grass of the forest that had so often been their bed.

'What if he has gone home?' Agnes's voice is taught with fear.

'He will find out what has happened before he reaches the village.' Gui wiped his brow, damp from the heat of their tiny room. 'He can't have gone beyond Philippe's trade routes. We will know where he is within days.'

'And then?'

'And then we will find a way.'

Gui brushed her mouth with his thumb. Lips soft against his unshaven skin, Agnes kissed his cheek. He brought his mouth to hers. Agnes slid her hand inside his shirt, and he felt the tension in his body drain away under her touch. A bead of sweat ran over her collarbone. Gui traced it with his finger until he found her necklace. Lifting it up, he placed the ring that hung from it on his palm. Against the pink of her cheeks, her eyes were a vivid blue. Slowly her lips parted as he reached around to release the clasp.

'Gui.'

He regarded her solemnly for a moment, his chest pulsing with the steady, rhythm of his heart. He didn't say anything as he lowered her down to lie beneath him, and taking the ring from the chain, slid it onto her finger.

*

The inquisitor flexed his spindly fingers against each other. The buzz of the new day drifted up from the street below. Just two weeks before there had not been enough chatter to disturb him at this hour. Now though, as the sun approached its midsummer zenith, he noted those few moments extra of peace had been lost to the hubbub of ignorant peasants. Face pinched, he thought of them in a few days' time, leaping over solstice bonfires chanting foul pagan rites.

Outside someone cried clear passage for their wagon and a gust of wind brought the smell of horse shit to his nose. It was only the thought of the approaching Quarter Day rent payments that prevented his mood from souring further. He reached for the parchment to check the amounts due as someone rapped on his door.

'Come,' he barked. 'Oh it's you. I thought you were supposed to be on the road earning the coin I paid you?'

A pair of generous lips parted behind the neatly clipped beard.

'Well I was, I was. And I believe you'll agree I've more than earned my stipend.' Uninvited, the spy drew up a chair and sat, ankle resting over his knee.

'I hope it is so.' De Nogent slowly withdrew his hand from the ledger of rent collections. Christian grinned. A smile that meant to imply he had learned more about his host than would be comfortable.

'Well, after the most unfortunate escape, they fled to Tours. He has surprisingly diverse connections, your priest.'

'Guessing games do not divert me.' De Nogent stared back at the mocking eyes.

'No need to guess I'm sure. They are currently staying at the pleasure of a certain Philippe de Champol, a textile merchant from Chartres with whose name you may be acquainted.' The spy studied his fingernails for a moment. Trimmed and polished like a courting troubadour. 'And the thing is, this Etienne you asked about, the missing boy.'

The inquisitor lent forward.

'He is indeed their son.' The plump lips broke into a smile, revealing the pearly teeth. 'There wasn't a single peasant in that village who thought otherwise. As clear as the nose on your face they said.'

'I see,' said Bernard de Nogent, ignoring the pun. He eyed the preening deviant before him like a kestrel assessing a rodent from a hundred feet.

'And where is the boy?'

The spy coughed. 'He went missing after the devotional processions at Easter. From what I can gather he joined a group of shepherds and other peasants headed to the Fairs in the Île.'

'The Île? For what purpose?'

'To petition the king to crusade.'

Bernard de Nogent let out a strangled yelp. It was the first time in years he had laughed in company.

'I know. Entertaining, isn't it? They are following a boy named Stephen, who claims to carry a letter from the Virgin herself for pity of the Holy Land.'

The reverend brow darkened.

'So I propose, for only the smallest of increments in my fee, to identify this Etienne in person. You can send a retainer to detain the couple.' The spy opened his palms. 'If only every case were so simply resolved.'

De Nogent pressed his fingertips together and looked out through the small, oblong window over the rooftops to the fields beyond. The fields that would soon, God willing, be covered with wagons full of masonry, horses dragging timber, labourers bent over spades and hammers. Rising up from the earth, a beacon of new monasticism to shine a light where heresy had been allowed to lurk unchecked in the darkness.

'I would require only a very modest increment,' the spy prompted.

The inquisitor's head indicated negatively. The matter of the Le Coudray bastard was a delicate one and not one he was prepared to chance to the devious criminal seated before him. With all that was at stake, the last thing he wanted was for Maintenon to add the boy's life as a precondition for his reward. No, until the boy was safely cloistered behind Church walls he was bargaining chip best protected by a professional mercenary.

De Nogent grimaced. 'I consider it highly unlikely that even the best spy would be able to locate a peasant child in Paris.'

Christian mouthed an 'Oh' of mock offense. 'Of all the other chancers claiming to be spies you are discerning enough to hire me, but now you doubt my skill?' He wagged his finger.

The inquisitor sighed. 'I consider it wasted coin. To pay you the travails of locating a child who can hardly be expected to survive alone on the roads of France.'

'That can be arranged if you'd prefer?' A flash of the teeth, but de Nogent didn't bite. The spy was unperturbed. 'I hope I have impressed with the speed of my results.' He threw a lingering look out of the window. 'Am I to understand that you require this matter to be concluded with a degree of haste?'

De Nogent's blood heated. Not one but two of the deadly sins; avarice and pride. The black, beady eyes blinked. Loathed as he was to hand further reward to the impudent thief, the end gain had no price.

'Perhaps there is another matter,' he said.

'Oh?' The spy perked up.

'The man who turned the Le Coudray whore over to the inquisition previously is a nobleman by the name of Amaury, Lord of Maintenon.'

'I've heard the name,' Christian said, his eyes roving over the gold embossed ledgers protectively wedged against de Nogent's arm.

'It has come to my attention that Maintenon's motives may not have been as righteous as they appear. That he may have committed certain indiscretions. And I want to know what they are.'

The spy looked up. 'His reputation does rather precede him.'

'Well, given his reputation I understand why you might be reluctant to take on the task.'

'That depends.'

'An additional livre per diem?'

'Three.'

'Two.'

Christian the spy tilted his head back as the sun made the roof top opposite, bathing his face in its warmth. 'By Pentecost,' he said.

Outside, de Nogent could hear a peasant woman whining her tale of woe. Lies no doubt, strung together in order to part gullible women from their coin. You can't hear this street rabble from the abbey, thought Bernard de Nogent.

'Pentecost,' he replied.

*

The knock of horses' hooves on the towpath broke the eerie silence of the pre-dawn hour. A whinnying snort and the beast emerged from the gloom, visible now under the bargeman's lantern, its harness straining under the tension of its load. The boatman squinted into the night, and there was something about the craggy face that told the spy the other man was more nervous than he ought to be. Aside the peculiar hour, he must have been navigating these rivers for many decades. What reason would he have to be anxious?

From the scrubland beyond another lantern winked. The boatman scanned the shore with a lighthouse gaze. Christian shrunk further back into the bushes and held his breath. Not a hundred yards ahead a richly cloaked messenger emerged from the darkness. One of Maintenon's men, he was sure. The message he intercepted had not been clear, and was all the more suspicious for it, so he permitted himself a wry smile of self congratulation as the boatman hollered the boat to a halt.

Christian the spy wet his lips for a secret about to be revealed; but a whole adult life of trickery, espionage and theft had not prepared him for the sight. Hand over his mouth, he watched as the old river rat flipped open the hold with a stick. At first all he could see was their eyes, glinting against the backdrop of night, then slowly, terrified faces emerged from below, two at a time, until there were six children of Moorish appearance standing onto the towpath - four girls and two boys. He guessed the eldest was twelve and the youngest no more than seven.

Maintenon's retainer approached the shivering children, clicked his fingers, and the boatman prodded the eldest boy and girl forward. The others cowered as the messenger bared the boy's unblemished chest, forced his mouth open to show a good set of teeth. An uncomfortable rush of blood surged to Christian's loins as the man thrust his hand into the girl's chemise and squeezed a breast. The girl began to sob. Three livres, Christian scoffed at the thought of his paltry stipend. To Amaury, Lord of Maintenon it would be worth more. Much, much more.

The messenger gave a hoot into the night, and to Christian's surprise, two more girls crept out from the treeline; French girls, bound together at the wrist, mouths gagged with rag. From where he was it looked as though they were wearing habits. Without warning, a strange magnetic force he didn't understand began to pull at him, as though it were trying to draw him out into the open to cut their bonds. Droplets of sweat seeping from his brow, he found himself in a panicked fight against his whim.

Squinting, the old boatman reached for a box, peeled up a sheet of parchment, scratched a mark and offered it up to the messenger. Manhandling the Christian girls onto the barge, the messenger departed from view with the six slaves in tow. Then, muffled voices, the sound of the slaves being loaded into a wagon, and the lap of water against the hull of the barge, and Christian the spy was left gawping into the night, a queer sensation throbbing in his groin.

Chapter Ten

It had been over a week since Philippe left for Chartres. He had given Gui some coin and instruction to wait until he heard from him. Under no circumstances, the merchant had waggled a bejewelled finger, was he to go asking questions in the town. For the first few days it had been easy enough to enjoy the tavern's respite. Their best chance was with Philippe, Gui told himself. If anyone could get them news from the roads, it was he. But soon the desire to scratch at the itch of his anxiety shrank the walls of the room and stifled what air there was circulating through the midsummer heat.

Gui poured a jug of water into the washbowl and splashed his face, pulling the cool wetness through his hair. His legs ached for movement, something to displace the note of alarm that chimed constantly in his gut. Every day he waited was a day that took Etienne further away, and no amount of water could wash away the images that hunted in his mind - his son lost, hungry, frightened, and worst of all, alone, not knowing he had a father, a protector in this world who would do anything to see him safe.

Gui glowered out the window, fury at his impotence bottle-necked within. In the courtyard below a few chickens scratched the earth and the innkeeper's guard dog panted in the shade of the wall. A kitchen boy came out and threw some slops into the compost pile. Agnes breezed in under the gateway, nose in a bouquet of herbs, a brooch of cowslip pinned to her dress. Wiping fresh beads of sweat from his brow, Gui felt his irritation rise at the little yellow flowers, heads raised gaily to the sun.

Agnes flung the door open, still sniffing at the posy. 'I had forgotten how differently people treat you when they think you have coin to spare.'

'Which we don't.'

Open-mouthed at his outburst, Agnes tugged at her new dress. 'You think I am pleased to participate in this…masquerade? It hasn't rained since we arrived. It's starting to stink. That's all.' She tossed the sprigs of rosemary and lilac onto the bed. 'I suppose you would prefer I follow your example and do nothing.'

Gui stood, charcoal eyes betraying nothing of the heat rising behind them. 'We have dragged Philippe into this peril. The least we can do is lend him our trust,' he said.

'You mean I have dragged him in,' Agnes said.

'I did not say that.'

'You didn't have to.'

'You think I blame you?

Agnes turned away, her hurt as evident to Gui as the red scars that still braceleted her wrist. He shut his eyes to the stab of regret.

'Agnes. I'm sorry. Please look at me.'

But the nape of her neck stretched downwards.

'You think I blame you? For de Nogent? For Etienne?'

The voice that replied was brittle, resigned. 'Perhaps if we had told him the truth. As you wanted.'

'You cannot know that. Etienne is nearly twelve years old. He is not the first to fall for enticing rhetoric about the holy land.'

'The rhetoric of your church.'

'My church!' Gui stalked the confines of the room. 'And you think I am not ashamed?'

'Of me? Of us?' Her voice rose.

Gui stopped in his tracks.

'Of myself.'

Agnes collapsed onto the bed, body folded over as though she were nursing a blow. 'I just want him back.' Her shoulders began to shake. 'Oh please God don't let anything have happened to him.'

Gui knelt down beside her and folded her hands into his. 'Nothing has happened to him. I am sure of it.'

'You really think Philippe can find him?'

'I know it.' Gui said. 'But, you're right. We should have heard from him by now. I want to take a trip into the country, back towards Vendôme. See what I can find out.'

Agnes scratched at her arm. 'On your own?'

'You'll be safe here. I'll only be gone for half a day.'

'It's not that.' She shook her head, defeated. 'I just feel so…'

'Helpless. I know. So do I. But one of us has to stay here in case Philippe's message arrives. It's safer for me to go.' Gui leaned forward and kissed her.

Long, slender fingers crowned his head, her touch cascaded down over his shoulders, his arms. Coming to rest at his hands, Agnes fingered the brocaded sleeves. Gui looked down at his shoes, their unfamiliar taper that pinched his foot.

'I think you look very handsome,' she said.

'I prefer black.'

'Of course you do.'

He took his rosary from his tunic and poured it into Agnes's palm.

Containing his smile, he fixed her with grave eyes and said, 'Whenever you feel the urge to tour the markets, please count them.'

Agnes laughed. 'And you, what will you count?'

'The knots in my gut.'

*

Agnes watched the party arrive; a drab troupe of pilgrims and a merchant's caravan, all wilting in the heat. The innkeeper's wife fussed around them, hastening a pack of urchins to help with the baggage. The merchant's clerk, shoulders bunched in a shrug of perpetual disappointment, surveyed the courtyard from beneath the peak of his hand. Dabbing his brow with a large square of linen, the man flitted an eye to his master's wagons as they disappeared into the stalls, then back to the lady of the house. Agnes smirked as the woman folded her arms in defiance of his judgement. She was sure her father wouldn't have coached here with a full train, either.

She wondered at the contents of the crates. Not salt, that was for sure. Tours was not on the network of inland roads and canals used to traffic that white gold. Fabrics, wine? A shipment of soft Aleppo bars perhaps, with creamy foam that formed as you turned it in your hands. A proper bath. At once she was back in her childhood house in Chartres, immersed in a copper tub, her nurse pouring a jug of heated water over her. She can't have been more than six or seven - still a child. *Before.*

The next memory came as jagged and inevitable as her breath. The last time she had laid hands on a bar of that soap. Frantically she had scrubbed her skin until it was raw, trying to get clean, as if it would somehow remove the stain. She was barely dressed when they came for her, hammering at the door.

Agnes recoiled from the window, stung by the assault of memories. How easily they had risen from their tomb. Was it those same demons, who, creeping unnoticed like assassins in the shadows of her life, had been somehow responsible for Etienne's flight? If only she hadn't panicked so at his disappearance. If only she had just waited for Gui to return from Chartres. She agitated at the ring on her finger. The worst of her past Gui didn't even know about.

Dread cramped her belly. A fear she could barely acknowledge; that ancient hands would drag her from this world and seal her in their graveyard, a ghost in her own life, forever beyond the reach of her family. If she could not rid herself of them, she would have to tell Gui. Taint him with her shame. A confession, she knew, would transform her in his eyes, make her his congregation and not his love.

At once she saw him, the dusty grime of the road in his hair, heat on his back, searching for their son. Her baby boy. She smeared her palms across her face, trying to wipe away her worst imaginings. Body rigid, she bunched her fists, pushing her nails into her palms. Stigmata. I won't just sit here, she thought. Sit here and let them win. She looked out at the caravan stabled below. The travellers' banter drifted up – men glad of a warm meal and respite from the long trade routes of France. Trade routes that might be carrying news of a band of child pilgrims.

Bullying her hair underneath a hairnet, Agnes secured her veil with a headband. Her role as Gui's housekeeper required only a simple cotton kerchief in public, and she muttered curses at the accessories of spousal modesty tugging at her scalp. She peered at her reflection in the hand mirror on the dresser, how small the fabric made her face seem, how timid. It also obscured her peripheral vision – she had to turn her head to see out of the corner of her eye. Heaven forbid you see them coming.

The smell of roasting meats was curling its way upstairs as she stepped into the corridor. She stalled at a bray of drunken laughter; ladies did not venture into taverns unaccompanied. The voice of the innkeeper's wife lifted above the babel, sharp then obsequious, taking orders, carping at the staff. Briefly she felt the tug of her room. The safety of an evening alone, the voice in her head mocking her with what ifs. What if, indeed. Straightening her back against the leer of men in their cups, Agnes went downstairs.

Rain has broken the oppressive air, and the hauliers were bunched, steaming, on a bench, forks stabbing at a plate of meats. Hands folded in a lady-of-the-house pose, Agnes asked, 'Pardon me. May I ask if you have come from the Fairs?'

The men looked up from their feast, exchanged a conspiracy of glances. From the table behind them, the clerk spoke. 'Indeed, Madame. We have come from Lendit.'

'I am sojourning here with my husband and seek news of our son. He took the cross with a group of shepherd boys. It is rumoured they were headed to the Fairs.'

The clerk patted at the forlorn lock of hair clinging to his pate and gave a dispirited, 'Hmm.'

One of his men wiped the dripping from his chin. 'We was there not a week

past. I heard talk of this shepherd boy who carries letter from the Virgin for the king hisself.' The man gave a wink and opened his palm.

Heart pattering, Agnes rummaged for a coin. 'What of the others with him?'

'We never saw 'em ourselves.' He eyes his colleagues. 'We heard talk though.'

Nods and leers.

'Talk?'

'From people they'd done jobs for and such,' added one.

'We heard they petitioned the king to crusade. A right old spectacle it was, weren't it, Eric?'

'That shepherd went off to Alsace seeking the emperor I heard. A king weren't good enough for 'im!' A piece of gristle flew from Eric's mouth as he cackled at his own joke. 'Most of 'em were headed south though. Headed for the ports. Reckon they're going overseas on their own account.'

A chorus of laughter from the others. Agnes snatched her hand to her chest as though someone were trying to rob the air from her lungs.

'Overseas,' she whispered.

'We got more to tell,' said one of the men, eyes resting on her chest. 'If you got payment.'

'We certainly do. An' with your husband not about an' all we'd be willing to negotiate if you can't spare the coin.' The man winked, rubbing the silver disk against his crotch.

Agnes drew back, her body heating with panic. The others began to call out their bids. Suddenly, the world was a wash of garbled shouts and the thrum of the rain on the windows. A hand thrust forward, grabbing her arm. She tried to thrash it free but the grip tightened.

Behind her the tavern door banged open. Shaded by the dull light, Gui stood in the doorway, water sheeting over the lip of his hood.

'Let her go.' He flicked his cloak aside, revealing a knife. A squabble of heckling voices rose. Gui unsheathed the blade, eyes riveted onto the man who had Agnes by the arm - *I can't take you all but I will take you.*

'Gentlemen!' The innkeeper bellowed. With the thump of a mace, he banged for order.

'The night watch will not take kindly to being called tonight.'

The pressure on Agnes's arm released.

The gates to Philippe's courtyard were locked. No lamps were lit within.

'Perhaps he is just delayed on business.' Gui said to Agnes.

'Then why are his servants gone? The boys were sighted at Lendit over a week ago. Gui, we have to leave.'

'I know.'

Gui pulled his hood up against the rain, casting around for reassurance from the mundane - a man trudging home with a bundle of kindling, drunken labourers arguing about a debt, the grating smell as the rain swept the shit down the street. Still, he couldn't shake the ill ease that cloaked him. His cassock had offered greater protection, he considered. One glance of recognition and it rendered its wearer invisible. Oh, just a priest, you saw the thought pass across their eyes, and then you were gone. Priests had no place in the world of things.

Everywhere he looked Gui thought he recognised someone. A man he had passed earlier in the street, someone he had seen by a tavern outside the town. Pretending to inspect a shuttered shop front he stared at his reflection in the beaten brass plates, asking the distorted image if he was losing control of his fears.

The answer to his question was the sound of urgent hooves beating above the traffic. Turning their backs on the approaching mounts, he bundled Agnes around the corner, and hidden by the angle of the bend, watched as four men stormed by. Their shouts told him they were from the Chartraine - feudal retainers.

'Wait here for a moment.'

'What are you doing?' Agnes pulled him back by his cloak.

'Our belongings, our money, they are back in our room. I need to try and get them back.'

The innkeeper was outside, protesting as the retainers piled in. From across the way Gui met his eyes - the eyes of someone who understood a man in need. The soldiers' horses were tied together in the street, and with an eye to the window above, Gui rifled through one of the saddlebags - no parchment, no seal or heralded flask.

'Quick!' The keeper mouthed.

Gui's hand caught the saddle as he snapped the bag shut. The inside flap was embossed with a coat of arms. It was vaguely familiar to him, but he couldn't quite place it. It would come to him once he had Agnes far enough away for his mind to unwind. The innkeeper wrung his hand in silent exhortation. Gui fled back across the road.

Once the echo of hooves on the cobbles had died, he stole back to the inn.

'Did they take anything?'

The keeper shook his head. 'I said you had left. Showed them an empty room.'

Gui took the stairs two at a time. Their bag was as it had been, untouched under the bed. Thumbing the sign of the cross, he swung it over his shoulder.

'Here.'

Gui turned to find the keeper at his shoulder.

'Someone left this for you.'

"*Dear friend. Please forgive my silence. I am bound for Marseille and have news of your merchandise there. I will await you at the Fountain, where the road from Aix runs into town. Godspeed. P.*"

'Who?'

'I didn't see.'

Gui glanced round the room, checking the anonymous faces and the places where the shadows fell. Marseille was a over a week away, even if they made some of the way by canal. Legs suddenly heavy, as though he were wading through a dream, he walked out into the darkening evening, a smear of crimson just visible over the rooftops.

A wet night's travel in the woods brought a cough to Agnes's chest. They offered a prayer at a roadside shrine to St Martin, but by the time they arrived in the next town three days later her face and chest burned. The evening air was full of smoke and the lingering aroma of spits that had been turning all day in village squares. It was Assumption; candles were lit and crowds of locals mingled with travellers from the main road. Easy enough for a scribe and his wife to pass unnoticed amid the throng.

Gui found them a room for the night in a saddler's house.

Once the man's wife put Agnes to bed with a feverfew tisane and a dose of silver, he slumped in the chair, letting the darkness come on before he took a taper. There was a peace in the transition between day and night that he could find at no other time. As a child, his nurse had told him it was the time when spirits walked. Not the restless evil that walked only by night in their bid to escape the Devil, but the contented spirits who had stayed on in their homes. They walked at dusk, and if you would only sit and listen you would hear them, hundreds of years, hundreds of lives, carrying about their business just as they had done before death. Although his Church would not permit such a possibility, Gui had never found a better explanation of that peculiar calm - the certainty that things did indeed go on, incorporeal.

The contented souls of the dusk evaporated as evening passed to night. Footsteps shuffled along the corridor, bawdy songs and beer-fuelled banter rang out from the street, punctuated by the occasional shriek of a fox. Gui sipped at a cup of wine, companion to his vigil, and the constriction in his heart began to loosen. Spinning the beads of his rosary he watched his love sleep, fitfully to begin with, but then a deep-enough slumber to stop her coughing fits. Once dawn was on its way, and Gui felt certain that his church was not coming for them, he tucked his rosary back into his shirt, laid down beside Agnes and, her breath soft in his ear, closed his eyes for an hour or two.

By the time he woke, the fever had lost its grip on Agnes. Bleary eyed he raised his head to find her sitting up in bed, sipping a fresh tisane. 'Forgive me,' she said. 'It is my fault we have found such trouble…'

Gui ran his thumb across her brow. 'Don't say that. This evil lies at the door of zealots like Bernard de Nogent and those who command him.'

She pressed his hand to her lips.

'The boys are heading south,' Gui said. 'I know we are on the right path.'

'Show me the note again.' Agnes studied the sloping cursive for a moment. 'It is Philippe's hand, you're sure?'

'I am certain. There is a reason why he didn't contact us in person.'

'On account of those men back at Tours?'

'I'm almost certain,' said Gui. 'There was a herald stamped inside one of the soldier's saddlebag. It was faint. An indented partition on the shield, the diamond pattern on one half.'

'Doesn't the Church use the Seneschal of Champagne's men to arrest blood crimes?'

'Usually. But no, I know the seneschal's herald and this was not it. I don't know who those men were.' Gui shook his head. 'It makes no sense.'

Agnes placed her palms together, fingertips at her chin.

'If you recognise it, it must be someone from your home.'

Suddenly Gui clapped his hands. 'Yes! The arms of Philippe's father.'

'Philippe's father? Agnes bit the quick of her nail. 'Then something has happened you don't know about.'

Gui was staring out the window, to the hubbub on the street. 'Or it is a trap.'

'We must go to Marseille if there is news of Etienne there,' Agnes urged. 'My aunt still lives near there, a small place near the marshes called Marignane.'

'We'll leave tomorrow. You have to rest properly now.' Gui tucked scrap of parchment back into his cloak. 'And I'll go to the meeting place alone.'

Agnes opened her mouth to protest, but Gui placed his finger to it. Then bunching her hair into a tail he said, 'I think a disguise might be the best way to help us move unnoticed until we find Etienne.'

Agnes took her hair from him. 'You mean they are not looking for two men.'

'A lawyer and his assistant perhaps?'

'Hand me your knife,' she said.

'In a moment,' he replied, and buried his head into the soft mass of gold.

Chapter Eleven

Amaury of Maintenon leaned back in his chair. Looking up at the chubby- fingered cherubs that danced on the ceiling, he said, 'So what have you done about it?'

De Nogent, who had not been invited to sit, gave a grimace of a smile that was not meant to conceal his affront. 'They have left Tours and are being pursued.'

'By the same retinue who let them escape?'

The inquisitor felt his jaw tighten.' You said they were your best men.'

The leather of the nobleman's glove crunched as he clenched his hand into a fist and released it. 'Their information came from you.'

'Le Coudray will be returned to Chartres by the end of the month,' the inquisitor said, folding his hands together with a finality he hoped would draw the conversation to a close. He had been working on his *Nogentian Creed* when Maintenon's messenger interrupted him. The creed was to be the founding stone of his proposal for a new monastic order. A statement of faith he hoped in time would be added to the other great creeds of Christendom. He intended to present it to the pontiff in person before the summer when his eminence retreated to the cool hills above Rome.

Pope Innocent had already begun what de Nogent anticipated would be a flurry of approvals for new mendicant orders. A couple of years before it had been the merchant of Assisi, and lately his female cohorts, the Poor Clares - this pope's reforming zeal extended even to women! De Nogent had spent hard years fighting the heretics of Provence alongside followers of the preacher Dominic, and now rumour had it the Spaniard was seeking approval for his own order - an order dedicated to the eradication of heresy no less. No, he had no time to tarry, least of all flattering the vanity of petty secularity.

'And the boy?' The gruff voice interrupted.

De Nogent pursed his lips. 'The boy?'

'Damn it man, you take me for a fool?' Maintenon banged his fist on the table with an unexpected force that, to his irritation, made the inquisitor flinch.

'My lord, the boy is an irrelevance,' he hissed.

'I'm glad you think so.'

'What I mean is that he is just a boy. The bastard of a heretic and a disgraced priest. Once his parents are apprehended he will find himself in the workhouse if not on the pyre. From what my informants tell me he is likely already dead.'

'Like the Le Coudray girl was dead?'

Before de Nogent could respond to the provocation, the bell outside the reception room rang. Forefinger resting on his temple, the nobleman raised his head and smiled as his butler announced the guest. The man entered, a large, ostrich feather, dyed cobalt, waving ludicrously from his velvet hat. He removed it with a flourish and bowed, bearing his polished teeth.

'I believe you are acquainted,' Maintenon said.

De Nogent flushed crimson as the spy who called himself Christian strode jauntily towards him.

'How very resourceful of you,' he muttered.

The spy grinned. 'I told you I was good.'

'My compliments on your excellent timing,' Maintenon said. 'We were just talking about the boy, weren't we, Bernard?'

The inquisitor scowled at the informant, loathing his foppery, his casual deceit, making himself an inward promise of vengeance.

'Ah yes, the boy.' The spy preened the feather in his cap and popped it back on his head. 'He is journeying towards Marseille with a band of shepherd boys. They seek transport overseas to reclaim the holy land.'

De Nogent could feel the blood pulsing at his temples, pumping the urgent desire to grab hold of the treacherous spy and shake the life breath from him.

Maintenon lent forward and said, 'Do they now. How many of them?'

De Nogent watched the machinations flicker behind the noblemen's eyes with a sense of mounting dread, as the spy continued.

'Well I came across two or three groups myself, at least ten score in all. The merchants I encountered told me the boys numbered in their thousands. Dismissed by the king, now each seeks his own way abroad.'

The inquisitor felt the dull knell of misadventure clang in his gut as Amaury of Maintenon rubbed his face and began to laugh.

'How can you be sure the Le Coudray boy is among them?' De Nogent snapped at Christian.

'I'm glad you asked that, your reverence.' The spy glanced back at him, mockery twinkling in his eyes. 'Le Coudray told me herself.'

De Nogent felt the air leave his lungs in a gasp of outrage.

'What?' Maintenon uttered a carnal growl.

'Yes, yes. I came across her by the will of the good Lord, in a tavern in Tours. Quite the beauty, isn't she?' the spy chirruped. 'Happenstance I was able to overhear a conversation between her and a gang of hauliers before her good priest arrived and I called in your retainers.' Eyes round with self-congratulation, he smiled at the two men. 'Some local inquiries and I was able to find a wealth of interesting nuggets.'

Interesting enough for you to seek a higher bidder behind my back, thought de Nogent as Maintenon studied Christian from beneath his brow.

'Were you really?' Maintenon said.

'Indeed so.' Christian tapped the end of his nose. 'Before your retainers bungled the arrest.'

Drumming his fingertips together, Maintenon cast a leaden look towards de Nogent. The inquisitor did his best not to let his indignation show.

'You saw at least two hundred of these boys?' Maintenon asked.

'I did,' said Christian with an emphatic nod. 'On the road to Bourges. In rag tag groups.'

'And there are thousands of these boys at large?'

'Scattered in various locations, but yes, most likely several thousand.'

The steel grey eyes narrowed lasciviously. 'How can you be sure?'

'I can only relay what I have heard.' Christian laid his hand at his heart. 'And seen with my own eyes.'

'Let us be modest then and say there are five thousand peasant children at large,' said Maintenon. 'It has been some time since I was in the Holy Land, but from what I remember from my time overseas, you would pay between four and eight ducats for a good, strong Saracen slave with plenty of work in him.'

'Up to ten for a virgin housemaid in Italy,' chimed Christian with a wink.

Bernard de Nogent closed his eyes.

'More for a mature, light-skinned convert. Isn't that right?' Christian addressed Maintenon.

'How would I know?' barked the nobleman.

'Enough of this blasphemy!' De Nogent interrupted.

'Really, your reverence,' said the spy. 'No need to be squeamish. Everyone knows the Venetians cater to… Moorish tastes. Every merchant household in Italy worth its salt has a pagan house slave.'

De Nogent noted that the sly nod Christian gave to Maintenon went unacknowledged by the nobleman. Moving a stack of parchment carefully to one side, Maintenon lent his arms on the desk and said, 'Please go on. You seem to know a lot about this trade.'

'More than most.' Christian puffed up his chest, warming to the task. 'Blond Christians fetch most in the Tartar markets, but the Egyptian market is booming too. Allowing a modest average of five ducats, minus shipping costs and expenses, currency exchange and so forth, even if we could only gather a thousand healthy boys...'

'Close on half the demesne revenue of the Champagne in a single trade,' Maintenon said, and he smoothed his hand along the ridge of his desk with a contrived tenderness that made de Nogent feel distinctly uncomfortable.

'Prices are rising all the time,' continued Christian blithely. 'Revenue from slaves is set to rival all the other markets. It's the next spice, everyone is saying it.'

'If the Italians are getting fat off it then why shouldn't we?' said Maintenon. 'Inquisitor de Nogent, I require your help.'

The inquisitor felt his heart grow heavy.

Ticking his index finger emphatically back and forth, Maintenon continued, 'Or rather should I say the capital for completion of the abbey requires your help.'

'My lord, I really do not see how I could possibly be of help with this.'

'I have connections from my time overseas, I'll admit, but with this sort of scale we will need a wholesaler of some means. You have connections with the bishops of the southern lands, whom, I believe from my experience, run a decent business in slaves from Mediterranean ports.'

'My lord, such as the Church may conduct commercial activities for its earthly mission, the trade in heathens only is permitted.'

'I know,' Maintenon said flatly. 'Nonetheless, I am sure the Church has connections in the mercantile world who show no such - how did our informant friend put it? Squeamishness.'

'Given my lord's desire to insert a third party between himself and the point of sale I suggest he seek someone of a more, secular disposition. The penalty for such a trade if caught would be excommunication!'

Heart pulsing, de Nogent smoothed down his robes. Maintenon licked his lips. Sensing a tirade, the inquisitor hastily continued, 'With your permission, I am sure I cannot assist with your plans of a more commercial nature. I will oversee arraignment of Le Coudray and Courville as I have said, but now I really must retreat to concentrate on spiritual concerns.'

'Perhaps I could make a suggestion?' The spy inserted himself into the opportunity. 'As you know I offer my services throughout the kingdom and beyond. I am sure that with the appropriate inquiries I could source us suitable partners.'

De Nogent noted the nobleman bristle at the word 'us'. The informant blundered on, not noticing the tap of Maintenon's foot under the desk.

'It would of course cost, my lord, but I can personally vouch for the discretion of my contacts.'

'If I require you to do anything,' Maintenon snapped, 'it is to make sure we have our net cast as wide as we can. Find out where these groups have gone so we can entice them all to a convenient location.'

De Nogent's mouth went dry as he felt his plans slipping from his grasp. The chances of this pompous spy finding the Le Coudray bastard seemed unlikely but such a risk could not be permitted. Swallowing, he said, 'My lord, should we not leave locating the shepherd children to someone with more…'

'This I can most certainly do, Lord Amaury.' Christian interrupted, clapping his hands with slow precision as though he were trying to prevent himself from rubbing them together. 'But, given the understandable reluctance of our reverend prelate to assist, I can assure you that I would be well able to source appropriate trading partners. For an increment in my costs that would be very reasonable. I believe fifteen percent is the market rate.' The spy encroached upon Maintenon's desk. 'Understanding what a prize it is you desire, my lord.'

Maintenon drew his head back as the spy approached, a veil drawing over his gaze. 'And what would you know about what it is I desire?'

What indeed, thought de Nogent as the spy offered a conniving smile. Instinctively the inquisitor took a pace back as Christian drew his shoulders back and opened his palms like an actor readying to address a crowd.

'Lord Amaury,' he began, his voice a little louder than was acceptable in nobler company. 'With an army of a size this revenue could bring you, think of the campaigns you could join. You could finally win lands and honour worthy of you.' Christian waved an arc with his hand as though narrating a story to a child. 'Why, you could attract a union with a family of such nobility that the court gossips of France would soon forget you gained your purchase into their ranks from the coffers of a salt trader …whose daughter and grandson are still at large.'

De Nogent's eye widened at the spy's audacity. What a pearl of information you must have found, he mused as the spy continued his theatre. Standing behind the spy, de Nogent could see Maintenon's attention was now fixed a few inches over the spy's shoulder, his pupils growing wider inside the disks of cold steel. He cast a glance out the window to avoid them.

'As I said, fifteen percent seems more than reasonable.' The neat moustached lips parted in a smile. 'Utmost discretion of all your dealings…past and present, included,' he added. 'A man of your standing must be permitted his mores.' Christian stretched out the vowels of the last word.

Before the inquisitor had time to digest the possible meanings of the spy's insinuations, Amaury de Maintenon stood, and in one slick motion retrieved a small hand axe from the desk drawer and cleaved it into the head of the man who was still leaning over his desk. Bernard de Nogent heard himself utter a cry as the spy reeled back, soaking the desk with an arc of blood. Heart pounding, the inquisitor forced his mouth shut. He was aware that he should be doing something, but he found himself unable to move, even as the body of the informant called Christian landed at his feet with a thud.

'Now.' Maintenon took a calming breath, pulled off his bloodied gloves and tossed them to the floor. 'Perhaps we can continue?'

De Nogent fought to suppress the tremor in his legs, a peculiar feeling of shock and fury heating his guts.

'You wish me to go south and consult with local traders?' he said.

'Yes, and now we will need someone else to round up the contingents of this shepherd boys' crusade.'

'We will,' the prelate said.

The assault on his nerves still throbbing in his bowel, the inquisitor's carriage departed for the city. Christian the spy was not possessed of a pious bone in his body, but to fell him without accusation or trial in front of a man of God! Clutching his crucifix, Bernard de Nogent crossed himself, and brought the trinket to rest on his lips.

Up ahead the sheriff's men were hooking down the remains of a highwayman from a roadside cage. At least the informant's demise had been quick, he considered – an altogether better end than rotting under the sun, or some similar fate as inevitably would have awaited a man like Christian.

What did you find out that he silenced you so? Did it concern the boy? Le Coudray? How was it Maintenon had put it when he had first told him of her capture? *She could have spread her lies to anyone who would listen.* The hair on his neck bristled with a cold shudder of anticipation. The Holy Ghost was moving within him.

He drummed his fingers impatiently on the rim of the carriage window. He would feel far better once he had that whore back in custody. And what better bait to draw her to him than her bastard son? Now the task of locating the crusader children had fallen to him, he could hasten directly to Marseille. With their contingents heading south, if he moved fast enough he would soon have his hands upon the boy. Le Coudray would surely follow. And if there were secrets to be told about Amaury of Maintenon, his techniques would prise them from her. The prelate cast his eyes heavenward in a prayer, asking that all he needed be provided.

The carriage jolted over the ruts of the dusty track, putting distance between him and the venal whims of Amaury of Maintenon. Slowly, he felt his stomach settle. Nothing but a test, he thought. For what man would be worthy of History who was not prepared to be sorely tested for his prize? Maintenon he could care take of in good time, and he would have to, no doubt about it now. But he was not yet ready. More information was required. And money. The inquisitor sighed. More money was always required. Such was the way of worldly existence, he told himself. Drawing level with the Sheriff's men, he watched them toss the liquefying cadaver onto the back of their wagon and cover it with a shovel of lime, enveloping his carriage in a choking cloud.

Chapter Twelve

'The storm will be over soon.'

All heads swivel towards Jean, now sitting bolt upright. Etienne's heart feels as though it is going to leap out of his chest. They have been on the road now for more weeks than he wants to remember and it has started to take its toll on the weakest among them. Jean fell sick after they were caught out in a storm. For three nights he has lain in their bivouac, barely breathing, pale as death, while the boys argue about how much longer they should give him. Most of them want to give him up to a local priest but Etienne has convinced them to wait until first light. Now, as he watches his friend rise from the dead like Lazarus, he isn't sure miracles as big as this one are even possible, and he mutters a prayer of gratitude that God has seen fit to answer him, a shepherd boy from a small village. He must truly be pleased at their efforts.

Jean coughs and asks for a sip of water. His skin is grey, eyes huge and sunken in his head. For a moment he surveys them in silence, then just as Etienne thinks he is going to slip away again, he squints at their amazed faces and he tells them that his soul departed from his body during the long sleep. Guided by angels - tall, graceful creatures that radiated golden light - he was shown places so miraculous and beautiful that they are impossible to describe. The angels said God was pleased and would bless their undertaking. They need the blessing of no earthly pope when Christ and his archangels watch over them.

Off in the distance, thunder grumbles. The rain has eased to a trickle now and a pale yellow sliver of light melts through the iron clouds. Their belongings are soaked – sleeping blankets, the tents, clothes, what food they have. Etienne lifts himself up on his walking stick and surveys the dripping fields.

At first he thinks his eyes are deceiving him, but as the silhouettes approach they begin to take shape - a group of young men, shoulders propelling them through the long grasses, boots laced all the way up to the knees, like the soldiers of some lost legion.

'Yes,' he mutters, and gallops out into their path.

'Daniel!' he cries and the convoy stalls.

The dark-haired boy at the front of the group laughs. 'Etienne!'

'We were half a day ahead of you when we heard that some children were hurt, so we came back.' Daniel's face softens into an apologetic smile.

He looks to his cohorts resting easy on their walking poles, their sympathetic gazes on Etienne as though he were a lamb stuck on a rocky outcrop.

'We have been blessed,' says one of Daniel's friends. 'And it's only right to share our blessings.'

'How blessed?' asks Etienne.

'This morning we came across a pious merchant who told us he had been at the Fairs,' says Geoffrey.

'He remembered our plight,' Daniel continues. 'He was so moved he gave us some money and told us to journey on to Marseille via a place called Vichy.'

'Huh,' says Etienne. 'Imagine.'

'He is going to leave us some more vittles there. We thought we might get some meat and rest for a day or so.'

'That sounds nice.' The last time Etienne ate meat was the rabbit a butcher gave them for St John the Baptist's day. He can almost smell it cooking in the pot.

'We set off as pilgrims together so it's only right that we help the weaker ones,' says Daniel. 'The merchant told us the rewards would be all the more if we spread the word and gather more of us.'

The other shepherds nod. 'That's the whole reason we are here. To show God that we are not all like those greedy lords who fill their larders and never return their blessings on those who tend the land.'

'We are all here together,' another says. 'And there are many others making their way south.'

Etienne's eyes widen keenly. He thrusts his hand into his tunic pocket, fingers searching until they find it. Turning his back on the older boys, he hunches over and in the pretence of blowing his nose, plants a kiss on the little gold disk. The sky always comes clear, he thinks.

*

The moon is full when they resume their journey; woodlands, vineyards, long, glassy rivers, and plains with views that look like they go on to the edge of the world. It is easier travelling with the older boys. The days pass faster and for the times when they have nothing to buy food with, the older boys know how to trap a grouse or steal without getting caught - a chicken from a courtyard, a loaf of bread left to cool by a window. Etienne knows that at other times stealing would be wrong, but this is different. If God allows them to take with such ease and not get caught, then it means that He favours their endeavour. He has lain it right there in their path so they might survive. All is forgiven anyway, once you kneel at the holy places.

When eventually they arrive in Marseille, Etienne is glad he isn't just with his friends from Montoire. He has never seen so many people, or even imagined that there could be so many, side by side in the same place and he is glad to have the protection of the older boys.

'It's just like Paris,' Marc says with a confident nod as yet another cart splashes them with roadside filth.

Etienne knows Marc has never been to Paris but he doesn't say anything as he can tell Marc is just as overwhelmed as he. At least Daniel and some of his friends from the Île know what cities are like. Etienne hopes as they trudge through the chaos that they know how to find them a place to stay. Somewhere that isn't like one of these hovels; crumbling, windowless lean-tos crammed either side of streets that stink worse than any animal barns he has ever smelled.

'I hope this air doesn't make us sick,' Etienne says.

'Don't be stupid,' Marc replies. 'How do you think all these people live here?'

'They don't look very well to me.' Etienne pulls his shirt up over his nose just in case.

'Look. Etienne.' Marc pulls at his shirt. The group stops in their tracks. The man is carrying two heavy pails, bare-chested with a scarf wound round his head, sweat running down his face and torso. He staggers past them, eyes lifting briefly to take them in. The urge to reach out and touch his smooth, mahogany skin is almost irresistible. The man turns into a courtyard, putting down one of his pails to pat the head of the small child who runs out to greet him. For a few moments, the boys stand dumbfounded.

'That's a Mohammedan,' whispers Etienne.

'Probably a slave carrying water for his master.' Marc replies.

'But he is like us.' Etienne is still staring at the entrance to the courtyard.

'No he is not. He is half naked with a cloth wrapped round his head and dirty dark skin!'

'That's not what I mean,' Etienne begins but decides it is too complicated to explain any further.

'What Etienne means is that he was a man,' says Jean. 'Flesh and blood.'

At the end of the street they find themselves on a promontory overlooking the harbour - boats of all sizes are lashed to the quay, labourers heaving over-laden barrows back and forth as seagulls dive onto piles of rubbish. The rotten smell of fish, human waste and salt that tinged the air in the back streets hits their nostrils full. Etienne kicks a discarded bottle into the sea and peers over to watch it fill with water and sink. The water is filthy. Unidentifiable objects caught in bits of rope slap up against the side of the harbour, bobbing in the foam that clings to the wall. It would definitely make you sick enough to die if you fell in, Etienne thinks before wondering how many people fall in each year.

Moored just beyond the harbour chain, two barrel-hulled merchant transports dip up and down in the water.

'Are they taking us to the Holy Land?' A small boy called Renauld asks.

'Maybe,' replies Daniel. 'They are merchant ships. The men who want to help us told us to meet here. One of the boats is called *The Peregrine*

Falcon they said.'

'Just think in a few days we could be out at sea,' says Daniel.

'A few days?' asks Jocelyn.

'Yes,' Daniel says. His eyes glow like polished copper. 'Isn't it exciting?'

Etienne nods vigorously, even as it hits him for the first time that he hasn't been on a boat before. In fact, until a few weeks ago, he hadn't even seen one.

'Why do we have to wait though?' Jocelyn persists. 'The ship looks ready.'

'We have to wait for all others will join us so we can pay something towards our passage.'

'Oh.' Renauld sounds disappointed. 'The shepherd boy said we wouldn't need money.'

'He also said the sea would part and we would be able to walk to the Holy Land.' Marc clips the boy's ear. 'He was a fake.'

Renauld cries out and a brief scuffle ensues as the others come to the boy's defence.

'Look over here.' Etienne shouts at the fray.

Guarding the harbour mouth is a large fortification. Far larger than any castle they have seen on their journey, huge, featureless slabs of stone lean up towards the clear blue sky. There are no doors on the harbour side, only archery slits way up high. Behind the ramparts a watchtower flies a black standard with a white cross.

'The banner of the Knights of the Hospital,' Etienne whispers. 'There must be an entrance somewhere.'

The stone blocks are the thickest he has ever seen, easily as thick as his arm span, and he wonders how long it took to build. He runs his palm over the wall and wipes the chalky residue on his trousers. At least the reign of the last king, probably. Around the back of the building a double-towered gateway is blocked only by a chain. From within the cloisters comes a low murmur. The knights are at prayer. Etienne feels his heart quicken as he realises he is going to jump the chain.

Suddenly his friends scatter and before he has a chance to flee he finds himself staring up at one of the knights; a giant of a man with a full beard and a scar that runs from his eyebrow to his ear. His arms are folded across his chest, sword swinging in its scabbard.

'Please, sir,' he starts.

The top of his head comes up to the middle of the knight's chest.

'What are you doing here?'

'I'm sorry, sir. I just…' He can hear his voice pitching higher, like a girl. 'I just…there was no one here. I just wanted to look. I'm not a spy or anything.'

The knight reaches down and ruffles Etienne's hair. 'I can tell.'

Etienne's body judders with relief. He wants to say thank you but the words won't come out.

'There should be a guard on the gate,' the knight says, 'to preserve us from attack by twelve-year olds!'

'There's not enough of us to attack anything yet.' Etienne decides not to tell him that he is only eleven.

'What do you mean?'

Etienne tells the knight his story. He can tell the knight is impressed that they have come so far. The big warrior's eyes shine as though he is looking at some amazing sight in the distance, and even though he must be very busy, which Etienne can tell from the way he keeps looking away, he stays quite still and listens until the end.

The knight kneels down so he is shorter than Etienne and says, 'Your endeavour is worthy of praise and I am sure the Lord will reward you for your efforts but what you propose is dangerous and by rights I should counsel you to return home.'

The knight's face is stern and Etienne's shoulders sag.

'But I too ran away when I was a boy, younger in fact than you. God, in his mercy, sent me into the arms of the good monks of St Benedict.' He pauses and crosses himself. Etienne thinks, if I didn't know any better I would say he is choked for words. 'From there, by and by, I found my way into the Hospital of St John and became a knight.'

'You are not rich?' Etienne's eyes widen.

The knight laughs. 'No, no. I was an errand boy at first. I learned to fight overseas. Then, as God willed it, another knight bequeathed me his horse when he passed away. Here.' The knight unsheathes the knife. 'The handle is oak from a tree of the Holy City.'

'It's for eating.' Etienne hopes he doesn't sound disappointed.

'And yet it has killed a man.' The knight pricks his skin with the tip and they both watch as a bright red bead blooms on his thumb. 'It belonged to the very same man who attacked me on my way to prayer at the Sepulchre. I have kept it as a talisman, but perhaps it is time to pass it on to someone who may have more need of it than I.'

Etienne watches mesmerised as the knight unties the sheath from his belt and attaches it to his own. 'My name is Etienne,' the knight says.

Etienne gasps, eyes popping. 'So is mine!'

'Well, Etienne, that is a fortuitous sign is it not.'

Etienne turns the knife over, the hilt smooth in his hand. 'I think it must be.' And in that moment, he knows, with absolutely iron rod certainty, that he will visit the tomb of their name saint in Jerusalem. If not then God strike him down.

Chapter Thirteen

'What do you mean not enough?' Inquisitor de Nogent said through clench teeth.

The trader rubbed at the mottled patch of purple skin that stained his neck.

'It's always the same with you French when it comes to delivery. I was a tax collector at the Venetian treasury when your armies came seeking passage overseas a few years ago. Ships for thirty thousand we built! But when it came time to pay up, nowhere near that number arrived.' The chubby jowls trembled as the merchant laughed. '*Cò l'acqua riva aea gòea,*' he said, placing his hand at his throat. 'When the water arrives here, we Venetians know what to do.'

'So they say, Signor Zonta.' The inquisitor sighed. 'So they say.'

'*Dunque.* You said there would be one thousand of these *pastorali* at the port?'

'I haven't counted the bodies myself but my scouts tell me that is the approximate number.'

'Well, my men tell me there's less than half that number.'

De Nogent arched his brow defiantly. The truth was he had no way of counting exactly how many of the peasant children had gathered there. With such a violent and unpredictable business partner as Maintenon, he didn't wanted to jeopardise things with inconvenient detail.

'Trafficking in Christians from Marseille is risky. I need a better numbers than that.' Without pausing for breath, Zonta rattled on. 'I can only take ten to fifteen percent of white faces in the hold of a regular shipment. I trade dark skins for the Church, pagan Slavs, but no whites from Marseille. I'll have to use pirate vessels to move your gang of minature crusaders. I need numbers. And a larger downpayment than I would usually take to make it worth my while.'

'First of all they are not crusaders. They are the bastard sons of heretics and thieves. Quiz one if you will and all you'll hear is pagan filth.' De Nogent's beady eyes flared. 'Secondly, who do you think I am? I can't summon money out of thin air. If you can't be of more help, I am sure the Bishop of Beziers would be pleased to reconsider his middle men.'

'And he knows about your little enterprise, does he?'

Bernard de Nogent glared back. 'Don't threaten me, Signor Zonta. I'll inspect the cargo on the dock myself if you require a certification from the Church.'

The trader shrugged. 'I say give me two hundred livres now and we'll make generous terms.'

*

Lifting his gaze up to the stained glass window, the inquisitor followed a vein of gold picked out by the afternoon sun. A triplicity of arches, each one containing a scene from the Scriptures; the holy couple on their donkey seeking sanctuary, the three kings, the Baptist preaching, lamb of God at this feet. Beyond the window loomed a shadow cast by crumbling stucco of a building that had once been a warehouse. Now it was a foundling orphanage established for the offspring of executed heretics. Bernard de Nogent prayed for a sign. He had been sent here to this cesspit on earth for Divine purpose, he knew it. Sooner or later the Creator would reward him with clear confirmation of his mission.

He had chosen to break the unhappy matter of the numbers to Maintenon via letter rather than risk a face-to-face confrontation. To his surprise, the nobleman had obliging packed up four score of brats from he didn't want to know where, and sent them south to the greedy Venetian via some beggar of a bargeman. However, with Zonta insisting on additional money for the risk, he was still at least two hundred bodies short of the minimum cargo.

Aware of shuffling feet, de Nogent turned, irritated, to see the Mother Superior of the foundling's home. He had seen her before, squawking at the wretches on the fondaco. His lip curled with disdain as he watched the old harridan bowing at the Crossing, face lined and shoulders stooped by the burden of bitterness. Just then, the sun re-illumined the window and it struck him. What a fool! What clearer sign than the golden pathway already made right before him? *The bastard children of heretics and thieves.*

Suddenly, his heart was thumping in his chest. An idea as terrible as it was exciting began to take form. The dried up hag was weeping at the feet of the Virgin as Bernard de Nogent rose from his prayer cushion and shook the creases from his velvets. Not an act of wickedness, he told himself, but an act with which he would smite the carnal greed of secular men; of men like Amaury of Maintenon.

'I didn't think you would turn up your nose at a guaranteed supply chain,' he murmured in imaginary discourse with the vulgar Venetian trader. In return, he would gain a source of income of his own from the ever-swelling collection of children left behind by Cathar heretics. Whether they labour here or on some other shore for the rest of their days, what difference does it make? It is the inevitable wages of the sins of their fathers, and he would put it to good use by spreading the Hallowed word and stamping out falsehood where the weak minds of the ignorant have allowed the Evil One a foothold.

Satin slippers whispering on the marble, he skated over to the nun, and squeezing a few drops of water from his tear ducts, knelt beside her on the cold, hard stone.

'Ave maria gracia plena dominus tecum benedicta tu in mulieribus et

benedictus fructus ventris tui jhesu.'
*

It was early in the morning when the voices came floating across the mist. French voices. The sun was beginning to clear the fog, and the train of boys appeared like an army of ghosts materialising from some unearthly realm. More than three score, they snaked along the riverbank with sticks and bags slung over their backs.

Gui slid down from his saddle. Eyes fixed on the convoy he raced towards them as though fearful they might vanish, a mere trick of the mist. Dressed in tunic and hose, men's boots laced up to her calves, Agnes stumbled along behind him in desperate haste like a battlefield messenger heading for his master's banner.

From a distance the boys looked gaunt but not sick; young men who had walked for too long with too little food. It was only once they reached them that the toll of their journey was revealed; hollow eyes robbed of innocence and light, greying skin, bones jutting from beneath ragged shirts. Agnes tore off the large cloth cap that was spilling over her brow and ran among them, searching their faces, oblivious to the doubtful looks that fell upon this strange woman garbed as a man.

'You are from France.' Gui grabbed one of the older boys by the arm. 'Are you travelling with the shepherd boys from the Chartraine?'

'We were but we were separated on the road.' Glassy eyed, he considered Gui for a moment, then said, 'We are bound for the holy places overseas.'

'Overseas?' The word bore down upon him, tight as a vice. It felt as though his skull might crack. When the boy's eyes widened Gui released his grip. Fingers laced together, supplicant, he said, 'I am looking for my son, Etienne. He joined a band just as yours. We are from Montoire. You must have heard something of the boys from our village?'

There was a hesitant exchange of shrugs. 'It's a common name among us but I don't think so. Most of us here are from Rouen.'

The weight of Gui's heart bowed his head. He could sense Agnes at his side, but he couldn't quite bring himself to look at her. She placed a hand on his shoulder, touched his desperation with the whirling current of her own. Emotion stung the back of his throat. Lifting his head, he spoke to the boys in the soft, low tones of a priest.

'You should gather your strength and return home. Crusade is the job of knights and their lords.'

'They have failed,' the boy said with steady-eyed conviction. 'The Lord will not release Jerusalem to the swords of the corrupt.'

'The Lord is not concerned with our toil for the earthly Jerusalem,' Gui said. 'Do not give your lives to endeavour that can bring you only hardship and loss.'

'We cannot return now,' was the boy's simple reply. 'We are so close.'

'Others are joining us from every part of France,' said another. 'A great convergence.'

'But look at you!' Agnes implored. 'Look at the little ones. If nothing else think of the suffering you cause to your family.'

'You think our families did not try to stop us?' One of the others spoke, his lips covered with sores. 'The Lord wants the proof of our sacrifice. The older generation don't understand. If we cannot change this world then no-one can.'

'Not in this way.' Gui drew breath for another line of his sermon but the vague eyes of the group told him that not even Jesus himself could turn these boys back. Gaze lifted to the horizon, he murmured, 'What have we become that our children should feel our burden fall upon them?

They were half a league away when Agnes said, 'I wish we had never come across them.'

Arms circling Gui's waist, she felt his body flinch at her words, but he did not slow their pace.

'Did you see the state they were in?'

'Of course I did,' he snapped. 'What would you have me do?'

'That's not what I mean…' The air wheezed from her lungs as her voice faltered. Gui stopped their mount and turned to face her. 'Are you alright?'

She tried to hold on the dark eyes, the deep groove between his brows, but his face was a blur. She blinked to focus.

Squeezing her shoulders, he said, 'He's not dead, my love. I feel it. Can you not feel it? He is not dead.'

Her head felt so heavy. She let it fall into the shield of his body.

'He is not dead.' Although his voice was steady, she felt a tremor from deep within his chest.

The lost faces of the boys harried her. One by one their features arranged themselves into the same face: Etienne. A sickness of the mind was attacking her body. She knew it would continue its assault until she held her son in her arms again.

Gui peered at her with a doctor's intense look of concentration. 'We have to rest,' he announced.

'Just a few more miles,' Agnes replied.

Her eyes burned, chest tight as she struggled for air. Marseille was so close, no further than two or three days' ride. They mustn't stop. Once they were together again nothing else would matter. All three of them could disappear. Bernard de Nogent and his hideous cohorts be damned. She tried to swallow down her cough but it would not be contained. A convulsion rippled through her. I am drowning, she wanted to tell him.

'It's nothing,' she said. 'I'll be fine.'

Shouldering her weight with one arm, Gui swung his leg round, ready to dismount.

'Please, Gui. We can't stop. We are so close.'

'No. We rest and take a drink here, then ride to the nearest village. You send word to this aunt of yours you told me about.'

'Margarida. No, I…'

'She can tend to you whilst I go on to meet Philippe.' The soft brown eyes surveyed her sternly. 'That is what we are going to do. You have to rest.' Gui reached over and in one practised movement, swung her down from the horse.

'Oh quick,' she said. In the next breath she was on her hands and knees, choking up the terror.

Chapter Fourteen

The Fountain stood at the intersection of a main thoroughfare and an alleyway. Lantern light made dim shadows of the men within but, swamped beneath a large cloak and a wide-brimmed hat, Gui recognised his friend immediately.

'All these theatrics for an old friend?'

The guttering laugh and the firm clutch of his hand did not hide the air of uncertainty that radiated from Philippe.

'My inquiries as to the whereabouts of your boy yielded much more than I bargained for, I can tell you,' Philippe began. 'I had to take every precaution.'

'Someone followed us to Tours,' said Gui. 'A retinue of retainers from the Chartraine.'

Philippe scratched at his hairline. 'I'm not surprised.' The merchant sighed, his attention drifting to the entrance. 'We should move from here.'

Gui stayed him with his hand, looked him in the eye. 'Philippe, one of their saddle bags was embossed with the arms of Champol.'

Philippe's face contorted in surprise.

'Why don't you tell me what is going on?' Gui said.

The broad shoulders slumped. 'My house at Tours was robbed. A warning or a search, I don't know which.'

'The men who followed Agnes and me?'

'It seems likely. As soon as I arrived in Chartres I began making inquiries as to this shepherd's crusade. At first all I found were other families who had lost children, young men. It was easy enough to establish they had headed to the Fairs.' He eyed Gui reluctantly. 'But before long there were other pieces of information.' The merchant took a long draught of ale.

'Such as?'

'The group had dispersed in every direction, some to Alsace, Rome, the southern ports. I also discovered they have come to the attention of others.' He lowered his voice. 'There are scouts along the routes looking for them, attempting to gather as many as possible into the same location.'

Gui's gut beat a pulse of alarm. 'Marseille.'

'From what I was able to gather the children are being corralled by men of little scruples to be sold.'

A hot wave pulsed through Gui's body. 'Slavery?'

'I met someone, a Sicilian oil trader who told me he had been offered a couple of northern house boys for six livres.'

'Less than the price of a palfrey.' Gui rubbed his face as though he were trying to wash away a bad dream.

Philippe pressed his lips together in condolence. 'He had the impression they were not in healthy enough condition to travel on.'

Gui drew close enough to see the red-rimmed fatigue in the other man's eyes and said carefully, 'But what of Etienne? Do you know if he is here or not?'

Philippe nodded, grave. 'It's likely. I think they are being bought to Marseille to be sold onto Muslim households in Spain or even further afield.'

The merchant pressed his palms together in prayer as Gui's eyes blackened. 'Gui, you have to understand, I don't move in this underworld. After the robbery…There was nothing more I could do alone.'

'Where can we find these scouts?'

Philippe stood, gestured for Gui to follow him. 'An errand boy I was able to encourage told me where to go,' he said rubbing his thumb and index finger together. 'Come.'

The cool evening air was a welcome respite from the smell of stale beer and bodies inside and Gui took a deep, steadying breath.

The bolt came silently. It wasn't until Philippe staggered round, clutching his arm, that Gui realised he had been struck. He lurched forward to catch his friend and a second bolt clattered at their feet. Braced against Philippe's weight, Gui scanned the alleyway. It was deserted.

Philippe's fingers curled around Gui's cloak. 'Go to the quay,' he mouthed. 'Now.'

'We have to get you back inside.' Gui edged towards the tavern, his friend's bulk resting on his shoulder.

'Go now. I can get myself inside.' Bent double, Philippe limped for the cover of the doorway, a deep red stain blooming on his shirt. Another bolt ripped through the fabric of Gui's tunic.

'The docks,' Philippe said through gritted teeth, 'where the porters load oil for North Africa.' He walked his fingers inside his cloak and dragged out a leather pouch. 'This should buy you what you need,' he wheezed. 'Now go.'

Numb with disbelief, Gui backed away as his friend stumbled back inside the tavern. Turning one way and then the next, Gui tried to guess the direction of the port. The narrow alleys were a labyrinth closing in around him, the sound of his own breath grating as his lungs dragged the air in and out. Don't panic, said the voice in his head, just run.

*

Gui scrutinised the old woman, challenging her certainty, but the sagging eyelids did not blink or stray. Stooped low, she interrupted his conversation with a dockyard porter to tell him there had been French children here. Not two or three days ago she saw them, two score, maybe more. They came round with the noon sun, looking for the late morning scraps from the markets. They were blessed; she could tell they were on the business of the Lord. The porter moved to shoo her away but Gui held up a hand of clemency. She was hard to understand. A gypsy, her skin browned and shrivelled by the sun. She stank.

'Do you know where they went?' Gui spoke slowly, inserting the bits of Occitan he knew from Agnes. The hag wrinkled her brow and sighed. Gui opened his pouch, certain that coin would reveal her answer, but before he could hand her the money, she nodded to the other side of the harbour, 'Behind the foundlings home.'

The porter's face soured as Gui gave her a coin. In return she made the sign of the cross and muttered something that was neither French nor Occitan. Although Gui did not understand the tongue, there was no mistaking the warning.

The warehouse behind the orphanage was empty. Gui stood in the doorway, short of breath, heart hammering in his throat. All around the vacant space were signs; a scorched patch where a fire had been lit, dirty straw strewn over the floor, empty clay bottles, crates brimming with rotting refuse. Something caught his eye by the bedding area. He squatted down and filleted his hand beneath the straw - a wooden spinning top, it's handle snapped. He brought his hands to his head.

'Can I help you?'

Gui looked up. The bright sun made shadow of the man's face but the black cross on his white tunic was unmistakable – a knight of the Order of the Hospital.

'There was a group of children here.'

The knight was a good head taller than Gui, his cheek scarred.

'I believe I know what has happened to your boy,' he said.

Gui felt his body jolt as though he had been struck by an external force. 'What do you mean my boy?'

'I guessed. Watching you with the toy, you have the air of a father. Am I wrong?'

Gui shook his head.

'If he was among the group camped here then I believe I may know something.' The knight extended his hand. 'I am Etienne of the Order of the Hospital.'

'Etienne is my son's name.'

'Then he takes his looks from you.'

Gui's eyes shot wide open. 'You have seen him?'

'He came with some others to the priory not a week gone. His hair was fair but the same curls. The brow, the shape of the eyes. I'm trained to notice such things.' The knight paused, then said sadly. 'And your accent. The boy said he had come from Montoire because he didn't want to be a shepherd.'

Mouth clamped shut, Gui held his breath to contain the wave that was building inside his chest, threatening to spill out and shame him before this stranger.

'Come.'

Outside, the glare from the sun was a blinding contrast to the gloomy warehouse. The air was a cacophony of merchants, seamen, peddlers, their cries now and again consumed by the crash of a ship's gangway hitting the dock. Etienne pointed at two fat-bellied merchant cogs anchored on the other side of the harbour.

'Those ships?' Gui felt the host of dreadful possibility bearing down on him.

'They run supply routes in the western Mediterranean. The boat I believe they boarded was bound for Corsica.'

'What boat?' Reaching for the support of shattered packing crates behind him, Gui blinked rapidly, trying to bring the world to order.

'The boat they boarded.' The knight bowed his head. 'I did not pay them enough mind. You have to understand there are so many groups of pilgrims here, young men claiming they want to go overseas….I wasn't much older than your son when I sought service myself.' The knight rubbed the back of his neck. The noose of guilt, thought Gui.

'We are in contact with the harbourmaster. So many slave ships come and go from this harbour, trafficking of Christians is always a problem.'

The cawing of the seagulls was suddenly very loud in Gui's ears. A rush of blood pounding at his temples, he whispered, 'I was told there might be children being sold into service in Spain.'

'Not just Spain.' The Hospitaller stood at the threshold of the warehouse entrance, grappling with his task. 'Alexandria, Crete, Venetian colonies on the Black Sea. These men are slavers and the truth is they profit from trade in Christians as well as Mohammedan or Jew.'

All Gui could do was stare back.

'Theirs will not be a fast boat. If you want to retrieve your son then you're best advised to leave as soon as you can. I can arrange passage for you on one of our galleys.'

'Dear God. Yes.'

'You'll need money but you should be able to purchase your son back without trouble if you approach them with one of our Brothers.' He placed a huge, knotted hand on Gui's shoulder. 'I know it must seem an impossible world away but we travel overseas regularly. The world is not so vast as you might imagine once you are used to it.'

'I can sell my horse,' stammered Gui. 'But my wife…she's sick. I left her outside the city.'

'The ship sails at sundown. If you want to see your son again you must be on it.'

Shielding his eyes against the sun, Gui surveyed the bay, the departing boats, how quickly they became black flecks on the horizon and then were gone. Drawing his shoulders back, he stiffened.

'Please arrange it,' he said. 'I will return within that time.'

The knight gave him a firm pat on the shoulder. 'I do not think you have to fear the worst on your boy's account. He has something rare about him.'

'He is a shepherd. He knows nothing of how to fight.'

'Yet I saw the same conviction in your son's eyes as I see in yours now. It is not a quality of one who easily abandons his faith.'

Gui laughed, a casual, self-mocking cough.

'You're a priest, aren't you?' said the knight.

'You are an astute observer of men.'

'I have travelled to many places, met men of so many different creeds, different lives. The priest who has tired of the Church wears a shroud that is impossible to hide. You should take this chance as an act of His mercy that you have not forsaken your faith.'

Before he realised it, Gui had pulled his rosary from his cloak. Eyes closed, he made the sign of the cross on his chest.

The streets of the city centre spun him a congested web; thoroughfares blocked by carts unloading, cut-throughs that ended in piss-soaked dead ends, beggars and drunks under his horse on any path wide enough for him to take some speed. When he broke free of it, he tore up the road back to the inn, making half a day's ride before noon. His mind tossed on the seas of fetid pirate vessels, the wide-eye trust of innocents and his own wretched guilt. There was no space left to consider the choice he had to face, so when he returned to Agnes, sweat-damped hair tumbling about her, he was struck unprepared by the sensation of being wrenched asunder.

Gaze searching for focus, she smiled. He sat on the bed, took her frigid hand and rubbed it in between his. These were the little gestures that had the power to slow time. Perhaps, if he could link up enough of them without uttering a word, his decision would never have to be made.

'Agnes, my love, can you hear me?' He took her fingers to his lips.

She nodded. He let out a laugh of relief. The thought that came to him next was so loud he could have sworn it was someone else's voice. *If you leave her now she will die.* Invisible hands squeezed his heart. Gui knew that if he tried to speak in that moment he might weep, so instead he smiled back, the well-practised consolation his profession had taught him. Stroking the hair from her face, it occurred to him that he could say nothing and she would never know. It would be his guilt to carry alone. Their son was gone - the chances he would ever find the boy alive, let alone reclaim him, were so small. But her life, right here, was under his touch.

'You should rest, my love,' he said, going over to the washing stand for the distraction of wetting a face cloth.

'What is it?' Her voice was weak but insistent.

Arms braced against the stand, head bowed, Gui could see his reflection distorted dimly in the pewter jug. He looked away from the darkly circled eyes staring back, challenging his selfish fantasy with the truth: as much as Agnes meant to him, Etienne was her world. What would be the more painful? A lifetime of guilt that he had not disclosed the slim chance in his power to find their son, or the knowledge that he would be riding away now from the only love he had ever known. It was not his choice to make and he knew what her choice would be.

Gui bit down on his lip and turned to face her.

'Etienne has boarded a vessel with the other children bound for the Holy Land.'

Agnes raised her head. 'The Holy Land?'

Gui nodded, throat clamped shut by the truth. He closed his eyes on his crumbling faith. Lungs battling for air, Agnes's sobs turned into hacking retches. Helpless witness, he pulled her to his chest. Then, blotting her cheeks with his hand, he said, 'The Knights of the Hospital offered me passage on one of their transports. They think the ship the boys have taken is bound for Corsica.'

She looked up at him. 'Corsica?'

'I believe it is a week or so under sail. The Orders use it as a supply station.'

Briefly her eyes cleared. 'And they could get us there before this other vessel?'

Gui nodded. 'I would likely arrive before the other boat if I leave immediately.'

Comprehension dawned on her face. He spoke before she had the chance to.

'You cannot board a ship, Agnes. The journey would kill you. The damp. The conditions…you don't know what it is like.'

It was when she raised no protest that he realised she knew how sick she was. She gripped his tunic. 'Then you must go alone.'

He swallowed. 'The chances of finding him…'

'You must go. You must find him. You must.' Her bright blue eyes were fractured with threads of blood. 'Promise me you'll find him. No matter what.'

'I will find him and I will return him to you.' He caressed her face. 'And you will be waiting .'

She nodded. 'I will be waiting.'

He emptied the contents of his money pouch onto the bedside table, then he reached for his rosary and folded it into her palm along with the coins.

'Don't sell it for less than five livres.'

'Please,' she offered it back. 'I would sooner take a finger from you.'

He stared at the miniature crucified Christ lying on a bed of coral beads - his mother's deathbed.

'If you don't take it back now Gui, I will think you don't mean to return.'

He picked up the beads.

'This aunt that you spoke of, have you sent for her? You will need help.' He smiled. 'And I will need a place to bring Etienne back to.'

'The keeper here sent a message, he can tell you where she lives. He is a good man.'

Gui looked around the room for something to do, some distraction that would stall him there.

'Gui, you must go. I will be well,' she said, but Gui saw her eyelids flicker briefly downwards.

'I know.'

Every moment he spent looking at her ebbed his resolve, so, suddenly, decisively, he picked up his bag. 'I love you,' he said.

'I love you, too.'

And he closed the door behind him.

*

Shrouded in a black cloak, the prelate stood on the harbour and watched the sun melt into the sea. Hand of God notwithstanding, the cargo would be well on its way by now, although you never could be sure what would happen at sea. Irritation needled his skin. Over five hundred miles, dispatched like an errand boy. He was a man of high standing not some roadside pedlar. He bit at the skin of his nail bed. The Venetian trader was late. May God grant the day when he no longer had to deal with middlemen. Calling in more favours than he wanted to and all for the acquaintance of a fat little fix-it man with bug eyes and grasping fingers.

He narrowed his eyes at the galley preparing to depart. A vessel of the military orders - he couldn't touch it. On the ship's prow, gaze cast out to the horizon, a black mop of hair caught bronze in the evening sun. The corrosive bile of hatred gnawed at his insides.

'Sorry.' The portly trader was sweating. 'I lost a Pisan cog and Hulk full of oil.'

The inquisitor blinked slowly, swallowing down the vitriol he wished to direct at the Italian.

'It was not my fault your men identified to wrong boy,' Zonta said reproachfully.

De Nogent inhaled deeply. He had sent two guards who claimed to be from Montoire to identify Le Coudray's bastard, but the brat they delivered turned out to be a Breton rag seller and completely worthless to him. Narrow is the way, he reminded himself. There would be other ways to lure Le Coudray to him.

'Please do not tax me any further, Signor Zonta,' he said.

'Easy to say when it's not your money,' Zonta retorted. 'You think you can get your cargo to market without me?'

There are always people like you, thought de Nogent, summoning a sneer.

'Unfortunately, there is someone else wants a piece of our merchandise,' he fingered towards the galley. 'And I need you to ensure that he never finds it.'

'I am not an assassin,' said the middleman, eyes round in mock offense.

'Deal with it as you wish.' The inquisitor gave a dismissive wave as a dozen seabirds took screeching to the air in the wake of the war galley reaming away from its mooring.

'Our target is the man with the black hair on the prow. Don't worry, he isn't a knight.'

'The one looking back to shore?'

On the deck, a man with black curly hair was staring out from under a shielded brow, as though he were scanning for a familiar face.

'Yes,' said the prelate. 'That's the one.'

PART TWO - The Banners of Hell's Monarch

Chapter Fifteen

'My poor child,' the voice said, placing a cool palm against Agnes's forehead. 'What is this ailment?' Without strain, the arms, strong from decades of supporting whatever burdens had fallen to them, worked their way under her back and lifted her up. The woman's face she had not seen since she was child, but as she peered over her, Agnes recognised her without hesitation. For all the weather and toil it had seen, her aunt's cheeks were still as plump and content as she remembered.

'How weak you are,' she heard the voice say, although it seemed more distant now.

Agnes tried to reply, but the sound that came out was a groan, carried away on a tide of relief that washed over her body.

Aunt Margarida was the eldest of Estève's sisters and she had lived on a smallholding with her husband since they were wed, forty years gone. Slight and sinewy, Arnaud was dwarfed by Margarida. Toiling content in the background, he reminded Agnes of one of the small figures in a grand wall painting, towing a handcart or scything wheat - he was always there, but you didn't always see him the first time you looked.

Forty years together and six children, two buried before them; little about their lives seemed changed to Agnes. For two weeks she had lain hidden under a mound of blankets while Margarida spooned her broth and angelica root to break the fever. In and out of the earthly realm she tumbled, rolling on waves of delirium.

Twice she saw them standing at the foot of her pallet, their shadows blanched by a halo of light. Gui's arm was around their son. 'Come with us,' they said. Extending her arm she tried to rise like Tabitha, only to find herself wrestling the staying hand of Margarida, who dragged her back down to her sickbed – and into the world of pain.

The fever passed, sobriety returned, and with it demons of the lower spheres. Announced by a terrible ache in her bones, they rode on the leaden weariness of her soul until she was paralysed. Her loved ones, far beyond her reach, were lost to the vicissitudes of Fortune. All she could do was pray. Around her, a lifetime of clutter and a warm hearth gave the living room a cosiness that seemed to stall time. The Sirens of a soporific eternity called her to yield - a deceit from which she knew she had to wrench herself free if she were ever to see her family again. What use is a sickbed? If pray is all you can do, then best you pray harder, Agnes Le Coudray.

Weeks later, when Aunt Margarida was certain of her recovery, she placed the walnut box before Agnes. It was enough to blanket the fatigue that still lingered from her illness. Decorated with brass and mother of pearl lattice, a neat cursive inscribed inside the lid - *For Agnes*. One of the many birthday gifts from her father that had faded from her memory. Now, as she fingered the engraving, it seemed to radiate a talismanic power. Conjuring her father's beaming face in her mind's eye, she felt the warmth of his hand on her shoulder, as real as the box before her. A breath of wind cooled her face. *Papà.*

'By the time it reached us we knew he was gone.' Margarida rubbed a venous calf. 'We prayed for you but we feared the worst.'

'Someone was listening.' Agnes nodded to the statue of Mary Magdalene, garlanded with small, white flowers on a plinth by the door. Margarida's eyes twinkled, and kissing her knuckle, she crossed herself.

'Holy mother is always listening.'

Agnes lifted out the contents with the reverent awe of a child opening a Christmas box. What was this message she had travelled a thousand miles and a sea of heartbreak to receive? The scrolls looked almost new, their browning ink the only clue of the time that had past since they were penned. She untied the ribbons and laid the curled parchments on the table before her - little shavings of a past forever snapping at her heels. They contained her father's will and the title deeds of his land holdings, along with pages roughly torn from his business ledgers - all of it long since carried off by the Church, she supposed. In addition there was a map, crudely sketched, its margins annotated in a scratchy hand that told Agnes of the pressure her father was under when he wrote it: *Six young ones. Saracens. De Coucy ?*

'Six young ones? It's so strange. There was nothing more?'

Aunt Margarida gave a soft tut.

'The map looks like the back of my grandparents' summer house. I only went there a few times, but I think this is it. It was part of my mother's castellany.'

'They left it to a woman?' Aunt's voice lifted in surprise.

'Her brother Geoffroi never saw adulthood. A cousin claimed it, but papà had word he died without heir. So it came to us.' Agnes shrugged. 'To me.'

A low susurration escaped the old woman's lips. 'Nearly ten thousand acres.'

'The yield didn't even match father's business...' Agnes rubbed at the base of her throat, her sentence choked off by the knotted vines of the past.

'But it made you a Lady,' Aunt said with a slow nod that seemed to Agnes to be an acknowledgment of what that really meant - a woman with a title was little more than chattel to be bartered for like livestock on market day. 'And we all know how those Northern lords love their titles.' The old lady burrowed a finger inside her bulky bun of hair and gave the back of her skull a considered scratch. Her shoulders dropped with a sigh, and Agnes could feel their communion of hurt spanning the silence.

She blinked back the sting of tears. 'I'm sorry…'

'Whatever for, my child?'

All Agnes could do was shake her head. I could have saved him, were the words she could not pronounce.

'There now, child, we are all better off without such false friends as riches.'

Agnes patted the damp from her cheeks. 'I know that, aunt. But there is more.' She traced the words Estève had scrawled onto the parchment. *Six young ones.* 'Father meant to tell me something with this. I know he did.'

Aunt Margarida raised her shoulders in long, elaborate consideration that Agnes knew was Occitan for a concession, reluctantly given.

'Who are these young ones?' Agnes's eyes returned to the parchment. She leant forward, her father's call from the grave kindling urgency. 'What if papà wanted me to do something?'

'The jealousy and greed of lesser men killed your father, my love. Lesser men, but better protected. How I wish it was not so. Your uncle Raimond told us they took Estève's holdings around here. Gave them to a Northern crusader. Raimond petitioned the Count of Toulouse, but….' Her brow drifted up.

'Count Raimond has bigger battles to fight.'

'Crusaders they call themselves, yet they slaughter God's children.' Aunt flicked her hand in disgust. 'What can the count do but fight? What can any of us do less we renounce our kin, our way of life? Rome sends inquisitors to denounce us as heretics, then they call in their French dogs to spill our blood and reward them with our land. It won't be long and our ways will be stamped out for good.'

The fire hissed as boiling water overflowed from the pan. Aunt leapt up and unflinching, lifted the pot from the flame with her bare hands.

'There is a new foundling house on your father's old estate now,' she continued, pouring the bubbling water into a bucket of nettles. 'Built by Rome for the orphans of those they burn as heretics.'

'Dear Lord. Those poor children.' *The young ones.*

'Let us be thankful at least that your father never learned of the evil they have turned it to.' Margarida placed her hands on her hips. 'With wealth comes power. And with power comes enemies.' She picked up the box, studying the lattice work as though there were something to be read in the pattern. 'Doesn't your Gui hail from the same place as your mother? When he returns, perhaps he…'

'Gui doesn't know everything,' Agnes blurted, heat colouring her neck. 'About the past. I mean there are some things…'

'Then who is there to tell him?' The old lady's wide-set eyes closed with a resigned smile.

'No one.' A dull ache spread in Agnes's chest, companion to her guilty heart.

'What is it, little one? You want to tell me something but you are afraid.'

Agnes longed to confess to aunt what no other living soul knew. Her lungs felt as though they were being crushed by the weight of what she would say, making it impossible to speak. The casket of shame had been locked too well, even for someone with the kind heart of Aunt Margarida to prise open.

'It's nothing.' She softened her brow and smiled for the old woman who would happily have hidden her and her box of secrets until they were all dead and long forgotten.

More than ever though, Agnes could feel the gnawing certainty in her gut that those secrets would not lie. That they would hunt her down, dogged as her pursuers. She also knew that if she did not leave soon, her presence here would bring the inquisition to aunt's door. And she could no more repay Margarida's loyalty with such risk than she could wipe the faces of Gui and Etienne from her mind.

The faces of those beloved she kept in close recall. In a blink of an eye she could walk in the woods outside Montoire with the cold mulch of leaves beneath her feet, feel the warmth of Gui's body as she slipped her arms under his cloak, or smile at her boy as he stoked the fire, his face the same look of studied concentration as his father's.

Perhaps that had been the real cause of her illness, she considered. Everything she could not forget. The idea that she might never hold them to her again flooded her with panic. Was their future in her hands? She cannot have come all this way, endured as she had for no purpose. What if this was the reason the Gui and Etienne had been separated from her? A test of her worth. A demand for action pit against an oppressive enemy whose name she knew was Fear.

She enclosed her face in her hands then peeled them away, seeking a new window on the world. A world away from Montoire. Why had it taken this for her to see? For too long she had allowed her family to shelter in the safety of Gui's office. The office that kept them all bound. The thump of her heart in the pit of her stomach told her that she and she alone could complete this task. She glanced over to the statue, then bowed her head in silent prayer that she find the strength to drink from the cup of courage. *Holy mother is always listening.*

Just a day or two more of rest was all she could allow. The longer she stayed, the more likely she would bring her troubles upon aunt. She had to uncover whatever it was the little map concealed. It contained the key to their freedom she could feel it. Whatever it was it had been important enough for her father to consign it to parchment and dispatch it to the future. Now, as the last rays of the sun's light dappled the table before her, she felt her blood stir with the hope that here would be the explanation for all that had befallen them. Something that, God willing, might recover her father's good name and set her family on a path to a surer future. She knew she had to find a way to lift the dark shroud of the past if she was ever to quieten the voice that told her the more righteous course would be to give herself up to the inquisition and set everybody else free. Perhaps the power to redeem the future for them all was in her hands after all. Perhaps then, God willing, her boys would be returned to her.

*

The messenger shrugged. 'We did everything we could.' He cast an eye to his colleague, but receiving no exchange of confraternity, jabbered on alone.

'The innkeeper said an old woman came to take her the day before. We couldn't find out who she was. It's Cathar territory.'

The other man shook his head sagely. 'They don't talk.'

'I am aware of the difficulties.' The inquisitor tapped his bony fingers sharply on the desk. 'Rest assured the armies of the Church are working as we speak to exterminate their contamination from the Provence.'

The two soldiers nodded stiffly.

'So we have two possibilities, don't we?' said de Nogent. 'Either she is still with this old woman. Or she has returned north.'

'Right.' They nodded keenly. 'We'll start asking around the Chartraine. We'll find out soon enough if she's come back north.'

The inquisitor forced a stretched smile. 'If we can avoid making our inquiries a public event.'

Both men gave a confused frown. 'But how are we going to find her if we don't ask about?'

The skinny fingers drummed.

'The arraignment of this woman is of the utmost importance.' A deeper sigh this time. 'Let us just say that it will be personally very unfortunate for me and personally very unfortunate for you were I to be forced to explain that she is lost.'

Nods of understanding. 'Right. Leave it to us, your reverence. If she's back in the Chartraine we'll find her, quiet as mice.'

Bernard de Nogent folded his hands together in an attitude of long-suffering patience. With Courville's bastard beyond his grasp for now, Le Coudray was the only leverage he had over Maintenon. That she was harbouring his secrets, wittingly or otherwise, he had no doubt. And if anyone had the techniques to prise such information from a person, it was he.

'Remember the Le Coudray girl is to come to me unharmed,' he said pleasantly.

'Unharmed. For questioning.'

De Nogent nodded slowly as his butler tapped on the open door.

'The wagon, your reverence.'

'Excellent. Unload it into the library. I will come immediately.'

The manservant dropped his head even lower.

'Gentlemen, other matters call.'

The retainers sloped off behind the hunch-backed butler, their path crossed by two coachmen, struggling with a large chest. The inquisitor cast a half smile.

'Excellent, bring it through,' he gesticulating keenly to the spot next to his desk.

Prising open the treasure chest he let out a grunt of delight. The first returns from his new venture. Delving his hand into the chest he picked up a fistful of coins. Fruits to be picked from the darkness and transformed into His light.

Bernard de Nogent placed his eyeglass down on the desk with utmost care and rubbed the bridge of his nose where the wooden frame had left an imprint.

'Impeccable hand,' he said, staring at the figures on the credit note that accompanied the cash payment. Set out in even lines, a tight, carefully rounded cursive, product of a thorough and considered mind. It was not in the same hand as the letter from the Venetian trader that came with it. A poorly-controlled stroke whose use of the vernacular showed the man for who he was – an ill-educated, guileful peasant who had harnessed his wits to serve his greed.

On the desk, a thick, creamy church candle he had lit just after Nones burnt brightly at the sixth hour mark. Six hours he had been locked in his study, re-imagining himself as the recipient of such unexpected wealth and the possibilities it bought him. The total sum was at the higher end of what he had been expecting. The banker's note was pinned down inches from his hand by a piece of gold-veined marble from the Tuscan mountains. Periodically he would stretch out his fingers and run them over the smooth, glittering stone and the irresistible allure of the parchment beneath, fighting to conceal from himself the unwelcome craving that had fallen upon him to keep it all for himself.

The note, as agreed with the Venetian, was made out to him. It meant that he would have to account for its disbursement cleverly. It also meant that Amaury de Maintenon would never see the true sum: Eight thousand eight hundred and fifty-three livres tournois. His venal partner was expecting just over half that amount. And why should he be due more? The number of shepherd peasants had been unsurprisingly exaggerated by the dull-witted spies, but with the addition of the heretic bastards from Church orphanages...well, they yielded more than he could have hoped.

Clearing six hours of library dust from his throat he said brightly to his imaginary interrogators, 'Donations. What else would it be? More and more lands are being prised back from the jaws of heresy into the bosom of the Church and the people are grateful. Donations are up.'

The rest was his to use in the advancement of Righteousness as he saw fit. It wasn't that Maintenon was not minded to complete the Abbey - no nobleman worth his salt is without an abbot or two in their pocket. He knew Maintenon well enough to know the prestige of founding a religion house was a powerful motive. But, as he cast his mind back to all the mockery he had been served, he would be a fool not to protect himself now he had the means. If nothing else this windfall was a sign that it was time to take charge of his own destiny. With the outstanding sum, he would purchase himself an audience with the Bishop of Chartres, and win himself a seat at the great tables denied to him only by the accident of birth.

The bell for Compline rang out. Stretching out his legs, he snatched up his letter to the bishop and scanned it one more time. Bishop Reginald of Chartres was a man of the sword, still down South fighting with the Crusader armies against the Cathar vermin. He was not expected back in the diocese for at least a month. One month in which he could unearth a nest of heretics significant enough to account for such an amount of money. It would need to be large enough to allow the bishop to impress the new pontiff with his zealous endeavours, but not so big as to alarm the Holy See into sending a legatine mission to investigate. By that time the Le Coudray whore would be under his arrest, and then there could be no more stalling.

Chapter Sixteen

The cabin is lit by the smoky flame of a lantern that gutters as it knocks back and forth above their heads. Although the only porthole is shut, it leaks as the grey swill crashes against it. Etienne wonders if they wouldn't better off trying to force the porthole open for a short while to get some clean air, even if they did get wetter. It might stop some of the boys from being sick, and maybe they could find a way of throwing out their waste. They all agreed, as there was no bucket, they would go in one corner, but with the lurching of the boat the sewage is starting to spread.

The boys draw closer together as the wind screeches through the timbers and the vessel sways and shudders. Now and then there is a big bang and the boat comes juddering to a stop.

'It's just the waves,' Daniel says with a soothing certainty. 'When the boat hits against the water in the strong wind it makes that noise.'

Etienne nods his head to no one in particular and repeats, 'It's alright, it's just the wind.' It still feels scary though, and the worst bit is they can't see what is going on. All they can do is trust that the boat is going to land safely when it topples over the crest of the wave.

'We must keep faith,' Jean says. 'The Lord always sends trials. Just like Paul in the Bible. The Lord struck him blind. He was even shipwrecked!'

'It will make our triumph all the sweeter.' Daniel addresses them, both arms braced against the ceiling, muscles popping as the boat bucks and rolls. He is trying to hold the whole world up, thinks Etienne. 'When the Mohammedans hear of our endurance they will all fall to their knees for Christ!'

'For pity stop!' yells Marc. It is the first time he has spoken since the boat left the harbour and the surprise of it is enough to draw their attention from the crashing and howling. 'Did you not see?' he rails on. 'Are you blind?'

Heads cast down, no-one responds. Etienne knows he is referring to the scores of olive-skinned children that boarded with them. Greying tunics, cheeks marked with livid, red slits – there was no mistaking they were slaves in transit. Separated into different holds, it was easy for the boys to convince themselves they were not bound for the same fate. But as the weather lashes the boat, Etienne can hear the frightened cries and whimpers of the slaves carrying through the timbers - cries that sound exactly the same as their own. He presses his face tight against a gap in the boards. On the other side of the wall, he can see the whites of unfamiliar eyes catching in the lantern light, the rest of their bodies consumed by the blackness.

'The only thing the Mohammedans are going to hear about, is how much we cost!' Marc continues.

'That's a lie!' shouts Daniel.

'We are Christians,' says Jean, his voice cracked with exasperation.

'They aren't allowed to sell us,' Jocelyn adds.

Marc guffaws, loud and spiteful. 'Why do you think they locked us away here?'

It is a good question thinks Etienne, and from the silence it seems no one else has an answer. Marc draws himself up, triumphant in his unhappy prophecy. 'In case they were inspected by the tax collectors.'

'Of course,' murmurs Etienne, as his heart sinks, heavy with the weight of the truth. He recalls the amber eyes of one of the girls that snagged his as she passed, a whisper on her lips. In that moment he hadn't understood the look of pity she gave him. But now he does, and he knows Marc is right.

'I heard them on the hard, talking about how when we get to Corsica they'll be meeting another boat. That was when those others arrived. So I didn't hear anymore,' Marc says much more quietly.

'Corsica, can't be far now. The moon was full when we left and last night it was nearly gone.' His mouth feels completely parched.

Suddenly there is a ripping sound, as though the sky is tearing open, and the boat spins round like an apple in a barrel. Etienne's heart is galloping but his body is frozen. The cabin fills with screams as the meek flame of the lantern flickers and dies.

'Water!' The word fills the cabin. Although it echoes around in a dozen different tongues, Etienne knows the language all too well; the language of fear. Eyes swivel over to where water is now spraying in through the hull.

'It may not matter anyhow. If the ship doesn't...' Marc's voice fades as the boat hurtles down into the pit of another wave. The boys cling to each other to stop themselves from skidding down into the bilge water. Etienne can feel Daniel's breath, hot and rapid in his ear, and he wants to ask the older boy if he is frightened. He is pretty sure he must be, that even a grown up would be. Still, it would be nice to hear him say it, then they could try to help each other not to be afraid.

Someone pulls out a whistle. The children sing along timidly to the thin, reedy note and Etienne remembers the times when they would sing to pass the time in the fields. But this is not at all the same hearty sound, and although he can hear a few voices rising more steadily above the din, he just wishes they would stop.

Beside him, Jean is turning his rosary beads. They make a soft clacking just like Father Gui's did when he was thinking something over. Etienne hasn't given two moments thought to rosaries in his whole life, but now he wishes he had some to concentrate on. Instead he closes his eyes, and tries to pretend he is back in his cottage, listening to his mother fussing and the clack, clack, clack of Father Gui's beads as he turns them through his fingers. For a half a breath it feels so real that he can see the little coral beads hanging from Gui's hand. Just as he convinces himself he might actually be able to reach out for that hand to hold, the vision evaporates. Instinctively he fingers the pouch inside his waist band where his mother's St Christopher is tucked away, but pressing the little disk does nothing to alleviate the nauseating dread in his stomach. Inevitably, he feels the tears squeeze from his eyes, and he buries his head into his knees.

'We will prevail. Take heart,' Jean says. 'To convert the infidel is the highest cause there is. God is just testing that we are worthy of such a task.'

'I know,' says Etienne, even though he doesn't. He doesn't know at all.

Jean folds something into his hand - a piece of felt that has something hard wrapped up inside.

'Don't open it, you might lose it.'

'What is it?'

'A fragment of bone from St. Martin. Don't tell anyone. It's real and people might not believe you. And if they don't believe then…'

'Then it won't work.'

'Exactly.' Jean draws his face right into Etienne's. The space around them seems to clear. Suddenly Etienne feels safer, like he is sealed off from all the fear circulating in the cabin, as cloying as the stench.

Fists clenched, eyes squeezed shut, they recite the Lord's prayer, over and over, as bodies and belongings capsize about them. Daniel shouts for calm, and tells the boys to steady their weight. Slowly their babble quietens, and soon the only sound left is Etienne's prayer. One by one the boys join in. Their voices rise together, a steadying ballast against the squall. Etienne can feel the prayer humming in his stomach, calming him. God must be able to hear us, he thinks, and he scrunches his eyes even tighter, until he can see right down inside himself.

If this is how it is to end, thinks Etienne, then why has God allowed us to come so far? God can't be angry with us, it just can't be so. So why? His heart thumps in his belly. But it is not a fearful fluttering, it is a driving, war drum of a beat that pushes up a lava of fury with it. He feels like he could punch a hole clean through the side of the boat.

'No.' He takes a furious kick at the water. 'No, no, no,' he yells.

The hold full of boys falls silent, and their eyes are upon him.

*

The light above deck is blinding. One hand raised against the glare, Etienne stands squinting with the others.

'Come pilgrims. We show you the way,' the sailor says, grinning like a man who has learned to smile by copying someone else. He gives them a horrible wink and mutters something that makes the other sailors laugh. The boys have agreed that on Daniel's signal they will make a run for it in the hope that their numbers will overwhelm the slavers.

They are penned in by the six hulking men who goaded them up from below, thick coils of rope in their hands. Etienne can feel alarm sparking as the children jostle and murmur like cows before a storm. He has tied the knife given to him by Etienne the Hospitaller inside his waistband, and he struggles to resist the infectious panic that would have him grab it. Two of the men are readying the gangplank and Etienne watches them haul it out as keenly as he has ever watched anything in his whole life.

'Let us out of here!' The cry comes from the middle of the group. Etienne snaps his head round to shush them and as he does he sees little Renauld shoot out from their huddle.

'Grab him!' says borrowed-smile man, and next thing there are three pairs of bulky arms pincering as Renauld weaves and ducks between them. Daniel, jaw and neck straining like he is shouldering a yoke, flashes a glance to the older boys. Etienne's legs tremble as though they want to start running by themselves. One of the men grabs Renauld who thrashes his legs out at the man's shins.

'You little bastard.' He flings the child to the deck.

'Run!' yells Daniel and they all rush for the gangplank as the slavers grab at whoever they can get hold of. Etienne doesn't look back. Eye trained on his exit, he swoops down to collect the bawling Renauld and, dragging the boy by his collar, charges forward. Two of the slavers are standing by the plank, tossing aside the approaching boys like they are sacks of grain.

A distant voice in Etienne's head is telling him there is no way he will make it past those muscly sailors, but it doesn't stop his legs from running like the whole world is on fire, a strange, metallic taste on his tongue as he drives forward, eyes fixed on the wooden beam that will take him to freedom.

He reaches into his tunic and pulls Etienne the knight's knife from its sheath. One arm stretched before him, he swipes the blade back and forth. Then, with a screech like he is wailing the dead, he dives headfirst onto the gangplank.

'Look out!' Jocelyn calls, as, hard on Etienne's heels, he vaults over the side. Landing on Etienne, he knocks the wind out of them both and they crawl away from the ruined vessel. Etienne hears a yelp and turns to see Jean writhing in the grip of a slaver. He races back as Jean sinks his teeth into the man's forearm. The sailor thrusts his arm up and Jean lurches forward, spilling over the gunwale and into the water.

'Take Renauld and follow the others,' Etienne shouts to Jocelyn. 'I'll be right behind you.'

'Jean. Over here!' Laying on his front, Etienne stretches his arms towards Jean's thrashing hands. But the water makes his grip slippery and Jean, eyes wide with terror, cannot get a firm hold.

'Come on!' Etienne screams. 'Take it!'

Jean flings his hand up. Their fingers touch. Etienne edges his torso out further until he is balanced by a hair's breath over the quayside. Delving his hand under the water he finds flesh and hauls his friend upwards. Jean's head breaks the surface and he takes a roaring breath that sounds as though his lungs are tearing apart. He is kicking furiously to keep his head up but the wash between the boat and the quay is so choppy he is taking in water with every breath. Twice Etienne drags him up above the foam. His body is burning with the effort, but he can feel his strength ebbing. His arms feel so heavy.

'Kick!'

'I can't,' the terrified Jean yells back, choked with his tears and the swell of the water.

Etienne takes a huge gulp of air and prepares for the biggest heave he can muster. The eels that are writhing in his stomach tell him he does not have many more goes left in him.

'On three this time,' he cries, but as he does so a boathook comes stabbing down, hard and sharp into his back. He cries out with the pain, looks up to see the leer of a slaver. The hook jabs down again, scraping his neck and tearing his tunic. He tries to grab the hook one-handed, but the searing pain in his shoulder will not let him. His chest is bursting with panic. He can't fend off his attacker and keep hold of Jean's hand. The hook swipes again, ripping his cheek. He screams, throws his hands to his face, then pulls them away, full of blood. He looks back down. Jean is gone.

'Jean! Please!' His hands flap uselessly back and forth, but nothing comes up from the bubbling water. Tears blind his sight.

Squatting on top of the gunwale, a crewman readies to jump. Etienne rolls to his feet and runs. It is only when he reaches the harbour wall and he sees the others that he realises it doesn't matter that he is being chased. Slumped at the foot of the wall, they all cower together. Around them, their sunburnt captors tether one to the other. Etienne's eyes dart in every direction. But even as he scans for an escape, he gaze is drawn back to his friends. Marc is among the captives - Jocelyn, Daniel, Renauld. Then, hands are upon him too, and there is no escape.

On the quay two men march up and down their lines, poking, squeezing, inspecting. They are wearing coloured tunics and pantaloons and go about their tasks silently under the watch of another man whom they seem frightened of. When he shouts his lip curls back, bearing his teeth like a dog. He has two fingers missing. Every now and again he taps his stick and the boy they are inspecting is shoved to one side.

Etienne stands firm in his legs as one of the baggy-trousers draws his bald, pocked head close to peer inside Etienne's mouth, behind his ears.

Then, with his stick, the chief taps for Etienne to stand apart with the others he has picked. When there are about two score of them standing apart, the men go back and start again. A little shiver runs up Etienne's neck as he realises they are being sorted into groups - the biggest, fittest ones, a medium group and a dozen or so of the very youngest along with some of the older boys who have sickened along the way.

Etienne is the youngest who has found his way into the strong group, along with Marc, Jocelyn and most of Daniel's friends. He can hardly bear to look at the weakest, their heads cowed like, round eyes pleading in their gaunt little faces. Etienne knows these men don't care about them at all, the ones who will be dead before they could give a week's work - the ones that probably aren't even worth selling.

It is the middle of the day and the sun is beating down on their heads hotter than Etienne has ever felt it. The back of his neck burns with sweat. His head feels as though it's cooking. The edges of the world are starting to look fuzzy. He knows that if he doesn't get a sip of water soon the heat will get the better of him. He will collapse and end up in the group of sickly boys.

The nasty stick man gives a command and his men approach with a large barrel. Scooping into it with a wooden ladle, they fling a powder at them that stings their eyes and instantly drains their skin of all moisture. Etienne recognises it at once as lime, the very same thing he uses in the lambing pens.

He scrunches up his eyes and seals his lips. From the group of the weakest boys he can hear choking. The sticks man hollers some fury at them and snaps his fingers at one of his men. Etienne's guts turn cold as the man uncoils a long whip and begins to thrash at the little boys while the stick man rages. As the lime dust settles, Etienne can see Renauld, red-faced and wheezing.

'The powder is making him choke,' calls Daniel. 'Help him!'

Renauld falls to the ground. Eyes bulging he gasps for air, hands at his throat. Etienne's mouth is open but he can't make any sound. Everything is moving very slowly. It feels like he is in a dream where he needs to run, but his legs respond as if they are sinking in mud. The men stand idle as Renauld's whole body spasms silently. When he has stopped moving, the stick man lifts up his head by the hair then lets it go with a casual sneer. Etienne flinches as the boy's head cracks back down on the stone. He can't believe what his eyes are showing him. He can't move. Not even to turn his head to the others. It feels like a horse is standing on his chest. Two of the slavers come forward and toss the limp body into the water as though it is a sack of spoiled goods.

'No!' Daniel cries and races forward.

The slavers fall upon him. Delivering kicks to subdue his struggle they spread- eagle him on the ground. One of them forces his trousers down.

105

Etienne's bowels churn. He turns his head away. His friend's screams are all he needs to know of the evil into whose hands they have fallen.

Huddled together like sheep under the crack of the slaver's whip, they are goaded aboard, heads hanging, shoulders shaking with silent sobs. Their captors are chatting among themselves, laughing, scratching, oblivious. Who are these monsters? Etienne asks himself, even though he knows there is no answer. Even God would have no answer. They didn't even call a priest for little Renauld, just tossed his body away like an animal carcass.

A priest. Staring into the fetid space before him, Etienne wishes very much that Father Gui were there, messy hair and black robes outlined against the night, eyes twinkling just as they always did when Etienne needed to know that everything was going to be alright. A hot lump snags the back of his throat. He scrunches his eyes tight.

As the men fasten them to iron cleats, Etienne can't help but think of all those cold nights sitting in the lambing barns back home, chopping logs in the snow, hands all blistered and raw; how he got a beating from the farmer for going into the village with Marc when they should have been in the fields. He misses it all so much. With all his heart he wishes he had known. He wishes that there was some way he could go back in time and warn himself that the chains of his circumstances really weren't that bad, that he would be trading them for chains much more terrible than anything he could have imagined sitting on his small little hillside wondering what else was out there. Well now he knows. He knows what becomes of you when you try to break free of the order God has set the world. And he would give anything to make it that he didn't.

He draws his knees into his chest and buries his head. Behind him he can hear the sound of retching, then a warm stench as someone soils themselves. Wiping his cheek with his hand, he smears a ribbon of snot across his cheek. 'If this is a test Lord then please make it stop soon,' he sobs. 'Because I know I can't pass. And I'd rather die now than witness anymore of this terrible place.'

Chapter Seventeen

Gui found the splintered remains of the vessel listing in the port at Ajaccio. Its mast split, the topsail hung limp, shrouding the foredeck. It looked as though it had journeyed the five rivers of Hades. You'll know it when you see it, the harbourmaster told him. *Please God, don't let this be it.* But he knew from the sickening weight in his heart that it was.

He jumped aboard and kicked his way through debris of wood and canvass to the gash in the deck where the mast had fallen. It was too dark to see below but the stench spoke loud enough. Stomach pulsing, he dropped down into the hold to find himself standing in a decay of sea-bloated wood, mouldy fabric, human waste. He inched forward through the slop until he found the forehead cabin.

Hand shielding his nose, he waded in, a current of dread sucking at his guts. Something in the bilge water caught his shin. He toed at the bobbing object and a handkerchief unfurled to yield a wizened stump of flesh; a relic, something once devoutly possessed. A blade of light from the battered deck above revealed iron manacles nailed to the bulkhead. The acid in his stomach surged up and he fled. Stumbling through the filth, he beat away the water in his path as though it were some living monster.

On his hands and knees he made it to the gunwale and emptied the contents of his stomach overboard. Skin cold and clammy, he wiped his face with an unsteady hand. A voice in his head was telling him it was not possible. He could not be on God's earth and witness what he had just seen. Then he heard the clunk of something against the side of the hull and there was no denying it. A mop of fair hair atop a coarse wool tunic came to rest alongside. The body of a child. Blood rushing at his temples, he tore off his cloak. 'Please God, no.' He hung his torso over the side and thrashed for purchase.

The body looked too slight to be Etienne, but still it took all Gui's steel to fix his eyes open as he heaved the water-laden cadaver onto its back. He did not recognise the features of the face that stared back, long-lashed and serene. Harbour lights gently dappling the water around him, the boy showed nothing of the horror that must have befallen him. Gui tugged at the boy, but before he could pull the body aboard, someone grabbed his legs. He torqued himself round.

His assailant, breath rank with alcohol, spat words Gui didn't understand as they wrestled.

'You are crew to this vessel? You know who that boy in the water is?' Gui shouted as he groped for his knife. The other man's eyes mocked.

'Boy?' he said slowly in French. 'Yes.' He rubbed a calloused thumb and forefinger together.

Gui slammed his fist into the slaver's gut. 'Where have you taken them?' His hand tightened around the man's throat. '*Answer me!*'

'Sold…they are sold.'

'Sold?' Every fibre of Gui's body felt as though it needed more air. Heart pumping a stinging brew of fear and rage, he stamped on the man's knee and the slaver sank down.

'Listen to me.' Gui steadied his voice. 'Tell me where they have gone and I won't kill you.' He pressed his dagger into the grease of the slaver's neck.

'*Misr.*' The man dropped his head forward. '*Misr.* Egypt.'

'Egypt?'

The man nodded violently. 'Two days.' He held up two fingers. 'Two days they go.'

Gui's guts were molten tar. *But for two days.*

'You pay to me. I take you.' The slaver grinned, showing the few sharp, yellow stubs that served him as teeth.

'Pay you?' Gui's ears were ringing. His mind emptied. His body felt remote, light, as though it were not under his command. He squeezed the hilt of his dagger, piercing the slaver's neck.

'No kill me. Pray...please no,' the man jabbered.

'*Take me to my son!*' Gui roared.

'Yes, yes. I take.' The blood shot eyes drooped pitifully. 'Please. Mercy.' The man began to weep.

Gui stared into the pathetic, sun-blistered face. *Thou shalt not kill.* In his breath of hesitation, the sailor jerked his fists upward, catching Gui on the chin. The men fell to the ground, wrestling in a tight embrace until Gui jerked free. His dagger plunged into the resistance of cartilage, and the man's screams faded to a gurgle.

Panting, Gui threw off his assailant. A dark crimson pool spread out over the deck. He tried to bring himself up from all fours but his limbs were shaking. He lowered his head to the man's chest. There was no life. Gui stared in disbelief at the body. The raw grate of his breath in his ears, he reached over to close the man's eyes. As he did so, he found himself making the sign of the cross.

Later that evening Gui sat on the harbour wall, watching as the shimmering black waters consumed the hulk of the slave ship. Two days before his son had stood on the very same ground, looked out over the same waters. Etienne was somewhere out there now, floating on this infinity of night towards who knew what fate. *Misr.* Gui breathed the strange sound. Egypt. If the slaver had been truthful. Numb, he considered the grimy soul now drifting down to feed the crabs. How quickly these new garments have become bloodied, he thought as he flipped his rosary over and over. Dressing up in Philippe's fine clothes had felt like something of a game, a short-term necessity of circumstance. When he pulled off his cassock all those weeks ago, Gui had not considered he would never wear it again.

Deliver the weak and needy from the hands of the wicked. His mother's words returned to him. He sought nothing less. Yet his Church would have him spill no blood. The same Church who rallied the faithful to arms in defence of the earthly Jerusalem. They preached the glorious rhetoric that captured the hearts and mind of children for whose fate they denied responsibility. Would God really see him stand by with incense and chalice in hand while evil men rained blows upon the innocent?

Gui studied his hand - the wide, muscular palm. They were his father's, the hands of a long line of warriors. Perhaps they were always destined to be bloody, he thought. Sealing his fingers over his eyes, he sought Agnes's face, the softness of her skin, the smell of her hair. He saw her as last he had, laying on the bed, burning with fever. The numbness in his chest began to sear as it thawed. A bruise that ached far worse than any slaver's blow. She was still alive. He could feel it. She would never depart this earthly realm without somehow letting him know. He had heard reports too often to doubt that. Mourners who, from afar, had seen their loved ones depart this world in a halo of golden light. If either she or Etienne had gone he would know it.

*

Gui folded the parchment in two, then immediately opened it and read it again. He had written to Agnes in the sleepless hours of the night before, when the stars of the firmament were shimmering so brightly it was impossible not to believe they were the immortal departed. He had wished on them with his life's blood that he might hold his loved ones again. The note was an imitation of all he needed to say, but like a conversation he couldn't bear to end, his eyes would not lift from the page.

He had nowhere to send it to, but the pretence that Agnes might cast her eyes over his words was all he had that afternoon to hold off the emptiness. He ordered a cup of wine, willing to accept even the false companionship of the grape, but all it did was fill his stomach with acid and fuel the urgency crawling in his belly that told him everything he needed to hold was slipping from his grasp.

Every flash of fair hair turned his head; a messenger boy tripping along the quay, a pickpocket weaving artfully among disoriented foreigners, a woman's voice, shrill with reproach, chasing behind. Each time hope sparked in his heart before his mind had a chance to snuff it out with the visions that hunted his sleep – of Agnes on her sick bed, of that ship.

He had arrived at the port of Messina a few days before, courtesy of a small grain-bearing galley. A late autumn tempest had closed the harbour shortly after, leaving him stuck. With the last of busy season's traffic dispersed by the storm, the captains of the vessels waiting to depart were few and they had wasted no time in raising their prices sky high. Soon, Advent would be approaching and it would be too late for sea-faring. If he could not find passage to Alexandria in the next week or so, he would be forced to winter in the Sicilian city.

Beyond the harbour chain, two large transports weighed anchor, their standards beating in the autumn gusts. The sun was flaming as it sank, but Gui could just make out the bold, red flags – one with two crossed keys beneath a mitre, the other a golden lion: Rome and Venice. They had docked together and he watched as they set their tenders to the water. Figures cast in shadow slid down rope ladders into the skiffs and sent glittering shards up into the air as they dipped their oars. Gui blew out the air from his cheeks. If they were his last chance before winter closed the seas, he doubted his pocket would stretch to satisfy their prices. Draining his cup, he crumpled his love letter into a ball.

'Never throw away a love letter,' said the foreign voice.

The man was dressed fashionably in a fitted doublet under a emerald green tunic.

'You can tell?' said Gui.

'I am a trader. How can I sell if I do not know what a man may wish to buy?'

Gui considered the stranger's accent, his showy clothes. 'And you are from one of the Italian states.'

The man wagged his index finger, decorated with a large garnet ring. 'The most important. *Venezia.*' He thrust out his hand. 'Enrico Zonta.'

Gui hesitated. The trader's familiarity aroused his suspicion but his appearance seemed too memorable for him to be anything other than he claimed.

'I am Marc,' Gui said.

'You look like a scholar. You are making pilgrimage?'

'I am.'

Enrico Zonta considered a passing Arab girl, hips swaying with the weight of the pail on her head, then he said,'Your clothes look borrowed.'

'They are.'

'I am intrigued.' The merchant pointed to a tavern along the front. 'Please.'

Gui told the other man just enough of his story to allow him to tell it convincingly. He was on his way to the Holy Land as penance for an adulterous affair.

'You should have bought an indulgence!' Zonta waved for a cup of wine. 'Or at least brought your lover with you.'

'Travel is a dangerous business.'

'So is love.'

The Venetian had a benign face, soft from the pleasures of life but not sagging or ruddy with excess. His business was whatever he could sell -

pearls, linen, perfumes.

Gui took a sip of wine. An earthy grape with a metallic after taste, it warmed his belly and softened his tongue. 'I don't believe that you can truly love more than one woman.'

Zonta heaved his shoulders in an exaggerated shrug. 'You only have one grand passion at a time, of course. But I have been to so many cities - Ragusa, Tripoli, Antioch, to the North. Each one a different pleasure.'

'I will never love anyone else.'

'Maybe, maybe not.'

'What of your wife?' asked Gui.

The trader patted him on the shoulder. 'She is the only woman I have ever feared.'

The merchant shifted on his stool and sighed. His cheeks bagged like a sail bereft of wind, and for a moment it seemed to Gui that he was looking at the real man behind the affable persona.

'Those transports harbouring over there,' Gui nodded towards the dock. 'I could get a pilgrim's passage?'

'They are merchant vessels but yes, if you have the coin someone will take you. You best be quick though. They leave in two days.' He hesitated for a moment. 'I could ask some acquaintances about a passage for you. You are staying here?'

'Just off the square.'

Zonta called over more wine. '*The Three Moors*? I know the patron well.'

Gui's head was already starting to buzz from the cup he was nursing, and he blocked the refill with his hand. The Venetian peeled it away and beckoned a serving girl to pour.

'She is Sicilian,' he said of the blonde-haired girl. 'Norman. Come now,' he grinned. 'Let us be friends.'

The merchant edged Gui's cup towards him, and there was something about the insistence of the gesture that sent a signal of alarm pulsing through the fog of Gui's mind.

He tried to wave the girl away but Zonta grabbed her arm. '*Resta. Resta cu' noi,*' he said, bearing his gums as he smiled. Turning to Gui he made a fist with one hand and squeezed the other over his bicep 'You are bold enough to cross the seas, but here, a thousand moons away from your love, you allow modesty to deny you?'

The girl fixed her gaze on Gui, reached out and touched his hair. His blood heated. The bitter aftertaste of the wine thickened on his tongue. He fumbled for his thoughts, but they would not come to order.

'*Veni,*' said the serving girl.

Instinct drew Gui eyes towards the tavern's exit but it was blur in the sunlight. He could feel beads of sweat forming on his hairline.

'You are very rare,' he said to the girl. Easing his stool away from the

111

table, pulled himself to stand. A griping abdominal pain forced him to take a steadying pace forward. The merchant's raised his cup.

Panicked, Gui looked around to find he was now the only customer in the inn. The next thing he knew, a bulky, donkey-faced man with a meat cleaver was standing on the threshold of the front door. The padrone emerged from the kitchens, showing a blade of his own. Digging deep Gui swiped up his bar stool. Holding it up as a shield, he backed away towards the side door the prostitutes used. The two thugs lunged towards him. Gui threw the stool at them, turned and fled, stumbling down an unlit corridor.

Shouldering open one of the doors, he found himself in a cramped boudoir. The window frame was rotten, and it crumbled as he kicked out the grille. A glance downwards, then he rolled out into the alley. Doubled over in pain, using the wall as a crutch, he staggered out into the labyrinth of the port town. Once he knew he was clear away from the tavern he gave into the burning in his guts. Mouth flooded with saliva, he forced his fingers down his throat, purging the tainted liquid from his stomach.

Gui drenched his head under a water fountain and hobbled on until he found an apothecary. It was then he discovered that his money pouch was gone. The Jew made Gui drink a foul, buttery emetic for the poison, and waiving payment, sent him on his way with an antidote of horehound and garlic to take after.

The next morning, under a head-baking sun, he scoured the port and its warren of thoroughfares in search of the man whom had so easily gained his confidence, and more pressingly, was in possession of the money he needed for passage to Egypt. The sun was mid heaven when, from the corner of his vision, a flash of recognition prompted him to turn. The Italian trickster was rounding the corner into one of the backstreets.

Gui raced over, but Zonta was gone. The passageway was barely an arm-span wide; shuttered and still. A fine place to disappear. He crept into the gloom. From up ahead, there echoed the murmur of voices. Gui pressed himself into the shadows. Padding forward, he glimpse the outline of a man vanish inside a low door.

He waited a moment in the penumbra of the doorway, then knocked. After some conference behind the iron grille, it inched open. Zonta's name was Gui's Abracadabra. Inside, the wooden walls were covered with embroideries of carmine and gold, faded by salt and damp. The air was thick with fumes of seaweed kindling and the gossip of men who threw half glances towards the entrance each time a new client entered. There were no windows, each table instead lit by its own candle.

Zonta sat in a corner entertaining another man with a carafe. Gui took a goblet from one of the whores winding around the tables. More important than having the money, he had learned, was acting as though you did. Another carafe spent, and Zonta's companion was stumbling towards the rear of the establishment in the wake of a pair of breasts. The

Venetian surveyed the room. Gui bowed his head, brushing some imagined dirt from his tunic. When the fraudster made to leave, Gui was in his path. The avuncular features opened briefly in surprise.

'Please sit down,' Gui said pleasantly.

Zonta clutched him as though he were an old friend. Gui pinned the Venetian's forearms to his side. 'You may well have reason to take me for a fool. But it is you the fool for showing your face today.'

'First calm yourself,' the merchant spoke softly, making no attempt to distance himself from Gui's grip. 'Then tell me what you are talking about.'

'It is your gamble,' Gui whispered. 'You can stop this game, or I reveal your trickery to the patrons of this establishment and you will find yourself alongside the other thieves baking in the square for public amusement.' Gui tightened his hold. 'Your man in the back room did not look like a humble pilgrim to me. He looked like a merchant who will not take kindly to being made a fool of, much less being drugged and robbed.'

The Venetian pouted. Gui guessed he had been plying his trade long enough to recognise a desperate man, and know that desperate men were dangerous.

'I sit,' he said.

He explained to Gui that he was awaiting a flotilla, in whose protection his small cog could travel safely back to Venice. His problem, and the reason Gui had caught him engaged in such an insalubrious activity, was the arrival of a 'rich, usurious bastard' on the island; an Apulian grain merchant to whom he owed money.

'He makes the Doge look like a pauper. Estates in Lombardy. Two villas in Venice. You think he makes all that from cereal?' The merchant's face coloured.

'So you swindle other men to pay your debts?'

'Swindle! I am in fear of my life for those debts. What would you have me do?'

'I want my things back,' Gui said. 'Now get up.'

The merchant held up his hands in surrender. 'Don't get carried away.'

'I'm armed,' Gui said. 'And I haven't begun to get carried away yet.'

'As you wish. As you wish.'

'Walk.'

'Where are we going?'

'To your rooms. To my money.'

'But I don't have it there.'

Gui patted the blade at his waist. 'Walk.'

Gui followed the merchant through the hive of backstreets. Low, dank tunnels, the tightest cut-throughs, steep, dog-leg pathways; Zonta made it hard as he could for Gui to keep his bearings. When they emerged onto a

113

small square, a water fountain at its centre, the Venetian carved a smile. In front of them was a building tiled in Moorish design. An ancient Sicilian answered the bell, saluting Zonta in dialect. Gui eyed their exchange for any hidden signal as the merchant breezed through the hallway. The floor was a mosaic of fractured terracotta tiles. A large fan, levered by an Arab slave boy, churned the air above them. The owner had once been a man of means.

Zonta's room held no such faded charm - a grubby linen at a window gave out over a shambolic courtyard, refuse mounting in one corner.

'You know this.' Riffling through a bag of rags, he handed Gui his pouch. 'He gave a lingering shrug. 'I had to make some interest payments.'

'Interest payments?' Gui said, shaking the pouch to gauge how much was gone. Ten ducats was the last price he had heard quoted for passage to Crete and that wasn't Venetian prices. He had had eight before the theft.

I want your cloak and hat as well.'

'What for? You're mad,' the merchant said, animated.

'Don't argue with me.'

'You're crazy. All I have to do is cry out…'

'And they'll come running to find a man with his throat cut. Now give me your hat and cloak.'

'This one?' He pulled at his cloak dubiously.

'Now.'

The merchant took off his cloak to reveal a large, purple birthmark on his neck.

'Leave the brooch,' Gui instructed as Zonta fiddled with the gold buckle at the neck fastening.

Gui made his move as the merchant was folding the garment. Wrestling the trickster to the ground, he silenced his shouts with a shirt sleeve and bound the thrashing man by the hands and feet.

'They'll find you soon enough,' he said over the merchant's muffled abuse. 'I have business far more urgent than you can imagine.'

Attention straining for sounds in the corridor, Gui tore through Zonta's belongings until he found another small purse and a garnet ring. Then, donning the merchant's garb, he was gone, swift as a deer, through the warren of streets, following the sun's clues towards the harbour.

In the early hours of the next day, dressed in the embroidered cloak and plumed hat of the Venetian, Gui stood on the stern of a merchant vessel flanked by a trireme. The landfall of Sicily just visible at the vanishing point of water and sky. The fleet was ultimately destined for Trebizond, but would harbour first at Alexandria two or three weeks hence. On his cloak was a brooch that would answer most questions and in his hand a large portmanteau: a prop of merchant's cloth, including a Templar's tunic that Zonta had clearly appropriated from the Brethren of the some priory. He also carried a letter of introduction stating that he was Roberto Blanchier, representative of a group of textile traders from Lille, bound for Alexandria seeking new export opportunities.

Chapter Eighteen

The moon was only a few days old. Its nascent light dappled the stones before her. A sliver of the heavens by which to see was all she needed. The map was tucked into her bodice, its contents already burned into her memory. Agnes had a stolen shovel strapped across her back, and a knife belted over the tunic and hose she borrowed from her uncle. Hair chopped to her neckline, enough to scrap under a headdress if need be, but not so long as to interrupt the masculine costume she now wore. She knew her best chance of surviving the long road home was to inhabit this twilight, to play with the shadows.

For all the planning, the hundreds of times she had played this route in her mind, she was shocked by what she saw. The house was a ruin. Not even fifteen years gone and most of the stone had been chipped away. The roof had collapsed in on the plundered walls, the remaining window frames gapped like eye sockets. Had it all been taken by local peasants to shore up their own dwellings? If so, it meant only one thing – there was no tenant farmer. Yet the surrounding land was farmed, that much was clear. Why would someone tend to the land but forsake such a valuable asset to demolition? For the first time that night, tiny beads of sweat prickled her skin as the steel vault of her purpose felt the smelting heat of doubt.

Agnes closed her eyes and listened to the night, determined not to feed the fear that was nagging her to turn around. She had been thirteen years old when she came with her father to view the unexpected inheritance, and now in the silence she could almost hear his footsteps beside hers, scraping at the leaves on the ground. He had been wearing a green Spanish doublet on that day, and she recalled how he pulled at his beard as he considered the estate.

'*E que fare*?' He made light of the castellany, but still she felt the unease beneath his casual bravado. A discomfort she knew came not from the task of managing the land but from the knowledge that it lifted his daughter into the ranks of men whose ideals and armies he did not trust. Her father had been raised in a land of the troubadours, a land that believed in love. The petty nobles who had considered his wealth too brackish to vie for Agnes's hand now had their permit.

The spot Estève had marked was a way on from the house, just beyond the confines of the estate. A dirt track took her through an abandoned orchard, its floor a mulch of fallen fruit that no-one had collected. The locals had stripped the stones from the house, but ignored a bounty of fruit? Fruit fit for a rat trap she thought as she edged onwards. All around her she could hear the twitching and rustling of the animals as they went about their hidden business, companions to the grate of her breath.

Up ahead she made out the silhouette of a bosk, its needled trees holding off the moonlight. A fortress of brambles covered the floor, tearing at her ankles as she waded through them to place her father had sketched out. The ground before her subsided sharply and she skidded down the escarpment, observed by sombre-featured guardians on the crumbling pillars above. It looked to Agnes like an old family sepulchre.

Beneath the slime of composting leaves her fingers met cold stone – the first of several steps that led down into the earth. A rising tide of panic pressed at the gates of her self control. *Where have you brought me, papà?* She shuffled forward, casting out with her feet to test the ground before her. Loose chunks of masonry disinterred as she skidded downwards. It felt as though she was raking the dead. When her foot hit the hollow knock of wood she cried out, her yelp ringing out amid the scuffle of the night hunters and their prey. How much easier it is to withstand the fear of a mortal enemy, she thought.

Finger snagging on a piece of flint, Agnes sucked on the warm, salty taste of blood. It was an unexpected, earthly comfort in this other-worldly terrain and for a fleeting moment the damp musk of the autumnal earth was transmuted into the rich smell of sandalwood. The smell of her father's pomander.

'Then you are with me,' she whispered to the night.

Tucking a few strands of loose hair under her cap, she rolled up her sleeves and scythed her spade into the earth until it hit wood. A flurry of wind agitated the trees. There was dampness in the air that told her a downpour was on its way. A patter of rain that would dull her hearing, conceal the tell-tale snapping of a twig, or an unnatural rustling. She scraped away at the earth, shovelling it aside to the rhythm of her own breath until a panel was revealed – the top of a hatch.

The night was yielding to a band of ultramarine on the eastern horizon. She was about to lose her cloak. If they had followed her, now was when they would strike. Agnes lay down on her belly as the first drops of rain began to fall. She rooted around until she felt a metal ring. The rain quickened as she tugged to free the handle, and soon she was enveloped in a muddy puddle, hair plastered to her face, blurring her sight. She drove the spade into the edge of the panel, levering back and forth until its prison of dirt was loosened. Aware only of her labouring breath, she hauled open the seal on a decade of calamity.

Cold damp earth and the stench of decay filled her nostrils. Momentarily she recoiled, shrinking from the task ahead, bone marrow frozen in grim anticipation. She pressed her hand to her chest where the map was folded, seeking reassurance. The rain pounded down in demonic baptism as she unbelted her tunic, secured the leather strip to the hatch and swung herself down.

The only sound in the chamber was the clamour of her own fear thundering through her veins. Muscles rigid, she squeezed her eyes shut, then open, adjusting to the dark blue light that filtered through the hatch. What she saw tore the breath from her lungs, then sent a shriek scraping through the tomb. *This is what father had seen.*

Time had melted the flesh from their bones, but she could make out distinct bodies amid the tangle. Stomach heaving, she turned to flee but her legs buckled beneath her. For a moment she was paralysed, the world reduced to the horror before her eyes and the roar of blood in her ears. Around her she imagined movement, the roots of the living earth reaching out to claim her. Her body began to shake with effort, as though she were holding up a dam against some monstrous tidal wave of memory.

Garnering all her strength she yelled at herself to move. It was enough to break the spell and free her limbs. Scrambling onto a pile of lime blocks, she pawed for the leather belt above her and dragged herself out of the chamber of forgotten corpses. The sound bubbling in her throat diminished to a groan as she emerged back into the world. Panting, she snatched up her belongings and kicked the trap door shut, pausing to make the sign of the cross before covering her tracks with hasty fistfuls of soil and leaves.

Muscles cramping with the violence of her shivers, she raced back along the road. She ran to the sound of her footsteps and scattered recollections from those childhood days - her mother's shawl of russet lace on her shoulders, the thick, comfy blanket into which she huddled on the journey home, a soft mist of autumn rain falling.

By the time she reached the main road the day had dawned. A liminal silence hung under the weak sunlight of a world that was at once exactly as it had been and at the same time forever changed. The cold wind of late autumn ripped through her damp clothes, the exhaustion of her labours and of her fear, like a hod of stones upon her back. The past months making her way back from the South, the lies she had to tell, the friendless places here she had lain.

She hadn't often wondered what life would have brought had her father lived, but she thought on it now as she stumbled across the fields; the hardships she would have been spared, the lover she would never have known, the child that never would have been. It had been her duty to make sure that child never lived a day to regret opening his eyes on the world. Tears blurred her vision as she dug for the strength to find the next step.

Resting against a tree, she tipped her head towards the heavens. The rain had eased, but the air was a damp vapour, smothering her as she sought to recover her breath. Her bones felt so heavy, as though they were answering a call to return to the earth – the call of those poor souls whose fate her father had discovered. Agnes reached into her bodice, drawn by the need to see her father's hand writing, to be near him. She felt for the parchment, warm and soft from heat of her body.

'Oh papà, why did you need me to see?'

Agnes scoured the plains around her. Shorn of their harvest, a horizon of stubble was relieved by small copses of woodland and thickets. The edges of a charred world beyond the reaches of her blackened past. She ransacked her childhood for some clue, but her mind was a swirling mist of half memories and lingering instincts that she couldn't quite shape into words.

Then, deep within her gut, a recollection stirred. Out of the void she felt the grip of his powerful hands on her neck. She clutched her hands to her throat. Suddenly, the mist about her was a torrent, pouring poison into her lungs instead of air. She pawed at the vision before her, just as she had done that night, wrestling uselessly to free herself from his bulk, the heat of his groin against hers, the tearing pain.

The fire-rimmed world began to darken, her stomach convulsing bile. Tiny circles danced before her eyes.

'Have mercy,' she whispered. Then there was nothing more.

Chapter Nineteen

The air is warm and sweet. Campfires punctuate the dusk. Smoke drifts in low banks, carrying unfamiliar aromas. Voices murmur in prayer. Away from the roadside, little stick figures rise then kneel in genuflection, their backs to the setting sun. Beyond the fires Etienne can see the outline of mountains rising up from barren, sandy plains. It is dusty, and the smoke from the fires stings his eyes. On the bench beside him, his companions sag as if in sleep, although sleep is not possible on this bumpy, parched journey, only exhaustion. Exhaustion and fear of what is to come.

Every so often, just before their prayer time, the caravan halts and their captors disappear under an awning of rugs. Through an air slit in the wagon's panel, Etienne watches them keenly - one improbably tall, his limbs waving as he strides off, the other, fat, barrel-chested, waddling behind. Etienne is pretty sure that no praying goes on inside. These roadside tents seem to be the desert version of an inn, and he has observed this routine enough times to know that shortly after the chanting stops, a servant boy will emerge from the tent-inn to bring them a sip or two of water. Usually it is just enough to make him wish he hadn't had it. Still, it lifts his spirit to see the water-bearer come shuffling out, bucket in hand. They never spill a drop.

'The water is coming.' He nudges Marc excitedly even though he knows Marc won't respond. He hasn't said a word for days. Still, Etienne refuses to believe that the spark-eyed boy, always so ready with a put down or a boast, won't rally from his glazed silence. Although he has often thought bad things about Marc, Etienne feels sorry to see him like this. Sorry and guilty that it has taken such a calamity for him to understand that being friends doesn't mean you have to like the other person all the time. He realises now that Marc was his friend all along, and he wishes he could have the old Marc back, even if he did say stupid, mean things sometimes.

'*T'shirabu*,' the water boy says, plunging a ladle into his pail. He wears a disc-shaped cloth cap and a long, white dress. He has the longest eyelashes Etienne has ever seen on a boy. He looks about the same age as Etienne and the sad sympathy in his smile makes Etienne think he is not that much better off than they.

'*Tashrab*,' Etienne repeats. 'Water?'

The boy nods vigorously. '*T'shirabu. Maa'*.'

He lets Etienne take an extra long sip. Etienne closes his eyes as he draws in the cool from the ladle. It feels like bathing in a stream. He wants to ask the boy what the other word, *maa*, means, but the boy is casting

120

anxious glances over his shoulder. Before Etienne gets a chance the water-bearer scurries off to the tent-inn.

'*Shirab, Maa',*' Etienne whispers, embedding the sounds in his memory.

Their captors saunter back. Bellies full, they salute their colleagues and ready the horses. Do they have children of their own back home? Etienne wonders. Do their children know what they do? Probably they do. He recalls the Moorish slaves he saw back in Marseille. It's not a sin to buy and sell Mohammedans in Christendom, so why would it be a sin to sell Christians in their lands?

Opposite him Daniel is trying to clear a fly off his face by shaking his head, but the fly keeps landing on a different part - his nose, forehead, hair line. The caravan hits a large bump in the road that sends them all bouncing up off the floor.

'At least the fly's gone,' Etienne whispers across to Daniel and the older boy smiles. A tired smile that makes wrinkles on his dusty face, but a genuine one. He badly wants Daniel to say something back so they can strike up a conversation. Anything to lift the dismal silence that hangs like a pall. But Daniel says nothing. It feels to Etienne as though no one wants to interrupt their misery with imitations of another, more carefree time. So they stare down at their legs, silent witnesses to their own private shame.

Etienne is pretty sure they are going to the slave markets. The place that, unknown to them, was their destination all along. The world he knew before he boarded that terrible boat feels like another lifetime ago. He has spent so much time since wondering about all the what- ifs. What would have happened if they had realised that rickety old ship couldn't possibly be a pilgrim boat, or if they had been a bit faster, a bit luckier on those docks in Corsica? What if that big storm had sunk the ship? Would any of them have survived, clinging to bits of wood until someone came to rescue them? What would it have been like to drown? Just like Jean did.

Etienne thinks about drowning a lot. He can still see his friend, gasping for air, throwing his hands about in panic, his terrible, wild eyes. He had tried to save him. His shoulder still hurts sometimes where he tried so hard to pull Jean up. If only he had been able to pull a bit harder, and those men hadn't seen him. If they hadn't jabbed at him like that he is sure he would have been able to pull his friend to safety. But then Jean would have known the shackles of that boat, and being beaten. And what it is like to be about to be sold.

Finally they arrive in a great city. Smoke and the sweet smell of incense mingle with the dirt and smell of decay. Naked, filthy children roam amid piles of rubbish and wild dogs. Worn down men with legs as thin and brown as twigs carry bundles of rags on their heads alongside donkeys, oxen and bawling, hump-backed beasts, their riders all wrapped up in black.

The wailing Mohammedan prayer punctuates the day, even in the most squalid places. As frightening as it first sounded to him, Etienne has come to anticipate it, almost look forward to hearing it. He doesn't understand a word and he knows it is the worship of a false god, but the devotion brings a comfort with it. He wonders if the Devil might be getting to him. Or perhaps it is a sign. If his God is more powerful than the one they call Allah, then might the Christian God of all things be able to speak to him, even through this Heathen prayer? He has some vague recollection of Father Gui once saying that God is in everything.

The caravan stops. Voices outside bark as though they are arguing. The lock on the door of their carriage rattles, then, harsh words from the barrel-chested man who holds a stick in one hand and a whip in the other. There is the usual jerk and stutter as they all try to stand and move forward under the burden of the shackles.

Blinded by the white-hot sun, Etienne squeezes his eyes shut for a moment. He opens them to find they are in a vast square. Before them is a towering stone building with huge domed vaults, and awnings that stretch half way across the square. Hundreds of people, black-skinned, brown-skinned, white-skinned, weave around the pillars; some are chained together as they are, some carry ceramic pots on their heads. It is so crowded there is barely space to stand. If only they weren't tied together, Etienne thinks, it would be impossible for their captors to keep track of them all. Most of the shouting seems to be coming from inside the building. It reminds Etienne of the sheep market at Illiers he sometimes went to when the farmer was down a hand. He feels his stomach flip.

'Look!' Someone nudges him. 'Over there.'

In front of them a chain of girls are being led around the other side of the building. They look clean and well fed, certainly not like they have just arrived from overseas, even though some of them are fair. A man with a stick beats a clear path through the crowd, slapping at the straying fingers that reach out to fondle the merchandise. Most of them wear a simple sleeveless tunic but as Etienne peers closer his eyes pop to see that some of them have their breasts exposed. Ripples of heat pulse through his body, and although he can feel his face turning crimson, he cannot look away. A slaver's sudden bark makes Etienne start. Head is still swivelled towards the naked girls, he has no time to find his feet as the others trundle forward and he has to scramble to right himself before a little bandy man with a misshapen hand reaches him with a birch.

They are marched up some stone steps, worn down in the middle from wear, and into a single storey, wooden annex at the back of the main building. Thin slats of brilliant sunshine pierce the gaps in the walls along the dismal corridor. It smells of lime and piss. The contrasting light makes it hard to see where they are going and the group edges forward, bunching into each other until another man, whom they have not seen before, tells them to halt. And then strip. Etienne feels a fist of panic bunch in his guts. He turns to Daniel.

'But my knife.'

'Your knife? Give it to me. Quick.'

Etienne has tied the blade to his inside leg with a piece of twine and his fingers work frantically at the knot as around him the other boys reluctantly begin to undress. Daniel secretes the weapon inside his shirt as he pulls it off, and when the guards are looking elsewhere, kicks it into the darkness.

Even though Etienne knows he would never have had the chance to use it, that Daniel has saved him from a beating by getting rid of it, as he watches it skittle across the floor beyond his reach, tears swell the back of his throat. He isn't sure why he feels like that about a knife, when much worse things have happened to them. But it was such a good knife, and such a great honour to receive it as a gift from a real knight.

When Etienne the knight gave it to him, he had such a clear picture of himself standing in that black and white uniform, over-looking some fortified promontory under the baking desert sun, defending the last pride of Christendom with that very knife belted at his waist. Being a knight of the Orders would have been a good thing to be. For some reason that he doesn't really understand, Etienne realises he had come to believe that while he had the knife with him, no real harm would come to him.

A brown-skinned man with a cloth wrapped around his waist steps forward with a bucket. A fat belly hangs over his cloth but he has strength beneath the flab. From the way his arm muscles pop as he lifts the bucket, Etienne can tell it is full of water. At least it isn't lime. Yet, as good as it feels to be free of the chains, Etienne feels more frightened now. There had been some reassurance about being all tied together, inseparable.

Eyes to the floor, they trail along a hallway, earth and sand at their feet. There is a double door at the end of the corridor, big enough to fit a horse through. From the other side a cacophony of voices echo, dim to a murmur, then crescendo once more. Etienne's heart thumps hard as they approach. It wouldn't feel any worse, he thinks, if he knew there were gallows on the other side of that door. He casts his eyes to Daniel, desperate for a reassuring exchange, but Daniel is staring at the ground, lips moving silently.

A tall man, clothed in billowing silk, comes to look at them. He has a long nose but it is thin and pointy, not curved and fat like a lot of the other brown men. It makes him look fiercer than the other slavers and Etienne guesses he is important. He is carrying a roll of parchment. He walks their line once or twice, lips pursed together like he is considering a choice between things that aren't all that good.

'Raise your hand if you can read,' he says in a crisp French that makes Etienne start. For a moment he is paralysed as he deliberates whether or not he should admit to being literate. Why would the elegant man want to know that? He wants to believe it will be something good but everything he has experienced so far tells him it can't be. Still, there is something about the man's expectant poise and the power of his own need to believe that somehow, despite it all, God has not turned His back on them that prompts him to raise his hand. At once, four or five of the boys raise theirs, including Marc. Etienne knows for sure that Marc can't read, and straight away the familiar tug of dread pulls in his gut as the man stalks over and flicks a sheet at Marc.

Marc screws up his eyes, trying to look like he is concentrating, and puts his finger on one of the words, as though touching it might make it easier to decipher. The man jerks the sheet away and shakes it at him again. Marc jabbers something about sheep from the Bible and the man blinks in disbelief, then nods at one of the slavers. The man pulls out his whip and beats Marc until he is scrunched up in a ball, crying out for mercy. Etienne stares at the floor in front, heart hammering guilty. One of the other boys who said he could read starts to cry.

Etienne looks up to find the turban man towering over him, eyes narrowed. His hand shakes as he takes the parchment. It is an extract from the Gospel of Matthew, the bit about the Magi visiting Jesus he has read a thousand times with Gui. His whole body melts with relief as he begins to read, and the man's withering squint lifts into a surprised arch. Etienne widens his eyes expectantly, but the man gives a curt nod and glides away without so much as a word. Mouth hanging open, Etienne has no time to articulate his confusion. The next thing he knows, the big doors open, and they are pushed towards the bellowing crowds.

*

Etienne awakes to the call to prayer. The room is hot. Geometric patterns of sunlight flicker through the carved lattice. He draws himself onto his elbows. There are five other boys lying on the ground with him, all asleep. He doesn't recognise any of them. Two of them are brown-skinned, the others olive, from southern lands of Christendom, he supposes. None of them seem harmed. He puts an eye to a star-shaped hole in the lattice. There is a dusty courtyard where two dogs lie under a feeble tree, its branches drooping towards the sun-bleached ground. In one corner there is a water pump, the earth around it dark with moisture.

A tiny, brown man wearing a long, white shirt and a piece of fabric wound around his head comes to the fountain. Etienne ducks instinctively, then, cranes his head up slowly to watch the man as he splashes his face and neck with water. The back of Etienne's neck feels sweaty and grimy - it would be good if they let him use that pump later.

'*Vuoi da bere?*'

Etienne jumps at the voice. One of the olive-skinned boys is talking to him. He doesn't understand the tongue but the boy is holding out a clay pot. Gingerly, Etienne takes it and noses the contents. It is water. Eyes on the boy, who is making cupping gestures for him to drink, he takes a sip. It is clean and sweet. He gulps some more and wipes his mouth with the back of hand.

'*Shirab. Maa'*,' Etienne says proudly. His face falls as the boy bursts out laughing.

'*Ma sei Francese, tu*?' The boy says. '*Français*?'

Etienne nods stiffly and the boy offers his hand in the way that men do.

'Alberto,' the boy says. 'That man,' Alberto nods to the courtyard. 'He is Abubakr. Is our boss!'

Etienne peers back out through the patterned shutters. It seems unlikely that the skinny brown man could be anyone's boss, but he shrugs congenially as the boy continues his introductions.

'I am from the island of Sicilia.' Alberto speaks slowly in a blend of his mother tongue and Norman French that Etienne can recognise. 'Maybe you have heard of it?'

A little shorter than Etienne, Alberto has huge, cow eyes and his face is framed by dark ringlets that tumble to his shoulders. Thick brows make it look as though he is concentrating hard, even though Etienne thinks he probably isn't.

'No?' The boy laughs and his heavy brow lifts.

'Where are we?' asks Etienne

Alberto lowers himself into a comfortable squat. 'We are in Cairo, Egypt at the home of the governor Al Kamil. You came from the market?'

Etienne contorts his face into a grimace he hopes will hide the shame that heats his guts whenever he thinks back to it.

'Is a terrible place I know.' The boy holds a smile on his face but Etienne catches his eyelashes flicker down. 'I went twice. My first time at the market I was bought by a *Tunisino. Bruttissimo.'* He puckers. 'But then I pray many, many times for God to take me away from that place and the *Tunisino,* his ship sink.' Alberto pats Etienne's arm, 'But here you have been lucky. The governor is a man of culture. That's why he wants only smart boys like us.'

'What for?'

'To do works. You know, cleaning, prepare some rooms. Carry food.'

Etienne hopes he hasn't understood well enough. Cleaning and preparing rooms is for girls.

The other boys begin to stir from their afternoon slumber.

'Sometimes we do reading to his children,' Alberto continues. 'You can read, no?'

Etienne nods. 'There was a man at the market. He asked us.'

'See, I know already!'

'Al Kamil wants his sons to learn all the knowledge of the world,' says another boy who says his name is Giacopo. He looks a bit like Alberto, with the same heavy brow and olive skin, but he has straight hair that hangs like a velvet curtain above his eyes.

Sitting in a tight circle they introduce themselves, jabbering in a mixture of their own tongues, Occitan, French, the odd word of Arabic. From what Etienne can tell they are glad to have another addition, someone to show the ropes to. He wants to tell them about his journey, the friends he has lost - Daniel, Marc, Jean. He wants to ask them about their journey, if any of them had to watch their friends drown before their very eyes, or left to choke in a cloud of dust, their small, lifeless bodies tossed into the water. He wants to know if it is possible to recover, if such memories can ever fade, or if they will always sneak up on him, ready to stab his heart and stop his breath.

Every morning, after prayers, Abubakr gives them their tasks for the day. Usually Etienne works with Alberto, or with a dark-skinned boy called Yossef from Catalonia who is a whole head shorter than Etienne even though he is fifteen. He has big owl eyes that it turns out are not very good at seeing, so he keeps an eyeglass in his tunic for any close up work like polishing the plates or dusting the ornaments. His mother is Jewish and he isn't too sure who his father is as his mother has never mentioned his name, other than with a curse beforehand. Yossef is the only one who speaks Arabic properly and he translates it into Occitan so they can all get a gist from there.

Etienne likes working with Yossef. He knows a lot of things - about different customs from different lands, the beliefs of the Mohammedans, the stars. Pointing out the different stars in the night sky, he tells Etienne that the Greeks worked out how the earth moves among the heavens. Etienne has heard them talk a lot about Greek this and that and finally, as they are on their hands and knees in one of the courtyards pulling up weeds from between the stones, he plucks up the courage to ask.

'Where is Greece. Exactly?'

Yossef sits up and grabs Etienne's arm.

'Look,' he whispers. 'There you are. There is Greece.'

They peer through a latticed archway that leads from the courtyard to one of the gardens. Two girls appears from behind a huge ornamental vase that stands in the shade of a palm. For a moment Etienne just stares. Petite, with long black hair wound round and round upon their heads in a plait, they wear belted white robes that cover everything but their feet and hands.

'You like them, no?'

Etienne blushes.

'They are Greek,' he says. 'Everyone likes them.'

'Do you lie with them?' Etienne tries to sound casual.

Yossef shakes his head. 'No one does. It's forbidden to talk to the personal servants of the governor's family. You would be beaten for sure if the governor heard of it.'

The girls pad back across the garden, carrying bunches of white flowers, eyes cast down.

'So you can never meet them?' Etienne asks.

Yossef scrunches up his eyes like he doesn't understand how someone could even think such a thing was possible. Etienne scratches at his neck and begins to stammer his way out of the blunder when Alberto comes racing over.

'Etienne! Come quick. There is another *Francese* arrived.'

Etienne leaps up. 'You're sure?'

'*Mah!*' says Alberto. 'He just arrive but he won't talk to us. Maybe he is from your boat, no?'

'Maybe,' he says, face breaking open with a smile. He can't think how else a French boy could have found his way to the palace.

Come,' says Alberto. 'He is cleaning silver plates.'

Etienne races along behind the Sicilian boy, elated. It has been days since Etienne has spoken French. He has even taken to talking to himself aloud to remind himself what it feels like to say exactly what he means without having to contort his jaw around sounds that leave him feeling as though he has been chewing a tough old shoe. His heart is skipping beats as he tries to guess who it will be. Marc? Daniel? There is even some small part of him holding on to the hope that it might be Jean. That would be just like him – frail Jean with his limpy leg and eerie see-through eyes, showered with another miracle.

Etienne comes skidding over the tiles to find the boy sitting in the corner, knees pulled up to his chest. He is a total stranger. Disappointment dips Etienne's shoulders as he takes him in. Pale, doughy skin, the boy has a nest of ginger hair and a dusting of freckles over his round face.

'I'm Etienne.' He cocks his head to one side. 'Alberto says you're French?'

The boy's face crumples like he is about to cry.

Alberto rolls his eyes. 'Maybe we leave you two to talk.'

'What's your name?' Etienne tries again. 'Did you come on the boats?'

The boy winces like he is trying to duck a beating.

'Please tell me your name. I've so wanted to have someone to talk French to.'

The ginger-haired boy mutters something into his knees. Etienne cranes forward and the boy repeats. 'Christophe.'

'Where are you from Christophe?'

The straw-coloured eyelashes blink rapidly. 'Saintes.'

'Saintes. You are not a shepherd then?'

127

Christophe shakes his head. Etienne instinctively wants to give him some reassurance, but as he reaches for it the platitude dies in his throat. He thought that meeting someone else from his country would make him feel better, but as he rummages up a smile for the terrified boy, he realises that the encounter has made him feel worse. What's the point of being able to speak your own tongue if you can't say what you want?

Just one look at the shell of a boy in front of him tells him he can't talk to Christophe, not properly, like you do with real friends. Christophe is too brittle for the truth. And the truth is that it is not alright. The governor's palace is not the slave boats, but the cool marble luxury that surrounds them, the rippling fountains, the lush gardens, the silver plates brimming with juicy little balls of lamb and dates are as far away from them as the King of France's table. The truth is they are hardly freer here than they were on the boats.

He thinks there is probably a way to leave the governor's palace, but he is almost certain that if he tried he would likely end up worse off, maybe even back at the slave market. It is funny to think that the best thing about Montoire had been the fact that he could leave if he wanted. That and his mother. The only person in the world who would still love him, no matter what idiot things he got up to. It makes him sad to think that she most probably thinks he is dead, or at least lost forever. Maybe I am lost forever, he thinks.

He looks down at the shipwrecked French boy slumped on the floor, and tries to shift the rancour he feels towards him for reminding him of home.

'I have to get back to find out my tasks before lunch is over,' he says. 'Alberto says it's the only break I'll get for a while.' With that he steps outside, pupils shrinking under the fierce, white glare of the sun.

Chapter Twenty

'Bad weather?' The old man's face was impassive, although Gui fancied he was amused. 'Well that depends on what kind of bad weather you're talking about. The wrong bad weather and you'll finish on the bottom of the sea with your Roman galleys and long boats from the North.'

'I'm sure of it. But what about a better starred, bad weather?'

The navigator sniffed the air. It was hard to tell his age. His skin was weathered and couperose but looked as though it had been that way for a very long time and would still have the same aspect in twenty years. The corner of the man's lip lifted and he nudged his cap up over his brow with a thick, knotted finger.

'You think it's not possible to smell fair weather after forty years at sea?'

'If you tell me it is so.'

The blue eyes crinkled. 'You are not a merchant, are you?'

Gui felt his neck prickle beneath the collar of his stolen cloak. 'What do you mean?'

'You're too honest. That is what I mean.'

'I am not a sea-farer,' Gui replied. At least that was honest. 'I'm journeying on behalf of my business partners.'

The old man's eyes travelled over Gui's clothes, and he gave a slow nod of comprehension. 'If you say so.'

A moment of total stillness radiated from him. Time itself seemed to part like waves about them. Gui felt his body yield its tension to the old man's unspoken understanding that before him was someone in desperate need of help. Gui heard a voice say, if you don't speak now, it will be too late. He drew breath, and staring past the other man's shoulder said, 'I need to get to Alexandria because there is someone I am looking for.'

The navigator's reply was a patient pause.

'My son has been taken.'

'Slavers?'

Shame cinched Gui's stomach. 'Yes.'

'I'll give false hope to no one, so I'll tell you the slave trade is rife and there's nothing those men won't do to defend their business.'

Gui's limbs felt weighted down, a lead line plummeting into the deep.

'I have to find our son before it's too late. My wife...I promised...It has only been a few weeks. There must be some way to trace him. Someone must know.'

'Slow down, son. The men who take these souls do not mean them to be found. Rushing will only serve to trip you up.'

'You know who they are?'

'I know most who hazard their lives on these waters.' The bright blue eyes looked right into Gui's, and he could feel the man taking the measure of his heart.

'Your son was taken from Marseille?'

'He was.' Gui answered abruptly, as though seeking to distance himself from the words. 'I think he took the cross with a group of shepherd boys and went to Marseille to find passage overseas.'

It still sounded as absurd to hear it aloud as it had the first time he was forced to explain. It prompted the same, unanswerable question he knew lay coiled in his gut and perhaps always would: how did I let it happen? The navigator rubbed his teeth with his tongue. Gui steeled himself for a paternal admonishment, but all he said was, 'And the man who robbed you?'

'A Venetian merchant he claimed. Dark haired, stout, well-dressed. I took his cloak and hat to disguise myself.'

'There are a thousand thieves at every port, but tell me more.'

'He gave his name as Enrico Zonta.' Gui spun the plumed hat around in his hand as though it might tell him something more about the man who poisoned him.

The navigator laughed. 'I knew Enrico Zonta.'

'You know Zonta?'

'Knew him. He had a small fleet. We used to ferry back and forth to Ragusa, Rhodes, Constantinople. Wool and salt mainly. Sometimes wine, dye, house girls from Azov. I scrubbed down his keels in winter.'

'You're Venetian?'

'Slav. From the town of Zadar. My father was a fisherman. He sent me to Venice when I was boy. Said its streets brimmed with gold.'

'I thought that was Constantinople.'

'It's all Venetian gold now.'

From the upper deck one of the crew signalled to him, a silhouette against the morning sky. The navigator tipped his cap in reply – their talisman, acknowledging all was well.

'I was a boy then. Enrico Zonta is long dead. Your man might be a Venetian slaver, but most of them that trade in Christians prefer to keep their identity to themselves. Their Senate may turn a blind eye until they have reason not to, but who can tell the why and when of that?'

'Well, this man has made that name his own. He had a mark on his neck. A purple birth stain.'

'I'll ask the crew.'

The galley was crossing the wake of a fishing boat and for a moment everything was drowned by the screech of sea birds. The coastline of Sicily lost to the waves, the boat it slid up and down on the swell.

'Which direction is Alexandria?' Gui asked, as if an answer might help him find his bearings.

'The same direction the wind is coming from now,' the navigator said.

Gui swivelled round to face the wind. The air sucked his breath away. He trained his attention on the furthest point he could see, trying to conjure the shore into view. But the only reply was the grey chop of the waves against the boat and the cry of seabirds. He peered over the gunwale. A shiver fingered his spine.

He knew how to swim. Unseated while crossing a brook one summer, his father had been seized by the whim to teach his sons. A length of rope at his side, he forced the boys into a pond, its waters green from the stagnant heat. Gui recalled the panic as the water folded over him, how quickly his limbs had tired as he thrashed to keep his head above the water's slimy coat. Lungs exploding, he and Simon had begged to be pulled out, pawing for the rope while their father barked at them from the bank. Gui had tried to beat away the water, the weight of his clothes dragging him down, confusion swamping his heart – is my father really going let me drown?

He had learned how to swim alright, but Etienne hadn't. The thought of it turned his stomach. Gui closed his eyes, trying to remove the distance between him and his destination. It felt as though the water of all the seas was pushing down on his chest. Eyes still scrunched tight, he whispered, 'Please hold on. Your father is coming.' The idea that his son may now never hear the words he longed to say made him want to howl.

*

The smell of the sea and spices mingled on the warm air adding a sweet fragrance to the stink of life. Gui scuffed his feet in the dust. Had this been Etienne's first sight of land? There were a dozen or so ships anchored; cogs from the North with their square sterns and round, cargo-hungry bellies, sleek-silhouetted galleys, the bearers of luxury goods, and behind them, drifting in the channel, the angled lateens of river-bound Egyptian vessels. What lay beneath their decks? Wine? Oil? A hold of frightened children?

Even if their cargoes were pottery from Iraq, linens from Flanders, salt from the Occitan marshes, someone must know of those other, renegade boats. Someone must hear the cries of their haul, like calves newly separated from their mothers, full of white-eyed terror. The urge to search each one of them tore Gui's gaze in every direction.

'Your man, Zonta. He's from Veneto all right, the mainland. Got as many names as he does tunics but we think he was born Roberto Sandolin.'

Gui started at the navigator's voice. The old man rocked back on his heels, inhaling the harbour air contentedly, as though returning to a once familiar hearth.

'He's a small time trader for his own account and does some legitimate

131

business with the Church. But makes his real money as a middle man to freebooters and slavers.'

Robbed of words, Gui found a business-like nod of gratitude for the mariner.

'I'm sorry, son.'

The man's sympathy stung Gui's eyes, forcing them to the horizon where the sun was emerging, a flood of light burning away the deep pinks of the dawn.

'Who is his master in this business?'

'Money.' The old man scratched his forehead. 'The slave trade is the fastest growing business in the world. Men are growing fatter than kings from it. They get greedy, take more risk. And they aren't going to let someone like you get in their way.'

Gui's jaw tightened. 'They took my son.'

'See them.' The old Slav's head twitched in the direction of a cog that had docked alongside them. A group of light-blind slaves shuffled down the gangplank, pooling on the hard under the eye of three dockers who set about inspecting them.

'They're going to the slave market. If your son docked here then someone there knows what happened to him.'

Brow pinched, Gui watched as the men prodded at the slaves, binding them in small groups while their other cargo was checked by a reed-thin customs inspector, a large pouch at his waist and an armed guard at his side. Light-skinned girls with slanting, feline eyes, older boys of North African appearance, and scattered among them, ebony-skinned children who looked no more than five or six years old.

'For the love of God, they're only children,' he whispered. The idea that his son had been goaded like livestock twisted his guts with a hot, urgent rage that made him want to tear them out.

'They are the lucky ones,' said the navigator. 'It means their households want them young enough to convert, teach them their customs. One day they'll be more than likely be freed.'

'Convert them? Are they heathen?'

'Some. The rest are Christians. It's forbidden for the Mohammedans to take a fellow Mohammedan as a slave. Unless they're skin is black enough. Then they make all sorts of excuses.'

'But those merchants are Europeans.' Even as he spoke Gui could hear the childlike outrage pitch in his own voice. 'It is forbidden for them to trade in Christians.'

'Not over here it's not.'

'Do they have no fear of the penalty back home?'

Sharp, blue eyes twinkling under sagging lids, the navigator's bearded lips parted in laughter. 'At the dock they sometimes send a local Catholic priest aboard to inspect. It's he who decides whether the slaves are

Christians.'

'And if they find Christians?'

'Depends where they are and who's paying. Sometimes they send 'em back to where they came from. Orphanage, workhouse. Or they lie and call them Mohammedans. Sometimes they'll sell 'em on undeclared as contraband. Tax free profit.'

'Sell them to whom?'

'Mohammedans take Christian as slaves just as freely as the Italians take heathens. Pagans in the Crimea will pay highly for a fair European.'

'Crimea? The land of the Tartars?' To his embarrassment, Gui heard the tremor his voice. He rubbed his palm over his mouth. Hidden under months of beard growth, his face felt as coarse and unfamiliar to him as the place he was standing.

The navigator let his shoulders slump in a sad pause. He put a hand on Gui's arm. 'If you need help, look for a friend of mine. A lady called Yalda. She works out of rooms at the end of the copperware market. You'll see the blue tiles that mark her door. She knows all you need to know about that market. Tell her Dušan sent you.'

The old man held out a flask. 'It's plum wine from my fruit orchard. In my land no-one starts their day without it.'

A slug of the fiery liquid shook Gui from his grim trance. He found a smirk for the old seafarer. 'There are many wars?'

The navigator nodded slyly. 'Fighting is good for men. Now and again.' Gui offered him back the flask and but he returned his hand.

'Keep it. And remember that each time you drink.'

*

Slender, painted fingers drew back the grille. 'Who is it?' The woman's voice was deep and soft, like an unspoken invitation to recline. It caught Gui off guard.

'The navigator of the Sea Phantom sent me,' he stammered.

'Dušan?'

'Yes.'

'Please wait.'

The grille closed, and Gui was left standing alone in the street. There was a dead seabird at his feet that had been part scavenged by a dog. It stank. Death smelt worse than shit, he thought. Two sets of brown eyes passed by, their owners concealed under black robes. Briefly they took in the foreigner standing outside the brothel. There was no mistaking the judgement they made as they hurried on. He turned his back to the street, arm resting on the doorframe, resisting the urge to knock again.

'I am Yalda.' The world seemed to stall as the beautiful prostitute opened the door. Her kohl-rimmed lashes fell down his body, in expert assessment of his means.

Yalda wore a continuous piece of fabric, wrapped skilfully over her body, permitting a glimpse of flesh at the waist and the cleavage. It was deep blue with a golden weft and it shimmered even in the dim light of her salon. Black hair loose beneath a gossamer veil, she wore a gold chain around her ankle. She looked the way that Gui had imagined a whore might look before he had encountered the bare-breasted portside workers at Marseille who called out for his coin with ribald laughter.

'I don't work in the morning. I can make you an appointment for this afternoon,' she said.

'No, no.' Gui coloured. 'I'm sorry. Dušan said you might be able to help me with some information. I don't want to take too much of your time.'

'Information?' Yalda cocked her head one side.

'I can pay, of course,' Gui said hastily.

She smelt of jasmine and she floated over the tiled floor as though she and the fabric were one. 'Payment won't be necessary. I am successful enough,' she said, melting down onto a floor cushion.

Gui felt his neck grow hot.

'Please, go on.'

'My son was taken in Marseille by slave traffickers. I have reason to believe he has been brought here. The navigator said you know something of this trade.'

'I do.' She ran a finger under her bracelets, dropping them as he noticed a silvery knot of scarring they concealed.

'I was taken from my hometown in Syria and brought here. Fifteen years gone now. I escaped, with the help of Dušan, and made myself a living here with the only opportunity I was left with.'

'I need to know where my son has been taken. Dušan said you might know who to ask.'

Yalda ran her hand over her arm, and Gui saw the accomplished mask of the courtesan slip.

'I knew. Once.' The beautiful prostitute looked away. Gui leant towards her, the quicksilver of desperation chasing through his veins. Fingers interlaced in supplication, he said, 'Please. I have no other clues. If you can help, then I implore you.'

Yalda moistened her lips. 'These men,' she began, 'you cannot imagine what they are.'

'Oh, I'm sure I can.'

'No, really.' Yalda stared back, eyes glistening. 'Believe me when I say you cannot.'

He glanced down. 'Back in Corsica, I found one of their ships.'

Gui saw her shoulders stiffen. She shook her head.

'If I help you, start asking questions, then…I have no other home.' She pressed her palm to her cheek as though she were blotting invisible tears. 'It's been many years since I have dwelt on it.'

Sensing that a clue to Etienne's fate was slipping away, Gui rose to his knees, suddenly animated. 'There was a man who tried to poison me in Messina, Roberto Sandolin. Goes also by the name of Enrico Zonta. I am sure he is involved in this trade. There must be other working with him here. This dog trades in Christian souls!'

Yalda's silence was all he needed to lift his eyes to the walls, where there hung embroideries of Arabic calligraphy. The designs he recognised from the Muslim quarters of Messina - prayers to Allah. He closed his eyes, cringing inwardly as the first sounds of the early evening *Adhan* rang out.

Yalda shook her head. Gui saw regret in her resigned smile. 'I suppose you have never seen the slave markets of Genova or Barcelona,' she said.

Gui swallowed on the prickle in his throat. When Yalda first opened her door for him, he had dared to hope that he might win himself an ally. Now, as the intonations of foreign prayer filtered into the room from the minarets outside, he felt the estrangement keenly.

'Forgive me,' he said. 'I have been a poor guest.'

As Yalda rose he noticed how diminutive she was, how slight her bones. She placed her hand over her heart.

'I am sorry. Truly I am. I pray that your son is returned to you.'

'I will find him,' he said.

Chapter Twenty-one

The low, reedy voice of an old woman was singing a lament of the peasant's lot. Agnes inhaled the smell of earth and horsehair. There was a hearth in the centre of the room. A vent above drew up the smoke through gossamer filaments of rain. No sooner had she opened her eyes than the old woman turned around.

'We found you out in the wet,' she said in a dialect Agnes could barely understand.

Agnes sat and looked into the ancient face. Watery eyes, fogged by time, stared unjudging from the deep creases of leathery skin.

'Thank you,' she said.

'She is awake?' A younger man stood at the threshold of the hovel, his face obscured by a full beard and a cap pulled down to his brow. Despite the cold he wore only a leather gilet over a shirt.

'Just now,' the crone replied.

The man came to stand by the fire, rubbing his hands until she shooed him away to fetch some water and fill the log basket. Agnes cast off her blanket. Instantly a chill air gnawed at her. The old woman tutted for her to cover herself.

'Where am I?'

'Near Houx. Three leagues from Maintenon.'

Agnes clenched her chattering teeth. She watched the old woman shuffle about the room, pushing at cinders with a broom, wiping out a pot with a greying rag. She longed to release the pressure of the silence, but the old lady seemed so self-contained, her chores a barrier of ordinariness against the torrent of all that Agnes might say. Silence settled upon them like layers of ash until the woman paused, breathless, against her broom.

'Have I been here long?' Agnes asked.

'We found you this morning. Your lips were blue.'

'I remember it was raining at dawn,' she said.

'Are you with child?' The crone asked. The question felt like a blade. Agnes shook her head in place of the reply that pricked her windpipe. The old woman approached her and squatted down. For all her years, her heels rested comfortably on the ground. She has ground wheat in that same position for decades, thought Agnes. The same grain that made the bread for my grandparents' table. The old woman looked into Agnes's eyes like a soothsayer looking into an obsidian tablet.

'Did you escape him, my child?'

Agnes's blood froze. Her lips parted, the truth upon them, but she could feel the sting of shame in her throat. 'Who?'

The old woman said nothing, rheumy eyes drooping sadly. She knows, thought Agnes. Moments passed like hours, until Agnes whispered, 'What is his name?'

'Amaury de Maintenon,' the crone said and another aeon of silence descended.

Several times Agnes drew breath, but each time she was defeated by the chasm that lay beyond. All the times she had lain beside Gui, close enough to hear his heart, longing to share this dread intimacy. Sometimes he noticed, a gentle query in his eyes, so full of adoration. Will he still look at me this way if I tell him? It was the thought that always turned the words to thorns.

The peasant woman was humming softly the way a mother hums to a babe after it has fallen asleep, fearful that silence will wake her child. If I don't speak now, Agnes thought, this malignancy will corrode my soul. Her heart quickened. The old woman's head nodded, almost imperceptibly. An invitation.

'It was a long time ago,' Agnes said suddenly.

'You're the old castellan's kin, aren't you?' She drew a circle around her face. 'I remember you. You came once or twice with the salt merchant.'

Agnes felt as though she was falling. 'My father. When my grandparents died, the castellany of Gazeran came to me... for my father to hold until I was wed.'

The old woman gave a sad shake of her head and muttered, 'And that's when he came?'

The air felt like tar as Agnes forced in a breath.

'My father's trade made him a rich man. After I inherited the castellany he was arrested, accused of heresy. The night after he was taken a man came to me. He didn't tell me his name. He told me that if I agreed to be his bride he would have my father released and I would know no suffering.' Tears ran down her face but Agnes's voice was steady. 'But I couldn't. I was so frightened, I just stood there. And he...' Now, she faltered. The old woman sat motionless beside her, an affinity in her eyes that said, you don't have to go on. But the dam was breached. The only way through the flood was to wade on.

'He took his pleasure with me. I fled to beg for my father's life, but the Inquisition arrested me... They said they had witnesses against me. That I loved the Devil...'

The old woman patted her hand with a rough, icy palm.

'If only I had said yes to Maintenon, I could have saved him.' Agnes wiped her face with the back of her sleeve. 'I could have saved papà.'

The peasant woman took Agnes in her arms and said, 'Don't you believe that. Maintenon meant only to torment you with those words.' She cast a finger in the direction of her grandparents' house. 'We know what he is. There is no inch of mercy in that black soul.'

137

'You know about the others?' Agnes asked quietly. Her father's map was scratching her skin. She knew the written word would be meaningless to the old woman, but the need to share her proof was stronger. She took out the parchment. 'My father sent this for my aunt to keep. I don't know how he found that place.'

'The old chapel? Gaston saw him arrive one night with a cart. There were three or four bodies. Girls. Dark-skinned.' There was a pause. 'What can we do? We barely survive.'

The old woman's admission relieved the tightness in her chest. She was believed. 'Saracens,' Agnes whispered, eyes on her father's note. 'There are others down there too. More than four. He wrote a name here, too. De Coucy.'

'The de Coucys married into the county of Dreux. Yolande de Coucy married one of the count's sons I believe, but my memory fades. Gaston will remember better than I.'

The old woman called out and her son appeared at the door, a basket of logs under his arm. A question lined his brow.

'Maintenon.' The old woman rushed the name from her lips as though it was an incubus she did not want to invoke. 'This woman is the Castellan of Gazeran's kin.'

The man poked his cap up and gave a nod. 'I remember them. They used to come here in the summer after harvest.'

'Her father found the old chapel. Reckoned one of those souls might be the de Coucy girl.'

'Could be. Margueritte was Lady Yolande's youngest. Maintenon took her for his bride. Came with a fine dowry. She died of plague that winter. Or so he said.' Gaston laid down the logs. 'Maintenon went on crusade in the Count of Dreux's retinue. Men like that don't doubt the word of a loyal vassal.'

'What of the other girls? The Saracens?'

'Maintenon gambled his wealth on crusade, returned with nothing. Rumour went round he liked the dark-skins for himself. We'd see 'em by and by, faces pressed up against the gaps in the coach. Young girls.'

'He trades Saracen slaves?'

'No. He don't trade the heathen ones around here. They're for his amusement.' He exchanged a look with the old woman – shall I tell her more?

A single nod of the head.

'Round here, he takes them what won't be missed – orphans, foundlings, destitutes. Children of serfs who can't pay their rent. The wagons come and go by night.'

Both of their eyes travel to the ground. The shame of their poverty. Their powerlessness. Agnes marked herself with the sign of the cross. 'Dear God, can no one stop him?'

The old lady seemed to be staring at some distant vision. Agnes could feel the power radiating from her shrunken frame. 'We may not live to see it, but one day the righteous of this country will rise up. Men like Maintenon will be skinned and pegged out in the fields like goats.'

'Amen,' said Gaston.

'But what if we could do something to stop him now? Prove Margueritte de Coucy was murdered and buried here? We could go back to the chapel, see if we can find something. I might be able to gain the trust of Margueritte's family. Would they not want to know that the lands of her dowry were as good as stolen? That she was slain by their trusted vassal? With people of such high standing, even the court of France would listen.'

The way the old woman and her son were staring at her made her feel like a madwoman, one of the wild-haired ascetics who roamed the byways of Christendom, eyes rolled back in prophetic ecstasy. Softening the edge in her voice, she continued, 'My father lost his reputation and his life trying to protect me. How many others have there been? There must be some way to end it.'

'Rest here for now, child. Wait for the shock to pass. Gaston will get you a fur. I'll put a pan of water on.'

'Let me.' Agnes stood. The top of the old woman's head barely reached her breast, but the time-twisted hands guided Agnes back down to sit. For the first time, the ancient face cracked with a smile.

'If events had not been so turned by the Devil, we would be your tenants.'

Agnes pushed the matted hair from her face, nodded in acknowledgement of her predicament. Exhausted and penniless, a wanted heretic- this tiny, smoke-filled hovel was her only refuge.

'The power of the Evil One grows every day. What can we do but till the land until God's hand returns to free us?'

'What can we do?' Agnes said as the old woman poured the water from the bucket into the pan and hoisted it over the spitting fire. Sit for now, that's what you can do she thought. Tomorrow you can stand.

*

Bernard de Nogent swallowed the humiliation that was burning, bottled at the base of his sternum. The young man before him was dressed in the livery of the Le Bar household. It would have been insult enough for the bishop not to meet the man who had made such a generous donation, but to send this pimpled youth was a well-calculated outrage.

'His Grace, Bishop Reginald sends his utmost apologies and gratitude, Bernard.'

Bernard! The inquisitor felt his teeth grind.

'But I am sure you understand the campaign is at a very delicate stage. There has been such a backlash after the events at Béziers and we cannot risk a revanchement,' said Hugh. A former junior Canon at Chartres, he was two decades younger than de Nogent, and did not have the natural merit to make inquisitor, let alone anything greater. But he did have one thing that all the merit in the kingdom could never buy: he was fourth son of Count Reginald II Le Bar, and his mother was the king's cousin. His eldest brother was Bishop Reginald of Chartres. In all likelihood, he would one day inherit the bishopric, and he knew it.

'Your reverence, the bishop wants you to be assured that anything you wish to say to him you may entrust to me.' The sallow, beardless cheeks broadened into an exaggerated grin. He hadn't even offered de Nogent any refreshment.

Struggling to keep the conflict from his face, de Nogent considered it almost too great an insult to convey his wish to this idiotic upstart, but he had travelled two days to get here and sent a thousand livres in charity as a sweetener. With all he had at stake, it seemed churlish to turn back now. Could it be this was a final test? He knew his faults well enough to know that if he had any failing in his virtue it was the sin of pride.

'My visit is with regard to the abbey at Maintenon,' he began, head inclined in respectful attitude. 'I have spoken with his Grace on this matter before. I believe that Lord Amaury is now in a position to complete the foundation. He may have mentioned my name in regard to the abbacy, it was my intention to discuss my plans to use it as a hub for fighting heresy in and around the Île de France.'

'Oh, yes, of course.' The youth smirked. 'Lord Amaury has indeed spoken to His Grace on the matter of the abbey's foundation.

'Excellent.' De Nogent beamed. So, money does talk, he thought. A moment of humbling himself was about to be rewarded.

'The thing is.' The youth pulled at his ear and de Nogent felt a knot bunch in the pit of his stomach. 'Lord Amaury also came to ask the bishop to bless his nuptials with Alice St Pol.'

'Nuptials?' The knot was a stone.

The youth nodded blithely. 'An excellent family, you'll agree. You may have heard, quite wicked fortune, but the youngest boy is an imbecile. Maintenon has offered the abbacy to him as a gesture to the count. Such a weight off his mind. I'm sure a man of your depth and virtue will understand.' Hugh Le Bar folded both his hands over his heart. 'Blessed are the poor in spirit.'

Chapter Twenty-two

The heat of the late morning about him like a cloak, Gui squatted, short of breath. A line of boys, stripped to their loin cloths, bunched together under the coiled whips of the market slavers. Beside them a small boy with soft, chestnut ringlets lay curled at the feet of an elderly man. He was chained at his ankle to a stick. Gui's skin burned as though it were being scourged.

Swiping away the flies, he threw his head back and took a gulp of air. Although his church held otherwise, he could not have children capable of sin, let alone sin great enough to explain this hell. Perhaps the Dualists of the East were right and he wrong. Perhaps the power of the Devil was equal to that of the Lord.

The market was vast. *How will I ever find my son in all this?* He surveyed the porticos where buyers crowded around platforms or took rest beneath makeshift awnings. Another sip of the navigator's plum wine and he threw himself into the tide of bodies. He shouldered his way through the huddles of human chattel, palming away salesmen who pushed almond-eyed children into his path. Eyes peeled for a fair-haired child, he tried not to see the forlorn looks of the others as they rubbed tired faces with chubby hands.

Taking two steps at a time, he entered the main building, passed the market administrators hunched over their ledgers like vultures. The roofless building was shielded from the sun by swathes of fabrics poled up into the sky like sails. They rippled when the air moved, dappling the heads below with flashes of yellow that made his heart skip a beat only to fall as the shadows closed in to reveal another olive- skinned youth blinking into the clamour of bidders.

Hours past and the sun moved from its position overhead. There had not been one white-skinned slave for sale. Was Etienne ever here? Heartsick, Gui withdrew from the gallery. Dragging his feet back onto the main thoroughfare, he took a pocket of flatbread and some spiced beans from the most insistent hand. The mixture burned on his tongue for a few moments, but was not dissimilar to the hearty dishes of home. French children would not be so fond of such highly spiced food though, unless they were hungry enough. His appetite died with the thought and he handed the cup of beans to one of the hot little hands that reached up, calling for his charity.

From the corner of his eye he caught a glow of white skin, the golden head of a child. His lungs purged themselves of air. From the depths of his guts he pulled out a hoarse cry. '*Etienne!*'

The boy turned around and Gui's heart cracked. His only thought had been Etienne. Despite all he had seen, he hadn't considered a different possibility, and the sight of the sun-bronzed child, crowned with a halo of angel's hair, numbed him. The ice blue eyes squinted cautiously at Gui. The boy looked about eight years old and there was a bleak resignation in his regard that hollowed the pit of Gui's stomach.

'Do you speak French?'

The boy gave a solitary nod. His grimy hand was covered with calloused nodes. It was a hand that belonged to a carpenter or a mason, not a child. Gui dropped to a squat. 'Where are you from, son?'

'I have to go.'

Gui felt the boy shrink from him. 'I mean you no harm,' he said. 'Will you tell me how long have you been here? You were taken away from your home?'

The boy's response was a silence as thick and oppressive as the market's air.

'My son was taken, just like you. Have you seen boys from France? Perhaps you know my son? His name is…'

'I do not know your son.' The boy's eyes darted over Gui's shoulder. 'I have to go.'

'Please talk to me. Were you among the shepherd crusaders?' Gui placed his hand gently on the boy's shoulder.

'Leave me alone.' The terror in his eyes scalded Gui as the child pulled away and scurried off, gaze fixed upon the dirt path.

'Wait, please,' Gui called after him. 'I have to find my boy…' Sitting on his heels in the dust he watched the golden head bob and weave through the crowds, a Willo'-the-Wisp flickering through the press of *souq,* carrying away with him the hope that for a brief moment had lit Gui's soul.

'I have to let him know,' he whispered, and for a heart beat the world stalled. Nothing seemed to move, although the sounds of hundreds of voices, of the beasts of burden and the clang of construction work bore down on him. Gui looked up. He still had sight of the little boy, swerving the obstacles of the grown-ups' world . *He has a father who loves him more than anything on this earth and I have to let him know.*

Rising from the dust, he shadowed the French boy until he arrived at a line of battered lean-tos abutting the western most wall of the town. Sitting on the threshold was a bald, overweight man in stained overalls, whose Mediterranean colouring could have made him Italian as easily as North African. The young boy set down his pail and emptied a few coins into the man's hand for which he received a pat on the head before disappearing behind the curtain of the hovel.

Gui purchased a bag of sugared almonds and a meat-stuffed bread. Then,

making use of great stone pillars that belonged to palaces of a forgotten age, he waited under the rays of a white, winter sun. Still, it was hot enough to burn his skin and his neck stung when, in the late afternoon, his patience was rewarded and the boy re-emerged. His blond curls were patted down with oil, his face wiped clean, lips a pinky sheen. He looked a grim imitation of a nobleman's child scrubbed up for Advent mass. A large, hide-bound portfolio was wedged awkwardly under his arm, and he cast around before he scuttled off, eyes to the ground.

A few streets on and the boy stalled at the threshold of a courtyard. Taking the document wallet out from under his arm he muttered a few words to himself. Gui seized his chance.

'Please don't be frightened,' he began. The boy's mouth opened, and for one dreadful moment, Gui thought he was going to shout out.

'Please,' he implored with a desperation that the boy seemed to sense was genuine. 'Are you hungry?' Gui asked and the boy nodded.

His conscience was a hod of bricks on his back as he offered the bribe to the poor urchin before him. The meat-stuffed bread glistened with the oil, and the boy's eyes lit up like Gui had performed the miracle of the fish and loaves. His leather wallet slapped onto the ground as the boy snatched it and began devouring the bread like a stray dog falling upon the contents of an upturned cart. For a heart beat the warmth of parental satisfaction spread across Gui's face as he watched the ravenous child. All at once, his mind flew to Etienne. Is my own son this hungry?

He squatted down on his haunches and said, 'Can you tell me how you got here?'

Inches from the boy's face now, Gui could see clearly the berry-pink lips were stained, the blue eyes lined with kohl. The world beneath his feet began spinning as Gui made sense of what the boy's appearance was telling him.

Grease dripping from his chin, the child raised his head reluctantly from the feast and threw a glance down the street. Hastily he crammed in the last morsels of the bread. His eyes darted down to the spilled wallet, face clouding – the happy interlude was over.

'I have to give these papers to a man,' he said.

'Let me do it.' Gui snatched up the wallet.

'No!' The boy exclaimed, alarmed. He wasn't able to meet Gui's eye as he said, 'No, he wants me.'

'But I don't want anything from you,' Gui insisted. 'If you come with me, I will make sure you are safe. I swear it.'

The boy hovered in indecision. Gui knew he only had a heart beat to sway him.

'What's your name?' he asked.

'Simon,' the boy replied.

'I'm Gui and I'm from Courville near Chartres.'

'Beaucaire,' said the boy as he wiped the grease from his chin with the back of his hand, leaving a pink smear across his face. Gui pulled down the sleeve of his own tunic and cleaned the remaining lip stain from the boy's face. Simon smiled shyly. Someone used to take care of you once, Gui thought.

'Were you part of the shepherd's crusade?' Gui asked.

'No,' said Simon. 'I'm orphan. I was taken from the children's home of the Sisters of the Good Courage not long after I arrived.'

'The Sisters of Good Courage?' Gui puckered up his face like he was sucking on a lemon and Simon laughed.

'They were horrible old crones with hairy cheeks,' he replied and Gui knew he had won. Gui chuckled along, a deep, jolly sound that made him think of his friend Philippe and wonder if he was dead or alive.

Simon took Gui to within two streets of where he said he was taken when he first arrived, but not even a whole bag of sugared almonds would make him go an inch further, so Gui dispatched the child to Yalda with a few dinar in the hope she would take pity.

A series of warehouses were set around a quadrangle. *Fondaco dei Veneziani* proclaimed the sign: The Venetian's Warehouse. Each large Mediterranean city had its own warehouse complex in major port towns. All traded goods from that city were logged and stored there, with an adjunct hostel for merchants and travellers.

The traffic ebbed and flowed - barrels, crates, donkey-drawn pallets. Simon said he had been unloaded there by an Italian merchant with a dozen others, but his account was inconsistent and he wasn't able to give Gui any kind of likely timeframe. Other than a Nubian slave carrying water, Gui could see no sign of trade in human souls.

It was nearly time for evening prayer and men clustered aimlessly on the streets, their arms full of the remnants of the day – bundles of mystery goods tied up in cotton sacks, carts with shaky iron wheels emptied of their wares, huge terracotta flagons that spilled fat drops of liquid. A couple of Mamluk officers exited a tavern opposite, weaving drunkenly. A man in the crisp, white religious dress of the Mohameddans crossed the street to avoid them.

Gui's shirt was stuck to his back. He slowed his breath to stop his heart hammering, pulled his shoulders back, and with military gait, approached the administrator's office at the Venetian *Fondaco*.

The man's faced was poised in outrage as Gui leaned over his desk and said, 'I'm the governor's new inspector and I'm here to renegotiate the rates on a few items.'

The administrator eyed him with distaste. Muslim governors only employed renegade Christians who had renounced their faith to deal with European traders. They were regarded with a mixture of contempt and fear.

'The tariffs were only revised last month,' the Venetian said cautiously.

'Not all of them, eh?'

'I don't know what you mean.'

'The alcohol you sell to the Mamluks, for example...prohibited by the governor.' Gui flicked his eyebrows up with a glare that said, see what you get for your own self importance.

The clerk blinked rapidly.

'And the European slaves you wouldn't want your Senate to find out about.' Gui sucked his teeth. 'I wonder what they would say if they found out you were short changing them with profit from undeclared booty that could get the whole of Venice excommunicated.'

The clerk's eyes widened indignantly. 'Wait here.' He snapped his quill down on the desk and pushed his chair from the desk, scraping it along the tiled floor.

The instant he was gone, Gui peeled up a fistful of papyri and began flicking through the ledgers. His heart sank as he scanned through page after page of receipts for barrels of wine, oil, linens, invoices for loans, inheritances. A breath or two later and he could hear voices echoing across the courtyard. He grabbed another ledger, this time stamped with the crossed keys of the Vatican that he had seen on a ship docked at Corsica.

Hungrily he scanned the script for something he might recognise. Jumping ahead to the notes at the bottom of the stack, he moved his thumb to re-order the papers, and his eye caught a familiar name: Roberto Sandolino. Footsteps were just the other side of the door. Stuffing as many of the sheets as he could into the back of his hose, he dropped the stack of documents as the clerk reappeared with a bull of a man who stroked his pitted head as the clerk said, 'This...gentlemen says he is the governor's new renegade, here to renegotiate some of the special tariffs.'

Even from several paces away Gui could smell aniseed and alcohol vapours oozing from the other man.

'Does he now.' Throat rattling with phlegm as he spoke, the Venetian soldier fingered his belt where his weapon hung. There was nothing Gui could do but double down on his gamble. He brought his hands together, interlaced his fingers and pinched his lips like a disappointed Latin master considering the cane.

'Muslim soldiers are rolling drunk in the streets, every corner you can find Christian boys peddled as concubines. The imams are blaming the current drought on sin. A public repentance has been ordered for next week and the governor intends to clamp down. It would be expedient to make sure you are not one of the ones he makes an example of.'

The clerk raised his shoulders in a mocking shrug. 'It is quite a serious thing for the governor to accuse us of profiting from piracy.'

Gui stood firm. 'The governor wants an additional ten percent on the alcohol and five flaxen-haired boys to gift to his allies.'

The Venetian soldier shook his head. 'Haven't got any left. The order book is already overflowing with requests from Tartar princelings and the blonds are not easy to get hold of. The only white ones I've got now are Slavs. Girls from Russ. I've got a couple of boys of around ten years from the Black Sea that aren't quite white.' He grinned, baring stained teeth. 'But they are ready to go.'

Gui's stomach turned. Slowly, he fingered the gold buckle on Zonta's cloak. No sooner had he suggested the trade than he saw a lascivious gleam in the other man's eyes. The bulky Venetian picked at the scab on his head in a pregnant, bartering pause. Gui felt his choler rise at the other man's greed.

'New shipments are over now until March.' The dealer raised his hands in mock regret.

Gui frowned. 'One of my colleagues took tax on a slave shipment this morning at the docks.'

'Nubians they were,' said the Venetian.

'Mainly,' replied Gui.

Shouts echoed through the vaulted porticos of the courtyard, metal ground against stone as the warehouse shutters were drawn up. The clerk studiously ignored the din but Gui noted a tension that crept into his countenance. The muscle man moved a pace to one side, blocking Gui's view - and his exit - through the half open door. Gui dug in against his instinct to flee and squared himself to face the Venetians.

'His Excellency, Al Kamil requires these gifts at the end of the week along with the tariffs from the wine and he will be very disappointed not to receive them.'

His saliva tasted like metal as he marched directly at the man in his path who checked him with a glancing blow to his shoulder but let him pass. Keeping a steady stride, Gui weaved through the jostle of newly arrived merchandise now being unloaded in the courtyard.

From one of the covered wagons he caught the sound of a child's voice. He span round to face the sound, only to find himself looking into the long muzzle and buck teeth of a face that he recognised but couldn't place. They played a brief game of dodge. Gui slid past. He had reached the entrance gates when it came to him: the man was one of the men who had tried to stop him leaving the tavern in Messina with Zonta. He could feel eyes at his back. Don't look round, he told himself, but it was too late.

'Oi! You!' The shout went up. One hand secured at his waist where the documents were stuffed, Gui broke into a run.

Up ahead he saw the brass and copperware shops, their frontage a jumble of cooking pots, jugs, lanterns. Although his knife was at his waistband it felt uncomfortably distant from his fingers as he chased along the funnelled passageways. The rhythm of his step metered against the call of the *Adhan*, the streets flew by. Like a spider's web, they all drew Gui back to the same centre point. Knowing this haphazard path might land him back at the *Fondaco dei Veneziani*, he cast around for a place to hide.

The last bronzed rays of sun were shearing off the buildings, and they picked out a shop sign, hanging just above him; the seven spheres of the heavens revolving around the ecliptic. Beneath the orbs, a line of spindly calligraphy advertised, Gui presumed, the services of an astronomer. The patter of approaching footfall echoed through the meander of passageways. He ducked inside.

Inside the closet of a room, columns of parchments sprouted up like the foundations of some building as yet unmade, and fine particles of dust hovered in the dying light.

'May I help?' came the disembodied voice.

Gui pivoted, looking for its owner. By the light of the only window, hidden behind a lectern, sat an old man.

'Ibn Ibrahim.'

The astrologer had a fierce intelligence to his face. Thick, white hair swept off a high forehead that lent emphasis to the sharp nose, and small, penetrating eyes that time had not yet clouded over.

'You are seeking someone.' He spoke in deep, considered tones, his French as precise as any Parisian scholar's.

'How did you know?'

'A man's thoughts carry a weight, as do the yearnings of his heart. These things carry life force and they are as readable as the written word.'

Ibn Ibrahim looked down at the papyrus spread across his writing bureau, symbols on it.

'I am correct?'

'My son.' Gui fingered at his waist for the girdle he no longer wore.

'You want to ask me to consult the stars but you are afraid.' Feather poised above the sheet, the astronomer waited. A bead of ink dropped and flowered on the parchment.

'My Church says prophecy is heresy,' Gui replied.

The astrologer massaged his lips together, as though he were preparing a sermon, and said sternly, 'This is a Greek science. Older even. Mesopotamian.'

'There are seven planets in our Heavens. 'At the hour of our birth, or the birth of any event or question, these planets lie in certain aspect. This tells us whether the enterprise be ill fated or at least how hard won must be the querent's victory.'

Gui's hand hesitsted at his brow. Once asked, the answer to his question would come – for good or ill.

'And mine? Will I find my boy?'

There was no sound but for the scratch of the quill as the astronomer consulted his grid of the Heavens, an eye glass pinched on his nose. Gui coughed to relieve the constriction in his heart. He could feel his need to know filling the room, announcing his desperation.

'Do you see anything? How does he fare?'

'What I see.' The man laid down his eye glass, 'is that you will find that which you seek.'

The pressure drained from Gui's chest and his throat filled with an exclamation of relief.

'When will we be reunited? Is he harmed?' The questions spilled out. Ibn Ibrahim held up his palm.

'My work is not prophecy. But I can say that your journey to find him is perilous. There are obstacles that must not be taken lightly. Your son has come to no physical harm. The child is fortunate. It is in his nature to act without calculation. Regardless, he is fortunate and fortune will come to him.'

It felt foolish to smile at such fanciful visions, yet even as he knew the old man was telling him exactly what he wanted to hear, Gui could not help but grin.

'And his mother? Is there anything in the Heavens?'

The old man pulled at the corner of his mouth with his fingers, then after a lengthy pause, said, 'She will once again hold her son in her arms.'

When Gui stepped out it was twilight. The pole star was bright above his head. Etienne would be able to see the same star with fine skies. So would Agnes. Perhaps the stars really did link men to their fate. Surely a man of science like Ibn Ibrahim could not dedicate his life to something he knew to be trickery. Had he really been told only that which he wanted to hear? That Etienne was safe. Fortune would come to him. Agnes would hold him again. It was something Gui needed to believe in, or rather the alternative was something he could not countenance.

The blow came over his right shoulder and it knocked him to the floor. He struck out at his assailant, but the other man had the advantage of surprise and skipped out of the way. Blood running from his nose, Gui drew his knees up to his chest to fend off a kick to his ribs. In the dim light that remained of the day, he saw the man draw a dagger. He fumbled for his own.

Vision blurring like a drunk, Gui made to stand but the other man caught him in the face with his boot. Gui clutched his hand to the pain. The man picked him up by his tunic. Is this it? Confusion rang in his ears. Have I really come all this way to die like this? He cursed himself for exposing his quest to strangers as his assailant's blade inched towards his eyes. The dull thud of a blow sounded in the dark. The man groaned and fell, a dead weight on top of Gui. Someone grabbed Gui's ankles and began to drag him across the street.

Chapter Twenty-three

'Shall I come down there with you?' The ruddy face of Gaston appeared in the orange glow of the torchlight. Earlier she had tried to stop him from accompanying her, but once he understood she was intent upon returning to the chapel, he bucked her insistence. Now, as she crept over the soft crumbling earth, she was glad of his presence – an earthly companion in this Devil's realm.

'No. Stay there and keep a look out,' she called, her voice a damp echo in the catacomb.

Her stomach tightened as she approached the bodies. It would not be so awful if all that remained of them were bones – clean, anonymous bones. But tatters of skin were stretched like drying animal hide over ribs, jaws, forearms. Colourless clumps of hair sprouted doll-like from their skulls; a whisper of their living form. They had been people.

'Courage, Agnes,' she reproached herself. 'If not you, then who?'

On one side a number of bodies lay tangled in abiding embrace - the Saracens of her father's note. How did he know? They must have been fully clothed in their skin when he saw them. In front of her, afforded the small distinction of solitude, lay Margueritte de Coucy, hands folded neatly on her lap in ghostly repose. Agnes scraped at the floor with her shoe, looking for a clue, but nothing sparked in the torchlight. She would have to get down on her hands and knees before the evil of Amaury de Maintenon one more time.

'You monster,' she whispered, trying to weave the hook of hatred through the eye of her task as the rich, fertile soil oozed through her fingers.

'Have you nothing to tell me?' She asked of the dead.

Margueritte still had her teeth. Good, strong teeth. But there was a fractured indent in her skull - the tell-tale sign of a blow. Some plague, thought Agnes. *Help me, my friend.* She wasn't sure how she was going to do it, but she knew she had to touch the remains. A prayer came spontaneously to her lips as she fanned her hands over the earth.

Let	nothing	disturb	you,
Let	nothing	frighten	you,
All	things	are	passing	away:
God		never		changes.

Patience obtains all things

Straight away she saw it. Dulled by the earth and the hand of time, it had no lustre but she could tell it was a gem. Muttering an apology she slid her hand underneath Margueritte to retrieve the tiny object; an emerald encased in a silver heart. She held her palm to the torchlight above. It looked as though it had been part of a charm bracelet, or a necklace. *Thank you*. She crossed herself, then turned as though guided by an unseen hand towards the others.

'What's that you say?' Gaston's voice boomed, too earthly to make her jump.

'Nothing. I was talking to myself,' she called up. 'I think I've found something.'

'Be quick now. I'm getting the creeps up here.'

'Just a moment more.'

Her eyes were well adjusted to the cavern now. There were five bodies that she could see distinctly. But they did not have the robust frame of Margueritte. No, these small, bird-like bones were the remains of slighter creatures. Children, sold to a demon in a strange land with no one to protect them. How frightened they must have been so far from home. Just like her baby. She bit down hard on the inside of her cheek. If I cry now, she thought, I will never be able to stop. The world will crack open and I will drown. Then this task will never be done and these poor souls will never have justice.

One of the young ones had a leather thong wound around their finger. Agnes followed the thread through the puzzle of limbs. It was too dark to see where it went, so she pulled gingerly and the mass of bones began to slide. She stifled a cry. At the end of the string there was a fragment of parchment. The edges, thin as a flake of ash, crumbled under her touch, but where the skin was better preserved a faint, foreign script could still be made out. She unwound the leather strip from the child's finger.

'You are with God now.'

Right at that moment she could not believe their God was different to hers. God of the dispossessed and the damned. God the Redeemer and the Judge. One day the man who did this will know Your law, she thought. Then she tugged on the rope that hung down from the hatch above, and the ox-strong arms of Gaston heaved her up, up, up towards the clear night sky.

Agnes broke the film of that winter ice with her fist and plunged her hand into the water, rubbing the little charm vigorously between her fingertips. A true cleansing. Next she polished the silver heart with a piece of leather until it gleamed as it must have done when Margueritte de Coucy first received it. A gift from her parents, Agnes was almost certain. Something her mother would recognise immediately.

'Come inside before the cold gets to your chest.'

'I'm coming.'

Agnes watched her breath blossom on the frozen air. It was mid winter and the muddy fields were hardened with a crust of ice. January was the month when the nobles sat before their great fires and feasted St Agnes's day. Martyred as a child, St Agnes was the patron of virgins. And violated women. Etienne was born two days before her feast. What gift will you bring me this year, my saint? Twelve years ago you brought me and Gui our son. I cannot believe you won't see him returned.

Her cheeks burned as she stepped back inside the hut. The smoke and tallow were a comfort now. Inside the old lady was shifting through a sack of barley. Her sight too worn to see the blackened ears, she rubbed her thumb and forefinger against the husks, head cocked as though listening for the blighted ones.

'The winter has hardened you as it does a sapling,' she said to Agnes.

Agnes squatted beside her, patted the rheumy hand.

'Not the winter,' she said, opening her palm to reveal the polished gem. 'The chance to stop him.'

'I wish I had the words to stop you,' she said.

'I know you do, *ma petite grandmère*. But these are people who can help us. Just think of it. If he is brought to justice you would be free.'

The old woman tutted. 'You dream as only the well born can.'

Agnes took the linen pocket she had stitched and dropped the gem inside. The note she would include in the parcel was already written in her head. Although there were feathers aplenty with which to fashion a quill, she had no way to get the ink and parchment. A local priest came for odd Offices in the nearby village, but peasants could not approach him for writing tools, and Agnes knew better than to trust an unknown clergyman.

In order to procure what she needed she would have go to the town of Maintenon itself. There she would write to Margueritte's mother in the hope that the bond of motherhood would ignite the fellowship she needed – and with it the weight of a noble house powerful enough to fall upon Amaury de Maintenon. She would offer Lady Yolande a rendezvous near Chartres. In the town, she had a better chance of being anonymous. It was also nearer to the safety of her godmother's cottage, where she would then go and wait. Wait to see if St Agnes would bless her with the only gift that mattered.

Chapter Twenty-four

'Etienne.'

Etienne opens one eye. A hexagon of sunlight twinkles through the shutters on the floor before him. Drifting through the corridors of half-sleep, he considers the honeycomb of light. Yossef once told him the Mohammedans use the hexagon to represent Heaven.

'Etienne!'

He shuts his eye.

'Come on. We have to collect the water.'

Etienne can tell from the singsong in the voice that it belongs to Alberto.

'Not yet,' he mumbles. 'They haven't called dawn prayers yet.'

'Any minute,' Alberto insists. 'Anyway, it's Thursday.'

Etienne sits up and rubs his head with both hands, scuffing off the fog of sleep as the first notes of the *Adhan* break open the morning.

'So it is,' he beams.

Thursday is his favourite day. On Thursday it is his turn to go to the markets with the men from the kitchens. Friday is a day of prayer for the Mohammedans, so the streets are always brimming with activity the day before as people prepare for their holy day. It is the only time when Etienne is allowed outside the palace grounds, under the eye of the governor's entourage, to view the many sights of this strange land. The city is vast. Its streets are so busy that it isn't possible to move without bumping the shoulder of another man.

Etienne is certain that in the bazaars of Cairo it is possible to buy anything you want on this earth. There is the tentmakers' street where walnut-skinned men sit cross legged, half hidden behind bold geometries of fabric, then the shaded rows of spice merchants with warming dusts of cinnamon that tickle his nose. Next they pass the *chandeliers*, whose brass lamps and braziers give a cosy glow to the tight, dark thoroughfares. Weaving through it all, like a unifying thread of the finest silk, are the sweet vendors, carrying trays of sugar-spun pastries, little balls of almond paste, pastel squares of softest marzipan. The sight of them makes Etienne's fingers itch, and his soul longs to be free of the hawk eye of Abubakr who would most certainly notice if he stole one, even if the vendor didn't.

They buy flour, beans, oil and chickens tied together by the legs that squawk and peck and shit everywhere. By midday the carts are fully laden and the gang heads back to the main *souq* for their final errands before the long walk back to the palace for the next part of the day. The afternoon is better even than the dizzying temptations of the market, for is also the day the maidservants go to launder the robes. After lunch Etienne has to polish the silver plates, and if he lingers on that job long enough, but not so long as to make Abubakr suspicious, he can catch the girls returning through the portcullis opposite which he sits, shining the plates, bowls, trays and goblets until he can see his face in them.

The beautiful Greek girls always come through the gates last. He has often watched them as they approach, crisp piles of laundry on their heads, talking and laughing until they get to the gate. Then they put a couple of paces between themselves and their faces falls into their usual, hard-to-read expressions. Etienne thinks the one called Adamadia is prettiest. He is sure that if he can get to meet her outside the gates, then he will be able to make her laugh just like she does with her friend.

He is fantasising about what he will say to Adamadia when his attention is turned by a face in the crowd. A young man, a European slave, arrives at the tailor's. Although Etienne recognises the chestnut curls and the square shoulders, he can't quite believe it. He stands staring, just to make sure his eyes are not deceiving him, even though he knows from the excited leaps of his heart that they are not. It is Daniel.

From behind his pile of newly darned clothing, Etienne peeps his head out to make sure Abubakr isn't around. He looks briefly skywards in a silent prayer. He isn't totally certain one of the others won't see turn him in for talking to a stranger but what he does know for sure, is that God doesn't make accidents like this for no reason.

'Hey! Daniel!' he hollers.

The young man turns.

'How are you?' says Etienne, throwing a glance behind.

Daniel's eyes are wide with surprise – or is it suspicion? 'Etienne,' he says a little too flatly.

Etienne pauses, thrown by the other boy's lack of enthusiasm. Although only a couple of months have passed, he looks older. His back is straight and he moves with the same languid grace of the youth who left the Fairs at Lendit. Once he is up close though, Etienne can see there is something far away looking about him, as though he has decided that it is better to stare at the horizon.

'I feared for you,' Etienne says, hoping Daniel isn't still angry with him for leaving him lying there in the slave market dirt. 'I'm sorry I couldn't help.'

Daniel dismisses his apology with a shake of his head.

'You are one boy, what could you do?' He smiles his wide, familiar smile. 'And besides, I have been blessed. Allah is merciful.'

'Allah?'

Daniel nods vigorously and Etienne realises that the distant look in his eyes is the sheen that separates Mohammedan and false believer.

'Allah sent my master to the slave market that day. A Mamluk warrior in need of a manservant. He saw me fight and took me away with him. I

153

realised then that the Christian God had enslaved me and I converted to my master's faith that evening.'

'I see.' Etienne scuffs his sandal in the dirt as the giddy joy evaporates. He was so pleased to see his friend alive, he was sure it was a sign – whatever mistakes they made had been forgiven. One by one, God would reunite them and they would find a way out together. Now his shoulders sink with disappointment. His friend after all, is still lost.

'Have you heard news of the others?' Etienne asks.

'I saw Jocelyn and Marc after the market…'

'Where did they go?'

'I'm sorry.' Daniel shakes his head. 'The men who took the boys did not look like good men.'

'What do you mean?'

'My master said they were heading south, where they take the cheaper slaves to sell again. For hard labour.'

A shock of panic surges through Etienne. 'South? Where?'

'We can do nothing.'

Etienne furrows his brow, trying to understand who this version of Daniel is.

'But if we know where they have gone we must try and help them,' he says, agitated.

The young man before him just shrugs. 'There was another,' he says with a sigh, almost as if he is offering Etienne a consolation prize. 'The other day, as I took my master's blades to the Smithy I saw a white boy. He was standing outside the Church of the Copts. I had no time to linger but he was shouting out.'

'Did you see who it was?' Etienne rises up onto his tiptoes in excitement, craning for a flicker of his old friend in the gentle, brown eyes.

'You know there has been a Christian preacher here. A famous monk come from Rome to convert the Sultan?'

Etienne is bursting to interrupt Daniel's diversion, but there is something about the stature of this slave-soldier in training that stops him.

'I think the boy was speaking of this monk. Anyway,' says Daniel, 'he looked an awful lot like your friend Jean.'

Etienne's heart nearly leaps out of his chest. 'Jean? But he…I saw him go under the water.'

'It looked just like him,' Daniel repeats, casting an eye to the street. 'Look, I have to go now but I come to this tailor once a week on a Thursday.'

'Where is the Church of the Copts?' Etienne shouts as Daniel strides away, but his old companion's reply is lost to the call to prayer.

Etienne, realising how he has tarried, races back to where the others are waiting. As he flies past the stalls, his mind is a flurry of questions. Is there any chance that the reason God put him in Daniel's path today is because the preacher boy he saw really *is* Jean? How he is going to find out? And, perhaps most pressingly of all, if it is Jean, how will he be able to persuade Daniel that they have to try and find all their other friends as well?

*

Alberto is slouched in the shade of the wall of their hut. He is on his own, but Etienne can tell he is biting his tongue. The rest of the household is silent in the warmth of the mid afternoon sun, their lunch consumed and their prayers said.

'What have you been doing?'

'Nothing,' Etienne grunts.

Alberto pats the ground beside him. 'Take a few moments. In my country this is the time for rest.'

'Not in mine,' Etienne says grumpily.

'Ah but we are closer to mine. Besides, it is getting hot now. You wait, soon the spring will arrive and it will be even hotter than you can imagine...*Mama!*' He flicks his wrist as though he is pulling it back from a scalding pot.

Etienne sits down. Alberto rattles on about his country - the afternoon sleep, the fish in the market in the morning, the lush fruit lying in the road just waiting to be eaten. Etienne knows what is coming next.

'And the girls. Aiy!' He flicks his hand again, pauses and lets Etienne's silence fill the space between them before he says, 'So, why you not talk to that Greek girl this afternoon, eh? You know she likes you. Maybe you don't like girls?'

Etienne knows the goading won't stop until he reacts. If that is what he wants, so be it. He jumps up, ensuring Alberto's foot is under his heel, and pushes with all his weight.

Alberto shoves Etienne's foot aside. Etienne responds with a kick. Alberto grabs his leg and next thing he knows they are rolling in the dust, trying to get enough distance to throw a fist.

'Hey, hey.' Yossef pulls them apart. 'What's going on, you idiots? They'll beat you if they see you fighting.'

Etienne spits the dirt out of his mouth. 'I don't care.'

'What's going on?' Giacopo arrives.

Alberto scrabbles to his feet. 'Etienne likes boys, that is what is going on.'

Etienne breaks free of Yossef's grip and plunges towards Alberto. Giacopo and Yossef try to wedge themselves between the battling pair while the perpetually teary Christophe wrings his hands, entreating them to stop.

'I'll tell you what's going on,' Etienne fumes. 'He is jealous because the most beautiful girl smiled at me and now he wants her for himself.'

'Eh, you didn't take her...' Alberto jeers.

'Because I have more important plans,' Etienne blurts, heart still pounding in outrage.

Alberto rocks with mock laughter. 'Like what?'

Etienne knows he shouldn't really say, telling anyone will just make it go wrong. But he can't help it, he is so cross with Alberto.

'Like sneaking out of here. That's what.'

Head cocked to one side Alberto frowns . 'Maybe you don't remember what we told you about how they treat run away slaves?'

'Back home I was a shepherd. We all heard stories about the lands overseas. How people made their fortunes, became someone important. I thought it was God's plan. I couldn't believe He meant for people to live like we do. Some born to be rich, some destined to die in the dirt, farming a few miserable fields for a fat nobleman. Maybe I was wrong, I don't know. But I do know this. I didn't come all this way just to become a slave for someone else. Maybe I have been lucky coming to the governor's palace, but this is not how I am supposed to spend the rest of my days.' He shrugs. 'I just know it.'

All four boys stare at him. No one says a word.

Chapter Twenty-five

Gui woke to a cool cloth on his forehead and the heady scent of jasmine oil. His chest was bound with a strip of linen.

'It was you?' he said to the green-eyed prostitute who was tending to his head.

'Who stuck your assassin? Yes.' Yalda pulled her hair free from its pin and showed the long, thin blade to Gui. 'In my profession, you must always be prepared.'

He shook his throbbing head, trying to wake from this strange dream.

'You thought I cared too much my own safety?' She pouted her generous lips. 'Of course I care. But that little blond hair boy you sent to my door told me you were going to the *Fondaco*. What am I to do?' She turned her face away from Gui, chest rising with agitated breath.

Gui forced himself up on the day bed, teeth grinding against the pain. Yalda wound a strand of hair around her finger, mouth twitching as though she were resisting the desire to speak. Suddenly she turned her head, eyes lit with conviction.

'I know the wicked souls of those who profit from the misery of children. I was very lucky that someone freed me. I can never forget that. Who am I if I cannot help another up from the same fate?' Her brow arched. 'Even if they are believers of a different book.'

Gui looked down. 'Please. I'm sorry. I didn't mean…'

'I know,' Yalda replied. 'Muslims are not supposed to enslave their fellow believers either. And yet they do. What is it your book says about money and a camel.'

Gui laughter snagged on his bruised ribs. 'It is easier for a camel to go through the eye of a needle than for a rich man to enter the kingdom Heaven.'

'Yes, that's it! Rich men. They are the same whatever faith they profess.'

'You know who my assailant was?'

Yalda wagged an elegant finger. 'No. But someone wants you to go no further.' She poured Gui a cup of warm lemon and aniseed.

Gui delved into the leg of his hose and withdrew the papyri he had managed to grab at the *Fondaco*. 'This man. This Roberto Sandolin,' he said, ordering the pages. 'Here it lists some slaves he declared to Venetian customs in his real name. Slaves from the Black Sea.'

'Are there any from your land?' She asked.

Gui scanned the documents, allowing each page to float down to the floor as he finished. 'No. All from Azov.'

'Does it say where they were sold on?'

Squinting to decipher the tiny script concertinaed at the margins of the pages, Gui hunted for a place name.

'Here. *Al Qa'hira.*'

'Cairo,' Yalda said. 'If your trader has links with the Cairo markets it's likely most of his business is done there. Further away from the Venetian administrators.' Her eyes brightened. 'Your son, how is he?'

'How do you mean? Physically?'

'Physically, yes, tall, strong? But also in the mind?' She pressed her index finger to her temple.

'He is blond, average height for his age. I think. Not especially strong but determined, resourceful,' Gui said, eyes wrinkling briefly in recollection, then falling solemn as he stared into the grave symmetry of the face before him.

'He can read?'

'He can,' said Gui.

'*Ma'shallah.*' She clapped her hands like an enthusiastic tutor. 'Then let us hope he has gone to the main market in Cairo. Sometimes the sultan and his governors take Franks to teach their own children. They select the boys and girls when they arrive. The best ones go to the bigger markets for the highest prices.'

'And the others?' Gui swallowed hard on a sip of the astringent drink.

Her eyelashes briefly covered her eyes. 'Pray to your God he is as strong as you believe.'

'I think he is. He is quick on his wits as well.' Gui rubbed at the back of his neck, reluctant to ask for more charity. Yalda anticipated him.

'When you get to the market in Cairo, you must check the ledgers. They record all the slaves sold there, the price, where they are from. A friend of mine can help you. Tariq, a eunuch. He is a free man now but he still works at the market as an administrator.'

Hands supporting his ribs, Gui tried to stand, but the stab of his wounds took the air from his lungs.

'Not yet. At least a day's rest.'

Yalda's hand glanced his arm - a gentle touch such as he might have used himself to console the ailing. For a moment Gui hovered in the sea-green eyes, the urge to respond to her beauty building like a wave inside him. The only thing he had to stop himself from being dragged into its swell was the truth.

'I was a priest,' he said. 'We are not permitted to marry but my son lived with me. And his mother.'

'That is not so rare.' Yalda raised a sculpted brow, closing her lips on a bite of sweetmeat. 'Your priests live also in my land. Who knows why they do not convert to the Greek Church and take a wife?' She paused. Gave half a smirk. 'All this nonsense about the nature of Christ.'

Gui exploded with laughter, delighting in her casual irreverence, and

158

the possibility that he could lay down his conflict so easily.

'You know he is a prophet in Islam?' Yalda shrugged. 'What difference does it really make to your church if the priests wed or not?

'Because in my land you leave your land to your first born son,' he said flatly, suddenly seized with ire at all it had cost him. 'The church does not permit priests to wed. It would lose too much land to their children.'

'And these were the people you worked for?' Yalda smiled broadly. 'I prefer my clients!'

The heat of the day was spilling in through the shutters, filling the room with a heavy stillness. Swallowing down the pain, Gui swung his feet to the floor and leant forward, taking Yalda's hand.

'You have put yourself in danger and shown me kindness. I must repay you with something.'

She leant forward to meet him, her hair brushing his cheek.

'I have all that I need,' she spoke softly. 'Let us say this is personal. It would warm my heart to see your boy returned safe to you and his mother…if she..?'

'Agnes.' Gui smiled with relief to speak her name.

Yalda nodded keenly. 'She awaits you in France?'

'She does.' Gui pressed his palms together and brought his fingertips to his brow. 'I pray.'

The feline eyes fluttered and Yalda's hands opened in prayer.

'*Alhamdulillah.*' Then, golden bracelets chinking, she reclined back onto her cushions and into silence.

*

The wind was like nothing she could remember. Surging in waves it battered the buildings and chopped at the legs of the pedlars and moneychangers, the messengers and soldiers all milling in a bottleneck outside the city gates. She had given Lady de Coucy four weeks to receive and deliberate upon her note. Now the appointed day had arrived and God had chosen to unleash his fury. *If I were a lady of a noble house I would stay at home,* she thought.

It had taken her just over half a day to walk from the cottage at Houx. Dressed in her tunic and hose, one of Gaston's woollen caps flopping over her brow, she kept mainly to the canal towpaths, as unremarkable as any bargeman's boy. Now she lingered by the well-furrowed bridge at the city's main gate and there were many more eyes to subject her to scrutiny. Her gaze stayed trained on her boots - she knew she did not have the eyes of a man. She would not be able to stay there for long.

Noon, her note said, but noon was long past. As the wind billowed at her clothes and stole her breath, she realised how fanciful was the notion that her avenging angel would arrive in the form of Margueritte's mother. *I have been a fool.* She scratched vigorously at her hip where the coarse belt was rubbing, enjoying the sharp relief of her nails and the freedom of

159

this mannish etiquette. The pale grey disk of winter sun was falling behind the cathedral. How much longer could she wait? Or, more importantly, how long would it take before she was able to tear herself away from this thread of hope?

'You walk well but your waist is too slender to be a man.'

Agnes lifted her eyes from the speaker's pointed footwear. A dark green cloak covered a velvet dress of the same colour. Well cut, elegant, but with no fur, it did not invite jealous stares. The elfin face wore its lines handsomely, kind, hazel eyes shone out from hooded lids.

'Lady Yolande de Coucy?'

'So you are Agnes.'

'Madame, I am.'

Lady Yolande nodded in approval and Agnes exhaled. The canny eyes flicked a sideways glance. 'We should move from here.'

They descended from the bridge and walked alongside the canal where the city's tanners had shuttered their riverside workshops from the weather. The punts that were ordinarily loaded with bundles of wool, hides, honey, were shackled to the bank. Marguerrite's mother stopped and pulled out the little emerald heart from her muffler.

'It is hers,' she said, voice betraying none of the emotion etched on her face. 'It was part of an earring. A betrothal gift from her father.' Lady Yolande was staring at it as though she expected it to speak. A gust of wind buffeted the pair and she clamped her fist protectively around the gemstone. Agnes could feel the weight of the other woman's heart, long submerged in a well of grief. The unaffected manner of the older woman encouraged Agnes to speak directly.

'You don't believe your daughter died of plague?'

Lady Yolande smiled at Agnes but there was no mistaking the scrutiny in her face. 'Your letter said you know where Margueritte is buried. But it did not tell me who you are.'

Suddenly Agnes's mind was racing. She had thought of little other than winning Lady Yolande's support. For a moment she stared back, adrift in the realisation that she must dredge her past once again before a stranger.

'Forgive me, Madame. There was much I feared to disclose in a letter.'

Lady de Coucy listened, composed, as Agnes began her story, but the petite face soon crumpled before the horror, her eyes glassed over with tears for the fate her daughter did not escape.

'I am sorry about your son. Some of our tenants lost children to this shepherd's crusade,' Margueritte's mother said, accepting the coarse, hemp handkerchief Agnes offered. Whatever distinction of status there had been between the women was gone.

'I never liked Maintenon,' she said stiffly. 'Margueritte's letters home, they were… There are some things only a mother can know.' She glanced down, momentarily bereft of words. 'Maintenon said she died of plague, but we were offered no chance to see her body. ' Lady de Coucy drew back her shoulders and set her jaw. 'I would very much like to have her back home.' She seemed to be throwing down a gauntlet to her years of incertitude, and Agnes allowed herself to take encouragement.

'Your husband?'

'He was on crusade with Maintenon. I am here without his knowledge.' Lady de Coucy raised a resigned brow.

'Even if you could show him Margueritte was slain?'

'He believes in honour. He is not the sort of man to open sealed boxes. I would need cast iron proof before he would even consider a fellow crusader guilty of such a thing.' She turned her head into the gusting wind, defiant. 'If I go to her what will I find?'

'There are some clothes, fragments...you may recognise them. ' Agnes spoke with Gui's soft tone of reverence. 'But the rest...'

Margueritte's mother nodded, stalwart. 'I will know if it's her,' she said. Lapsing into silence, she stared, hollow-cheeked, at the river. A gust of wind spat a plume of water at them, soaking Yolande, and she turned instinctively for the steps. Agnes could feel her chance slipping away. Her mind raced for a way to prolong the exchange.

'There are others too, young children, buried with your daughter. If you were able to alert someone, we might be able to stop him,' she blurted, willing the other woman to give her something more. 'It might help you to find some peace.'

'Young children?' Lady Yolande raised her hand to her chest. She opened her mouth to speak but no words came.

'My lady?'

Yolande looked away. Her gaze seemed fixed upon a memory as she said, 'In Margueritte's letters to me she talked of house servants. Moorish boys and girls. How often they came and went...' She sealed her fingertips over her mouth and Agnes knew she would say no more.

'Merciful Lord,' whispered Agnes. Just as Gaston had described. 'You have to stop him!' She had not meant to say the words aloud and she felt the other woman flinch beside her. The instinct to apologise for the unintended sting parted her lips, but she found she could not recant the sentiment. 'If we don't stop him...' she said quietly.

Yolande de Coucy studied Agnes. Her face seemed aged. Will that face be mine ten years gone? Agnes thought. A child lost, the will for justice ebbed too far from reach. There was a moment in the silent exchange that followed when Lady Yolande's eyes seemed to catch fire, and Agnes thought she had changed her mind. All at once she straightened her back, business-like, and said simply, 'Madame Agnes, if there were any way for justice to be done, please believe me when I say it would be.'

Agnes tried to smile as they reach the road, but as she did she felt her lips tremble and she pressed them shut. Lady Yolande withdrew her hand from her muffler and folded it over Agnes's forearm.

'If you hoped for more, I am sorry,' she said.

Agnes managed to reply, 'My godmother has a little dyer's cottage on the bank of Eure, on the Courville side of the town. If you are able to help...I will be there.'

Yolande halted abruptly as though she had forgotten something, and said, 'I won't forget you, Agnes Le Coudray.' Then, Margueritte's mother nodded grimly, and Agnes fancied she was thinking that she had not done as much as she ought.

*

Agnes found her godmother's grave at the back of the little cottage half-covered by a mulch of leaves. Someone had laid a boulder and scratched a simple cross upon it. She knelt and brushed away the debris, closing her eyes as Marie's copper ringlets filled her vision, bouncing gaily in defiance of a life that had delivered as many cruel blows as it had kindnesses. If she had any tears left to cry, Agnes would shed them for the woman whose kindness shielded her when the world was baying for her blood. But she did not. All she had is was the numb exhaustion of someone who had walked more miles than she could ever count only to find her final refuge was a desolate and forgotten past, her only companions ghosts. All that was left now was survival. Will there be no one left at the end? she asked of the woman beneath the earth.

The room where Marie lived was coated with dust and leaves, long vacated.. From the accumulated dust and cobwebs, it looked to Agnes as though it had been several months since there had been anyone living there. A three-legged pot stood in the hearth with two clay bowls. There were three wooden vats and a stirring ladle in the eaves where Marie fixed her dyes. Apart from fabrics, succumbed to damp, her tools had been left as they were - a shrine to her godmother's endeavour.

It was near dark and there was no mattress in the house, no blanket. Agnes knew she must find a firesteel if she was to save herself from freezing. Tomorrow she could find some hawthorn for tea, set a trap, scrape at the earth where Marie grew her vegetables. Perhaps she would find some beets. The firesteel and flint were tucked inside the dry-stone oven with a pair of bellows. Agnes gathered some twigs and the driest leaves she could find and sparked a flame in the upstairs hearth. The room filled with the smell of burning dust and smoke from the part-blocked flue. Another job for the morrow. All she could do was hope she had pulled away enough debris to stop it catching fire.

It crossed her mind that the smoke might alert someone to her presence. She would have preferred to wait until morning when she could investigate the woods, but she had no choice - it was too cold to forgo the fire. She curled up as tight as she could. There was nowhere else she could go and more importantly, this was the place she had told Margarida to send Gui and Etienne to, if ever they found their way back to her aunt's hearth. Gui, she knew, would not return alone.

Chapter Twenty-six

Etienne hasn't slept since the night before his escape. Too scared to steal, he hasn't eaten anything other than some stale bread and a rancid onion. He has spent the best part of the morning hiding among the market stalls, making sure he doesn't linger anywhere long enough for someone to notice him. He needs to find Daniel. As much as his friend's strange, far away stare troubles him, Etienne can't quite believe the old Daniel isn't in there somewhere, waiting for the right amount of hope and good fortune to throw off the circumstances the new Daniel decided to accept. The young man who kept them all together and led them with such calm can't be lost. He just needs to find the right moment.

Etienne winds his way through the market's labyrinth with an air of business. By early afternoon the canvas awnings trap the day's heat. It's stifling. His mind turns to what he is going to eat. The fruit and vegetable stalls are closing now the sun has peaked, so he heads to the nearest square. There are always some good bits that get thrown away at the end of trading. He wanders along the channel between the vendors and their carts, selecting his target. Squeezed in between two well-manned stalls packed with bright citruses, plump squash and shiny legumes, is a wizened old man who sells only cucumber and tomatoes. If he can find some curd, there is a meal.

'You risk too much.'

The voice makes Etienne jump. He spins round to see Daniel, a pail of water balanced on his head and a thick length of rope in his hand.

Etienne beams. 'I went to that church to find Jean but…'

'If they find you a beating will not be the worst of it.' Daniel heaves the pail from his head onto the ground. Etienne can tell immediately from the grave look on his face that this isn't the right time.

'I don't care,' says Etienne defiantly. 'We all came here together and now that we have found each other things will get better. Can you not see? I know you do. I know you can't think it is an accident. Out of all the places in the city we found each other. There must be a way for us to find the others too. We can't just leave them to… suffer.'

Daniel takes the giant coil of rope from his arm and sits.

'Etienne, I know you have a bold heart, that you want to believe in miracles. But you have to understand you have been lucky. Very lucky. You have no idea what you are risking.'

Rivulets of sweat run down Daniel's brow. 'Curse this heat.' He wipes his face with his hand and laughs, and for a moment Etienne sees a spark that is not only his old companion but the ardent, kind eye of Father Gui. Immediately he is cast back to his lost home. Out of nowhere, he remembers Father Gui's gentle mocking when his mother's cake didn't rise. Unexpected tears sting his eyes. Daniel places a warm hand on his shoulder.

'I am sorry that this has befallen you,' he says. 'But stay strong and you will be blessed. This is all Allah's will.'

'Allah's will? I know you don't believe that. Why won't you help?'

Daniel throws an anxious look around. 'Be careful with what you say, Etienne. It is foolish to speak like that around here. I'm sorry. What you wish for is…it just isn't possible. The sooner you accept that and make the best of it the better it will be.' Daniel falls into silence and Etienne can sense his resignation. The cross weighted on his shoulder that he can no longer see.

'I can try and help you get a job with my master if you want, but you must promise not to run away.'

And with that Daniel stoops down and hoists up his burdens, muscles bulging as he walks off into the glaring sunlight.

'Wait!' Etienne cries out, but the Mamluk's manservant does not turn around.

'Daniel!' he screams. His insides are squirming. He feels utterly bereft, like a small child who looks up from his game to find he is alone. He had convinced himself that Daniel and he were going to find a way out of this together. He has no plan for this - adrift, rudderless in this teaming, hostile city. Strange brown faces stare at him as they pass by, and his ears ring with the harsh, guttural tones of the Arab bargain hunters.

'We can't just abandon them,' he sobs into his hands. 'We just can't.'

His head feels so heavy now he can hardly hold it upright. He feels sick with hunger and with fatigue. Behind the tailors' shops there is a big pile of off-cut material. It calls to him, an enticing refuge from this sea of disillusion. With barely a glance to check if the coast is clear, he nestles down into it until he can no longer see out.

Drifting off to the buzz of the day's trade, Etienne falls into a daydream about stealing rose perfume. He will steal a bottle and send it, unmarked, to Adamadia. She will know it is from him, of course. He pictures her face, broad with delight, hand on her racing heart. It will be the best and most daring thing she has ever heard of. News will pass around the governor's palace quicker than a forest fire. The boys will be so jealous. They will do their best to pretend it isn't a big thing, but secretly they will be wishing it had been them with such courage. It will be the talk among the servants of the palace for years to come, for sure.

Cocooned in the folds of cotton and linen, his eye catches on one of the patterns cushioning him. Black, red and orange flowers swirl against a white background, intertwining, then separating back into their distinct forms. Round and round they wheel, tumbling through the drowsy corridors of Etienne's mind, until the pattern becomes a mosaic on the palace floor, the one in the main reception hall with long vines wrapped around a hunting scene. A perfectly manicured pair of feet pad silently over the tiny tiles, and then, there is only the deepest sleep.

*

'*Seize him!*'

Etienne jolts awake. He can hear angry voices approaching and he knows their wrath is directed at him. He jumps up from his makeshift bed, fighting the urge to look back and see how close they are. What an idiot to fall asleep right there in the market where the servants of the governor's household come every day. Curse it. Curse everything, he thinks as he scrabbles out of the fabric tendrils. Please God, Please Allah, don't let them get me.

He scuttles from the rows of market stalls where there are too many locals willing to stick out their hand and grab hold of a runaway slave for the governor's pleasure. Across the open ground by the Coptic church and into the maze of backstreets that make up the old medina he flees, ever more like a rabbit trying to bob and twist its way out of the fox's path.

He runs and runs. His lungs burn, his tongue aches for water and his legs feel as flimsy as a newborn foal. Dimly aware that he has no idea where he is, he takes each turn as it presents itself, skipping over doorsteps and the legs of beggars, scampering over low walls, through courtyards and even through a lean-to hut that turns out to be someone's house. It is only when he rounds a corner, heart strained to breaking point, and sees the same sycamore and the wide open square, that he realises he has run himself in a circle back to the church of the Copts.

Both the men chasing him are waiting. One is the eunuch who looks after the governor's harem and the other is Abubakr's right-hand man, a stick of a man with big horse teeth who sprays spit when he speaks. Through the sweaty film that stings his eyes, Etienne makes out a third man who has caught up with them; Abubakr himself. His eyes dart in every direction. There must be a way out, an exit not covered. *Please God, show me which way to go.*

'The love of Christ needs no sharp blades.'

Panic coursing in his veins, Etienne almost doesn't hear the voice straining above the bustle of the square. It is only as he hovers in indecision, his breath catching up with him, that his surroundings cease to be a blur and he realises he is listening to the French of the Chartrain. He spins round. Despite his predicament, the men closing down on him, the inevitable capture and beating, he can't run now. He screams out.

'*Jean! Over here! Jean!*'

The small figure standing before the church ceases his sermon and looks over.

'It's me. Etienne. Over here!'

The eunuch arrives between Etienne and the French preacher. Etienne sizes up a route. Maybe I can dodge him, he thinks. God will clear a path. He races towards the church. All three of the governor's men are tightening the circle they have made around him, shouting out to each other.

'Jean! It's me!' Etienne yells.

The preacher peers at him as he draws closer. Etienne sees his lips move in a whisper. The eunuch is upon him now. Etienne ducks his first lunge, and runs wide. The eunuch makes another grab for Etienne from behind. Etienne thrashes and writhes but the other men are upon him too. He is about ten feet from the boy now - the withered leg, those pale grey eyes. His heart soars and despite his hopeless predicament he begins to laugh.

'The governor's palace!' Etienne screeches as they drag him away. 'Come to the palace. It's me. Etienne. Remember?'

The last thing Etienne sees as he is hauled away is the diminutive figure with the translucent eyes raise a cautious hand and make the sign of the cross.

*

Etienne doesn't know what is worse, the pain of the beating itself or the example that is being made of him in front of all the other boys. They all feel sorry for him, he knows that, but he also knows that from now on, no matter what happens, they will never be able to look him in the eye without remembering this moment. Even if he ever manages to escape again and even if Adamadia comes with him, there will always be this. The moment he failed. Failed in front of all these people.

When he was small, he had been playing with some older village boys and as he chased one of them into his house, the boy had slammed the door on his hand. It was an accident, but he knew from the searing hot pain and the blood smearing the doorframe that it was bad. He had been so desperate for them not to think of him as a cry baby that he bit down on his cheek so hard it took weeks for the ulcer to heal. He had managed it though, all the way back through the village and across the field to his house. He opened the door, still chewing on his mouth and telling himself to be brave. Then his mother had looked up and there was something about her face, the way she was looking at him. 'Oh my poor baby, what have you done?' He couldn't help it, he had started to sob.

And now, as he is released from the whipping post, he prays to God not to cry as he is led back along the corridor lined with the pity-filled faces of his friends. But all he can think of is his mother's face, so sad for him. She is the only person in the world who has ever felt his sadness as her own. Who probably ever will. He bites down hard on the inside of his cheek, just as he had done then, but he cannot stop the tears squeezing from his eyes. He clamps his lips shut, determined not to make any sound, so maybe people won't remember it so badly.

Chapter Twenty-seven

The basket weavers' stalls were on the corner of the square, shaded by the same sycamore that gave shelter to a Coptic church. Gui gave a wry smirk. Is this how God answers a beggar on his knees? He thought as he crossed over to the shop fronts, their thresholds covered with nimbly-wound trays, spiral-lidded pots, loop-handled infant cribs.

He was expecting a small man-boy, but Tariq the eunuch was ageing, and he carried a perfectly rounded pot belly on the jewelled waist of his pantaloons. It was hard to picture him as a friend of Yalda, sipping mint tea in an elegant harem, but circumstance often made unlikely allies. When Gui told him who he was, the man was polite but nervous. His keen smile belied by the way his shoulders drew away from Gui and his eyes refused direct contact, preferring to hover at the entrance of his stall where a young boy sat braiding long reeds into baskets.

Tariq worked as a clerk in the main slave market, he explained. Hundreds of slaves came through the market, all documented; the weight, height, provenance and condition of the merchandise, the price paid and the name of the owner. If Gui's son has passed through the market between October and November as he believed, then his sale would be recorded in one of the ledgers.

At a cost of the remainder of Gui's coins, Tariq said he would leave the door to the administrator's room unlocked that night and the ledgers on his desk in the far left hand corner of the room. Guards patrolled the Treasury next door, as money was held there overnight. It would be to Gui's skill to take what he needed undetected. The ledgers, of course, were in Arabic. Gui could tell from his apologetic shrug, that the eunuch was offering no further assistance.

Gui meant to head directly back to his room after the meeting but the ground of Coptic church, sticky with sap from the tree, halted him. Pausing, he could not help but wonder at the interior, the cool, silent wood. Outside there was a boy bent down to drink at the fountain. His skin was light brown. Gui narrowed his eyes against the light trying to determine if the skin was naturally brown or a white skin, darkened by the sun. Still stung by his encounter with the young European slave, he watched as the boy wiped his mouth and hobbled on.

Hovering by the church's porch, Gui wondered if someone would hear confession. Did they hold the same Hours as he once had? His feet felt glued to the stone. The power of consolation wrestled with shame at his appearance. The fine velvets of Zonta's clothes were worn and dirtied from his journey. He looked exactly as he was – a world-weary outlaw with nothing in his purse and nowhere left to turn. How different a welcome might he receive were he to step through the threshold as a cleric of Rome? He pulled his hand over his face, admonishing his vanity, and shouldered open the door.

Cool air and frankincense bathed his face. It roused the most terrible longing to be standing in his church at Montoire, rosary in his hand, knowing for certain that there was redemption in suffering. He approached the iconostasis. It was decorated with the abstract geometry of foreign meditations, not the unforgiving eyes of ancient martyrs. First he knelt, then he touched his forehead to the ground at the crossing.

'Christ. God incarnate. Pardon this sinner.'

The relief that soaked through him felt like a sin. He felt like a drunkard, lips touching a long-denied draught. Heart cramped with conflict, he rose to find himself under the gaze of a priest whose eyes looked right through to everything - the black eyes of the ancient martyrs.

'What are you seeking, brother?'

Gui put his hand to his head as he stood, dizzied by the great, domed vaults, the vibrant arcs of coloured light at the windows. For a moment he thought he might vomit.

Then he said, 'My name is Gui. I am an ordained priest of the Holy Catholic Church. I was a Canon of the Cathedral of Chartres, exiled to a small parish because I freed a woman, falsely accused of heresy. She is the mother of my son. For ten years I lived in the betrayal of my parish as I did of my own family. My son joined a crusade and has been brought here by slavers. I don't know if I have forfeited the salvation of my soul but I cannot, will not, see my son forfeit his for my crimes. If it is anyway in your power to assist me in this, then I beg you now, in the name of God's love, do so.'

The priest listened unblinking as Gui told his tale - his grim discovery of the slave ship at Corsica, how he chased it to Alexandria, his encounter with Yalda and the eunuch who directed him to the slave markets. For what seemed like an eternity the priest stared, saying nothing, until Gui became aware that the only thing reflected in those pitch black eyes was the guilt he harboured in his own soul - his own worst judgement of himself. Once Gui had seen his devil, the priest spoke.

'Return here with the ledgers from the market tonight. I will read you the Arabic.'

Gui fortified his stomach with a carafe of date wine, arriving at the market in the long hours of night. A pair of guards stood outside the treasury entrance just as Tariq had said. Every half an hour, one of them made a tour of the building. In time, with his colleague mid-way through his tour, the remaining guard sloped off for an inevitable piss.

Walking swift and light, Gui entered the building, footsteps echoing through the corridors. The auction room with its rows of benches and horseshoe dais shimmered empty and innocuous in a flood of moonlight. It could have been a theatre. Time pressing at his chest, Gui slipped behind the dais. There were two corridors. To the right were the administrator's offices, the airy salons where the wealthy were tended to away from the sweaty chaos of the main market. To the left, a narrower passageway wound back to the tradesmen's entrance; the pitch-dark corridor through which the human merchandise was funnelled for sale.

Gui paused, momentarily transfixed by the gloom. He reached out to the wall for support, fighting the imperative to inch his way along that corridor so he might walk on the same dirt as his son and inhale the same fetid air, just as he had on that boat at Corsica. Although he could barely admit it to himself, there was an unquiet corner of his heart that needed to check his son was not still cowering in some filthy, forgotten room, waiting for the hand of God to deliver. Both hands pressing against the wall, he let his head hang down heavy on his neck. Etienne is gone from here and so will your chance to find him if you don't hasten, he scolded, then turning his back on his guilt, he stole towards the offices.

The door to the administrator's room was unbolted, as the eunuch had promised. Gui grabbed all four of the hide-bound ledgers on the desk. Unbolting the wooden shutters, he threw the ledgers out in front of him and was gone before the guard came round to complete another tour.

The Coptic priest flared a torch over the table and searched the scrolls with his Hellfire eyes.

'This one.' Gui's intuition guided him to the tenth month of the previous year. Lists of names. Endless lists. Etienne, if he were even among them, would be near impossible to identify. Gui watched over the priest's shoulder as he read out the descriptions one by one, and shook his head to each. When they had done it a hundred times over, the bell sounded out some minor Hour of the night.

'Go to your prayers. Please,' he said to the priest. 'I have seen enough to recognise the words I need.'

Gui scrutinised every entry with burning eyes, as desperate to read a description that might match Etienne's as he was terrified. *November.* He tried to remember where he had been. Aboard a boat? Already in Alexandria looking up at the stars, wondering if Etienne and Agnes were seeing the same heaven?

He turned another sheet and recognised one word, copied out a dozen times - *Origin : France.* His hand shook as he scanned, right to left, finger wavering beneath the ornate cursive. Could it be? His heart was thudding high in his chest even before he finished reading: *Male, Twelve years, Blond, Good health, Literate.* Gui closed his eyes and rested his face on the page. The pulse at his solar plexus told him without doubt it was his son.

'Etienne.' He re-traced the entry with his fingertips as though he were touching his child. *Good health.* His eyes moistened. The dreamed-of euphoria at proof of his son's life locked fingers with the dread fist of all the cruelty he had witnessed. He looked back down at the ledger, needing to reassure himself it was as he thought. Two more words jumped from the page: *12 dinar.* He reeled backwards, body shaking, and for the first time in his life, he invoked the Devil.

The pressure of the priest's hand on his shoulder made him flinch.

'I am so ashamed I let this happen,' he whispered. 'He doesn't even know I am his father.'

The priest peered over the ledger, then turned his eyes onto Gui. There was no judgement but neither was there pardon.

'He was sold to the slave master in the household of the governor Al Kamil here in Cairo,' he said. 'He has been lucky.'

Chapter Twenty-eight

The sun had shone in a cloudless sky, but now its rays fell below the treetops, the temperature was dropping fast. A figure hastened along the path, a shadow in the gloaming. Agnes caught the motion from the corner of her eye just as she was about to lock up for the night.

'I am Octavia, a novice with the Benedictine Sisters of Blessed Virgin at Houx,' the nun said, eyes hunting fretfully. Framed by her wimple, the timid face was still plump with youth, belying the austerity of her black and white uniform.

Agnes's heart skipped. 'Near Maintenon?'

The girl nodded quickly, as though acknowledging some indiscretion it were better not to dwell on.

'Lady Yolande de Coucy sent me.' Retrieving a scroll from her satchel, the nun extended it stiffly; a mission accomplished.

Agnes let out an audible gasp. Weeks had gone by, rolling back the winter darkness, and she had pushed the flicker of hope that was Lady Yolande from her mind. Now though, as she heard the name again, she felt a corner of her heart lift. *I told you so.* Neat and concise, the letter was a commendation of Sister Octavia, and an thickly-veiled offer of help.

Agnes studied the girl before her. *Her menses cannot have long begun. To charge such a young girl with such a task?* Responding to the scrutiny, Octavia said,

'My sister Isobel was Lady de Coucy's chambermaid.' She gave a fragile smile, and Agnes could tell there was a story too difficult to begin.

Agnes threw a handful of camomile into the pot that swung over the hearth, and ladled out a draught for the girl. Red-raw fingers pressed around the wooden cup, the nun took a cautious sip. Eyeing her host from over the rim, she put Agnes in mind of the deer, eyes glinting in the woods, whenever she put out food for them. How still she had to stand, how patient, before they would trot forward.

'If anyone knew about this place, I wouldn't still be here,' Agnes reassured her. 'There's a forester nearby, a good man. He keeps an eye out. You've walked a long way. Please, sit.'

Octavia lowered herself reluctantly onto the chair by the fire, knees knocked together as though honouring a half-recalled etiquette lesson.

'My Lady asked me also to give you this,' the nun whispered into her satchel, rummaging until she found a chunk of bread wrapped in cloth. Carefully, she picked apart the hard crust to reveal a bundle of scrolls. The girl turned up the corners of her mouth as she handed the package over, but her eyes held an apology. Agnes felt the cauldron of dread stir, thick as tar, in her belly.

The first two documents were extracts from a ledger of household accounts, for the purchase of Moorish house slaves. They were dated the summer of the previous year. Agnes paced backwards and sat on a wooden chest:

"One boy, two girls, 12 years, 8 years, 10 years, Mohammedan, 20 livres; three girls, Mohammedan, 25 livres."

The sober lines of Yolande de Coucy's face appeared in her mind's eye. *Moorish boys and girls. How quickly they came and went.* It was him. Amaury de Maintenon. Agnes looked over at Octavia, now sitting on her hands, eyes to the ground. There's worse, thought Agnes.

The next sheet was a remittance for goods transported overseas for the sum of five thousand, six hundred livres tournois. Appended to it was a letter in the same hand. Agnes's heart gathered pace before her eyes had even met the page.

"Amaury, Lord of Maintenon and Chatelain of Gazeran, Greetings. I am detained in the Occitaine but have now secured a fair contract for the transport of the shepherds' merchandise from Marseille overseas…"

Her eye sank to the end of the document. The signature was an elaborate design of interlocking circles but the name it spelled out was so well known to her that she needed no scribe to decipher the clerical flourish: Bernard de Nogent.

Her chest felt as though it were being crushed. She stared at the letter. *Five thousand, six hundred livres tournois…. transport of the shepherds' merchandise from Marseille.* She flicked back to Maintenon's ledgers: *slaves.* Her mind didn't need to make the reckoning. The documents shook in her hand. The goods from Marseille were shepherd boys, sold as slaves. Hundreds of them. Dear God. Etienne.

She clapped her hand over her mouth. Her stomach heaved. Another convulsion and the acid rose up.

Octavia sat, her arms hovering, readying for action, unable to take it.

'Madame Agnes?'

Water ran, silent, from Agnes's eyes. She wiped a bile-covered hand on her apron. Picking up the parchments now fanned out across the floor, she stared at them as though they were a keepsake. 'My son,' she breathed. 'They sold my son.'

'Merciful lord.' Octavia crossed herself.

Agnes tried to stand, but her gut felt as though she had ingested poison, forcing her to remain doubled over. Through the tunnel of pain she felt an invisible presence cloaked around her, shrouding her from the world. 'Gui,' she mouthed. His face appeared, exactly as it was when he left her on her sick bed outside Marseille. Dark, serious eyes that were trying to shut out the fear. He knew it, she thought. He knew Etienne had been sold. 'Can you bring him home?' she implored the empty space.

'There now, Madame Agnes,' the girl consoled. Crouching at her side,

Octavia laid her her small, child-like palm cautiously on Agnes's arm. Awkward in such intimacy, but insistent. The wimple-framed face squinted with concern. 'There now. 'You must drink a small sip of this,' Octavia said resolutely, in imitation of her Abbess.

The command brought Agnes back into the world. She blinked. I am still here. She took the tiniest sip of camomile as the child-nun instructed, then exhaled through her mouth; a deep, shuddering breath that carried away some of the shock. Nothing has changed, she told herself. Except now you know. Once she was sure another torrent of bile would not erupt from her stomach, she said to Octavia, 'Where did Lady Yolande get the documents?'

Octavia gave a small shrug. It was not a denial.

'Does anyone else know you are here?' Agnes tried another way.

'No. Lady Yolande told the Mother Superior she was taking me to collect my sister's belongings.' She paused. Sensing there was more, Agnes pressed her gently.

'She came in person to tell you when your sister passed?'

The novice nodded. 'When Isobel went missing. She'd been in service with Lady Yolande for six years. She loved her. She'd never have run away. There were rumours...' Octavia's eyes flickered away. 'My lady said she'd made some inquiries, that she had an important task for me.'

Agnes steadied her hand well enough to draw another sip from the beaker.

'Rumours?'

Octavia hesitated, eyes rolling heavenward.

'Please,' said Agnes. 'If you can.'

'Isobel had been sighted...near the chateau Maintenon.'

'You know?' Agnes searched the girl's face. 'About Maintenon?'

The novice pressed her lips tight. Agnes followed her gaze to the fire. For a moment it seemed as though the hypnosis of the flames would transcend the need to speak. But it did not. The time for silence was over.

Octavia drew breath as though she were inhaling ice. 'He brings them to the woods at the back of the convent.'

Agnes exhaled audibly. The Saracens at Houx.

'Moorish girls.'

The girl nods, wordless.

'Mother Agathe tried to chase him away. She went into the village one morning...We never saw her again.'

Agnes marked herself with the cross. Girls shipped from foreign shores and slaughtered alongside the poor woman who had the misfortune of an attractive enough dowry. She rubbed her forehead, trying to comprehend how, by the incalculable Grace of God, she had been one of the lucky ones.

'The week after, he took a novice from the orchards,' Sister Octavia continued. She took a weather-chapped hand to her face.

'You saw him?'

A single nod. 'I was seeing to the hens. I hid inside the coop. But I saw.' Her knuckles whitened around her habit. 'I saw it all but I didn't say anything.'

The pain on the girl's face had Agnes searching for words of consolation, but they all clanged hollow so she held her tongue. What the girl really needed was for her to be another witness.

'When the new Mother Superior arrived it got worse. She pretends not to notice but we all have ears. We all have eyes.' She let out a tremulous sigh. 'He hunts the heathen ones through the woods at night… hunts them for sport like dogs.' Her voice broke. 'We found one once, Sister Clarissa and I. We were collecting brushwood. Naked in the woods. She was beaten so badly, her face...'

'Dear God.'

'How can it be true?' The small, plump face looked at Agnes gravely. 'Sometimes I think I have gone mad.'

'It's not you.' Agnes folded the girl's hands into hers.

'I didn't think anyone would believe me.' Sister Octavia said urgently, 'I am so frightened.' Then, before Agnes had a chance to react, she launched herself into her arms.

'You're safe here,' Agnes repeated, rocking her gently. It seemed aeons since she had held a child in maternal consolation and it made her heart burn; for the son she might never see again, for the daughter she was denied, for the children stolen from their homes and sold on foreign soil. She lifted her eyes skyward. Guide me, Mother Mary. There will be a lifetime to grieve.

Dabbing her cheeks with the sleeve of her habit, Octavia turned her face to Agnes and said, 'You are afraid of him too, aren't you?'

Agnes scrunched her eyes shut. Even now, cocooned in this dwelling, unnoticed by even the closest passers by, was fear really a better master than hatred? The thought of it made her want to scour out her insides.

'I am more afraid for my soul if I do nothing,' she whispered. 'My son joined a group of shepherd boys from the Chartraine who wished to take the cross and was taken by slavers. Maintenon's slavers.'

'The Pastoreux. I've heard talk of them. He must be brave.' Briefly, panic moulded her face - was it the wrong thing to say? 'To have joined them I mean.'

Finding a smile, Agnes nodded. 'He is that. My husband left in pursuit, but I've had no word. I don't know whether I will see either of them again. Likely as not I won't.'

She took a breath that was steady and furious. It was the first time she had allowed herself to say it aloud, express the nagging fear she had tried so many times to vanquish. How many times had it woken her in the small hours of the night, robbing her of sleep for weeks on end? Now she had exposed this terrible half thought to another, she was surprised that a river of tears hadn't come pouring from her eyes. Instead the bold, sad truth of it felt like ballast, a weight of constancy on the roiling seas of doubt.

'There is nothing more they could take from me,' she said. 'Once a mother has lost her child, what else is left? My life?' She scoffed at the thought, and a queer elation bloomed with the realisation that she was impervious to the blows of Amaury de Maintenon. Should I cower in this cottage until my hair turns white and my fingers too gnarled to work? She looked at the girl in front of her - another victim of Maintenon in her way. How many more, Agnes? How many more will you allow?

Rising to her tiptoes, she reached for the shelf where she had put her father's wooden box.

'I begged Lady Yolande to tell the Count. I found the bodies of those poor girls buried with her daughter and I begged her.' She sprang the lock on the box and gently lifted out the miniature book. 'I found this tangled up among the bodies. I believe it is the Mohammedans' holy book. Only the Lord knows how she managed to keep it about her.'

Octavia crossed herself and instinctively drew her head back. Agnes laughed gently, and, hovering her finger over the sweeping script, said, 'I remember my father telling me once the first line in it says, "There is no God but God."'

She stared into the hearth flame once more, entranced, allowing her thoughts to become one with the darting tongues. She wasn't sure where the words came from, if she was speaking to Octavia, to herself, or to God but as the words came, they were forged steel.

'I don't know what happened to change Lady Yolande's heart. Perhaps your sister's death was one too many. There is only so much blood a person can wade through. But I do know this. On my heart, and on the heart of the Virgin herself, I will do all I can to ensure Amaury de Maintenon never takes another innocent again.'

Octavia looked down. 'Would that God grant me your courage.'

'Did it not take courage to come here? A day's travel, alone. With nothing but the vague promise of an address, a monster in every shadow?'

'I was so scared,' the girl said. 'It didn't feel courageous.'

'It never does.'

Agnes smiled warmly at Octavia. 'Lady Yolande gave you no further instruction other than to come here?'

'No, Madame. Only to tell you she is ready.'

'Then she must means for me to...'

'To what?'

'To stop him.'

'But how?'

'I must ask you another courage, dear, brave, Sister Octavia. Go back to your convent. Get word to Lady Yolande. She must find word as to when the next shipment of Moorish children is arriving. Send word here via the forester. I will take you to meet him tomorrow. He will let me know. Tell the good Lady Yolande that in the name of Margueritte, your sister, and all the others who could not be saved, that I will go to that same place as bait to try and draw out Maintenon in person. Tell her that if she be so pleased, to send the bailiffs that night to my aid.'

The inflated loops of de Nogent's signature stared up at her from the pile of parchments. And if I have to face you and your dungeons too, she thought, then so be it.

*

There had not been many moments when Bernard de Nogent was sure that God loved him, but this was one. He folded away the letter, and sighed out the first lines of the *pater noster*. For weeks his scouts had scoured the roads for news. Finally, they found a suspiciously-armed wagon of vagabonds heading to the convent at Houx. Then all it had taken was one careless slip and a weak-minded local bailiff who was only a few whores and a night of gambling away from the debtor's prison. The result was a copy of an intercepted letter from a barely literate nun to Le Coudray via some hovel on the banks of the Eure that, irritatingly, appeared unoccupied.

Bliss poured through his veins. Now I have you both, he sang it softly to himself. The Le Coudray whore and, more importantly, everything she knew about Amaury de Maintenon. Judging from the sketchy details he gleaned from the poorly copied letter, it would be enough to finish him. He closed his eyes and he could see every detail:

He stands over Bishop Reginald of Chartres at his desk. The bishop's face is black as thunder as he signs over title to the Maintenon Abbey. Chartres looks up, finds a thin smile as he offers up the quill. Savouring the triumph, he adds his own signature: Abbot de Nogent. He can hardly bare the ecstasy as the man who has insulted him more times than he can recall signs away his authority to the Bishop of Rome.

The bells for Nones began to clang. Hurriedly, de Nogent locked the letter away in his drawer. Rising for the Office, he rubbed at the prick of emotion that had bloomed in the inner corner of his eye. Rome.

PART THREE – Consolamentium

Chapter Twenty-nine

There is no shade from the glare of the sun. Beyond the bastions, the palms trees in the palace courtyard are visible. Somewhere within there is a waiting salon. Shuttered in cool, marble repose, basins of rosewater awaiting those whom governor wishes to compliment. But Gui is an uninvited visitor, a supplicant to be reminded at every moment that Al Kamil is a powerful man upon whose mercy his future well being now depends.

Shadows ripple on the inside of the arches; water from the courtyard pool. Gui tries to swallow but his mouth is parched. The heat of the day and the sweat of his anxiety are trapped under the robe he has borrowed from the Coptic priest. Black dots swim before his eyes. His head, robbed of the ability to form coherent thought, feels as though it is baking in an oven. How is he now to plead for his son's life? Closing his eyes he tries to conjure up the brittle, mid-winter landscape of home; the throb of his frozen feet, the numbness of his rag-wrapped fingers as he walks home after evensong, but still the sweat runs, gluing his clothes to his body.

Eventually a dainty man dressed in a crisp, white tunic appears from behind a column and beckons him. Gui falls in behind his host, averting his eyes from the glassy waters of the pool, fearful of the urgency with which he must slake his thirst. His guide holds up a perfectly manicured hand and halts Gui before a large double door, its iron-studded hinges polished to gleam. How many servants are there in the employ of the great governor? Gui wonders. Are these sparkling doorknockers the handiwork of my son? The blood pools in his calves as once more he is left to contemplate his insignificance before the opulence of the governor's wealth.

Finally the doors open and a flood of cool air washes out from the high-ceilinged chambers. Gui can barely restrain the moan that escapes his throat as he steps over the threshold and the infernal exterior is banished behind him. Inside the reception room, latticed windows are shielded by date and citrus trees from the courtyard. A subtle scent of orange blossom perfumes the air. The floor is carpeted with an exquisite rug; floral motifs of red, white, black, green, framed by a series of ellipses and rectangular borders. Still dizzied from the heat, the pattern gives Gui the impression that it is expanding infinitely in an explosion of perfect symmetry – the mind of God, the glory of the governor. It takes several long, uncomfortable moments for him to traverse the hall to greet a second man who stands hands clasped in elegant expectation.

'I am Ibn Al Tayyib, secretary to the court.' The man speaks the French of the Île de France. 'I am told you seek information about a slave?'

'Thank you for receiving me.' Gui bows. 'I am most grateful.' A film forms on his palms and he fights the itchy compulsion to wipe them on his tunic. He knows he only has one chance to ask for his son back. A set of words that he will have no chance to reframe if they do not give him the result he needs. He draws a slow breath.

'I believe that my son, who was unlawfully taken from his mother and me, may have found his way into this household.'

Ibn Al Tayyib lets the room fill with silence. The call of exotic birds floats in from the gardens. The urge to embellish his speech compacts in a knot at the base of Gui's throat. He is making you sweat it out, he thinks. That is a good sign. Patience.

'All the members of the governor's household are purchased legitimately.' The secretary offers up the statement to Gui with open hands.

The dry tickle in Gui's throat forces a cough. 'Forgive me if I do not explain myself. I have no wish to imply that the household of the noble governor is in the business of illegitimate trade. Merely that the boy came to be at the market on account of those men engaged in such traffic.'

The other man's eyes rove in slow contemplation. 'It is true that we have acquired some boys from your lands.'

Gui's body sighs with relief. 'Then it is possible that the one I seek may be among them?'

Ibn Al Tayyib arches a thick, black brow. 'His name?'

'Is Etienne.' Gui's heart hammers to speak his son's name. The dream he has hardly dared to hope for feels within his grasp. 'I could easily identify him if you would permit me to view the boys that you have from my country?'

'It is not in my power to grant such a request.' The governor's secretary purses his fleshy lips. Gui knows he is playing a game of hazard. Keep steady. He lowers his eyes to the spiralling rug.

'But if you will be patient, I will make an inquiry as to this Etienne.'

Gui's legs feel as though they are going to buckle beneath him. All he can do is bow as the administrator turns heel and leaves him once more, a lone figure swamped by crested stone columns and an ocean of lush embroidery.

'Quick! Quick! We have an inspection,' Yossef rallies the boys.

They leap to their feet, throwing off their mid-afternoon lethargy.

'Come on. Up!' He offers a hand to Etienne. He takes it and gives Yossef a smile because he is trying to be nice. It still hurts to stand up straight, but more than the discomfort, he just doesn't feel like it. He has more duties than ever now and he is so, so tired. Everywhere he goes it seems that one of Abubakr's men is lurking, pretending to be doing something else.

181

Abubakr instructs them to form a line, then, one by one, he checks their dress is in order, their nails clean. Usually this inspection is done once a week, on Saturday. Etienne can't work out why, it being only Tuesday, they are doing it all again.

'You.' Abubakr fingers Etienne. 'Come here.'

What for? Etienne wants very badly to ask. He hasn't done anything wrong, he is sure of it. Stepping forward, everyone's eyes are upon him, exactly like when he was beaten. The only glimmer of salve for him is the knowledge that for all the trouble he has been in, he is sure that Abubakr has been in just as much. Even if it is a different sort of trouble and not the sort where you get whipped in front of all the people you know.

'You.' Abubakr beckons grimly at Christophe, who wears the same wild look of bewilderment as always. His pale hazel irises rove about his eyeballs as if he has just woken up from a dream and can't work out where he is. The slave master dismisses the rest of them with an angry flick of his hand, as though he is having to tell them for a second time, even though he isn't.

'Follow me.' Abubakr barks at the boys. Christophe begins to quiver as they file out of the servant's courtyard towards the main palace.

'Psst.' Etienne tries to engage the taciturn boy from Saintes. Christophe doesn't even turn round. He has been even less willing to talk to Etienne since the botched escape. All Etienne knows is that Christophe hasn't been on crusade or followed any shepherd boys. Shepherd boys! How stupid that sounds now. As if a shepherd could get to the Holy Land. Etienne isn't really sure how Christophe came to get sold. Whenever he broaches the subject, the boy mumbles something about errands at a port and a man who said he could become famous. Etienne figures it must be some really embarrassing mistake, maybe even more stupid than following a shepherd on crusade.

'We are both French.' Etienne shares his observation anyway.

'So what?' Christophe whispers, his cheeks reddening. It must be hard not to be able to hide it when you feel flustered, muses Etienne as Christophe swivels his eyes in just about every direction that isn't looking at him.

'Silence,' Abubakr hisses out from the front. Etienne gives a quiet sigh. No doubt that means more latrine duties for him. Latrine duties are bad anyway, but now the weather is warming it is nearly more than he can stomach. Plunging his hands into the black, fetid holes to free a blockage he has nearly thrown up his lunch more than once.

'Stop.' Abubakr raises a white-sleeved arm and his gown ripples down to reveal his bony, brown elbow.

They are told to face the doors that open out onto the gardens. From the other side of the terrace, Etienne can make out three figures silhouetted behind the shutter. Maybe someone is looking to buy French boys because they are better workers than the others Etienne thinks, even though he knows it is as untrue as it is unlikely. Maybe they need boys who can speak French for some reason. A French merchant in Cairo? It has to be better than this place. Please God let it be something good like that.

The shutters swing open and three figures step out. One is a bureaucrat from the governor's personal staff, the other the burly, tall Egyptian called Nasir - the Mamluk in charge of all the guards. The third is a man dressed in a long, black robe who sways slightly as he steps out into the bald glare of the Egyptian sky. Etienne narrows his eyes. The man is white skinned. The robe looks like a priest's, or a lawyer of some sort – has someone come to take them back on the orders of the pope? No. That doesn't explain why they haven't selected the other Christian boys.

The black-robed man squints directly at Etienne. What on earth have I done now? he thinks.

Like a rider emerging from heat haze on the horizon, at first it is just a ripple in the air. The impression sharpens as it draws nearer until, finally, it takes form. He knows that face. He knows it nearly as well as he knows his own. If he hadn't been standing in this foreign place, he would have recognised him instantly.

The governor's secretary gives a sweep of his arm. Gui steps from the cool serenity of the palace onto the terrace, caught momentarily by the fierce heat that pricks his skin. The boys are standing before a stone wall overlooking the governor's private gardens. A swarm of men below bathe the verdant lawns and bright flowerbeds with the water of life. He knows, even before he has the chance to survey them properly, that Etienne is the one on the right, twiddling his fingers and gazing about as the other boy stands rigid.

Gui gives Ibn Al Tayyib a nod that he hopes gives nothing away of the magma surging within him, scorching his lungs and deafening him to all else but the rush of blood in his ears. A bead of sweat trickles down from his hairline. Quickening his pace as if the scene before him is a mirage that will dissolve before his touch, Gui skates over the terrace. All the long-rehearsed words evaporate as he reaches Etienne and his son flings his arms around him.

Laughing in wonder, Etienne says, 'Father Gui, it's really you!'

Disoriented by the flood of relief, Gui draws his son in tighter. 'I've come to take you home,' is all he manages to whisper.

Etienne pulls free. Open-mouthed, he inspects Gui as though he can't quite believe the man before him is flesh and blood.

'You feel boiling hot!' Water runs, silent, down his son's nose. Gui palms the tears away.

'How in heaven did you get here?'

Gui beams at his son, swallowing on the emotion of everything he

183

cannot yet say. 'I have come on behalf of your mother.'

'My mother? I knew it!' An excited grin flares on the boy's face. 'Is she with you?'

Gui rocks back on his heels. 'It is not safe for a woman to travel to these places.'

Etienne's face crumples into query. 'So she sent you alone?'

Gui gives a string of rapid nods. 'I came because she wants you back more than anything.'

Gui's chest feels so tight it feels as though his ribs might crack. He pauses to breathe. Somewhere in the garden a peacock shrieks. He can feel the governor's men watching with inscrutable stares. The currency of restraint his highly valued amongst men of rank in Al Kamil's court. Much like the nobility of his own land, displays of emotion are considered a sign of weakness. His son is not yet free. Keenly aware that Etienne's fate is balanced on the whim of the artful secretary with whom he must barter, Gui squares his shoulders and turns to Ibn Al Tayyib. He bows his head politely. Someone barks for Etienne to return to the ranks.

Etienne stares at his father in utter bewilderment, and Gui has to fight with all he has to prevent himself from reaching out a consoling hand.

'I must speak with the governor first,' he whispers. 'He has paid for you and…'

'Can't I come with you?' The look of injury on his son's face is almost more than he can bear.

'I won't be long. I swear it,' he says, trying to conceal the pressure of the negotiation to come.

His son raises a trusting smile. Gui closes his eyes as he walks away, praying with all his heart that if he is to fail, God take him right there on the very spot he stands.

*

The governor's secretary pulls at his coiffed beard. Gui smiles patiently. He has spent so long waiting it would be pointless now to lose his composure.

'The governor is a merciful man.' The man sets to strolling back and forth in front of his huge walnut desk.

'I am certain of it.' Gui folds his hands together - the priest preparing to address the congregation.

'But he has status. Great status in this city,' the secretary continues.

'His name is known throughout the world.'

Al Tayyib turns to face Gui and places the tips of his fingers together precisely. The skin on the back of his hands is as smooth as a child's. 'So you will understand that he has rivals. Friends and rivals that observe his every deed. To free a slave in such a manner would be perceived as weakness.'

'If you permit me, can it not be seen as an act of charity in keeping with the texts of your faith?' Gui keeps the smile, but in his voice there rises a note of agitation. He has not come this far to be turned back by the false courtesy so favoured by those of high privilege. How ironic, he thinks, that these men fight against the counts and kings of Christendom who practise the very same codes of honour and leave the very same rank trails of death in their wake.

'A foreign, low-born slave? It would be considered beyond charity.' The secretary's face is impassive. Gui's blood heats. Don't give in to it. He looks at his feet. The room fills with the clicking of an elaborate water clock, marooned in the middle of the vast space.

'Very well,' he says to break the uncomfortable pause. 'So do you have a proposal, or does the governor exercise his right to refuse further discourse on the matter?' Gui knows the latter isn't true. The governor would not have permitted him to view the boys at all if it were not to propose some barter.

'As you have nothing of value to offer His Excellency for the boy, I propose an exchange of a different sort.' The secretary spins a sheet of papyrus on his desk, aligning the edges exactly with the top of the desk. 'You are a clerk?'

'A scribe, yes.'

'So you are educated, literate in several of the Christian tongues?'

'I am.'

'Then Al Kamil, the grand governor, in the name of Charity, permits the boy to return to his mother.'

Gui hears himself utter a soft groan of relief. The secretary offers the governor's generosity with palms open, in the attitude of Mohammedan prayer. The corner of his eye tails slyly, allowing Gui to guess at the 'but' before it comes.

'But you will remain as tutor to his sons. That is the exchange. The life you so desire to set free in exchange for your freedom.'

The blow has physical force and he feels his shoulders slump. 'Remain indefinitely?'

'As the governor sees fit. Not indefinitely. His sons will grow into men.'

Gui's mind races. How can he ensure Etienne's safe passage to France? Impossible. Can he keep Etienne safe in Cairo until he is able to escape himself? Is it even possible to escape?

'The governor offers your Etienne safety of passage to Gibraltar. He will work on one of his ships, of course. From there he can find passage to Marseille.'

'The governor is generous and merciful and I thank him for his offer but Etienne is too young to travel safely alone.'

'I would say his resources are perfectly adequate. Cairo is a long way from his home.' The same sly look. Gui holds his tongue. Etienne is safe for now and it gives Gui time to form a plan.

185

'Quite so. Then, I gratefully accept.'

'Splendid.' The secretary claps his hands, summoning the butler who had first greeted him.

'Khalid will show you your room.'

Gui bows to his new employer. In substance, Gui reflects, not so very different from the Bishop of Chartres. Richer, certainly, and the guardian of a far more elegant prison. One that he must now inhabit alone.

'If you permit me, when does this boat leave for Gibraltar?'

The secretary plucks a sheet from his desk.

'In one week.'

Panic crowds Gui's mind. It is a bitter enough draught that he must give up his son in order to free him, but the idea that Etienne will once again be taken from him without knowing the truth is intolerable. 'Am I able to see the boy before we bid farewell?'

Ibn Al Tayyib looks up form his paperwork and leaves Gui's heart stalled for a long, considered breath.

'Very well.'

*

'So we can go now?' Etienne asks.

'Not quite.' Gui presses his lips together in apology.

The boy looks crestfallen. 'Why not? You said you had come to get me.'

Gui feels his shoulders tighten.

'Are you too poor to buy me back?' Etienne asks the question casually.

'Almost certainly.'

Etienne shrugs. 'What are you doing here then?'

Gui tugs at the neck fastening of his robe. He feels like a man called to mount to gallows. The pressure building inside him is making him nauseous. *Set it loose it will defend itself.* He recalls his promise to Abbot Roger, made a lifetime ago. He looks into his child's eyes, so full of hope. It can no longer be held back.

'Etienne?' He pulls his hand over his jaw. His son is too smart for roundabout jabbering and half explanations. 'There is something else…'

Etienne looks alarmed.

'I came to find you for Agnes that is true. But there is another reason. I came because I had to make sure you were safe for myself.' Gui's heart is in free fall as he looks right into the bright blue eyes. 'Because I am your father.'

Etienne cocks his head to one side as though he hasn't quite heard right. The laden silence makes Gui's skin itch like no anxiety he has ever known.

'I am so ashamed I kept it hidden,' he says. 'Please forgive me.' He rubs his fingers over his forehead. Etienne is looking at him as though he is searching for clues he should have seen long ago.

'But you are a priest,' his son says eventually.

'Yes. But I love your mother just the same.'

Etienne squints up at Gui, hands searching for non-existent pockets in his tunic. He gives a half nod. 'How is she?'

'That last I knew she fares well,' Gui says buoyantly. Etienne eyes flicker down as he replies. 'I am pleased of it,' he says, and Gui knows that the boy has seen through him.

'She was not well when I left Marseille. I had to leave her with an aunt to come and find you.'

'I see,' says Etienne. The same deep-set eyes as his own stare intently from beneath the ridge of his son's brow. A moment of silence passes, then Etienne says, 'You know, Father Gui, I think maybe I always knew.'

Chapter Thirty

'So, this priest from your village, he just came here by chance?' Alberto sounds incredulous.

'Yes. I told you, he was following the old preacher from Italy. The one who came here to convert the Sultan,' says Etienne even though he knows Alberto won't be so easily fooled.

'Hmm.'

Etienne knows Alberto is angling for him to say more. He desperately wants to share the truth with his companions but he knows he cannot. The lesson has been far too painfully learned for him to forget it now. He doesn't know what Father Gui has planned, but the solemn wink he gave him as he went back inside the governor's palace said that it isn't going to be as simple as just walking out. Although he knows Abubakr would be glad to see the back of him, they are not going to let him go for free.

There is no way he is going to risk getting found out, so he smiles back at Alberto. A little smirk that says, I know you know I'm not telling the truth but I'm still not going to say anymore.

'*Ba ben'* have it your way.' Alberto slopes off with a shrug like he doesn't care.

Etienne slumps down on the shady side of their hut. He knows he should get about his duties so as not to draw attention to himself, but he needs a few moments away from the eager faces of the others to get his head around what has just happened.

Although he has seen it with his own eyes, there is a part of him that still can't quite believe it. Father Gui boarded a boat and travelled all the way over those weeks and weeks of water to find him. His own father! Right there, all along. He shakes his head at the enormity of it. He never even guessed at it. All that time, all the terrible things that happened, if only he had known. His head hurts. He wishes he could reach up and put the sun out. Getting a bit of cool air into his brain might help him think more clearly.

He isn't upset. At least he doesn't think he is upset. But what he can't make sense of was how come he hadn't put it together before. He suspects that in some corner of his heart he did know. When he told Gui that maybe he had always known it felt like he was telling the truth. How it is possible for some part of you to keep something so thoroughly hidden from the rest of you?

The other boys back home always teased him about Agnes and her priest. Maybe that was it. He understands how dangerous it would have been for them to say anything. Everyone knows priests aren't allowed to get married. Still, they could have told him as a secret. He wouldn't have said anything. Didn't they trust him? Perhaps not when he was small but more recently, he could have known and sworn not to tell.

He knew how much his mother loved Gui. *He knew!* What a prize idiot. It is as plain as the nose on his face. He reaches up and feels along the ridge of his nose, the narrow, angular bridge that is forming now he is no longer a boy. He pushes his hair off his face, the same crazy ringlets as Gui. Father Gui. His father. The man who came all this way to rescue him.

He laughs out loud. Part of him feels so happy, he can't stop grinning. But there is some other part, hidden beneath the joy bursting in his chest, that is making him anxious and he wishes he knew what it was. Etienne beats the earth beside him with a half-hearted fist. He feels tired. It is as if just knowing the truth is tiring. His eyes want to close so he can sleep. Then he won't have to think about it anymore.

'That man who came to see you...' Christophe approaches him shyly, a bucket in one hand and a fistful of rags in the other.

'What of him?' Etienne sighs.

'He looks like you.'

'No he doesn't,' Etienne snaps back.

'I mean you look like him. Not quite as serious and you are blond. But yes.'

Etienne shrugs and turns his head away. Christophe puts down his pail and kneels beside him, freckly face all full of concern. A stab of guilt turns Etienne back towards his countryman. The frightened boy from Saintes really does look worried on his behalf.

'Are you in trouble? I won't say anything, I swear on my mother's life.'

Etienne smiles against his will. Poor Christophe. What a terrible story must he have, thinks Etienne. He has guessed that a relative of mine has arrived at the palace, and his first thought is that I might be in trouble. He looks so forlorn it seems unfair to deny it. Of all the boys, Christophe is least likely to foghorn the news around the palace. In fact even less than the least likely, Etienne decides - the most impossibly unlikely.

'Is it that obvious?' he says.

'To me, yes.'

'Alright then, you promise not to tell?'

Christophe's watery eyes widen in earnest and he nods.

'He is my uncle. He comes from a rich family in the Beauvais.'

'Really? Has he come to free you?' Christophe's face is shining as though he has just been told that someone has come to free him.

Etienne shrugs. 'He isn't sure if he can. The governor hasn't decided yet. And he wants compensation.'

'Oh. Your uncle is rich though?'

'Yes but...look I don't know what's happening. Please don't say anything.' Etienne instantly regrets wading into the lie. Just by hinting at the truth to the friendless Christophe, he can feel the cogs of what is supposed to happen start to slip.

'Of course not. I swear it. On the lives of my mother and sisters and the Holy Virgin herself.'

Etienne smiles at the other's boy's excitement.

'When are you going?' He asks.

'Shhh!' Etienne throws a glance around.

'Sorry, sorry…' The boy's face falls apologetically.

'I told you, I don't know anything more.'

From across the courtyard they hear raised voices. Abubakr is on the warpath. Hurriedly, Christophe reaches into his tunic.

'Please do me a favour when you do go.' He plucks something out from his undergarment. Etienne frowns. 'Sorry,' says Christophe. 'I have to keep it safe.'

Etienne holds the golden disc in his palm. It is the front part of a cloak pin, emblazoned with the heraldry of some noble house he doesn't recognise.

'Please give this to my mother if you ever get back to France. It was hers. Let her know that I am alive.' He picks up his bucket and rags.

'This is your mother's?' Etienne tosses the pin over in his hand. It has good weight - real gold. 'Who is your mother?'

'The Countess of Saintes.'

'What?' Etienne chokes. 'Why didn't you say?'

'What does it matter?' Christophe replies.

Etienne's mouth falls open, his mind spinning with a carousel of possibilities. 'What do you mean what does it matter? Are you mad?' He pushes his hands through his hair to stop himself from grabbing useless Christophe by the collar. 'For a start, if the governor knows you are from a noble house he might write to your father for a ransom!'

'My father would never pay anything to rescue me. He'd be too angry that I had shamed him.'

'Shamed him?' Etienne shakes his head.

'I have three older brothers. They are all better and at riding and fighting than I. Even the one who is for the priesthood. My father doesn't care about me.' He rolls his eyes. 'Believe me.'

Etienne scratches his head. He feels bad for Christophe. What kind of father would be ashamed his son was captured, even if he was a bad horseman? He can't imagine. Maybe Father Gui will have an idea how they can help him. The idea that he could share Gui with Christophe to make up for his own father makes him smile inwardly.

'Please don't say anything,' says the red-haired boy urgently, as though he can sense Etienne might be hatching a plan. And he is.

'You know I told Alberto the man who came for me was a priest?'

Christophe nods cautiously, in exactly the same way Etienne used to back home when he was sure the other boys were about to play a trick on him.

'Actually that's true.'

Christophe's face crumples in confusion.

'In fact, he's not really my uncle at all. He's my father.' He laughs a little too heartily. 'I didn't even know that until today,' he says as, inexplicably, his eyes begin to fill with water. Christophe's mouth is agog as Etienne continues.

'Back home I was a shepherd. My mother was Father Gui's house keeper.' He gets to his feet, suddenly compelled to convert Christophe to this unfamiliar new feeling of hope. 'He's come all this way for me. I know I've been lucky in that. But even if it seems to you that you are not so lucky, it doesn't matter. You can't just give up because of your father.' He shrugs. 'You just can't.'

The pale, freckled boy's lip is trembling and Etienne can tell it is the first time anyone has ever spoken to him like they cared. He reaches out and an uncertain hand and pats Christophe's shoulder.

'If Father Gui can get me out of here, then I'm sure he can get you out too,' he says. 'And if you really don't want me to, then I won't say a word about your father. Please say you'll come with me.'

All Christophe can do in reply is nod.

From around the corner, the sharp, thin shadow of Abubakr sweeps over the path like a torch. Etienne slips away, whistling a little ditty that his mother used to sing when she did the laundry. He heads for the gardens with his brushes, planning to sit underneath the purple tree by the fishpond until it gets a little bit cooler, and watch the flashes of orange and gold dart by. He doesn't even care that Abubakr is lurking across the way, scowling at the prickly pears.

*

'We don't have much time,' says Gui. 'And I must have your full attention. Do you understand?'

Etienne nods. Father Gui has clipped his hair and beard, so he looks a little more composed now and less like one of those crazy desert men. He has a plan for them, Etienne can tell from the serious and distracted way he is talking.

'I understand,' he replies solemnly.

Gui's attention flickers to the servant who is pretending to inspect the floor tiles.

'In three days you are to board a ship bound for Gibraltar. From there you can find passage to Marseille with the coin that you earn aboard the ship.'

Etienne's blood fizzes with panic. 'What do you mean me? Where's Gibraltar?'

'It's on the southern most tip of Moorish Spain.'

'Aren't you coming?'

Gui ticks his head negatively. The room begins to spin. This can't be right.

'What do you mean you're not coming? How do I know it won't be another slave ship? That I won't be bundled down to the hold with no chance to see any coin at all?'

'Because the governor is a man of honour.'

Etienne widens his eyes.

Gui looks stern. 'And so we must trust him,' he says as he inclines his head ever so slightly in the direction of the loitering servant.

'Right. Yes…' Etienne stalls, and there is an awkward moment as he realises Gui knows he was about to call him 'father'.

Gui's eyes are smiling, even though the rest of his face is expressionless, and Etienne notices a slight colour to his cheeks as he leans in and whispers, 'Will you call me father?'

'Yes, Father,' Etienne says and they both laugh - a low, nervous laugh of relief that attracts the attention of the man who is now bent over, peering at the door handles.

'What are you going to do?' Etienne asks.

'I have agreed to remain as tutor to the governor's sons.'

Etienne hears his own intake of breath. 'But I thought…'

'Enough.' Gui eyes rove to the door before he gives a subtle nod down to his hand. 'Now let us pray.'

They kneel, and without taking his eyes off Gui, Etienne snatches the sheet that his father offers, folded in his palm, and secrets it up his sleeve.

Gui begins the murmuring of prayer, then mutters, 'Go to the docks as you are bid, then follow the instructions on the map I gave you. You will be safe there until I arrive.'

Etienne's hands are still clutched tight together, feigning worship.

'How long must I wait?'

'However long it takes me to get away from here.'

Etienne can feel the pressure of a thousand questions fighting in his throat.

'I will be there,' Gui says.

'What about the other boys from France who were sold here? We could all go back together.'

'We don't have time.' His father looks alarmed. 'Do nothing until I arrive in Alexandria.'

'But my friends…' Seized by the memory of what he has promised Christophe, Etienne's skin feels like it is crawling with lice. How in the Devil's name is he going to get Christophe out of the palace without Gui's help? He scratches fiercely at his shoulder.

'Amen.' Gui raises his voice.

'Amen.' Etienne mumbles.

'Go with God,' Gui says gravely, and they rise to find their observer has retreated. Lowering himself to Etienne's height, he kisses his palm and takes it to his son's cheek. 'I will see you soon.'

A shadow of anxiety creeps over Etienne's face. 'Father?'

'Yes?'

'God be with us,' he says, then turns to go.

Suddenly his father pulls him back into a fierce hug and it catches him by surprise. At first he stiffens against the constriction, unsure of how to respond. He is holding onto me like he might never see me again, Etienne thinks, and the demon of panic begins to beat its wings in his gut. He encircles his arms around his father, and finds himself thrown back to what seems like twenty life times ago, to the last time Gui embraced him at their cottage in Montoire. It was right after the fight he'd had with Marc about his rude woodcuts and he had been afraid he was going to get in trouble. He realises that squished against the body of this man he feels safe. Please God, he mouths into Gui's chest, don't let anything else go wrong. He cranes his head up underneath Gui's chin.

'Please come as quickly as you can,' he says.

'I will, don't worry.' Gui rubs his back, and he cannot help but flinch as his father's hand meets with the scabs that still remain from his beating.

'What is it?' Furrows of concern dent Gui's forehead.

'Nothing.' Etienne's stomach churns. He doesn't want his father to bear witness to his shame on top of everyone else.

'Etienne, let me see.' Gui spins him round by the shoulders and lifts up his tunic. Etienne hears him gasp. He snatches back round to face his father.

'I tried to escape,' he says with a shrug.

Gui blinks several times and Etienne feels as though he is looking right into his soul. The look on his father's face reminds him of the time he was playing on the weir with the village boys and one of them slipped on the moss. The boy threw out his hand and Etienne grabbed it, just a reflex, without thinking about it. For a moment, before the others reached them, they had been in perfect balance, the boy hovering over the weir, Etienne pulling the other way. The boy looked up at him and Etienne could tell that he wanted to throw up his other arm so he could grasp on with both hands. But he knew that if he did, he would have pulled them both in.

'I will be there. I swear it.' Gui whispers, almost as if he is talking to himself. Etienne can see that his gaze is fixed far away, eyes as black as the onyx stones the countryside pagans use to make their spring sacrifices.

Chapter Thirty-one

The spring winds are screeching like a graveyard of demons when the message comes. It has been almost a year since those accursed processions came trumpeting through the Chartraine, with their bright banners, gay pipes and beguiling promises that carried away her son and a thousand other sons.

The forester has offered to come with her, but as much as she would like the company, she cannot risk it. She has walked from the Languedoc alone, over five hundred miles by the rough reckoning of the roadside milestones. Experience has taught her that the only way to tell if you are in danger is when you, and you alone, are responsible for every single step.

Once more she slips into a man's hose and binds her breasts with a linen bandage. There is a reassuring discomfort to it. It has been so long since she has seen her true reflection that briefly she wonders if she still makes a plausible youth; for as a grown man, she knows she will never convince. Not without garb far finer than she has the means to acquire. A foppish jongleur or pampered merchant perhaps, but never a man who toils. She has neither the forearms nor the shoulders for it. There is a subtle discord that the eye of any keen spy would spot a league away.

The letter she received looks as though it has been written by someone self–taught. Sister Octavia, she presumes. Its half- invented abbreviations and words spelled in haphazard, local dialect make it hard to decipher. She understands that she has until the half moon in the second week of Lent to get to the rendezvous. The place, roughly sketched, indicates a triangle of land between a tributary of the river Eure and the convent near Houx. All the 'apropos gentlemen', she is assured, will be waiting. Her Madame, pays compliments. Agnes commits the spindly map to memory, throws the note on the fire and crosses herself that the 'apropos gentlemen' will indeed be there.

*

Clouds flit like ghosts past the pale semi circle of moon. Damp vapours rise from the cold, mossy earth. It is not late, the bells for Vespers have not yet tolled. Still, it feels like the kind of evening that makes people believe witches can depart from their sleeping bodies and fly on broomsticks to make communion with the Devil. If she had not walked through half a lifetime of these nights already, Agnes fancies she might believe it too.

Her enemies though are all too material; for them she has a hand axe and a slim arming sword she found in one of her godmother's chests. The hand axe she has wielded often enough chopping wood, but the only experience she has of an arming sword is watching Gui act out his youth. How he would laugh to know she had it clanging from an ill-suited tooling belt at her side, causing more chaffs and bruises to her thigh than it will likely do to an enemy. 'More likely to injure myself, I know', she says aloud to the man who is left only in her memory.

The conversations she still has with him are a necessary comfort. They are so real to her that when the whistle comes, shrill on the cold air, it makes her start and scalds her blood. The man who canters up on an expensive stallion wears a well-tooled leather hauberk, armed with a true long sword that only a well- practised feudal retainer can carry.

'I am the bailiff of Dreux,' he says and Agnes's heartbeat dips a notch. Lady Yolande has kept her word.

He swings himself down from his mount and leads it into the shadow of an oak. From the half-light of the moon, she can see he is a man in his twenties with a full beard, chest well-lifted, and firm muscles that say he is no idler.

'Are you alone?' she asks.

'For now,' he begins, but with the approach of a wagon he brings his finger to his lips and they duck into the cover of marshy grasses. There is an air of calm authority to his actions. Finally, it seems the Lord has sent her a champion. Agnes makes the sign of the cross in her mind's eye.

A voice carries on the air. The reply skims back over the heathland. It is the cry loaders make as they barrel merchandise through the streets of busy towns. The glow of a lantern appears, hovering like a willo' the wisp, and a wagon emerges under the pale yellow circle of light. Agnes watches as a man steps out from the brush. He converses briefly the wagon's driver, who dismounts. Bulky and squat, the driver strides around to the back of the coach, arms swinging. He opens the doors.

Although she has been expecting it, Agnes is still shocked as the whites of an eye catch in the light. It is impossible to tell anything of their owner – is it a child? She hasn't thought that far ahead. Her heart gathers pace as she takes stock: in a few moments time she will have a group of frightened children in her charge. In all the months they have been separated, never has she wanted Gui to be at her side more than she does now. Salt stings the back of her throat. There is a gift to giving comfort without revealing the sorrow in your own heart, and Gui is a master of it.

Her stomach flips as the first, thin pair of legs appear on the wagon's step. She gives an audible gasp. The bailiff extends a low, restraining palm. She looks at him - are you going to do something? Keeping his eyes fixed on the scene, he brings the tips of his middle and index fingers to meet them. Still watching. The body descends from the wagon. This she is not prepared for. It is Sister Octavia. Her coif and wimple are torn away, a thick mass of red hair falls across her bruised cheek. She cannot help it, Agnes lets out a stifled cry.

The wagoner spins round. Beside her the bailiff tenses, shrinking down lower as the wagoner kicks his way through the scrub towards them. Barely upon them, the bailiff grabs his ankles, pulling him flat on his back where he lands a brutal punch on the side of the man's head.

'Drop your weapons!' The bailiff springs up as the other delivery man draws his dagger, swiping it to and fro. He is no match for a professional. The bailiff smirks and repeats, 'Drop it.'

The man grabs Octavia as the bailiff strides forward, his knife quickly at her throat. 'Make another move against me and you'll kill yerself a woman of God.'

The bailiff shakes his head. 'Her blood will be on your head as surely as yours will be on mine,' he says.

Rousing up, the wagoner comes at Agnes square on, growling like a mastiff. Both hands clenched around her hand axe, Agnes readies herself to meet him. She strikes out, catching his hand, hears the crack of his knuckle. The big man cries out angrily. Pawing at her like a bear, he finds the axe, rips it from her grip. Momentarily her mind empties. She has no way to fight this hulk of a man. She fills her lungs to scream and she remembers – the arming sword. His arm extends to her neck. She thrusts the blade from its belt, swiping it across his flesh. With a roar, he throws himself upon her.

Seizing the distraction, the bailiff slams his elbow to the face of the man holding Octavia. He pivots back to Agnes. Octavia runs free, weeping blindly. The bailiff jerks the wagoner back by the neck, then delivers a double handed blow with his sword hilt. Agnes reels from the spatter of blood, turning just in time to catch hold of Sister Octavia who collapses into her.

'They caught me outside the convent,' Octavia sobs. 'The children were already in there.' She flaps a hand in the direction of the wagon.

Agnes races over. Four girls, cower in the wagon behind a large chest.

'It's gold,' Octavia stammers. 'I saw them load it…'

Agnes beckons to the slave girls, encouraging them to her. But she has no moment to order the world as the bailiff grabs her by the waist, pinning her to him.

The force of his grip hits her like a branding iron. Briefly she struggles, but he is too powerful. She fights to turn her head. 'What is this?'

'You'll find out soon enough,' he says, without meeting her eye.

'Run!' She yells at Octavia. The novice stumbles over the scrubland and into the night. The children scatter in different directions.

'Go to the forester!' Agnes calls, summoning the energy to try and squirm free.

'Cease your struggling,' the bailiff hisses into her ear. 'Where do you think you can run to?'

He hoists her up on his horse, and she knows he was not here to free those children. He was here for her.

Chapter Thirty-two

The governor has twice as many servants as there are rooms in his three hundred- room palace. It is impossible to turn the corner without finding one of his pristine men hovering with a tray, stooping over a floor tile, or flicking at a bit of imaginary dust with a cloth. Gui knows it will take him weeks to familiarise himself with all the short cuts, dead ends and secret passages; weeks more before he has any chance of passing by unremarked by the staff. Before then it will be useless to contemplate escape.

Servants are chattering in the courtyard below in a mixture of Occitan and Arabic. Gui paces his cell. Barely wider than the span of his arms, it contains a mattress and a washing bowl. A space designed to clip the wings of the mind. It presents him with two choices - quieten his thoughts or go insane. The governor's birds have wider horizons, he thinks, placing an eye to the window. Covered in a lattice of eight-pointed stars, it interrupts a proper view of the boys lined up outside. Etienne is among them, awaiting orders to depart, but he is at the back of the tail that snakes beyond Gui's sight.

The window does not allow him to stick his head out, so Gui pulls away and sits back down on his pallet. All he wants is one last look, a nod of reassurance to his boy that all will be well, that he will be thinking of his every step. A man shouts out and there is the shuffle of footsteps as the governor's convoy of slaves moves off. Gui shuts his eyes tight. Usually he would pray, but he finds he cannot. The frustration of powerlessness courses through him - a livid brew sparking in his veins, demanding action that he knows he cannot take.

At the conclusion of afternoon prayer he must descend from his tiny garret and cross the gold and ivory serenity of the palace complex to the salon where he instructs the governor's young sons in French - the language of their enemy. They are seven, eight and ten years old. The older two sit cross-legged, staring out to the gardens at the array of house servants, gardeners, traders and courtiers that scurry to and fro. They are the middle sons of the powerful administrator and their path in life is spread comfortably before them. Chins jutting, aloof, there is simply no reason to believe the ramblings of this foreign servant could offer any advantage. The younger one is different though, alert, full of wide-eyed nods and endless questions. He reminds Gui so much of Etienne that the idea of facing the curious little boy now makes him want to weep.

His skull feels tight, as though it is bearing down upon his brain. He rubs his brow, seeking a balm, and it conjures an image of himself and Etienne aboard a boat. He, in his tattered merchant's garb and, at his side, Etienne wears an oversized cloak that trails on the deck. *Are we really going home, father?* Gui pulls the cape more snugly under his boy's chin. *We are, son.* Etienne laughs into the stinging wind that is blowing away the foul stench of the port, carrying them towards France. And to Agnes. Out of nowhere her face appears so vividly he extends his fingers to touch the golden braids. His breath tightens as the muezzin's call shakes his fantasy.

*

Etienne feels sick. The dust and the jolts are bad enough, but it is the thought of the waiting boat that really churns his stomach. He feels as though he is already aboard, being tossed and slammed by the waves, not knowing for sure that there isn't some storm brewing which will see the end of them all. That, and the fact he really has no idea where the governor's ship is going. He has never even heard of Gibraltar, much less how to get back to France from there. That's if the governor even keeps his promise and lets him go. He clears the dust from his throat and checks his thoughts. Father Gui will come. It won't be like before. Father Gui will be there, just like he said. He will find a good boat and everything will turn out just fine. You don't have to worry about the rest.

Except he is worried about the rest. The map on Gui's note clearly shows where he is to go and wait, but it's vaguer about how he is supposed to escape the governor's convoy. When you are loading up the boat, his father told him, there will be a lot of traffic and confusion at the docks. Use that to pick your moment. Easy for you to say, thinks Etienne. He knows that imagining how things could go wrong is often worse than what actually happens. Still, he can't help it. His insides feel like gelatine. Please God let this be over with soon. And please make it obvious when I am supposed to run for it.

They are sitting in a cart, a heavy cotton tarpaulin overhead. It is hot as Hades. Etienne shuts his eyes. It makes his nausea worse. Please don't let me be sick, he asks of no one in particular. One of the other boys was sick earlier and the warm stink is getting unbearable. We must be nearly there by now. Peeling back the cover he peeks outside. All he can see are the dust and stones from their convoy skittering about in the wheels. The air smells of shit. Maybe they are passing an animal transport. One of the boys jogs his elbow and he re-ties the flap of the canopy.

A couple of hours later he can hear sea birds squawking in the air currents above raucous, busy streets. His backside is completely numb. He pulls the canopy back again - carts, camels and donkeys jostle for space along the dirt track. Not long now. Etienne bites at the skin on the side of his nail. Please be here soon, Father Gui. I just don't think I can get on another one of those boats by myself. As far as he has come, he can't remember feeling as nervous as he does now. Perhaps it is the knowledge that freedom is so close. For the first time since his journey began, he actually has something to lose. If it goes wrong now, he isn't sure he will be able to live with it.

Light floods the cart and someone barks at them to get out and get on with it. There is always slaving to be done, thinks Etienne as he shuffles along the bench and stretches his legs to stand. They feel like they have been in irons. His back aches too. By the side of the road, an old beggar with a withered arm rattles a can. Is this how old people feel all the time? Like they just rode two days solid through the desert on a wooden bench?

He surveys the governor's four wagons, all fully laden with crates, barrels, and bags, and sighs. Now they are portside, the aroma of bread and stew curls its way over from the eateries. He realises he is ravenous. Some bean stew would be good, even heavily spiced like the Mohammedans eat it. He doesn't mind that anymore.

'You, boy. Get moving!'

Etienne feels a prod. The others already have their backs into offloading. He slopes off to join them, casting a glance around for the places that Father Gui has marked on his map. He has memorised them as well as he can, but amid the thump and yell of the port's daily business nothing looks like it fits. Etienne heaves up a box and troops off behind a boy he hasn't seen before.

The governor's boat is a fine vessel. A sleek, single-decked ship, brightly painted with two sets of sails and a proper enclosed wheelhouse at the back. A red and gold canopy covers the whole stern, so at least they won't get burned pinker than a spit roast washing down the decks. Down below the hold smells of new wood and nutmeg, not piss and fear. He dumps his box down. There is no one else there, so he sits down and wipes his brow. If he wasn't just about to escape this wretched household forever he would lay down right here behind these boxes - to Hell with it if they find him.

'Boy!' The holler comes from outside. 'Get back here!' Etienne jumps to his feet and scuttles back down the gangplank. He is just about to heave up another crate when he hears a commotion.

'Christ,' he mutters as he sees Christophe fleeing across the quayside, Nasir the slave master in his wake. Instantly he regrets encouraging his friend to stow away with them. What now? Instinctively, he feels for Father Gui's note at his waistband. Is this it? His opportunity? A quick cast around. Everyone's head is turned, watching the debacle unfold. It is.

Darting through the busy docks, he finds himself on the other side of the main square. It is easy enough to hide behind the stacks of crates and pallets waiting to be loaded. Eyes fixed on Nasir, he watches as the slave master inevitably chases down Christophe. Head in his hands, he tries to talk himself out of it - it is far too dangerous to try and save Christophe when no-one has even noticed he is missing yet. But Nasir is already showering blows with his whip upon the hapless French boy and Etienne knows what they do with runaways.

'Hey! Over here!' he yells.

Before he knows it he has thrown himself back into the crowd and is engaged in a game of dodge with the hulking Egyptian while Christophe runs round and round on himself, like a beetle that has fallen on its back. The map says they have to exit by the copperware stalls, so on his next pass, he grabs Christophe's sleeve and flings him in the right direction.

'Follow me,' he hollers, and they chase down the alleys towards the main market. Dull thumps and shouts tell him that his pursuers are not far behind. Heart racing in his throat, he doesn't dare look back. He doesn't want to see how close they are in case it makes him trip.

Out of the covered market they swerve left where the men are weaving reed baskets, pass the mosque with the blue tiles in the courtyard and straight on until they reach the alley where the cobblers sit. Second right now and one, two, three, four doors down, a threshold with flowered tiles and a red painted grille on the door. He pounds on the door. The grille slides back.

'I am Etienne,' he pants. 'Gui's son. He told me you would help. Please let me in! They are chasing us.'

He hasn't even drawn breath when the door opens and a bare, olive-skinned arm snatches him inside. He grabs the wheezing Christophe and they tumble in, nearly barrelling over the woman called Yalda. Flinging her arms around him as though he were some lost relative, she offers him comfy cushions to lie on and some sugared almonds. Yalda seems to think he has suffered something terrible, and coos at him in a soft voice, leaning over him so her breasts are practically in his face. How brave he is, does he want more to eat? Something to drink maybe? He is fairly sure from the way she is dressed that she is a prostitute, all wrapped up in a tight silk robe that draws the eye to her bosom, and necklaces of large gems and jangly gold coins. Etienne can't imagine for the life of him how Father Gui came to know her with his serious face and his awkward manner.

'Don't worry, little one. He will be here soon.'

Etienne wants to tell her that he isn't little but then thinks better of it. He isn't sure what Gui has told her and he has no idea how long he is going to have to wait with her. She squeezes her eyes at him. Etienne shifts uncomfortably on the cushion.

'He is a brave man, your father. He would do anything for you.'

Outside they can hear Nasir the slave master and his henchmen hollering dire warnings in the streets to anyone who gives harbour to runaway slaves. Yalda presses her lips together and gives a wan smile that Etienne imagines is supposed to be reassuring but isn't anything of the sort. How in heaven are he and Christophe supposed to pass the time sitting here with this woman?

Someone knocks at the door at Etienne's heart leaps into his mouth. Yalda adjusts her cleavage, blots her lip line with a finger.

'Through there,' she mouths, stabbing her index finger towards the courtyard door.

Etienne and Christophe scurry outside. It is a very small but beautiful garden, crowded with lush plants and herbs. They squeeze between a spiky aloe bush and two fig trees with big, wavy leaves, and crouch down. It is the middle of the day and the sun's rays reflect off the walls of the enclosed space. Itchy beads of sweat run from Etienne's hairline into his eyes but he is far too frightened to move. He can hear Yalda's voice drifting from within, and although it doesn't sound as though there is any shouting, in the tongue of the Mohammedans you can never really tell. He squeezes his eyes shut and prays to the one true God that it is not Nasir the slave master.

When it seems like an awfully long time has past and Etienne's shins are burning beyond endurance from the confined squat, he looks over at Christophe, who has the same look of expectant misery as always. He is desperate to say something aloud, if only to reassure himself that even if it was Nasir come to search Yalda's rooms, there can't possibly be that many places to be search – and wouldn't they have come out here to look anyway? In the end he mouths, 'What's going on?' even though Christophe's wide, robin's egg eyes are glued to his feet, so he can't possibly have seen.

Behind them there is a large clay pot of rosemary, its small blue flowers in bud. It reminds Etienne of his mother's herb garden back home. Stripping the spines from a twig, he releases the oil into the palm of his hand and inhales deeply. It is the smell of his old kitchen in the summer. It still bothers him that he cannot recall even one time when he had an inkling that his mother and Father Gui were lovers. Why hadn't they told him? If he hadn't been captured would they ever have told him? He massages at his brow as though it might somehow rub out his confusing thoughts. Maybe he would just have realised when he got older. It must have been so obvious to see them together. He scratches at his shoulder – what else has he pulled the wool over his own eyes about?

Suddenly they hear a man cry out, a low, enduring groan. Christophe twitches in surprise and throws out a hand to steady himself, catching Etienne, who topples into the aloe bush.

'It must be a customer,' Etienne whispers to Christophe.

'What?'

'Never mind.'

*

A rap at the door jolts Gui from half sleep. It is still dark outside. He peels himself up, and clothed in his nightshirt, opens the door to find himself squinting into the flare of a torch. Nasir the slave master pushes him aside and enters the cell. Forearms covered with scars and burn marks, he towers over Gui - slave master now because he had once been

202

the best slave.

'It will be better for you if you tell me the truth.' The way his voice grinds conjures up instruments of torture.

'The truth,' nods Gui. 'With regard to..?'

'The boy has escaped and you will tell me where he has gone.'

Gui tries not to swallow as his mouth runs dry. His son is free.

'Escaped?'

The slave master stays silent. With his unusually wide-set eyes, he resembles one of the animal-gods of his people's ancient religion.

Gui shakes his head in confusion. 'I have travelled from the other side of the world and given up my freedom so an innocent boy could win his. Why would I see him escape from safe passage back to his home?'

Arms folded before him, Nasir growls. 'If you want I can beat it out of you.'

'Beat me?' Gui's voice pitches in outrage. 'Your master, the great governor himself, guaranteed the boy's safety, and now you want to beat me because you have lost him?'

The slave master's jaw tightens. 'We will find him. But until we do you should remember...'

'You should remember that I agreed to remain here only subject to Etienne's freedom and well being. Am I to go and find him myself?' Gui pulls on his robe.

The Egyptian's eyes narrow. 'When we find him we will bring him back here and then...' He draws as breath, and Gui detects an uncertain thought travel across his face. The governor doesn't know you have lost him yet, he thinks as he looks into the dead eyes of the other man. Nasir lifts his chest, but an invisible shift in the balance of power has taken place. He is not able to threaten information out of Gui, and now he knows it.

'We will be merciful when he tells us how he came to escape.' The giant slave master sneers as he closes the door behind him.

Gui sits heavily on his pallet and rubs the knuckles of his hand. It has been three days since Etienne departed through the portcullis with a dozen other slave boys and an eight-horse baggage train. He has been anticipating this news, holding his breath every time he is summoned to receive his duties, or sees a member of the household running across the gardens. Now it has come, he feels the throb of apprehension. Somewhere out there, the governor's men are hunting for Etienne while he is trapped in this gilded cage, under suspicion.

Gui had planned to wait a few days before he attempted flight, but the news of Etienne's escape has brought with it a sense of urgency that he knows he cannot resist. The chances of the governor's men tracing Etienne to Yalda are slim - if Etienne has managed to find her. But the longer he leaves it, the more likely it is that his son will be caught. He peers through the heavenly patterns of his window. The lights are on in the servants' quarters across the way and he can sense dawn hovering just beneath the blanket of night.

Soon after his arrival, the governor's librarian approached him. An Italian holy man, Francis, had arrived, seeking to convert the Sultan by preaching poverty and peace. His curiosity aroused, Al Kamil asked his clerics to interrogate Gui on the beliefs of this mendicant to ensure that the Sultan gained no advantage of secret knowledge. Thus Gui's duties have been to assist the librarian in the quest for all books on the matter, ferrying parchments back and forth between the palace and the libraries, church vaults and private residences of the great city.

Stooped by age, the librarian does not always accompany him, and the guards pay him little mind as he comes and goes, trailed by an entourage of servant boys with boxes stacked upon their heads. They have been nearly a week in this task already and he does not know when Al Kamil will decide this particular avenue does not contain the mystery of the Ages and tire of it. Is this his best chance?

The call of the muezzin rings out. It is the only time the servants' entrance is unguarded. His head is still buzzing from his encounter with the slave master and the fog of sleeplessness. All at once, the scourge marks on his son's back harry his sight. His body heats with fury. *God so loved the world He gave His only son.* Gui knows it is a lie. What father would sacrifice his own son? For what? For this greedy and reckless world? 'Do you ask me to give mine?' he hisses. Above his head hangs a mahogany crucifix that the governor has provided. He wants to throw it at the wall.

'Enough,' he mutters and stuffs his few possessions into his bag. Slinging it over his shoulder, with a couple of large prayer books under his arm, he winds his way down the narrow staircase of the servants' wing. There are two men at the entrance and he recognises neither. Inwardly he curses. He should have waited a few moments longer for them to turn to prayer. He raises his eyes to the graver looking of the two and salutes with a nod. The man raises his chin in query. It is the toss of the dice.

'Books to be returned to the Coptic monastery,' Gui says, hoisting up his bag. The men exchange glances. His heartbeat surges.

'Where is the librarian?' the guard asks.

Gui rests his hand on his stomach and mimes sickness.

The other man returns a nod and it is done.

Outside the palace gates, Gui sheds his black robe and flees north, a fleeting shadow among those who must rise to prepare the day for those of greater means. Men are already gathered beneath the buttresses of the Citadel, seeking the labour that drives them to risk the disease and dangers of the city.

On the other side of the road, a group of tribesmen are packing away their belongings in the dawn light. Scarves flick into place for travel, their eyes fix on the path ahead. A cloud of dust rises up with their beasts as they depart. Gui feels a weight at his back; the weight of someone's attention. His peripheral sight detects no one but still, he can feel someone watching. His nerves? Perhaps.

Gui knows he will not be missed until the boys' lesson after their morning prayers - the governor's children do not have to rise before the dawn. Once his absence is noted, the governor's honour will require that he send an outrider to find him. Such a man will travel twice the speed of a coach. He has two hours advantage, three at most, and the journey is two days long. If Etienne is to remain free, he must get to him first. The penalty for failure he has no time to imagine.

Chapter Thirty-three

The place she does not recognise, but she does know it is not the ancestral home of Amaury de Maintenon. They have turned off the main road to Dreux, and Maintenon's chateux is a league or two behind them now. The bailiff has seated her in front of him as make their way along a track, cut with deep furrows of mud, the sky a canopy of gold dust above them on this crystal clear night.

At first, she gripped the pommel's horn tightly, barely daring to breathe, doing all she could to prevent her body from touching his. But the anticipated violence has not come, and now she does not think that it will. Her captor has taken her hand axe, but not the arming sword she resheathed beneath her tunic. It is possible that he simply hasn't seen it she supposes, but that does not seem likely - not a feudal retainer of his rank and practise.

He rides at a steady pace, just enough to keep the worst of the chill at bay, and the easy rhythm gives awkward comfort to this unexplained journey. Although the enigmatic bailiff has not said a word, he has wrapped a blanket around her shoulders, and she fancies she can sense something troubling him. Remorse? Sharing a saddle is an act of such intimacy, it would require a person to toss away their soul before they could blot out their awareness of the other.

It prompts her to risk asking their destination. Twice she has tried to get an answer. Although he raised no impatient hand, he will not speak. Perhaps he knows the dangers of striking up conversation with a captive you are inclined to pity? She doesn't believe the man who steers the horse is soulless - heaven knows she has met plenty of them. No, rather it seems to her that he is lost, as though he has hazarded his lot on a game that he has no way to cease playing, even though he has long since tired of it.

The eerie song of a wolf pack has been following them since they turned onto the track. Suddenly, a howl from the alpha sounds, just paces away. The stallion shies and takes a stumbling sidestep, forcing the bailiff up from his seat. As they both grip the horse, the corner of the saddle cover peels back. Agnes reads *Michel de Plaissis* carved into the leather. Her heart skips. Now she has a name.

'Michel?' she blurts out, before the courage of impulse deserts her. The bailiff draws an audible breath.

'The saddle bears your name.' She cranes round to face him. His eyes are a soft brown. Not as dark as Gui's, and without their ardent spark, but there is a warmth to them that tells her he has a good heart.

'Will you not tell me where we are going?'

'What does it matter?' Michel replies. 'Besides, we are nearly there, look for yourself.'

The row of timber dwellings look as though a series of labourers' cottages have been refashioned as one building. Opposite, Agnes makes out the frame of an empty stable; no one of means lives here, or visits often. Michel dismounts and draws his horse to a trough of rain water. There is a dim, yellow glow at one of the windows. They are expected.

Drawing the blanket around her more tightly, she shambles over to Michel.

'Why are you doing this?' she asks. 'What of those children?'

His eyes dart to his boots. 'This way.'

The old woman who answers the door is almost invisible. She doesn't stoop, but her hair, scraped up into a cap, is completely white. There is a soft down on her wrinkled cheeks. Agnes imagines she is well into her eighth decade and has been in service all her life. The housekeeper gives a bob to the bailiff and says, 'I've prepared a room for the lady as you asked. Will you take supper now?'

'No, thank you,' he says, and she shuffles off, a small bird of a woman dwarfed by the low beams of this modest place.

Michel stands before Agnes in silence. For a moment she thinks he isn't going to say anything at all. Then, he lifts his hazel eyes to hers and says, 'I'll do my best to find the children.'

'Who..?' Agnes begins, but she does not need to finish the question.

'Inquisitor de Nogent,' he cuts in.

Agnes closes her eyes. Of course.

'I will be here until he arrives.'

Michel reaches the door before he turns and says, 'I'm sorry.'

Although he leaves without another word, Agnes is left with the impression there is more he wants to tell her. Much more.

Agnes thinks she must have dozed for a bit, but the sound of hooves on the courtyard do not wake her from any dream. Quickly, she rises to peek out the window, grateful that the lord has given her these moments to prepare as Bernard de Nogent steps down from his carriage. She was expecting to feel only fear, but to her surprise, she finds it mingles with the warm seduction of hatred. Her hardships have had their purpose, it seems. All her tears have dried diamond hard.

Although she has had half the night to ponder it, she has no answer as to why he has brought her to this place and not the dungeons of the Inquisition. Was it at the behest of Maintenon? It seems unlikely that Maintenon would have her deposited in this secluded cottage instead of the comfort of his own manor. Rather she feels as though she is being hidden, and her instinct tells her that guessing why may be the difference between life and death.

The slam of the front door shakes the building's timber frame. Agnes returns to her pallet, pulling the cover back up over her in the hope that a feigned sleep will give her a few more hours. But it does not. Bernard de Nogent is well versed enough in extracting confessions to know that interrogating the weary yields results more effectively.

When she enters the room he is scratching his eyebrow like an impatient tithe collector awaiting payment. First, Agnes feels dread stir in her gut. Then, she remembers his signature, looped over documents that sold her son. The choler rises. He has come alone with his driver, a middle aged man already bowed down with the cares of too many mouths to feed. Apart from the old woman and the driver, it is just she and de Nogent in the house.

'Admirable,' de Nogent says, 'your tenacity.'

'What have you done with my son?'

The wiry eyebrows jolt up into his forehead. 'Your son?' He pauses, grimaces. Agnes feels cold fingers of uncertainty grip her insides.

'You did well to evade us for so long, waiting for your idiot of a lover.'

He doesn't know where I was, she thinks, and smiles inwardly at this small victory.

'I'm not waiting for anyone,' she says.

He laughs, a hoarse, mocking sound that grates in the back of his throat. It makes her want to spit at him. The inquisitor steps in front of the hearth and warms his hands behind his back. Silence. Refusing to give him the satisfaction of her confusion, she stares, mute, at the floor in front of her.

'You want to play games with me?' he says. 'You don't remember what it was like last time?'

'What are you going to do?' Agnes says. 'Try me again?'

'You know I don't need to try you again. No one knows you are here. I can dispatch you when I am ready. No one will notice.' Now, standing erect, he steps forward, rubbing his warmed hands together.

'You have kidnapped me just to dispatch me unnoticed?'

The inquisitor purses his lips. 'That was a very daring rescue you were attempting, the bailiff tells me. What were you planning to do with a gang of heathen children. Or hadn't you thought that far ahead?'

'Anything would be better than the evil you have devised.'

'I have devised?' He tuts at her. 'No, no. I was hoping that you were going to tell me who devised it.'

'Why are you asking me when you must already know?'

'I do know who,' he concedes. 'But I don't know why. And that is what you are going to tell me.'

There is such awkwardness to his question, it strikes her that he is trying to extract information without revealing his purpose.

She feels certain that if de Nogent were planning to dispatch her tonight he would have made his move by now. As the acid brew of fear ebbs in her veins, there creeps the exhaustion of this sleepless, disorienting night.

bringing its own menace. The flames of the fire are the forked tongues of dragons, strange shadows race up the walls, the room feels alive, as though they are not alone. She stretches open her eyes.

'How should I know?'

De Nogent shakes his head. There is a viciousness to his smile and it starts her blood pumping again.

'You've been such a busy bee haven't you, Agnes de Coudray? You are going to tell me.' Unexpectedly, he takes the poker from the fire grate and smashes it down on the tiles with such force that a chip of flint flies off. She flinches at the assault. Now she is wide awake.

'You are going to tell me everything you know about Amaury de Maintenon.'

Finally she understands why she was brought here, out of sight of Maintenon and his retainers. Their partnership of convenience, it seems, is no longer so convenient.

'You've had a tiff, haven't you?' she says.

The perfect way to dispossess people of their land: have the Inquisition condemn them as heretics. The Church must hand its victims over to a secular lord for blood punishment. Then, really, who is watching what becomes of their property? Lord knows how much stolen land Maintenon is sitting on by now, she thinks. He doesn't need a dangerous zealot of an inquisitor to help him steal more.

'He has tired of you, has he?' she says. 'Do you think I know something that you can use to condemn him?'

The stony stare tells her that is the case. It also tells her that once she has told him what he needs to know she will no longer be useful.

'Do not test me,' de Nogent spits. His black irises are a pinprick; no light of a soul behind them.

Agnes's mind flits back to her arming sword, now secreted under her straw pallet. An admixture of hate combines with the fear swelling within her. Is it fierce enough to overcome this desiccated old vulture? Even if escape from the cottage were possible, with such zealous enemies and the isolation of this unknown terrain, would she last the night out in the open? Fleetingly, the bailiff's last glance returns to her mind's eye. It is an imagined promise, hardly a hope, but it is all she has. If she can keep de Nogent waiting, will that be enough? She has no choice, she has to keeping playing his game. The blood rushes in her ears.

'Even if I did know something useful about Maintenon, why should I tell you? Once you have what you want, you have no further need of me.'

'Think of it more as a simple choice. You can tell me your tale here by the relative comfort of this hearth, or you can tell it harder, later. Much harder.'

Agnes fights the urge to swallow as saliva floods her mouth. The inquisitor gives his rictus grin; a menace that tells her he will torture her anyway. Her heart thumps in her stomach. There is only one way to delay this she can think of. He is just a man, she tells herself as she feels her insides shrink away. He has no way of knowing whether you are lying. Agnes speaks slowly, buying herself all the precious time she can to think.

'What if I do give you information that condemns Amaury de Maintenon,' she says. 'But in condemning Maintenon, you will also condemn yourself?'

'What?' The top lip of the inquisitor peels back.

'I will give you the information you require about Maintenon. But when, and only when, I am released unharmed, will I give you the proof I have that links you to his crimes.'

'You dare to threat me, Agnes Le Coudray?' The inquisitor's eyes are on stalks, his sickly pallor mottled pink.

Now he is off centre. Agnes allows the possibilities to tumble through her mind. Lady de Coucy's parchments. The sale of Saracen slaves is not a crime, and the

reference to the shepherd crusaders in de Nogent's note is too oblique. At least without witnesses. Noble witnesses. Hastily she sifts through her memory; her meeting with Lady Yolande, the letter, the bailiff. There must be something she can use.

'If you do not release me, those to whom I have entrusted the evidence will see you hanged.'

De Nogent shakes off the threat and approaches Agnes. He leans right into her face so she can smell his sour breath. He pokes his index finger into her jaw.

'Enough stalling. You have nothing to barter for your own life.'

Agnes fights the urge to close her eyes. If she withdraws now she is dead. She stares ahead, seeing nothing. Think, she instructs herself. The bailiff's reluctance, poor Sister Octavia taken with the children to be traded. The chest full of gold. Gold that was to be delivered to Maintenon along with the human chattel? The money he made selling her son? The urgency of it fogs her mind. Think! She has no more time, she must hazard her guess. Turning to de Nogent, she looks right into those reptilian pupils, still probing her.

'I have proof that is…solid gold,' she says, and she sees the muscle around his eye socket contract involuntarily. It is the tiniest quiver, but his reaction makes her bold enough to risk the number she does have. 'Five thousand, six hundred livres worth.' Now de Nogent backs away. It makes her want to roar in triumph.

'The thing is, inquisitor, you have been in partnership with a murderer for decades. Despoiling the innocent and making enemies you don't even know you have.' She leans into the bluff. 'Some of your victims escape, don't they? And no matter how hard you look, you can't find them.'

The inquisitor exhales a long, wheezing breath. 'The truth is always mine in the end,' he replies. 'And there is no better truth than the rack.'

With that he reaches up and tugs the bell pull for the old serving woman, leaving Agnes standing alone in front of the last embers of the dying fire. Will her bluff be good enough? Has she unleashed the dogs on poor Octavia? She heard a man being tortured on the rack when she was in de Nogent's dungeon ten year's ago. It is not a sound you hear with your ears, it is a torment you feel in your innards. She knows there is no lie – or truth – good enough to withstand it. She crosses herself.

'God help me,' she whispers.

*

Someone is hammering at the door.

'Quick!' Yalda's voice rises urgently from the boudoir. Etienne can tell from the heavy, insistent thuds, that it is not a client.

They have the routine well rehearsed. Grabbing a flask of water, Etienne and Christophe race out into the courtyard and pull themselves up a trellis to the balcony above, where Yalda's neighbour lets them hide under her canvas awning. It's hot under there, and boring, but after one near miss when a local administrator nearly found them in the courtyard, Yalda insists on it.

Etienne and Christophe arrange themselves cross-legged, ready for the time takes Yalda to dispense with the visitor, but no sooner have they sat does her voice ring out, shrill and unexpected.

'Boys! Come down now!'

She is waving and grinning like a long-lost aunt on Christmas Eve, and as Etienne lowers himself down to make the short drop from the mezzanine floor he sees why. His heart skips as he stumbles over the plant pots and ornamental stones.

'Father!' he cries. 'You took so long. I thought you might never come.'

Laughing, his father raises an eyebrow. 'It's only been five days,' he replies.

Gui turns to Yalda. 'What do I owe you?'

A smile hovers on her lips. 'Your faces are payment enough. I have gems and coins aplenty from my admirers. '

Hi father's shoulders sag in a concession he does not want to give. He draws Yalda to one side. Etienne can tell he and Christophe aren't supposed to be part of the conversation, but the space is so small there isn't really anywhere else to go. They shuffle awkwardly towards tiny courtyard, pretending to admire the overcrowded family of plants, even though he has spent so long staring at it over the past few days he is sure he will remember it until the day he dies.

'But the boat passage… Really, it is too much,' Gui whispers.

'Let us just say I know the harbour master,' she replies. 'Once you are home perhaps you will be able to warn people. Stop others from suffering the same fate.'

'You have my word,' Gui says solemnly. From the corner of his eye, Etienne sees his father take Yalda's hand and bring it to his lips. He knows his father feels guilty that Yalda has risked so much to help them. Still, the way he is staring all moon-eyed at her makes him cringe. Although he is pretending to inspect a collection of tiny mosaic boxes on the table by the window, there is only so much Etienne can do to distance himself from the embarrassing goodbye.

Gui's eyes narrow accusingly at Etienne - I know you were watching me. Priests are good at making you feel guilty, even though you haven't really done anything, he thinks.

'The boat Yalda has arranged for us is leaving now,' Gui says. 'We must hurry.'

All at once there is an explosion of sound. Heated voices intrude from the street.

'Al Kamil!' Yalda shouts. She nods upwards. '*Amshi! As-saqf.*'

'The roof!' Etienne repeats.

One by one they haul themselves up onto the balcony above and clamber across onto the flat roof of the building next door. It is easy enough to negotiate, and Gui drops to the ground first.

'Hurry!' Etienne hisses at the prevaricating Christophe as angry tones caw out like seabirds from the street on the other side. The boys slither down via Gui's shoulders and away, streaking through the maze of the old city, its streets in afternoon slumber.

Gui grabs Etienne and Christophe by the hand. It makes it harder for them to run, but there is something about the insistence of his father's grip that prevents them from pulling away. They lollop along, half a step behind, skipping over the loose stones and the feet of the beggars.

When they reached the dock Gui holds up his hands and they clatter to a halt, panting.

'You are my servants, remember. Now, let us take a steady pace to where you see that merchant cog flying the flag of Marseille.'

Although they are trying to walk casually, Etienne notices there is a hitch to Gui's gait. He is holding his head completely rigidly, as though he is trying to stop himself from looking about.

'It's him!' Etienne yells.

They spin round to see Nasir the slave master cantering towards them.

'Run!' Gui pulls the boys onwards and they weave through the bustle of the port. The sailors on the dock are untying the cog's mooring ropes.

'Jump!' Gui hitches both boys aboard. He vaults onto the gangplank behind them, now under the protection of the blue cross of Marseille. Nasir is left cursing on the quay as an inch of water appears between the boat and the hard. Breath ragged, Gui comes to kneel and gathers the boys into him as the first strokes of the vessel's oars dip into the murk below: dark, foamy, stinking port water that will soon become the beautiful, boundless, clear sea.

Over a bowl of spiced goat soup and some hard bread Etienne persuades
Christophe to tell his tale. Having been allowed to accompany his father's
squire to a saddler's in La Rochelle, he wandered off when he shouldn't
have. He found himself at the dock, where a fat man with a fancy coat
promised him many fine things. Christophe rubs at his arm. Etienne
winces for him as he explains how he ended up following him into a trap.
He didn't like the man, and when he realised what was happening he tried
to run for it.

'I even made it back down the plank. I had a foot ashore.' Christophe
stares off to the horizon as though he is still searching for a way back to
that day, before everything went wrong. 'But there was another man, a
French noble man, as finely dressed as anything. He was talking to the
man who tricked us. I ran right into him.' He looks down at his soup, then
up at Etienne. 'I wish I hadn't. I wish I had run off the other way.'

'Well, you've escaped now!' Etienne says brightly. 'Just think, people
will be so impressed with your tales.'

'What? That I was taken as a slave?'

The boy shrugs and glumly submerges a piece of hard bread in the stew.

'No. Don't tell them that bit. Tell them you went on an adventure and
saw things they could never imagine in their whole boring lives.'

'My father will be so ashamed.'

'No. No he won't,' says Gui.

Christophe shakes his head. 'I wish you were right.'

'His father is the Count of Saintes, see?' Etienne says. 'It's not like
having an ordinary father.'

'Count of Saintes?' Gui eyebrows fly up.

Christophe nods. 'Third son.'

'No matter that,' Etienne chimes in. 'I'm sure there will be a reward,'
he says to Gui.

Gui cuffs him across the head.

'And this noble man you saw, Christophe. You would recognise him
again?'

'Yes,' the boy replies, eyes once again trained back on that fateful day.
'I am sure that I would.'

Chapter Thirty-four

Amaury de Maintenon stares at the inquisitor as though the forces of the Dark One are massed in his heart and being directed out of his eyes. He is sure it is not the first time that someone has been looked at the treacherous prelate with such malevolence, and he is sure it will not be the last.

'So, you see, my men are at the site. Whether or not I apply for permission to exhume the bodies is down to you,' purrs Bernard de Nogent.

Maintenon's eyelids fall, heavy. He rubs the fist of one hand into the palm of another. Never before has he been required to employ such self restraint. He ensures his tenants provide what vittles the Count of Blois's household requires, he raises the feudal retainers due under his ban, and rides to war as gladly as any man when called. Who has there ever been to stay his fist?

'I have never set foot in that place. It is not on my territory,' he replies.

'It's close enough,' says de Nogent.

'You will find no evidence of me in that place,' he says coldly, mind turning on who could have alerted de Nogent to the crypt on the Gazeran estate.

The inquisitor smiles with checkmate satisfaction. 'You might find it hard to deny given your men have been caught red-handed taking delivery of wagon load of heathen children. No doubt the same provenance as the dozens of dead ones we found buried there.'

'What court would prosecute the death of heathen slaves?' Maintenon growls out the last words, challenging de Nogent to defend such a thing. The inquisitor is too well into his game to be distracted by the other man's menace.

'It is good evidence of depravity,' de Nogent replies. 'And besides, they would prosecute the murder of one of France's noble-born daughters. A de Coucy for example. I hadn't realised you were such an unlucky spouse. Perhaps St Pol's nephew should know before he commits his daughter to you?'

'So, you've been digging in more ways than one, inquisitor,' says Maintenon, inwardly cursing the prelate's uncharacteristic display of boldness. Still, the de Coucy girl's death could be a lucky guess. He has never hidden the fact of his first marriage.

Maintenon leans back in his chair, arms folded behind his head. 'I am held in highest account with all those knights with whom I took the cross. I fought at Acre with the Count of Dreux.'

'Seeing the cadaver of your kin with her head staved in does funny things to a man.'

Maintenon nods, a long, slow gesture that buys him the time to channel his anger. There was only one other he knew of who had seen the de Coucy cadaver. And he is long dead. So, he muses, the salt seller had told his daughter. Maintenon allows his eyes to cloud murderously. He smiles slowly, letting de Nogent know he has seen his hand.

'It's the Le Coudray girl, isn't it? You've found her.' He laughs. It is loud and callous enough to have de Nogent shifting in his seat. 'You are prepared to take the testimony of a heretic who whored herself to a guileless fool of a priest as the footstool of your ambition?'

De Nogent draws himself as upright as he is able.

'There is always one that gets away, Lord Amaury. And I am tired of your half promises. You thought you could discard your contract with me to suit your new marital interest? If you do not relinquish the abbey and all it's territory to me, along with half of the original Le Coudray estate I will release the whore from her penalty and put her in the dock to testify against you. Along with a pile of cadavers that make the latest plague rolls from Paris look modest.'

Blinking like a sparrow hawk shocked at the size of the prey it has baited, the inquisitor turns on his heels and hurries out. Perfectly still, Amaury of Maintenon stands by the window and watches as the quisling inquisitor ride away. Then, in one stride, he crosses the floor, seals his fingertips beneath the lip of his oak desk and hurls it into the centre of the room. He stalks over and hurls it again, and again, until the top has come away from the legs, the drawers lie shattered, and the whole piece is utterly broken.

*

It is hard to tell how long it has been since she has seen another soul. A few days? A week? This cottage chamber is not the stinking dungeons of the Inquisition but it is cold and dark. Her window has now been shuttered. Even though a sliver of light prizes its way through the slates, the days are still too short and the light too dull for her to be able to gauge time.

When de Nogent had heard as much of her story as he required, he stalked away, presumably to Gazeran to verify her account. Sooner or later he will return though, to demand the evidence that links him to Maintenon's slavers. By then she must be able to provide him with a solid reason as to why he should keep her alive.

She hears the carriage approaching from some distance away. The wind carries the scratch of wheels and the crunch of hooves along the tree-lined lane. It must be nearly evening by now and Agnes is tired. There is still a tiny corner in her heart where hope resides, where she presses her lips into the soft hair of her son's crown, the man she loves standing over them. But the bone-aching damp of these grey-washed walls are tearing at her will. She knows what is coming next.

Beneath the mattress, her arming sword pokes mockingly into her back as she turns over. If there is nothing else to hope in, then why not run him through? It would take all her cunning and power - there would be no romantic flight - but her death would have some meaning, some dignity. She could stand alongside the martyrs of her father's soil unashamed. Who knows, perhaps it is they that reside in Paradise after all, for there is no God she can believe in who would provide an escort of angels for the torturers of the Inquisition and shun the children orphaned by their pyres.

She slips out of bed and kneels. The cold floor sends blades into her knees. Hands clasped together, she bows her head and closes her eyes, as though it might shut out this mercilessness world. What comes to her is the blond angel curls of her boy, the thrill in his eyes as his father presents him with a toy trebuchet he spent weeks perfecting. She meant to say the *Pater Noster*, but now water squeezes from her eyes. What has she done to bring down Hell upon those she loves? What has she done but be a daughter? There are voices out in the hall. Prayer is all that is left, so she prays to the one Grace she knows will not abandon her. To Mother Mary.

She pretends not to hear the door open. He gives a cough and she rises to uncertain hazel eyes. Spirit roused by the possibility that her hopes could be so swiftly answered, she quizzes the bailiff with a curious frown. All that returns is tension in his jaw, his stiff-shouldered gait.

'Come with me,' he says.

The table is laid out in the middle of the room with buckled straps attached to the legs. Although she expected, her heart begins to thump at the sight of a newly-lit fire in the hearth and the array of smithies' tools in the grate. It will be pain, that is all, she tells herself - a passing torment of the flesh. She stares defiantly at the scene as though that might temper its menace. Is this Our Mother delivering strength in her last hours? Will she feel as brave once it begins?

She suspects that if the bailiff has anything to do with it, it will not last long. The only armour she has for her bluff against de Nogent is the letter Lady Yolande sent her that ties him to Maintenon, now in the safe hands of the forester. She must play it well enough to convince the inquisitor it is worth her life.

She can make out three distinct voices in the corridor beyond. They rise from hushed formalities to an agitated competition, and for several ridiculous minutes she and Michel de Plaissis stand and wait. The man whom she suspects is just as much a victim of circumstance as she, does everything he can to avoid looking at her.

When de Nogent appears, she can tell at once that something is wrong. Face puckered, his body is coiled like a viper readying to spit venom at a larger predator.

'Unfortunately, I am called away on other business,' he says. Hand

216

behind his back he strolls over to the fire. Any relief that Agnes should be feeling at his announcement is kept in check as he bends down to pick up a smithy's iron. She feels the bailiff tense beside her. De Nogent inspects the tip, raises a brow. The fire is not yet hot enough.

'Still.' He sends it clattering back down on the grate. 'My men will see you tell us all about this information you claim to have.' There is a scrutiny to the black, glassy beads that has her raking up every doubt she has ever held about herself. 'It never takes as long as you think,' he says, withdrawing his hand from behind his cloak. 'Once it begins.'

He presents a linen cloth, smeared with the unmistakable rusty stains of dried blood. Instinctively Agnes averts her eyes. Her heart begins to jump.

'Something for you to consider while I am gone.'

With a flick of his wrist, de Nogent unfurls the package: a female hand. Agnes hears her lungs dredge up a cry. De Nogent throws the grisly package at her feet.

'She's still alive. If you do not tell me where the letters are, I'll feed the rest of your little nun accomplice to the hounds.'

Agnes can hear the protests and jeers from the other side of the half open door.

'Can't we join in?'

'What sort of cousin are you?'

'Later,' Michel replies, 'if you behave. Now get on with you!' A ribald cackle echoes through the walls.

The bailiff returns, shutting himself in the makeshift torture room with Agnes. She holds her breath as he picks up the hand and studies it. Then, he carefully wraps it back up and places the bloody parcel on the table. The reverent way he handles it drains the fear from her.

'It is a woman's hand,' the soldier says. 'But it looks like it was cut from a body that is long dead. Probably taken from a graveyard.' He speaks matter-of-factly, showing nothing but the restraint he has already shown.

'Why are you doing this?' she asks.

The bailiff stands mute, and for a moment Agnes thinks that any sympathy he had for her is lost. He wipes his forehead with the back of his gloved hand, leaving a smear of dirt, and says, 'Because I am a fool.'

He looks like the weariest man on earth.

'I have gambled away more than I can ever repay, and stole from Amaury de Maintenon to pay the debt. We have ridden out together a few times, local skirmishes. I do the jobs he doesn't want anyone else to know about. He was an easy target.'

'De Nogent found out what you'd done?

'You don't get to be in the position I am for long without other men learning something about you they can use.' His smile is full of self-reproach, but it makes him look handsome. Agnes feels a tug of guilt that she is glad to hear of his misfortune. It means she has found a victim of sorts who might be in a position to help her.

'Do you know where de Nogent has gone?'

'South, was all he said to me.'

'South? Did he say why?'

'No. I was only given instructions to interrogate you.' Michel nods towards the table and there passes an uncomfortable moment as they both consider what he has been tasked to do. He shakes his head, as though in denial of what she knows he must be capable of.

'What of the slaves that escaped the night we freed them?'

'No trace. There's only so much I can find out without running the risk of talking to the wrong person.' Michel presses his lips together as though he is considering her words, but his gaze rests elsewhere, far beyond the confines of the room.

'We found the bodies at Gazeran where you said they would be,' he says suddenly, almost as if it is a confession. He leans his ear to the door, listens for a movement. Satisfied there is no-one beyond, he rests both hands upon the frame, head hanging down between his shoulders. 'Fourteen in all.'

'Fourteen! As many as that? I saw six.'

He eyes her wearily. 'And how many mass graves are you familiar with?'

'De Nogent is trafficking slaves with Maintenon,' Agnes says urgently. 'My son was with the shepherd's crusade. The nun who escaped, Sister Octavia, she was sent to me by Lady Yolande with some bills of sale. I think the boys were sold overseas.'

Michel raises his eyebrows. 'I'm glad I didn't have to raise my hand to you for a confession. I must be getting better at this.'

Agnes does not concede him the joke. 'If Lady Yolande sent you to help me that night then she must trust you.'

He looks down, body weighted with shame. 'Lady Yolande's niece is my wife.'

Agnes glares in disbelief. 'Then you know what happened to Margueritte!' Her voice is shaking. 'What's wrong with you?'

He turns his face away. She comes in closer.

'Look at me,' she says through gritted teeth. 'Would you be afraid if you were me?'

His eyes creep back, taking her in. The slight, half-famished woman standing before him in a torn shift, with wild, matted hair and an even wilder stare.

'Well, would you?!'

'I'll think of something to tell de Nogent,' he says, pivoting for the door. 'Stay put for now, I'll return when I have something useful.'

218

'What about the guards?'
'They're my kin,' he replies. 'They'll do as I say.'

Chapter Thirty-five

The afternoon sun sparks the water. Seagulls bomb the wake of returning fishing boats, turning the sea to foam. Etienne leaps up onto the gunwale and points. "Look! Look! It's the Hospitaller commandry over there. Do you see?'

'I see. I see.' Gui laughs. They have been standing on the bow of the boat all morning, competing for the first sight of the great stone landmark. The sun's rays bathe the harbour's promontory, making a golden palace of the fortress.

'I win! I saw it first!' Etienne is tearing around the deck like a puppy. The corners of Christophe's mouth peel up. It isn't quite a smile, but it is a start.

The details of the shoreline are visible now; boats line the womb of the port, the great domes of the Cathedral rise up above a maze of wooden shacks. From astern Etienne hears a fisherman's cry - Provençal, a cousin of his own tongue. It will never sound foreign to him again. Am I really nearly home? he asks himself, and with it finds himself caught in a concertina of time. It feels as though it were only yesterday he stood on the quayside, all full of anticipation and adventure. Stupid, stupid adventure, he chastises the former version of himself.

His father is at his side, staring at the approaching harbour with a strange, far away stare. Etienne realises they must be thinking the same thing. He watches Gui inhale the tang of the salt air and press the heels of his hands to his eyes.

'Are you crying?' Etienne asks uncertainly. His father laughs, but the deep crease in his brow makes him looked pained.

'No. I am just very relieved.' Gui draws him in. 'When you have had moments where you were sure that everything you ever loved was gone. When suddenly you find you have it back within your grasp but...' he trails off.

'Most of it.' Etienne exhales deeply against his father. His father rubs his back – they are thinking the same thing.

'Do you know where she is?' Etienne asks, gripped by the need to know that wherever his mother is, she can feel them. Feel their return.

'Not long now,' his father says.

'Imagine the look on her face.' Etienne forces a grin, trying to imagine her reaction when they meet again. Rooting around inside the lip of his breeches, he offers up the little gold St Christopher. Eyes round in wonder, his father looks at it as though it is a thorn from our saviour's crown. Gui takes it in his palm, passes a fingertip tenderly over the detail.

'I stole it from mother,' Etienne confesses. 'For luck.' The corner of his lip lifts at the irony. His father hands it back.

'Then see you return to her when we get home,' he says with conviction, and for the first time, Etienne begins to believe that home might actually be there after all.

The port is brimming with merchants, sailors, port hands, pilgrims and vendors hoping to catch the passing footfall. Etienne wonders when they will be able to get something good to eat. It's been weeks since he has tasted anything other than rock hard fruit bread and salt fish. He spots a stall selling roast pork belly.

'Let's go.' Etienne tugs on Gui's arm.

'Etienne, stop that for a minute.'

'But food!' Etienne hangs his head, accusingly. Gui looks at his feet in a way that tells Etienne he is trying to be patient. 'Let me think for a moment. We are going nowhere until I am sure it is safe.'

Etienne casts around. 'What do you mean safe? We are in Provence!'

'We are in the port of Marseille, which is a long way from home if you remember.'

'Of course I remember,' Etienne mumbles. Why wouldn't I remember, he thinks, anyone would remember. He rolls his eyes at Christophe who is swivelling his head back and forth, blinking like one of the birds from the governor's aviary.

'What?' asks Etienne.

'It's him! It's him!' the boy cries.

'Who?' Gui scans the scene. He stops dead in his tracks. Despite the warm weather, the man they are staring at is dressed in a fur-trimmed cloak, gliding through the crowd, a silk scarf around his neck.

'The man with the fur cloak,' Christophe says, wringing his hands. 'He was at the port when they took me. Let's go, please, now. We have to go.'

'Stay here. I'll be a moment.'

'Don't leave us! Please!' Christophe's voice cracks and he lunges at Gui's tunic.

'Don't worry, I'll be right back.'

Gui gives Etienne a grimace, entreating him to help Christophe. 'Keep him safe behind these barrels. I recognise the man too. I just want to see where he is going.'

'Let's sit here and try to guess at what all these people are up to,' Etienne suggests brightly.

Christophe manages a wary smile. He allows Etienne to pull him towards a row tavern empties stacked against the wall, but his eyes keep darting off in different directions, like he is expecting the governor's men to appear and grab them back. Besides, Etienne knows the game isn't all that good - there are only so many maidens trying to escape evil lords or adventurers in search of the true cross that you can make up.

Etienne finds himself looking over to the Hospitaller commandry at the mouth of the harbour. It would only take them a few moments to go and see if any of the knights there can help them. No doubt they would be impressed with the tale of their escape. Etienne looks at Christophe. There is no way he is going to be able to convince him to leave their hiding place. He flops down on the ground and decides that if Gui isn't back by the time the sun has made the other side of the harbourmaster's tower, he is going to go to the Hospital by himself.

'It's Father Gui, over there. He's coming back!' Christophe is flinging his arms about like he has just witnessed the Madonna weep blood.

'Where?'

'By that bank of food stalls.'

Christophe swivels Etienne's head round. Gui is nodding thanks to a group of sailors as he sculls his way back through the crowds, a bag of roasted nuts and some clothes bundled under his arm.

'Now then,' Gui says, sounding like he is about to perform a magic trick for small children. 'Who wants to come to the Hospital with me?'

'Yes!' cheers Etienne.

'Who were those men?' Christophe asks.

'Just some sailors. Come on.'

'And that merchant? The one I saw at the dock? Where did he go?'

'Don't you worry about him.' Gui smiles and Etienne thinks he looks very pleased with himself.

*

Gui waits in the shadows outside the tavern. The sailors are drinking inside. Earlier in the day he had watched as they exchanged Zonta's pouches of coin for smiles and pats on the back. They hadn't even blinked at Gui's story – a bankrupted merchant with servant boys he could no longer afford to keep. Come with your cargo after dusk they told him. We have the connections you seek, middlemen to some of the richest in the kingdom. Well there's no point in suffering it, they all joined in the joke, there's a shipment due to sail. Bring them along and you'll be paid fair.

Bide your time, Gui thinks, pacing the quay. Get them properly in their cups. The evening is just beginning and there are still messenger boys scurrying back and forth, crewmen sluicing down decks, baggage handlers heaving bundles of canvas over the dirt. He strolls among them, trying not to scratch at the itch of his anxiety, trying not to look over at the fortress of the knights of the Hospital.

It would be easier to have ice in your veins, he thinks. Complete indifference to the suffering of another. He has known enough men like that. How easily they pick life's fruit. He feigns a sip at his flask, glances over to where the men are drinking, eating, laughing. It is not indifference staying his hand. No, it is satisfaction at the thought of their suffering. He tucks the empty flask away. He waits.

When the appointed hour arrives, he eases himself into the tavern with a crowd of revellers. Zonta's back is to the door. He curls his fingers around his dagger and all the pain of the past year courses down into his fingertips. His blood is molten iron, the knife is the lodestone. The sailors recognise him, throw up their arms in drunken greeting. Before the spy has a chance to turn his head, Gui's knife is out.

'Do you want your crew to see you die?'

Zonta places his palms down on the table in surrender. The sailors' mouths shape their surprise, but before any words are spoken Gui raises his finger to his lips and says softly, 'One word and I announce to this pissed-soaked den that you trade in the souls of Christian children. I would like that.' He finds a grin. 'Now, this boat they were telling me about?'

'The people I work for will kill you. You think they care if I am dead or alive?' The merchant's voice is smooth as velvet but Gui can see his breath, high in his chest.

'I'm touched for your concern. Now get up.'

The man who calls himself Enrico Zonta rises, gives a little bow to the dumbstruck sailors and, scraping the sticky sawdust from his shoes, steps out into the street.

Outside, the cool night air is a welcome contrast to the foul breath of the tavern.

'What do you think is going to happen when we get there, eh?' Zonta says jauntily.

'Walk. Don't talk.'

The merchant leads them to the warehouses on the far side of the harbour. It is the maze of buildings where Gui first learned of Etienne's fate. He feels the spectre of calamity throb in his belly as Zonta draws him into the warren of streets, silent but for their footsteps and the scratch of night scavengers. The stink of rotting fish and effluent mingle with the smoky sweetness of cedar, myrrh, and cinnamon bark.

'State your business?' The voice is gruff.

Gui pivots and blinks into the glare of torches. 'Gui of Courville.'

'Then it's you.' A barrel-chested man armed with a light sword sits at the front of four mounted men.

'I am the city provost. The commander of the Hospital raised the night watch for you. Said you told them there was trafficking in Christian souls here?'

'That is correct.' Gui elbows Zonta forward. 'This man is a slave dealer. I met him overseas when he tried to rob me.'

'A slanderous lie! I am an Italian merchant. An honest business man. I trade only in glass and perfumes.'

'We've seen nothing irregular tonight. I hope we do not waste our time here. There would be a penalty for that.' The provost's horse snorts in response to his rider's irritation.

'A dozen men can bear witness that I returned today on *The Lady Isobel* from Egypt. I don't know where they are keeping them, but I learned from this man's crew that they have a shipment of children planned to sail tonight.'

The provost dismounts, eases one finger between his belt and his belly. He nods for Gui to retract his dagger. 'We'll take your man in. See what he has to say.'

'This is scandalous. I refuse to assist you with this falsehood.' Zonta waves a haughty hand.

The provost taps at the hilt of his sword. 'You'll help us if you wish to wipe your own arse for the rest of your days.'

Zonta's body is unflinching, but Gui sees the bulging eyes chase down towards the quay at the end of the street. It dawns on him.

'He's coming tonight, isn't he?'

'I don't know what you mean.' The merchant purses his lips. Gui can feel the other man's anger radiating towards him. Now he knows he is right.

'He's come to collect his money, hasn't he?'

'Who?' The provost shoulders forward. For sure he wouldn't be as quick as he was in his prime, thinks Gui, but no one would relish a well-landed punch from him.

'His paymaster.'

Torches arrive on the docks, casting the mouth of the alley in a Devilish glow. The provost raises a warning hand to his retinue. Voices float across the water. From a nearby street they hear the screech of metal on stone. Orders hiss through the night like arrows in flight. Suppressed whispers break into cries. Children. Gui feels a hot fist bunch in his stomach. The provost prods Zonta on.

'Go to your business. Give them a clue and we'll run you through.'

Zonta flicks a glance back towards the night watch. One of the soldiers raises a crossbow and a wink. The levy advances behind the broker, as silent as the dead.

A vessel bobs in the water, anchored to the jetty. It doesn't look sure enough to make it to Nice, let alone North Africa. There are three figures on deck, their shiny, sun-flayed skin reflecting the torchlight.

'Hold until the children get here,' the provost murmurs to his retinue.

From behind the soldiers Gui sees Zonta nod his head in a fleeting courtesy. An instinct of precognition hums deep within Gui. He empties his lungs with a hissing breath.

The provost fingers for three of the men to approach from the flank. They inch forward. Now Gui can see him - a figure in a long, black cloak. A visceral hatred stirs in his soul, like some ancient beast uncoiling from sleep.

'You know him?' The provost turns to Gui.

'I know him.'

The horses of the night watch stamp in anticipation.

'Halt in the name of the Count of Provence!' the provost bellows. The soldiers surge forward with a cry, blades unsheathed.

Gui's body shakes with fury at the sight of the vulture robed in holy garb - Bernard de Nogent. There is no time for thought as the night watch canter in from each side. The air fills with panic, sobbing children pull frantically at their ropes.

'We're the night watch. You're safe now.' Gui surges forward, trying to scoop up the score of hands extended to him. Two of the watch ride in between the children and the slavers while the others flee to the vessel.

'Look! He's getting away!' Zonta yells out, inching away from the provost's stallion. Gui looks up to see the inquisitor fleeing. He runs him down before the provost is able to pick a path through the chaos of bodies. He has a swath of the other man's cloak bunched in one fist and his dagger in the other. Momentarily he is paralysed by his own rage. If he moves a muscle he knows he will stab de Nogent in an ecstasy of violence that every fibre of his being longs to submit to.

'You think this will save your whore?' de Nogent whispers.

'My soul is likely bound for Hell, what harm would your blood do me now?'

Gui launches at the inquisitor. A searing pain shoots through his flank and he buckles. Next thing he knows he is wrestling with the provost, trying to fight his way back to the man in the cloak.

'Who is your master?' Gui kicks out towards de Nogent from behind the provost's restraining arm.

'The Vicar of Christ.'

Gui roars, 'You don't have the means for this trade. There is someone else. He was seen at La Rochelle. Who is he?'

'How do account for yourself?' The provost says to the inquisitor, measuring out a length of rope.

'I was making payment to the Italian for ornaments on behalf of the Church. I have never seen these others before in my life.' De Nogent, lips pressed white, stares unblinking at Gui as the provost binds his hands. 'This is an outrage. I have nothing to do with those men. I am a man of God!'

'You'll talk,' Gui hurls after him. 'You'll talk when someone gives you a taste of blood punishment.'

'That's enough,' says the provost. 'We'll take him in.'

Gui slumps to the ground, hollowed, as the prelate is lead away. His lungs feel too tight to draw breath.

'He'll talk,' he mutters to himself. 'Bastard.'

Gui wipes the sweat from his brow. It won't be long before de Nogent's co-conspirators find out about his arrest. The idea of standing feels almost too exhausting to contemplate, but he knows he has to get back to the boys before anyone else does. He swings his legs to kneel. Pain shoots through his side. He fingers his flank. It is wet and bloodied. De Nogent has put a blade to him.

Chapter Thirty-six

The bird is soaring beyond the sight of man. Every now and then a speck flashes on the floor of the heavens. Only briefly is he able to track it, squinting into the sun. He blinks and it is gone again. Amaury de Maintenon closes his eyes and lets the sun's rays bathe his face. It allows him to imagine himself back at Acre where first he learned this sport of Mohammedan royalty, under a baking sky, waiting for the Lionheart to arrive. Patience - then, as now. His bird will come. Although it has the vast canopy of freedom before it, Maintenon knows the falcon will return to his arm. Freedom is but a terror for those who have known only slavery.

Again he calls out. A flash of black appears. At first moving too fast for the eye to follow, he catches it as it dives, then it is hidden once more by a cloud. It emerges, swooping, to return to his arm, the stringy corpse of a fledgling magpie in its claws. Maintenon tries to quash the superstition that the magpie is a lucky bird.

In the same moment as he is telling himself that there is no such thing as an unlucky portent, a messenger rides up. All his years of experience allow him to read the man's news before he opens the note. The rider is composed, but it is the studied composure of a professional who has ridden long and hard with important news.

Feeling the flutter of anticipation, Maintenon rips open the sealed parchment. The grey eyes shine, almost translucent in the sunlight, and he begins to laugh. A raucous, mercenary yowl that has his men exchanging glances. The note, bound with the Bishop of Chartres' seal, is confirmation of the appointment of Gautier de St Pol as Abbot of Maintenon. The letter continues; *Item, Regretfully, we inform you that Inquisitor de Nogent is arraigned in Marseille for the crime of trafficking in Christian souls. Appointment of a new inquisitor for the lands of the Île de France and the counties of Blois and Champagne is pending.*

How thoughtful of someone to draw his enemy to a convenient location. What easier place is there to have a man silenced than in prison? He promises himself a trip to the bishop's palace to reveal in the prelate's downfall. All he has to do now is ensure that the source of de Nogent's information is similarly snuffed out. He is certain it is the de Coudray woman. There is no one else it could be. Better he get there sooner than risk the loose thread of a desperate harlot trying to talk her way out of her gaol. The inquisitor is not his only enemy.

'Send a note to bailiffs at Dreux,' he instructs the messenger. 'Tell them Inquisitor de Nogent of Chartres has been arrested. I believe he has taken a captive who must be found. Tell him to search the church lands around Maintenon. Any abandoned buildings. Use as many retainers as they need.'

*

There is something strange about this delivery wagon that Agnes cannot quite put her finger on. Usually, it arrives in the early afternoon on a Monday. Its regular appearance is the only reason she can be sure she has been at this place for three weeks now. It is not quite spring but the worst of the winter is past and the hardiest of the daffodils are readying to poke out their pale heads amongst the lengthening grasses. Dandelion clock clouds skip along fast, chasing past the sun, which is not yet high enough in the sky to mark noon.

The man who steps down is not the usual farm hand who brings the supplies. Although his features are concealed beneath a hat, pulled well down against the early April bluster, he is familiar to her. Opening up the rear of he coach, he heaves up a large bag of flour as the charwoman comes out to meet him. From their exchange Agnes is sure the old woman cannot know him. She points to the scullery entrance and he waddles off. This is not a man who is used to lugging sacks of flour.

She glances out to make sure the old woman is busied elsewhere, then creeps into to the scullery. She watches the man from the door. He lets the flour drop with a thump. Bends over, winded. He looks up, catches her.

'Dear Lord!' cries Agnes, and runs into the soft, corpulent belly of Philippe de Champol.

'Philippe!' She covers her mouth with her hand to stifle the cry that is building inside her.

The merchant's eyes twinkle. He takes her by the shoulders as though he is checking she is real. 'I have been trying to find you ever since he departed,' he says.

'You've had word of Gui?'

A quick twitch of his head and her heart sinks.

'I've heard rumours about a scandal that erupted at Marseille though… Someone trafficking in Christians. I've got scouts there now. If he's returned, I'll know soon enough.' He pats her hand with his chubby paw. 'Let's just say I've got a feeling in my bones.'

Agnes nods, mute. His childlike certainty is infectious. She wants so badly to believe in it, but all she can feel in the pit of her stomach is the nausea of disappointment.

Rubbing at his shoulder, Philippe continues, 'Last time I saw Gui, I took this arrow. I knew then we'd stumbled on something grave. I never thought I'd trace it back to my own kin.'

'Bernard de Nogent is your kin?'

'No, Amaury de Maintenon.'

Agnes gasps.

He nods, half admission, half apology. 'Still, it's how I was able to find out he has raised a retinue, looking for an escaped heretic.' The merchant chortles. 'So come, it's time. Get your cloak. The wind is chill and I am not sure where we will be able to stop.'

Agnes races back to her room, retrieves the cloak that she arrived in and searches under the mattress for the arming sword that has lain useless beneath the straw for so long that she has a bruise on her thigh where it digs in at night. Her palms are slick with the anticipation of escape, her heart flooded with the possibility of Gui and Etienne.

'I haven't seen the guards this morning,' she says.

'Good!' Philippe hollers.

She shakes her head. 'Something's happened.'

'Then let's away before we find out what it is.'

Puffing from the urgency of their task, Philippe flicks the horse on with his crop. The cottage clears from sight and Agnes feels an alchemy of relief spread through her body. But they are not two hundred yards on and the merchant lets out a cry. Agnes cranes forward and sees them; a levy of mounted men heading across the boggy plain.

'Get out!' Philippe yells, uncoupling the wagon from the horse as two of the men gallop towards them. He points towards the cover of a copse, but the men are upon them now. Hauling up her shift, she runs for her life, leaving Philippe to mount the mare. Sword unsheathed, she swings round to face the rider as he catches up with her. It's Michel de Plaissis. For a moment they stare at each other.

She raises her weapon. He casts a fleeting glance behind him. Then, clamping his hand firmly over her wrist, he forces down her arm with a strength he has not used against her since the day they met. There is a wildness to him, she can see the tug of his breath in his chest. His eyes are fixed on her and she has no idea what he is going to do.

'De Nogent has been arrested in Marseille,' he says. 'I have alerted the Count of Blois's constable to the burial site at Gazeran, it's in his county.'

Then, before she has time to take stock of his words, he turns her hand and plunges her weapon into his own thigh. He grunts through clenched teeth as his clothes turn red. The hazel eyes are still on her, and they are telling her to run.

It is not until she reaches the cover of the copse where Philippe is waiting that she realises how violently she is shaking. The portly merchant kneels down and makes a stirrup with his hands. She places her hand onto the dappled mare and leaves her print in blood upon its haunches. Two of the horsemen have cantered up the path to the cottage, another is scouring the gorse. Philippe walks the horse along the other side of the hedge line, until they hit a rough track, then he mounts as well, and they are away.

Chapter Thirty-seven

Gui kneels over a faltering tower of sticks and moss, trying to kindle a fire. He has been used to the desert air and the crackling grasses of the south where fires near light themselves. Now they are further north he sighs at the reluctant woodland moss, inserting more twigs into the smoking pile.

'We should be there by this evening.' Etienne's eyes flicker in contemplation. 'Are you sure she will be there?'

'Of course.'

'You don't sound very certain.'

Gui laughs, a harried cackle. It is impossible to hide anything from the boy. 'I am as certain as any man could be.'

'Alright.' Etienne picks at a scab on his leg. 'The fire's out again. I told you that moss isn't dry enough.'

'Why don't you get it going, then. You are better at it than I.'

Etienne beams. 'That's because you never had to set a fire in a damp shepherd's hut.'

Gui's side aches from being hunched over and he is relieved to stand. It has been nearly two weeks since they left Aunt Margarida's cottage, keeping to the less travelled roads and waterways. Despite the ease of their pace and the red, garlicky balm he coats it with daily, his wound has refused to heal. Some days he near forgets it is there, but a few days later it swells and begins to weep anew. The pain that gnaws at his side tells him how badly infected it is.

Gingerly he stretches, watching as Etienne dismantles his stack of tinder and begins to rebuild it. His son has an instinct for practicality, a natural skill with the physical world. *Nonetheless he is fortunate and fortune will come to him.* He recalls the words of the astrologer from Alexandria with a wry smile.

They are camped on heath land, a disk of wild grasses surrounded by gorse. Gui scuffs at the earth with his boot – garlic, yarrow leaves. There is a cattle pond on the other side of the scrub where they might find some asparagus. If Agnes were here she would already have rounded them up a feast. He raises an involuntary gaze in the direction of the city. Up until now he has been able to bury his worst fears beneath the urgencies of survival, but by tonight he will have no more hopes to sell. The lion of truth will be upon them once again. He cannot contemplate the possibility that she will not be there. Brow furrowed, he resumes the pretence of forage.

A noise breaks his distraction. Too clumsy to be an animal, it halts him in his tracks. He unsheathes his knife.

'Get down.' He ushers the boys to the cover of the gorse. There pass a few breaths of ominous silence before he sees them. 'Beyond the trees, over there.'

'What is it?'

Gui holds his finger to his lips as two mounted men emerge from a canopy of trees. One is a hard-eyed feudal retainer - hired muscle. The other rider lingers by the tree line, a tall, thick-set silhouette in a fur-trimmed chaperon that he has wound around his head like a Corsair. Amaury de Maintenon. Philippe's cousin.

Still as statues, the trio watch as the retainer dismounts, inspects the cooking pot and scours the ground for tracks. Gui points to a faint path through the scrub and whispers, 'Take that path for less than half a league until you meet a stream. Cross it. It's shallow but fast running so take care. Then turn right and follow the track. You should be able to see the spire of Chartres' cathedral above the trees. After another league or so the stream widens and branches into two. Take the right hand one. Two or three leagues on you will see the mill. That's the place. Now go!'

'You aren't coming with us?' asks Christophe.

'Come on.' Etienne yanks Christophe by the hand and they are gone, a whisper on the trodden-down grasses that cover the earth.

The dismounted man is standing a few feet away. Gui can tell from the way he is poking casually at the shrubs that he hasn't seen them. Boots stamping down the bracken, he draws near enough for Gui to hear the slow grunt of his breath. The temptation to crouch lower is almost overwhelming. A searing cramp spreads down his flank, igniting his laceration. Much longer folded over like this and it will disable him. *Damn it man, move on.*

Finally, the retainer turns his back. There will be only one chance to ensure the boys are not followed. He cannot fail. Grim determination is his splint as he rises up and, with the force of his whole being, sinks his dagger into the soldier's neck. The rider jerks at his companion's cry and charges. But the heath is not easy terrain for a horse. The pathways through the briar have been made by peasants on foot and it gives Gui an advantage. Maintenon will have to dismount to follow him.

Gui scrambles through a cathedral of ivy and brambles until it spills him out into woodland. There he pauses, catches his breath. It will take Maintenon a few minutes to circumnavigate the pond and come round to his flank. Up ahead is the stream that leads to Marie's cottage. Etienne and Christophe cannot be far down the path. He belts his dagger onto a fallen branch as a makeshift lance and finds a hiding place. Ambush is the only tactic he has to unseat his opponent. His ears strain for the dull echo of hooves but he hears nothing except the drum of his own heart and the shuffle of small creatures. He should be here by now. Understanding sinks in his gut like a stone. Maintenon knows where the boys are going. He

knows where Agnes is. He is not chasing Gui, he is heading to the cottage.
*

The light has begun to turn, draining the array of woodland colours into shades of grey and brown. Agnes stands barefoot in the doorway, watching the blades of the water wheel turn in the stream. At first she pays no mind to the two boys lolloping along the path. Now the sun's rays have dried the thoroughfare, she often sees children chasing along, voices shrill with laughter or song, arms stacked with piles of wood, fruit, laundry. But there is something about the flashes of blond that snag in the kernel of her heart and she pads out for a closer look.

Every day she has dreamt it. A dream so vivid, so lived-in, that she is sure it will never come to be, for it has already been birthed into another realm. Squinting through the trees she tells herself they are two local boys who have been out for longer than they should, hurrying home against the light. Still, there is something about that hair, the gait that sends her heart pattering. 'It cannot be,' she says aloud and sets out on the path towards them.

Next there is the pause between breaths, the silence before the thunder, the hair's breadth between life and death, and she knows he cannot be anyone else.

'*Holy Mary! Holy Mary! Etienne!*' Her cry is a screech that barely sounds human. She tears along the path, her bare feet oblivious to the prick of the thorns and nutshells beneath.

'Sweet Lord. Etienne!'

Etienne summons a burst of speed, and, as he stumbles over the last few paces of uneven ground, she hears the words she had forbidden herself to hope in.

'*Mama!*'

He throws himself into her arms and time rolls away. The hot, clammy embrace of her child, the sweet smell at the nape of his neck, and the pain of everything she feared she had lost, sear her chest. She feels a tremor go through her body - a demon taking flight.

'Oh thank you, sweet Lord. Thank you.' Agnes rocks him to and fro, tears running down the side of her nose, leaving a salty tang in her mouth. 'I thought you were lost.'

Head still buried in her shoulder, he squeezes back and she can feel him shaking his head. Etienne straightens himself up and beams at her, a damp-cheeked smile of wonder. But she can see there is a question in his eyes. He casts over his shoulder.

'What? What is it?' Agnes's fingers grip Etienne's tunic as she peers down the path. 'Gui? Where is Gui?'

'He was with us. But men came and he stayed to fight them.'

'Men?' Agnes's hand circles her neck.

'Yes. There were two of them, weren't there Christophe?' Christophe,

232

half camouflaged by the trees, steps forward and gives an uncertain smile. 'This is Christophe. He came back with us on the boat to Marseille.'

Agnes gathers the boys to her, and says, 'There is something very important you must do. About half a league along the river, you will see a track that goes uphill. It leads to one of the woodsman's cottage. Tell him what has happened and that we need help. Tell him he is not to come alone. We need at least three or four men. Armed.'

'You cannot stay here alone,' Etienne says. 'Father said.'

Her chest hollows to hear the word father. He knows. A breath releases from some long-sealed cavity of her lungs. It is the weight of a press being lifted.

'Your father,' she whispers.

There is an unfamiliar flint in her boy's eyes. He is not going to let her stay here by herself.

'Christophe. Do you think you can go alone?' she asks.

Christophe nods mutely.

'Etienne, untie the mule.' Agnes disappears into the mill and re-emerges with a branding iron.

'We will be faster without the mule,' Etienne says.

Agnes looks back at the cottage and for a moment all she can see is the same ruin that greeted her arrival. Before she has a chance to respond, Etienne has read her thoughts.

'But we will need it if we can't come back.'

'Saddle him,' she says. 'I must fetch my shoes.'

The pair set off at a brisk walking pace, the mule trotting behind them on a rope. Its load is a flask of water, some bread, two rolled blankets and the branding iron. The sun has left the sky now and a lilac hue paints the woods with a vivid luminescence, like a strange, future land. In a matter of minutes, the light will leaden and they will have darkness on their side.

A few hundred yards on from the cottage and she hears the beat of a fast-moving horse through the trees. It thrums inside her - the taut drum of war.

'Over here.' She leads them to a makeshift bridge where the stream runs shallow and a copse of oak and laurel will better shield them. Barely are they over the brook when the clattering hooves is upon them. Instinctively they crouch as the silhouette of a horse canters by.

'It looks riderless.'

'I can't tell from here,' Etienne replies. 'Both of the men who arrived at our camp were mounted...'

Agnes hears her son exhale a long, whispering breath. 'I hope Christophe is alright,' he says.

'I'm sure he is. There is always someone in the woods, especially this time of year,' she says, and in truth it is not Christophe she is worried about. The boy, she knows will stumble across someone soon enough.

'Let's cross over here just to be safe. We can cross back over again just before the river forks.'

The bridge is a fallen oak, spliced and bound, and it takes both of them to persuade the mule to cross. Around them, the sharp shadows of the evening are receding and Agnes breathes a little easier as a mantle of deep blue folds over them. She takes them into a natural archway, thickly garlanded with leaves. Roosting birds quieten their evening song amid pitter patter and shuffles; the change of guard between day and night hunters. For half a mile they walk on beside the stream, the living forest a low hum all around them.

Agnes's longing to talk to her son swells with her every breath, each inhalation an invite to release the stream of questions trapped inside her. How can she ever begin to explain, or to understand? All she has is a mother's need to know her son's ordeal, to share whatever it is she must. The good Lord has delivered a blessing, greater than any other she could name, but still she must wait before she can get to know this young man striding out ahead into the penumbra.

'Nearly there,' she whispers. 'Can you see a stone bridge up ahead?'

Etienne turns, the whites of his eyes picked out in the shimmer of the rising moon. Frowning in concentration, she sees a new angular slope to his nose, his brow, and it sends her heart into free fall. She could be looking at Gui. He cocks his head towards the stream, listening.

'Over there.' He raises his hand, sharp. 'Quick!' In the same moment he reaches for his mother there is a loud crack. Branches snap aside to reveal the bulk of a stallion and rider, his head covered by an elaborate chaperon. He paces the mount forward into their path. Agnes expels a primal cry as she finds herself looking into the distended, colourless eyes of a face that has haunted her ever since their only encounter: Amaury of Maintenon.

'Run!' She pushes her son aside. Maintenon cannot follow them both. The nobleman hesitates, the point of his sword moving from one to the other in a mock counting game. Agnes takes the start he has given her and flees towards a circle of silver ash whose tall, narrow trunks he will find hard to negotiate. But he is a skilled horseman, and he darts between the glinting poles, snapping at her heels. Abruptly she bolts to one side, turns to face him. His personal mores, she gambles, will not allow him to crush her with his horse. He paces his mount before her, lips puckered in a fleshy pout.

Agnes's heart is in her mouth as she watches her son from the corner of her eye, a grey shadow skimming over the soft forest floor behind Maintenon. She has no idea what her son's experiences have made him capable of. The best she can do is be ready.

Maintenon bears his teeth. *Get off your horse you bastard,* she wills, but the gloved hands stay laced over his pommel. Briefly their eyes lock

As much as she longs to engage this ancient enmity, she can do nothing that might expose Etienne, so she stares past him, a veil drawn over the hot brew of hate in her veins. A low hum escapes Maintenon, as though he were mulling over a number of appealing choices. He reaches for his saddlebag. Agnes's blood freezes; if he looks up now he will see Etienne. But he does not. He is too intent on withdrawing a length of rope. Carefully he coils it over one hand, then he turns back to her with the same, silent grin. He is not going to dismount. He is going to rope her like an animal from where he sits.

All at once Etienne strides forward, and with a battle cry, he punches the branding iron into Maintenon's knee. Howling, he slumps forward, groping for his reins as mother and son tug furiously at his legs. His mount kicks out with a blow that unseats him and sends Etienne flying backwards as if struck by lightning. Snorting like a bull, Maintenon draws himself up and throws himself at Agnes. She calls out to Etienne, who lays motionless a few yards away, but there is no reply. Thrashing in a deep well of panic, she tries to free herself, but Maintenon asserts his weight and seals her mouth with his hand.

'And to think poor old de Nogent wanted to burn you.' The low grate of his voice is like a bed of worms in her gut. She wants to claw his eyes out. 'But this is going to be much more fun.'

The only weapon she has is her teeth, and as he nuzzles his face into her neck she sinks them into his cheek. The blow of retribution is still pounding inside her skull when suddenly Maintenon's weight is peeled from her. She sits upright to see a wraith-like figure hurl him to the ground. Scrabbling backwards on her haunches, she reaches Etienne and presses her hand to his chest.

Gui grinds his knee into Amaury of Maintenon's throat. The protruding eyes and the strangulated cry pump hot satisfaction through his veins, as beneath him the big man thrashes with all his force for his life's breath. Hampered by his injury, Gui knows he will not be able to contain his opponent like this for long. He glances up. Agnes is cradling Etienne's head against her body, rocking him to and fro. The fury flows up through his core. With all the force he can muster, Gui lands a punch on the side of his enemy's head. Momentarily, the body beneath him ceases its bucking. Snatching the length of rope, Gui loops it around Maintenon's hands.

'*Father*!'

The sound of his son's voice sparks through him like a charge from amber, and instinct turns his head. What happens next unfolds like a dream, a series of images flickering against the night to which he is helpless witness. Etienne rises to his knees, his mother's hand hovering uncertain at his side. Agnes turns to Gui, her expression transformed by the light of recognition in her eyes. Stay where you are, he wants to shout out, but in the half-breath it takes to form the thought, it is too late. He feels the thrust of his opponent's arms push up against him and then a searing pain in his belly that he knows is a blade. The grip of his knee begins to fail and he gropes for the dagger inside his belt like a drowning man. The next thing he knows he is on his back.

'You know I had her when she was a girl?' Maintenon rubs his neck, laughing as Gui's face hollows. 'She put up a lively fight then too.'

The world is reduced to the rush of blood in his ears, the scalding laceration in his gut. He shakes his head, trying to throw off this madness like a rabid dog. But even as the edges of his world begin to darken, this red-eyed rage will not submit. It froths within him until it finds form, narrows to a single, inevitable point. Lungs releasing an animal cry, he rises up and plunges his dagger into Amaury of Maintenon's heart. *Every garment rolled in blood...* A smile cracks on his lips. *For unto us a child is born.* And then the world falls black.

*

'Gui?'

The hands on his face are cool. He nods. The soft warmth of a sigh kisses his cheek. Agnes presses her forehead to his. Time stalls. There is just the two of them, each one held in the world only by the other.

'Yes,' he says. 'And Etienne?'

'Here, papà.'

Etienne skids to his side. Gui tries to sit but he is beaten by a tide of nauseating pain.

'We need a compress of garlic and thyme,' Agnes says quickly. Gui winces as she peels away his tunic and he sees his son's face fall. He looks down at the macerated flesh.

'A compress and all will be well,' he says, but his eyelids flicker. He knows the damage done is far beyond repair.

'He will be well.' Agnes reassures their son, but her big, blue eyes are full of tears. 'I'm sorry.' She brings his ice cold hand to her lips. 'This is my fault. Maintenon…'

'None of this is your fault,' he whispers. 'I know what Maintenon was.'

'I tried to tell you so many times.'

'Shhh.' Gui puts his fingers to Agnes's face. 'We have our son. All the rest…It's over.'

He lifts his other hand, wrapped in the clammy warmth of Etienne's grip. Tears spill fast down Agnes's face as she fights to hold her smile. A breath later and she is laughing, laughing and crying at the same time.

'Please stay with us,' Etienne says, his voice beginning to falter. 'I would like you to help me make a sword when you are well.'

'That would be a fine thing. I should like that very much.' The corners of Gui's mouth lift, his breath suddenly buoyed. His son's face opens with joy, and for a second he thinks he might be able to cheat this fate. But almost at once he can feel his chest straining to rise anew, and he realises it is not the surge of his breath returning, but the effort of summoning his last. He turns to Agnes. Her face is the same beatitude that met him in this house all those years ago. Now it is a halo of light. His Father's house. He sighs. And his eyes are closed.

Chapter Thirty-eight

His mother stands at the back door beneath a bower of ivy that drips from the mossy roof. A chemise hangs loose in her hand and it looks for all the world as if she is about to peg out the laundry. But he knows she is not. She has been standing on that same spot for at least as long as he has been chopping wood beneath the lean-to. Mostly she seems lost in thought as she absent-mindedly fingers the shirt, but now and then her eyes flit over to the spot where the boundary of her godmother's dwelling merges with forest - to where the newly turned patch of earth marks his father's resting place. It has been four days since they laid him in the ground and she has hardly been able to pass an hour without returning to it, as though she is frightened he might not be there. Or perhaps it is just to be near him, Etienne isn't sure.

They dug the grave the day after his passed away. He, the forester and Christophe, all sweating under the rays of the warm, spring sun, heads bowed in a silent commune of endeavour that gave consolation as well as any eulogy. At first Etienne swallowed down his own grief, tried to comfort his mother when he saw her out there, adrift in a sea of loss. The touch of his hand on her shoulder made her smile, but he could sense it was not enough. Unlike his father he had no words, no extreme unction at his fingertips.

What she really wants, he knows he cannot give. All he can do is make himself useful, limit himself to the odd glance in his mother's direction as he chops wood for seasoning. In this hidden refuge there are plenty of tasks; chopping wood, ripping out the damp timbers of the wheel house, cutting back the rampant foliage that fingers at the window frames and pokes its way in between the timbers of the house. These are the tasks that root him into the earth, allow him to think about his father without feeling as though his world is in free fall.

He can't yet make sense of the fact that Gui, the father he has only just found, has been taken from him. He is not sure if he ever will. The loss of his father is a riddle with no answer, a bottomless well that never returns the toss of a stone with a splash. How is it possible that the man who had been at his side since he was a babe is gone? The man who provided for him, who taught him so much, taught him how to read! Why had he never truly understood what a marvel that was? Who knows what might have happened to him that day in the slave market if he hadn't been able to read the lines thrust before him.

Etienne pushes the heel of his hand into his forehead. A thousand memories flood in; the little cottage in Montoire, that safe feeling he used to get as he came down the lane at the end of the day knowing he was going to find Gui frowning over his parchments. The steadfast ally who helped him shrug off the barbs and punches of other boys in a way that a mother's worry never could.

Etienne raises his hand axe, strikes ferociously at a log and watches the splintered pieces go spinning to the ground. He bends, retrieves another branch, strikes, and for a moment all his thoughts are lost to this easy rhythm. Then, unexpectedly, the tentacles of grief entwine themselves about him and he sways, heart quickening as the hurt pounds his solar plexus. Next, he is back on the scorching terrace of the governor's palace, scalp prickling, looking into fierce, jet eyes that brim with remorse. *You know I think I always knew, Father Gui,* he remembers the mumbled response to his father's helpless confession.

For everything his father gave him, had he ever really let him know how thankful he was? More than anything in the world Etienne desperately wishes he could let Gui know. And the fact that he can't feels like it is wringing the very soul from him. Grip loosened by the wave of emotion, he lets the hand axe fall and he sinks onto his haunches. You came for me, father. He wipes the blur from his eyes. I thought I was all alone, but you came for *me.*

'Etienne. Someone's here.'

Etienne lifts his gaze to see a sad consolation in the round, freckly face of his friend. For a moment he burns with shame that Christophe has witnessed this private distress, but there is something about the kind way the boy presses his lips together and offers his hand. It reminds Etienne that his friend knows better than anyone what it is like to be exposed, unable to hide your despair. He allows Christophe to heave him up onto his feet and they exchange a look of camaraderie. An understanding that makes Etienne feel guilty about how transparent he has made his pity for the boy from La Rochelle.

'Thanks,' he begins. 'I'm sorry…'

'You don't have to say anything,' Christophe replies and they hover, uncertain, around the embrace that is asking to be exchanged, until the moment passes.

'Who is it?'

Christophe shrugs. 'A lady.'

Although she is wearing worn clothes there is no mistaking the tight, cushy weave of the fabric any more than there is her porcelain skin, or the meticulous way her hair is swept beneath a gossamer net. A lady indeed. The women clutch each other by the forearms and it isn't at all obvious to Etienne whom is consoling whom, for they both grip each other with the same ferocity – the shipwrecked clinging to jetsam. Although it is his mother recently bereaved, large tears spill from the eyes of the other woman and Etienne is reluctant to interrupt their exchange of womanly intimacy.

'Maybe we should go and make some cordial,' Christophe says.

They retreat indoors. 'Do you know who she is?' Christophe asks as he pouring out a jug of pressed fruit, one hand behind his back, deft as any butler.

Since they have been home Etienne has noticed this about Christophe. There is a neat economy to everything he does; his bed sheets turned down just so, dinner plates whipped away to the washing tub before his mother even has a chance to stand, the way he jumps aside, as though he is dancing an *estampie*, to let her pass first. Unexpected mannerisms and quirks that Etienne has never noticed before give glimpses of the boy Christophe must have been before Cairo. All the relics of his courtly life, Etienne supposes, are his way of trying to restore some familiar order.

'I've never seen her before.'

'Maybe she's something to do with Maintenon?'

Etienne's shoulders twitch. He has done all he can to shut out the stare of those lifeless fish eyes from his mind. But no matter the distractions he provides, they seem to find him, just like the wash of black blood that spread like tar over the ground, and days later still seeps into his dreams.

He shakes off the visitation and replies, 'I doubt it. She looks like a good woman.'

Christophe nods sagely. 'Perhaps she doesn't know what he was. Would you believe me if you didn't know better?'

Etienne ponders the question and shrugs. For it had been Maintenon Christophe recognised instantly as the fine-robbed man from the docks at Saintes who had trapped him in the hold of a slave ship. If the truth be known, Etienne isn't sure what he would have believed it, if someone had told him there were noblemen and clerics who turned profit in the sale of stolen children.

If Christophe is right and the lady outside is connected to Maintenon, it begs another question, one he is not sure he wants to know the answer to: what business did Maintenon have with his mother in the first place? When the chatter of female voices ceases, his feet take him outside to the ivy bower where his mother still stands, watching the noble woman depart, as silently as a ship gliding over smooth waters.

'Who is she?'

Agnes looks back at him uncertainly. She doesn't want to tell me, he thinks. Part of him wants to change the subject, find some urgent domestic task and duck the uncomfortable burden his mother now baulks at laying on his shoulders. He waits. His mother nods. A precise, downward stroke of the head that could be the end of the matter or the reluctant start to a long tale.

'Lady Yolande de Coucy. Her daughter Margueritte was married to Maintenon.'

'*Was* married?'

240

'She was killed. By Maintenon.' A ridge forms in the smooth space between her eyebrows, as though she is fighting with the words in her head. Etienne presses his lips together like a bather standing on the edge of an icy lake. The wind breathes over the bower, fledging blackbirds shrill in the ivy. Agnes sighs. Is it resignation, or an invitation? He can't tell.

'What has this got to do with you?'

The furrow deepens, and for a horrible moment Etienne thinks he has made his mother cry. But suddenly her face opens as if she has been struck by some revelation.

'There are many things I should have told you.' she says. 'That *we* should have told you.' A shadow of a smile passes her lips as she mentions his father. 'First you were too young and then....Your father wanted you to know.'

Softly, Etienne says, 'So tell me now.'

'My father was a merchant,' Agnes begins. 'He became a very wealthy man.'

'He did?' Etienne feels his eyes widen at the allure of a family fortune and he checks his enthusiasm with a studious frown that makes his mother laugh - the first genuine, unguarded laugh he has heard from her since he fell into her arms on the pathway.

'He did. He began as a pannier in the south.'

'Where aunt lives.'

'Exactly. He started there and began to trade. Salt from the Camargue, from Saintes, up the Rhone, over the mountains to Piedmont. After twenty years of trade he had exclusive rights to sell to some of the highest tables in the land. He was wealthier in fact than my mother's parents, the castellans of Gazeran.'

'Castellans of Gazeran,' Etienne pronounces the words with slow wonder as though he is trying on a vastly expensive robe.

'After I inherited the castellany Maintenon asked for my hand. When papà refused, he denounced us to the inquisition.'

'Why did he refuse?'

'I didn't know it then, but papà discovered Maintenon had been married before, to Margueritte, and that she had died. The villagers told him rumours that Maintenon had murdered her.' Agnes exhales, a long, impossible sigh. 'He discovered Margueritte's body along with the bodies of several others. Moorish slave girls I think they were. Maintenon denounced us and shared the spoils with the inquisitor he used to condemn us.'

His mother pushes an imaginary strand of hair from her face and suddenly she looks very weary to Etienne, as if she has reached the top of a mountain only to realise there is another peak to climb.

'My father helped you escape, didn't he?'

241

'Yes. Yes he did.'

'But your father didn't escape, did he?'

Hands pressed together in prayer, fingertips resting at her mouth, all she can do is shake her head.

'I'm sorry, mama.' Etienne puts his arm around her. 'The evil in the hearts of some men is so strange.' He feels his chest sag, defeated by incomprehension.

'It is the Devil, I suppose. I have no other account for it.' Agnes palms the dampness from her cheek.

'Do you think so? I am not so sure.'

His mother's lips twitch with a smile. 'That is what your father used to say. God is in everyone but the power to choose evil is man's alone.'

'Really?' says Etienne, comforted by this unexpected inheritance of belief. 'Well now Maintenon is dead, do you think Lady Yolande will help you clear your father's name. Maybe even get back Gazeran?'

Agnes gives a cough of laughter. 'You know I think you must get your optimism from my father.'

Etienne beams at this other nugget of inheritance. 'But mama, the land is yours. Your father would want you to fight for it. If Lady Yolande will help we could appeal to the court of Champagne. Tell them what Maintenon did. They would believe her.'

'Very possibly, they would...' Agnes's smile is soft and patient. It is the same smile she used to give him as a small child when he made a mess trying to help her, and he knows a but is coming.

His mother continues, 'But even if they believe that Maintenon murdered Margueritte de Coucy, the court would still have to find us of good standing and rule that we did not then kill Maintenon for the land. To them, I am still a convicted heretic who sired a child out of wedlock. You don't understand what they are. What we would be risking. The chains of society bind us as well as any gaolers shackles.' She takes his hand. 'We have our lives. Our freedom. Each other. That is enough for me.'

'But don't you want to clear your father's name?'

His mother nods and he can feel the conflict in her heart.

'Of course,' she whispers. 'There is nothing would please me more than to see my father's name redeemed. He toiled his whole life to achieve what he did. To win respect from those who despised his kind as peasants. "If I can come from the salt marshes of the south to win all this, then so can anyone," he used to say. He believed that one day any man will be free to achieve through toil what the nobility achieve by the accident of their birth.'

Her eyes are almost translucent, glittering with icy conviction, and as she pauses Etienne fancies he can feel this unknown grandfather standing there in the silence, adding the weight of his approval to her words.

'But you know what else he used to say?' Agnes continues. 'No matter a man's coffers, it is all for nought if you aren't surrounded by the love of your family. So no, now I have you back I won't risk it. I won't risk you. For all the land in the kingdom of France, for my father's righteous name. For everything thing your father did to bring you back to me. I would rather die on the pyre than stand before them at Judgment and tell them I risked you for a patch of soil.' His mother's voice is utterly steady. 'How I wish papà could have seen you, Etienne. He would have been so, so proud.'

Etienne rubs his eye. 'Very well,' he says. Then he pats his mother's hand. 'I wish I could have met him too.'

Chapter Thirty-nine

The Lady of Chartres has a very large nose. Fine boned, noble even, but still, Etienne reflects, it is a man's nose. No matter where else his eyes wander, it is very hard to keep them from straying back to it. Lady Isabelle keeps coughing too, and the dry irritation in her throat distracts him as he stands before the court, adrift in a starched formality that is utterly unfamiliar to him.

The court is a long, timber-framed hall, which, he imagines, is also used for feasts or similar occasions of noble delight. High above his head, birds nest on beds of straw stolen from the steep thatched roof. Now and then the beat of wings echoes in the rafters, and Etienne wonders if the venerable panel before whom he stands have ever been shat on.

The Count of Blois has a leprosy so hideous it keeps him confined to his castle, so it is his niece, Lady Isabelle who presides from a long trestle on the dais, flanked by long-faced advisors and a scribe who looks too ancient to see, let alone write. At Etienne's back a congregation of plaintiffs and vassals fill the hall with fidgets and whispers. It reminds him of being in church – a room full of people gossiping their way through a boring lot of lecturing that still manages to give you the uneasy feeling you have done something wrong. On the witness bench beside him sits Christophe, who upon sight of the crowd and the pinch-faced scrutiny of the judges, blanched a shade of white Etienne had never seen before, even when they were in captivity.

Lady Isabelle peers down the length of the bench at the men still shuffling the parchments he pilfered from his mother to make their case. When the rustling has ceased, she raises her voice above the hum of the crowd and says, 'Etienne of Courville, what is your age?'

Etienne lifts his chest. 'Sixteen, my lady.'

The Count of Blois' niece lifts her brow into the dome of her forehead and turns to her advisors who offer dour nods.

'Very well. These documents you present are the title deeds to land in the name of Agnes Le Coudray. She is your kin?'

'My mother, my lady.'

'And she is not here?'

'No, my lady. She suffers ill health such as she is unable to attend.'

'And your father?'

'Is deceased.' Etienne clasps his hand before him and lowers his head in the same way Gui use to when he was trying to get rid of troublesome local officials.

'And you have a witness of good standing to vouch for this?'

'I do, my lady. Christophe of Saintes, son of Count Roger of Saintes.'

The Lady of Chartres's thin lips round in surprise as Etienne turns to his pallid friend.

Christophe manages to stammer out the testimony they have rehearsed before collapsing back down onto his seat. It is hardly convincing and Etienne knows it. The members of the court exchange grave-sounding whispers, and Etienne can feel the prickle of sweat at his collar. Lady Isabelle flexes a finger and a page boy scuttles forward. Eyes narrowed on Etienne, she issues an order and flicks the boy away. The urge to wipe his hands down his tunic is almost as strong as the desire to close his eyes and remove himself from this committee of noble vultures about to peck out his birth right.

One of the hunched-shouldered, black robes speaks.

'According to the documents, these lands to which you claim title on behalf of your mother come from her uncle, Hugues, Chatelaine of Gazeran, held jure uxoris by her father, whom we find to be Estève Le Coudray, a deceased heretic.'

Etienne's breath tightens as he fights to keep his concentration against the flood of panic swamping his thoughts. Of course, they would have records of what happened to Estève, he scolds himself. Why hadn't he thought of that? The long-faces shuffle the parchments and utter low coughs. Etienne folds his fingers into his palms and squeezes, trying to imagine his father's steadying hand on his shoulder. *Just keep your countenance.*

'That is correct.' To his surprise he sounds remarkably composed. 'When my grandfather refused…'

'You will refrain from speaking unless requested to do so,' snaps Lady Isabelle.

'Yes my lady. Sorry.' Etienne attempts to shift his weight, but his feet feel as if they are encased in lead boots.

The black-robe continues. 'Land which now belongs, at the reckoning of our tithe collectors, to Lord Amaury of Maintenon.'

Etienne tries to swallow but his mouth is completely dry. Beside him Christophe makes a strange choking noise, as though he is about to expire. Please don't, thinks Etienne. With all the strength he can muster, he steadies his voice.

'If you will permit me to explain, my lady?'

Lady Isabelle arches an imperious brow. 'Go on.'

'Lord Amaury of Maintenon made an offer for my mother's hand, and when her father refused, they were falsely arrested for heresy and the land was stolen. The deed you have in your hands shows it to be true. I believe under the circumstances the land should be released to my mother and me as proven heirs and good Christians.'

'All land belonging to heretics in this county is handed over to Count of Blois's fisc for safe keeping until such a time as they are exonerated or condemned by fair trial. We have no record of such a transfer.'

'It is usual in cases of contested land for the other party to present themselves when summoned,' another advisor intervenes, his voice cracking with age.

Lady Isabelle blinks at the interruption like a raven eyeing carrion. 'Indeed. But as you can see, Lord Amaury of Maintenon is not here.' Her eyes ping wide open. 'And neither can he be found.'

The thrum of the court falls silent. Etienne feels the heat surge up from his gut. His heart is beating so loudly he is certain it is audible. *What have you done?* The sweat runs down his tunic. Everything seems to be moving very slowly and he wonders what his mother is going to say when she learns that he has hazarded his freedom with her parchments.

He draws in a deep breath. The moment has arrived when he must flip the coin of Fate. If he tells the truth then he will likely be condemning himself, and possibly his mother, to prison. If he lies and his lies are uncovered, then death is almost certain. He feels as though he is falling.

'Lord Amaury of Maintenon is dead, my lady.'

The court gasps. Christophe lets out a ghostly moan.

'Dead? How do you know this?'

Etienne does not know what he is going to say, he has no time to think, but when he opens his mouth, he finds an unexpected jumble of the truth pours out.

'This lord was engaged in the traffic of children. Of Christians to the Mohammedans and visa versa... as slaves...of boys that are not his chattel. And some girls. But mainly boys.' To howls of outrage he continues, 'It is true, my lady. I swear it. Christophe and I were among the stolen. We were planning to go to the Holy Land to persuade the Mohammedans to relinquish the City of God...'

A ripple of mocking laughter rings out. Etienne frowns.

'What nonsense is this!' Lady Isabelle interrupts shrilly, her head craned forward like a marsh bird.

'We did believe such a thing was God's will,' he says to the astonished faces. But even as he speaks he can tell that no one believes him. The Lady of Chartres is casting her attention elsewhere, scanning the hall for vassals of importance who might be offended by the spectacle. Her eyes alight on the quivering Christophe.

'What say you, Christophe of Saintes?'

The question is met with silence. Etienne feels his insides flip over. He gives Christophe a gentle poke but, stare fixed on the back of the hall, Christophe stays mute.

'Even if this unlikely tale is true, none of it explains how Maintenon died,' Lady Isabelle prompts.

Courtiers are twitching in their seats. The lady of Chartres perches forward. Etienne can tell she has had enough. He presses his lips together and braces himself for the certainty she is going to have him arrested.

'This accusation is of the utmost gravity and you bring nothing against the Lord of Maintenon but this jabbering boy, whose identity we cannot yet verify. Can you tell the court how Maintenon died? Was he killed?'

Etienne's whole body feels like it has been taken over by a demon, tossed high up into the air and is now plummeting back down to earth. *You don't understand what they are.* His mother's words come back to him. *The chains of society bind us as well as any gaoler's shackles.* He digs his heels into the floor and blinks away the watery film he can feel threatening his eyes. *I am so sorry, mama.*

Suddenly, Christophe raises up his arm and points to the back of the court like the ferryman on the river Styx. Etienne feels his blood run cold.

'Yes, he was.'

All heads turn to the gravelly voice. Standing at the back of the hall flanked by four retainers, is a broad, full-bearded man with a look to pierce armour.

'Father,' Christophe mouths, staring at Etienne with a mixture of apprehension and disbelief. Etienne's body heaves with relief. 'I told you he would come when he got our letter,' he whispers, stifling a grin at the memory of how he had coerced poor Christophe into writing to his father weeks before.

'What is the meaning of this? State your name.' Lady Isabelle snaps her fingers at the court guards who stiffen their grip around their hilts.

'I am Count Roger of Saintes and I killed Amaury of Maintenon to save my son.'

Christophe's eyes look like they are about to pop out of his head as his father shoulders his way through the hall towards them. He has the same red hair as Christophe, but his eyes are green, feline almost, and they narrow with a predatory playfulness as he approaches the open-mouthed Isabelle of Chartres. For all the intimidating stories he has heard Christophe tell, it's all Etienne can do to stop himself from running up to embrace the battle-scarred man striding towards them.

'Over a year ago, I took my son to La Rochelle on household business. While I was occupied he strayed.' A devilish flash of green flicks towards Christophe, who does not lift his gaze from his feet. 'We searched for near on a year, but heard nothing until a letter arrived.' Roger of Saintes beckons his son with a click of his teeth, as though he is coaxing a horse. 'Tell the court what happened.'

Christophe looks as though he is going to vomit.

'That's when they took us, my lady. At the docks,' he mumbles.

'Speak up, boy,' bellows the count.

Christophe wheezes and Etienne wishes he could speak for him to spare his friend's suffering.

'That man, the Lord of Maintenon, he was there.' Christophe casts a desperate glance to Etienne.

'It's true,' Etienne chirrups, 'he was working with an inquisitor, caught red-handed with a cargo of Christian children to be sold.' He halts abruptly as he catches himself about to blurt something about his father. He coughs. 'By the provost of Marseille, my lady.'

The Lady of Chartres massages her sharp chin with her index finger.

'If my boy says that is what happened then that is what happened!' roars the Count of Saintes.

'No one voices doubt, my lord Count.' Isabelle of Chartres blinks furiously.

Etienne rocks forward on the balls of his feet, fighting back a smile. He, Etienne, illegitimate son of a priest, might just be about to turn this game.

'If you permit me to continue?' Etienne dare not leave the narration of this tale to Christophe.

'Carry on.'

'We were taken to the palace of the governor of Cairo as slaves, but by the will of God were able to escape on a boat bound for Marseille. From there we wrote to Christophe's father who came to our rescue even as we were being chased down by the Lord Amaury of Maintenon, who wished nothing greater than to silence us *forever.*' He embellishes his speech with a hiss that draws the breath of the bench as the hall erupts.

'Silence in the court!' Lady Isabelle throws her voice above the din.

'I also have a testimony with your permission.' The voice is barely audible above the chatter. Christophe's father has such magnetism that it is only now she speaks that Etienne notices the small, neat woman standing with the count's retainers. He recognises her at once.

Isabelle of Chartres wrinkles her forehead. 'Lady Yolande de Coucy?'

Lady Yolande bobs. 'As you know, my lady, my daughter Margueritte was married to Amaury of Maintenon. And died soon thereafter.' Her white-knuckled hands agitate together as she continues. 'One day, this arrived by mail.' Lady Yolande opens her palm to reveal a jewel. 'This is Margueritte's earring and it was sent to me by Agnes Le Coudray, the mother of Etienne here. She claimed that my daughter had been murdered by Maintenon. She told me the same fate had nearly befallen her. And that she knew where my daughter's body was.'

'Lord in Heaven,' whispers Isabelle of Chartres and Etienne notices she makes the sign of the cross.

'At length, I persuaded my husband to accompany me to this place, situated on the estate of Maintenon, where we found a hidden catacomb. There we were able to identify Margueritte from the gold thread that remained on the scraps of her skirt. ' Lady de Coucy clutches her hand to her mouth. 'She lay there with several other children. The side of her head bludgeoned. It was such a terrible sight, it will never leave my eyes. The bodies have been exhumed by the Church, my lady, pending investigation by your uncle's constable I believe.'

Christophe's father glares viciously at the judges and he ushers the sobbing Lady de Coucy to sit. His face turns puce, and, veins bulging in his neck, he turns to address the assembly.

'By God's will I came upon this scoundrel about to take his revenge on my boy. I felled him where he stood and I challenge any good Christian to condemn me for it!'

A murmur of admiration ripples through the spectators. The Count of Saintes extends a vice-like grip and shakes Etienne by the forearm. 'When this fine young man told me of Maintenon's other crimes I contacted the good Lady de Coucy, who was brave enough to come and accuse him as you hear today.' Count Roger gives Etienne a crafty wink and takes up a stance of wide-legged defiance.

Etienne's head is spinning at the audacity of such an accomplished lie. His body feels almost weightless with exhilaration. Poor mild-mannered Christophe, he thinks, it must be nerve-wracking for him to labour in the shadow of such a relentless force. From the way his friend's gaze is fixed determinedly on the ground, Etienne half wonders if he would prefer prison to another one of his father's jousts.

There pass a few moments of total silence. It appears Lady Isabelle of Chartres is at a loss for words. Etienne prays silently, his lungs ready to burst with anticipation. He is almost certain that the leper count's niece is not going to take on the Count of Saintes over the killing of a vassal accused of multiple murders and the slavery of Christians to boot.

'Well,' Lady Isabelle exclaims as the crowd begin to shift in their seats. 'These claims against the Lord of Maintenon brought by such esteemed witnesses are far too grievous to dismiss. We will contact the Provost of Marseille who may also be able to corroborate these young men's testimonies. In the mean time the authenticity of the deeds of title for Gazeran and the other lands will be verified by my clerks.' She fingers the parchment. 'If the claim is found to be good, the land will return to the Count of Blois' fisc and leased to Mistress Agnes for a percentage of yield to be arranged, if the charges of heresy are then confirmed to be false by the Bishop of Chartres.'

'Which they will be,' adds the Count of Saintes.

Etienne can hardly believe what he is hearing. The urge to jump into the air feels like it is pulling him off the ground. Heart soaring, he looks to his friend in wonder. A smile playing on his lips, Christophe returns a shrug. Isabelle of Chartres coughs.

'Thank you, my lady.' Etienne bows to the Lady of Chartres. The hall rises for Lady Isabelle and her entourage to depart. Etienne runs his hand through his hair to find his head is damp with sweat.

'That was too close,' he says to Christophe as they file out. 'Your father is crazy.'

'You have no idea.' His friend shakes his head and they begin to laugh.

Outside the late afternoon sun is casting an amber glow over the rooftops and it looks as though the world is encased in bronze. Etienne inhales the warm, sweet air of this new world. He has seen a thousand sunsets like this but somehow everything looks different to him, as though a film has been peeled from his eyes. He feels as though he is everywhere and nowhere, as though time itself has come to a standstill and everything is hovering on the promise of something new.

Still light-headed with euphoria, he doesn't notice her at first. It is only when Lady de Coucy calls out a greeting that he takes in the woman standing on the path ahead with one hand at her hip, the other at her brow, scrutinising them.

'Mother!' He races towards her, but she doesn't move, and suddenly he is hit by a jolt at the memory of her words. *I won't risk it. I won't risk you. For all the land in the kingdom of France.* With all the high emotions he has forgotten how much he has risked. He knows he has been irresponsible, how badly wrong things could have gone if it hadn't been for Christophe's father. His gait sags at the possibility he has not had time to consider: that his mother will be impossibly furious with him for defying her wishes.

As scary as it was to face Isabelle of Chartres, his heart feels like it is racing twice as fast as he approaches Agnes. Lady de Coucy reaches her first. She takes his mother's face in her hands and he watches them embrace like old friends, realising that Margueritte's mother must have told her their plan. Still, his breath is in suspension as he looks at Agnes, her face a solemn mask, just like his father's when he didn't want you to know what he was about to say.

'I am sorry I defied you, mother,' he mumbles at the ground, even as it occurs to him that she is just mimicking Gui. Agnes, expression still grave, presses her lips together and he braces himself for the worst, but when she opens her mouth, her lips part to a grin.

Etienne leaps into the air. 'We won! We won back your land!' He throws his arms around his mother, and she yelps in surprise as he picks her up and twirls her round. She is shaking her head at him and he knows she meant to tell him off, but she can't, because she is laughing too much, laughing at the tears of joy that she is trying to blink away.

Suddenly he remembers. He rummages around inside his tunic.

'I'm sorry,' he says, offering up her St Christopher's pendant on his palm.

Agnes brings her hands to her mouth. 'Dear Lord. That was my father's.' She turns it over in her palm. 'It has been all the way to Egypt?'

Etienne nods sheepishly. His mother unclasps the small silver cross from her neck and threads the golden pendant onto the chain. Etienne gives his best smile. For all the times he had held it, praying for it to send him home safely, he feels a twinge of sadness to be losing it.

'Then truly, St Christopher has delivered a miracle,' Agnes says, hooking the chain around his neck and placing a kiss on the crown of his head. 'Quite literally.' She presses a kiss into Christophe's russet thatch as well. Christophe blushes furiously.

'He is a fine young man, you boy.' Count Roger strides over and takes Agnes's hand to his lips for a moment that lingers a little too long.

'Do you think your father will let me ride one of the stallions?' Etienne whispers.

'Maybe,' he says.

*

The city jail in Marseille is below ground. What little light there is comes from a small vent that takes its breath from the street above. Bernard de Nogent is tethered to the wall directly beneath it, privileged to the sounds of the world outside; seagulls screeching over the city's harbour, stray dogs barking late at night, the low rumble of cart wheels bringing their load to port. On occasion, he catches the agonising smell of fresh baked bread as its vendors trudge by in the early hours of the morning.

It both surprises and troubles him that he has fallen such easy prey to this carnal torment when he has never had any difficulty in keeping his dinner plate abstemious. Could it really be that the Devil has come so soon to tantalise him with a fantasy of the senses? It is effort enough to keep thoughts of the Evil One at bay without these additional temptations. Why, after all he has done in the service of the Church, has the Lord seen fit to abandon him to this squalor? How can it be that he deserved such a rigorous test? Ever has he pursued false believers and sinners with all the vigour that his faith requires.

The business with Amaury of Maintenon was regrettable, that he knows. But what price the souls of a few abandoned heretic children when the gain is the eternal righteousness of the word of the Lord? A momentous new order, a magnificent shrine to eclipse all those that have come before it, stamping out the new falsehoods that bloom like mushrooms in these fetid days. An inspiration of monasticism before the glory of God.

The Lord, who knows all, must know that it was never his intention to become embroiled in this trade, that it had been his full intention to turn Amaury de Maintenon over to the authorities when the time was right, and repurpose all his ill-gotten gains in the service of God. *Amaury de Maintenon.* Bernard's face pinches as he mutters the name aloud. How long will he have to languish here before Maintenon sends men to pay for his release?

Above his head de Nogent hears the familiar positioning of feet over the grate, as a man calls out to his friend to wait. A contented murmur of relief accompanies the warm liquid that comes splashing in through the vent and down the walls to bathe the former inquisitor.

'De Nogent?' The coarse vowels of a southern peasant holler his name.

'Here!' The inquisitor squawks. Is this it? My prayers answered?

He can feel the foul breath of the guard in his face, but no matter he thinks, Christ sends his mercy disguised in many ways. The bald headed man leans over him and picks up his chains with a gloved hand.

'It's time for a few questions,' the man says, and fondling the handle of the baton that hangs from his belt, begins to chuckle.

*

Half a day into the journey home they stop to eat, pulling up their wagons under the crumbling stables of a small, forgotten village. Christophe is buzzing around the food hamper, announcing the buffet as his father's manservant withdraws cloth-wrapped packages. 'Soft cheese! Game pie! Rouen caramels!' It warms Etienne's heart to see his friend's eyes flood with delight, but there is something dismally familiar about this ramshackle village that prevents him from truly being able to share his friend's joy.

Perhaps it is the two old men who sit motionless, watching as a villein tills his strip of earth beneath the accumulating clouds. Most likely they have been there all day and will be there again tomorrow, as fixed a part of the landscape as the oak tree they are sitting under. Or maybe it is just the emptiness of the place - the grey, unchanging skyline that makes his skin itch to move on. Etienne sighs.

'Cheer up, lad. The soil of Gazeran is good,' Count Roger says, rubbing the dark brown earth between his fingers. 'But you'll have to get on to harvesting. This wheat won't wait.'

'You mean we are still in the castellany of Gazeran?' Etienne makes a peak of his hand at his brow. As far as he can see, plains of golden wheat sway beneath the fast moving clouds. 'It takes half a day to ride through it?'

The count smirks with one side of his mouth and nods his head towards Agnes, who says, 'It's three manors if you count your grandfather's land on the other side of Maintenon.'

For the first time since Lady Isabelle of Chartres bestowed her judgment, the reality of their boon hits home. Etienne scratches his head. He had imagined himself standing in fields under a soft, setting sun, two or three men gathering in the bushels with him. But not this. These fields go on forever.

'How are we going to farm all this land?' he cries.

Count Roger of Saintes breaks a chunk of bread and laughs.

'Don't mock him, father,' says Christophe. 'You're not. Look.' His friend points vaguely towards the figure toiling beyond.

'The land is already farmed, Etienne,' his mother explains. 'We wil collect the rents and the yield and the County of Blois will give us a percentage back.'

'Right,' says Etienne, and he feels his cheeks colour. 'That's good. I was just worried about you having to work as well,' he says chewing on a fresh bread crust. Buoyed by this news he picks himself up and saunters over to get a caramel from Christophe. He is itching to ask his mother and Count Roger how much they think all this land will yield once the Count of Blois has taken his share, so he can work out what sort of horse he can buy. He is almost certain he will have enough to buy himself whatever horse he likes. Not some short little working palfrey, but a fine destrier, jet black, a fearsome beast that only he can ride.

Above his head a pair of swallows dart between the rooftops, shrilling as they ride the oppressive air currents. Instantly it reminds him of the birds in the governor's garden. All the horrors of his journey seem so far away now, lost to the memories of vast desert landscapes, the sweet smell of frankincense burning in roadside campfires, domed minarets against the warm, pinking skies of evening. And the girls, their deep, velvet eyes and their glowing brown skin. It's funny how you never remember the bad things, he thinks popping a caramel into his mouth.

The heavy clouds above them yield to rain, sparsely at first, but the big, heavy drops tell him a proper summer downpour is coming. It only rained once in Egypt the whole time they were there. It probably doesn't rain in Spain much either he guesses, otherwise the Moors wouldn't care to stay there. He wonders how much further Spain is from Marseille. Not too far probably. The knights of the Hospital there would surely be glad of a young man with a fine destrier to help them fight the Moors. And once the Moors were vanquished in Spain they could set their sights on the North African coast and the Holy Land itself. Who knows, maybe he would see Jean again. They could go and find Marc, and even persuade Daniel to join them.

A vein of bronzed light spills from a fracture in the dark grey clouds and it catches on the horse's mane. Etienne feels his heart warm. He inhales deeply, a smile breaking on his face. His mother wanders over and drapes her arm over his shoulder.

'What are you plotting?' She asks.

'Nothing,' says Etienne as he stares out across the endless, golden plains. 'Nothing at all.'

Author's note

In the spring of 1212, a young shepherd called Stephen of Cloyes began to preach Crusade in the Chartrain: his mission to recover the True Cross and liberate the Holy Land. According to the accounts of contemporary chroniclers, this popular movement attracted several thousand "pueri" or youths, whose number included shepherd boys as well as urban underclasses. Simultaneously, in Germany, a boy named Nicolas of Cologne began his own children's crusade, mirroring Stephen's success.

Although the Pope had forbidden them from continuing, their zeal to fulfil their holy mission remained undimmed. Some made pilgrimage to Rome, others went to ports such as Marseille, seeking a way Oultremer. The vast majority of them were never heard of again. Chroniclers provide us with a smorgasbord of tragedy: some starved en route, or whilst attempting to return home, others fell prey to sickness, others still were forced into domestic servitude in Italy, or were sold by unscrupulous merchants into slavery abroad.

Whilst the events that set the background for this novel are real, the characters are all works of fiction. Some of the family names of French noble houses are real, as are some of the Christian names, taken from genealogical registers. However, in no way are any of these characters based upon the lives of their namesakes.

I have endeavoured to keep the chronology of events and the details of medieval life as close to historical reality as possible. Some creative license has, of course, been taken to serve the story in a number of places. For example, the incipient Inquisition was not yet the dread and coherent organisation that it would be later become. The historian in me would also mention slave prices and the use of currency. Source materials from this period are scanty, accounting practises not uniform and currency exchanges for the myriad of different coins in use fluctuated greatly. The prices of Mediterranean-trafficked slaves generally appear in Venetian ducats - and I have exchanged them into French livres parisis or tournois only on a best endeavours basis.

Of the countless atrocities and victims of the Crusades, the so-called Children's Crusade holds its own particular, emotive horror. It is remarkable in itself that thousands of France's youth, already labouring under an oppressive feudal system, found the spirit to turn their outrage at the corruption around them into action by undertaking such a perilous journey. Led astray by those holy men whose message had so inspired them, only to be exploited by a cynical world, it is perhaps not surprising they met the fate that they did. If it seems unimaginable now that children could rally courageously or be so cynically exploited, it should not

According to Save the Children, 168 million children are victims of forced labour today, many lured into it by false promises of a better life.

For those interested in conducting their own research, I would recommend Gary Dickinson's, *The Children's Crusade* (Palgrave Macmillan 2008). For the Crusades in general, the sweeping study of Sir Steven Runciman, *A History of Crusades, Vols 1-3*, (Penguin 2016) is a comprehensive introduction. Additional reading could include Christopher Tyerman's, *God's War: A New History of the Crusades* (Penguin, 2007). For Arab perspectives, see Carole Hillenbrand, *The Crusades: Islamic Perspectives* (Routledge, 1999) or Amin Maalouf, *The Crusades through Arab Eyes*, (Saqi Essentials, 1984). Those wishing to investigate the history of the slave trade, could look at Bernard Lewis's work *Race and Slavery in the Middle East* (Oxford University Press, 1990). Estimates of the revenues of the French monarchy and nobility came from John Benton's article on the revenue of Louis VII in *Speculum* (1967, vol 42, 1).

My thanks go to my husband Patrick, for reading early drafts, his nose for story and the juggling he does to accommodate my juggling. Thanks in equal measure to my daughter Eleanor, conceived at the same time as this novel. The knowledge that there are still millions of children who fall prey to the modern day successors of medieval child traffickers was, in many ways, the engine that drove this work to completion.

Printed in Great Britain
by Amazon